THE TRUE PICTURE

ALISON HABENS

A Life Is Amazing Paperback

The True Picture

First published 2021 by Life Is Amazing
ISBN: 978-1-913001-02-5
First Edition

Cover Art and Design by Matt Wingett
Central image courtesy Shutterstock

THE TRUE PICTURE

TRUE – *VERA*

PICTURE – *ICON*

VERA ICON – VERONICA

CHAPTER ONE

I sing to sell my wares. My product is a best-seller and it doesn't need the muse of marketing to help shift the quantities I'm currently shipping out of here. It's just that, in my old job, chanting was top of the to-do list, every day and double on holidays; so, between sales, I start a song to help the business along, like I did when I was assistant priestess at the temple of Venus.

From a pink granite counter in the city centre, I ply the purple dye; advertising my trade with the voice I used at the high altar. Doing booming business with the commercial criers of Tyre:

'Golden sand, silver sea; Hercules picks up the first spiny shell of this immortal industry.' Loin-clothed, with his hound unleashed, he was off to meet a nymph he fancied, a date in the deep, where the Mediterranean waves are sewn, in and out, to the edge of our stone city. Tyrus, original mermaid of that place, wooed him with the jewels of the sea, sapphire wink and salty twinkle, as he walked his dog on the beach.

'Hercules' pet, let's call him Rex, hunts in the surf and comes when he's called, spitting the colour of kings on the sand. He runs to the heel of his hunky master, still crunching *murex* bones and dripping on that shoreline, for the first time ever, the shade of an emperor's hem. Earth's heavenly dye was sniffed out by – let's call him Rover.'

And all the gold diggers of Phoenicia have fetched sea snails from those shallows ever since. I bellow my holy pitch but this produce needs no selling, here at the reeking seam where it all began and is still smelling, down at the docks and in my high street store.

I first saw this story painted on the wall of my father's study in Rome. I was there as the artist slapped colour on wet plaster, sitting under the table, chin cupped in my hands. I watched him apply umber and ochre to the Phoenician coastline where Dad was making his fortune.

God's dog, how that *pictor* inspired me. In the cheap hues he provided for free, he showed Hercules' mood as clearly as his muscles. Framed by painted pillars that looked real, entwined with vines that seemed to grow as me and my sisters did, I saw Tyre on the wall of our *tablinum* long before I sailed towards it.

Temples and tower blocks, high walls and thick fortifications, no fresh paint smell could have prepared me for the salted ferment of the city where, once, resisting an advance by Alexander's army, two thousand Tyrian men were crucified on the beach. Vats of the famous local dye now stand there, gore to glory, *hexaplex* glands, festering night and day.

That fresco was paid for with new money, though our family was old and named after a painter, Fabius Pictor. All my father's wealth, his silver, ships and slaves came from one colour; purple. Importer of single stripes on plain white togas to the senators of Roma: the year Tiberius succeeded Caesar Augustus he had cash to splash on azurite for a bright blue sky in his office. *Pater* could even cough up for a spot of cinnabar to do the bloodstains on Hercules' sword. The droplets on the dog's whiskers were not the real thing, though. I saw the artist mix a little indigo with a lot of red madder in his pigment pot.

Luckily, I got my chin off my knees before I took up my first position, as a temple dancer. I needed my mouth free to sing, drink and kiss. I need it to sell, now, in my high-end purple dye store in Tyre, as I reconstruct the facts for my customers:

'From stinking slime came something sublime. The purple was so pretty, a nymph Hercules was courting swore their love would cool unless he could make her a dress in the colour of his dog's drool.' Contrary as the mermaids, this liquid. And you can never lick it from your chops.

Two hundred snails for a drop of the dye [1]; best gathered after the Dog Star has risen. I reconstitute the tale for my crowd as they queue out of the door: 'Here, boy! Come buy; this essence will make you master, half-man half-god.'

In the story, it doesn't say what became of the glamorous girlfriend but we know Hercules gifted a cloak, soaked in this merchandise, to King Phoenix. They called it 'purpura', worth its weight in gold, but did Tyrus ever get her dress made?

Sometimes I pretend to be that princess, dropping a tear into the same sea. I have lived for two years in the city that is two thousand years older than Rome. It survived the siege of Nebuchadnezzar, still flogging the precious dye that seeps from here. It survived the sieges of Alexander. I, too, have been attacked by many men, so the fallen stones of one defeat are the foundation stones of a new-built me.

These gritty plots were never outlined on my father's study walls; only Phoenix (which even *means* purple) and his sister Europa, painted expensively in every buckle and broach. She was raped too, of course, in another scene, not shown. And half-naked, half-invisible in the water; Tyrus, the sea nymph, simmering at Hercules till he takes her shopping for clothes.

I present myself like that, sometimes, as I can't afford to wear my favourite shade, earning a top salary though I do. Instead, I drip with semi-precious gemstones; my weakness the amethyst, like crystalised snail slime for the wrists and ankles, at a fraction of the price.

But I never say that to my customers. I spin purple so they get the look, not the smell, though the muse of consumerism doesn't need my help with the magic. I would probably trade my own voice for a tunic in that colour.

Across the shop counter, cluttered with calculators for the huge numerals I have to reckon, I join my buyers in their desire. First I had an old Babylonian abacus with beads but then I got a Roman hand abacus which is quicker. It's made of bronze, fits in my palm and the beads slide up and down in slots; so I can even deal in negative values, not that I normally need to. I still have a standard reckoning board on the counter with stones to move in columns; just plain beach pebbles, as some of my clients prefer to see the calculations in simple terms.

At closing time, I stack my papyrus scrolls, my stylus and wax tablets on a shelf and lock the money in a strongbox. This little safe, built into the mud-brick wall, doesn't feel secure enough for such a large amount of gold, but I can't bank it with Abibaal because he had too much wine at lunchtime and I can hear him snoring in his luxury *domus* next door.

With less racket than he is making, I pull down the wooden shutters, padlocking them to the pavement. The greedy eye of my shop closes. At the top end of town all the store fronts look smug, advertising things that Philistines from up the coast and Plebeians everywhere can only dream of: get your coral and pearls, your lapis lazuli here.

I wait on my doorstep for ages after I've shut, sweeping with a broom of tamarisk twigs that makes as much mess as it whisks off the kerb. The road is full of people going home, walking in a slow procession of traffic, hailing and cursing and conversing with each other. The late afternoon light makes the stone edges of ancient Tyre look newly-hewn.

I'm trying to sweep away my worries: first that my hard-earned gold will be stolen, second that it won't be. The thief would probably be thin; my father is definitely fat. The thief might be homeless; my father has a big house. The thief could survive on that cache; my father can live without it.

He has a bronze statue of himself in the *ala*, back in Rome. When people said it was boastful, he had four more statues made; his wife and three daughters, but they were marble and on a much smaller scale, so didn't seem to fit in the same alcove as Numerius Fabius Pictor.

I am the second sister; not the eldest or youngest, not the prettiest or naughtiest. The middle statue made me look better than I actually am; the nose was nowhere near as big as my real one. But dad insisted it was a good likeness and joked that she should be called 'true picture', a play on my name, Veronica; this pun as corny as any of his, and so fitting for the clunky statuette.

Art made me a singer and it sent me into temple service. With florid histories smeared on every wall of the family home, I grew up hymning Hercules' buttocks whenever I was summoned to my father's office for discipline; humming the scary Cerberus (a three-headed hell hound) in the *vestibulum* when I went out and came in. I learned curiosity from Pandora's Box pictured in my mother's room, creativity from the Muses on my bedroom walls.

Art made me a saleswoman and it saved me when I was abducted by Hades, like the painting of Persephone in our old dining room. Bold, against a black background, she nibbled pomegranate seeds painted red with heat-treated hematite. I grew up spitting those pips out.

Just before I took my next position, minding my father's business in Tyre, I tied his Veronica statuette up one night. With strips of a sheet, I bound the cold hands and feet and would have made her chin touch her knees again, if I could. Chill marble is not my style, nor were the unnatural eyes and lips the painter added. I thought then, of all the colours, the one I knew best was darkness; but when they sent me away to deal with it, turned out I really do have a way with the purple.

I've just done the biggest deal of my life. My father will be well pleased. A firkin of dye, buyer to collect, for two gold talents. It's Tyrian cash but I'm going to offer a sacrifice for the day's commercial success to a Roman god.

I stand my brush on the doorstep and set foot in a street thick with dust, scuffing up a cloud as I join the traffic behind a fellow businesswoman, the lady from Sepphoris who deals in flax. She stops suddenly and I nearly bump into her.

"Watch it," she says.

"I like your new shoes," I apologise.

"Jackal hide," she grins, "but don't you know it's dangerous to walk with your eyes down in these godforsaken streets. You've got to keep looking skyward."

She speaks a tradeswoman's Greek with a Galilean accent that makes everything sound like she's selling it. Her slogan is true, though. I glance up nervously at the multi-storey buildings leaning over us.

This is a city of high rise blocks, *insulae* with shops on the ground floor, lock-ups like the one I live in, and overcrowded flats above. Balconies lurch over the street, airborne gardens with birdbaths and terracotta flowerpots. But when a balustrade breaks, and crashes to the pavement, it can take out all the porticoes below. I have seen a whole tenement building crumble.

The temples don't often tumble and they are even taller. There are many, many stairs to climb; either that, or people get smaller and smaller as they reach the foot of the pillars chiselled like a deity's legs. Before I go there, though, I must arm myself. The wine shop is three doors down, and I hurry in.

"You're late, Veronica. I was starting to think you must be sick."

The wine merchant is a good friend of mine. Her name is Tanis, which means 'serpent lady' in Phoenician, apparently. She is a temptress, a bit like that snake in the Jewish story. My downfall is not an apple, though.

Sometimes I sing in Tanis' shop as well as my own; many nights I have hymned to Dionysus here. She doesn't mind; my ode to the drink, my praise of the drunk, brings in more customers. Sometimes she even advertises me.

I think our real lingo is wine, a universal language of *vinum,* with which we can pour out the truth. Tonight I pay for one goatskin bag of it. As my copper *as* crosses Tanis' palm she asks if this purchase is for sacrificial purposes.

"I've made a proper killing today," I smile, "so am going to pay my dues."

"You want Melqart then," she nods, "halfway down East Street, near the baths."

"I always go to Hercules," I say. "My Hercules, like he was in Rome, not Abibaal's version in a pointy hat."

The temple I attend has god as I knew him in babyhood. Pretty pictures show scenes from his labours, laid in mosaic on the forecourt. As I arrive in front of the steps, the crowds are thinning and the air is clearing. No special holiday, hardly anyone is burning their offerings to Hercules tonight.

The way I walk across the square takes in my favourite episode, his fifth labour. I surge into the stables of King Augeas, which haven't been cleaned for thirty years, on a great gush of water from the rivers that Hercules has rerouted to flush out the dung. Alpheus and Peneus; they pour through the stable door, a flood picked out in aquamarine pebbles.

In this mosaic, Hercules is half-naked and so hot. The trickles of sweat seeping into his loin cloth are made of the same sparkling droplets as the river stones.

Always, on my way out of the temple, I walk a different line across the square to take in the eleventh labour, my next favourite. Here is a hop, skip and jump on the golden apples of the Hesperides, which have the same sea-green tesserae for dewdrops in their leaves.

Of course, I have an eye for colour; at work, it gets in my eye. I dedicate every day to dye. It gives me the gleaming pouches and glinting pockets in my office-to-evening attire.

As I start to climb the temple steps in the setting sun, two slim brown feet in sandals, I can see myself casting a long shadow. Tunic too sheer to stop the light, a saffron *peplum* drawn in very tight at the waist and bust with silken cords; head the shape of the temple itself, with my curls piled atop a silvery diadem.

Over *XV* steps high above the pavement, the temple doors are standing half open. From here, it looks dim inside but I know it seems full of light once we've entered. I pull my *palla* closer round my shoulders; dyed a deep woad blue, it wraps me in the night's own shade. Taken already, I hope the shadows of the temple won't take me.

I trip on a step; silly girl to fear the dark ahead of my date with a giant golden statue of Hercules, lit by lamps left by other successful saleswomen, kneeling thankfully at his feet. So I run up the steps, earrings and bracelets jingling; rich girl. My bells chime with the sound coming from the temple, a lone voice in evensong, the last watcher at the shrine as the candles of commerce give in to the dusk.

Tip-toeing between carved cedar wood doors, I give in to the musk. There is that particular scent in temples, more lingering than incense, less intense than smoke, more fragrant than altar flowers, less pungent than the offal of sacrifice. It's a smell that seems to thrive out of natural light, nurtured by worship, encouraged by ritual. I find it relaxing and draw on it deeply, then fall to my knees.

The priest pauses for a moment to check me out but, as I bend down to the great god's big toe, his song continues: 'Hear, powerful Hercules, untamed and strong, to whom vast hands and mighty works belong...' [2]

When I've kissed the earth, I clutch my new wineskin. This is the correct way to pay homage and the priest's chant seems to speed up as he watches me unlace the bag and pour libations on the feet of Heracles. Purple wine, it flows into a trough at the base of the statue where it mingles with the meat and grain, burnt offerings of the day. With my head bowed, I smell compost and cold toast.

As the priest's beat quickens, an assistant appears from behind a beaded curtain; one of the temple dancers to do her other job, cleaning. She starts with her holy rags on the far side of Hercules, a discreet distance from me.

One of the temple dancers. That used to be me. Not at this altar, not in Tyre; in my old life, in Rome, at the temple of Venus. I knew how to dance to the goddess, then, and how to dance for her followers. I didn't have to wipe up the spills of their sacrifices, like this helper of Hercules. But she is dressed as a priestess, at least; I was dressed more like a prostitute.

The hymn the priest is singing was sung by Orpheus himself; so old, the lyrics are from our creation saga, and the singer originally appeared in the story. The padre's voice seems to have been going since then: 'Father of Time, the theme of general praise, ineffable, adored in various ways.'

When he sang those words earlier, a crowd of two hundred in the temple forecourt had killed a bull and were sending an extravagant smoke signal to heaven. And now he sings them to a lone trader, whose capital weighs so heavily she can't lift her head off Hercules' plinth. The same words, he'll sing again at nightfall in a small ante-chamber with his personal assistants kneeling.

I can still smell the bull burning, though I wasn't here before. 'Untamed and effing strong'; this is the kind of god-smoke I coughed when my livelihood was temple dancing. I believed it because a goddess gave me faith in myself. I know it's not meant to be that way round.

I used to live under Venus' roof, between the pillars of her temple in Rome, a regular at every daily ritual and nightly reprise. I was not chained to her columns but I was tied to her calendar; April 1st, her feast day, the *Veneralia*.

We carried her statue through the streets to the baths where we washed it and dressed it in garlands of myrtle. The business of purification as usual, working closely with my sisters, the goddess's staff, all concentrating hard on the rites. None of them noticed when I myself was carried off, a fleshy and flawed statuette, into the men's *caldarium*. Stripped of my garments, everything Venus stood for was shattered there on the hot tiles.

There were five verses in this rapists song and the rhythm stopped my heart beating. There were five men in the steam room, and there's no rhyme for what they did to me.

I couldn't believe it was happening: my faith in the goddess of love was abused. What good are those beautiful statues if they can't come to life and assist their servants when they're turned to stone? I plunged from the temple life of the soul to the bath time of the body; and was submerged long after my breathing somehow started again.

When I eventually found my way back to my father's house, I still felt that my face was pressed to the scalding hot-room floor. He raised me again, a second upbringing, this time not for gods but for money, not for spiritual but financial gain. Numerius gave me a job in his business, importing purple dye from the heart of its production in Tyre back to Rome.

We bring the great and glorious their stripes of office. Senators, magistrates and priests wear a purple strip on their togas, from a finger to a hand-width according to their goodness. Only a conquering general can wear the *toga picta*; purple all over, embroidered with gold.

Now Hercules' one-thin-stripe priest is trying to beat my dark thoughts with uplifting hymns. His breath makes the oil light flicker over the golden shins of the statue that is dwarfing him. The temple girl has come closer, sweeping charred grain from its base with an ibis feather duster. My libations have sunk into the stone trough. My spirits seem to have sunk with them. Getting to my feet, I decide to go home via the wine shop again and, this time, drink it.

From the top of the temple steps, I can see across the city to the sea in every direction. The sunset grinds pepper pink between the tower blocks. The fumes and the fury of Tyre drift upwards as I walk down, coming back to Earth; so fast and loud compared to Mount Olympus, though its population is dimmer.

In the street next to mine an *insula* is on fire, a tenement built of brick and iron just like the one I live in, and I bet I can tell why it's burning down. People believe they can bake upstairs but they can't. People think it's okay to light an oven on the third floor, with no hearth or chimney or source of water nearby, but it's not safe or healthy. I'm on the first floor of my block and I'll have a lamp at bedtime but I would never try to cook bread or meat in that flat.

Its shuttered windows in sight, now, I stop three shops before mine for more wine. The first person I see on entering sees me first; "She comes at last! The evening is lit up by her jewels."

My Phoenician landlord, business partner, relation by marriage, Abibaal. His house is next door but he lives in this store, too. I'm most likely to meet him out shopping, he's well known up and down the street, though it is always a special treat to visit his home. In a *domus* that takes up the whole ground floor of the neighbouring block, my boss has built a magnificent country pile. Squeezed into inner-city Tyre, he has established a great villa.

It is partly an optical illusion, painted cornices and columns giving depth of character to the flat walls. But he also has real bronze statues and pillars of Phrygian marble in there. He's got a very elaborate shrine to Ba'alshamin, the sky god, with blue ceiling and white clouds, though he swears he doesn't believe in heaven.

A big man, quite butch, but when he's swearing, when he's barking out orders or breathing out innuendos, he talks in a surprisingly high voice. Both sides of Abibaal, the filthy-rich purple tycoon and the sex-addicted buffoon, speak in the same falsetto tone. It's what we Romans call *superanus*. And that is the only reason why I even slightly love him, because he just makes me laugh so hard.

"I've had a message from Balthazar and your sister. They're at Hazor."

"Where's that?"

"We trade there," he says. "It's on the Damascus road, dear, about three days from here. Apparently they need to buy a new donkey."

"Did they say anything about business?" I ask him.

"Coming with a big order."

"Going to need a big ass."

"Want to come and do your banking tonight?" He's bought three jugs of wine. Even I'd have a job to bank those now...

"Oh, I've locked the shop already. There haven't been any robberies round here for ages."

"It was last month," says Tanis, "remember; Urbana, the ivory carver."

"Some shit made off with her entire stock of Sphinx figurines," Abibaal trills. "Must have gone way out of town to sell those babies on. Heard if they've been caught yet, Veronica?"

"Don't think so," I murmur, making my own guilty purchase quick as I can.

"Inscrutable, though her dress is see-through," says my landlord. Even when he thinks he is looking me straight in the eye, his gaze settles on the full folds of my tunic, as if he is blind to any pair of orbs but those.

"I'll come at dawn, Abi." I crack one dazzling smile because my commercial success still depends on his goodwill and walk out of the store slowly, calling over my shoulder; "I spent it all on Hercules tonight."

More reason, then, to recover on couches with ebony feet at Abibaal's, served every delight from dormouse to peacock by his slaves. But I need to be alone now, if that means a hard bed and some stale bread. There is wine to soften both.

I go up to my flat and fling open the shutters. The evening air, as light and scent, fills the room. I untie my sandals and kick them off by the door. Pouring a cup of water from the silver jug, I sip half before wandering over to the window sill and tipping the rest into my flower pots.

Sweet hyssop and heliotrope flourish on my shop-front; advertising the purple trade by day, disguising the smell of my piss pot in the night.

I sit on my bed and unstop the wineskin, mixing it with water for a while. On the table in front of me are displayed my treasures; and now I can be at one with myself, looking at my many things.

Standing on three lion's feet, this table is my only proper piece of furniture. I have invested my money in objects of art, collecting items of lust and envy and greed. I love to look at them, to touch and feel them, to tweak their positions on my display table.

I posses a set of glass vases, their shape sexy, their substance smoky. I own a bronze bust of Bacchus. I've got a Gorgon's head in ivory. I have a decanter made of *Terra Sigillata,* a fine red pottery from Rome. My best thing is the jewelled sword hilt, long and thick as Hercules' thing. Anyway, I love lining them up with geometrical precision.

When it is dark outside, I take wine without water and lie on the bed. My sheets look purple but they're just cheap, dyed black with nut-gall. Its shade comes off on my body as if all the dead snails in Tyre are crawling on my skin. But I'm so stained already it doesn't make a difference.

Their shells are pierced with an awl first, stabbed in the side so it's easier to prise out the gland. One shellfish might not feel too much. But so many; they make it impossible not to notice the pain.

When I lay down at night, the five pricks become five thousand, the snails I've smashed and grabbed today, singing to sell their product. The purple empress; wall-painted with the blood of a *murex* massacre.

But I'm not really the empress. My big sister is. She was here before me. She prepared the way.

CHAPTER TWO

Publia was here three years before me. Lived in this *insula*, in the apartment over the shop; fended off the advances of Abibaal but not of his brother, Balthazar. Younger, handsomer, sexier; whatever. His better-looking kid brother fell for Abibaal's first floor tenant, hard and fast. They married last year and left for a lucrative new position in Bethany, just outside of Jerusalem.

Publia said it was too easy, shipping purple back to the heart of the Roman Empire. The finger-striped linen, folded togas stacked as high as the *Colosseum*, the lengths of dyed woollen cloth stretching across the Mediterranean Sea like a net, so our ships never sank any more.

She wanted a new challenge. Now she's selling purple to the tribes of Israel. Her wares will never make a stitch in the tabernacle curtain, a knot in the rabbi's prayer-shawl, but there's a lot of Roman sewing up in the courts of Judea these days.

As sisters we were strands of the same thread but the fates have untwisted us till we're trading along completely different routes. Publia is more business-minded than me. All the time I was in the temple, dancing and singing to the goddess of marriage, she was buying and selling. While I was having a mental breakdown back home she was about to get married and move on. Not just one step ahead of me, Publia is running on a much faster track.

The day my sister is due to arrive in Tyre, I rise with the sun. As it starts to light up the stone faces of the city, I lay my *alabastrotheca* on the table and begin to do my make-up. In this carrying case, locked in the strongbox with my money overnight, are all the pots and flasks and alabaster jars that I need to be me.

I start with a little ground horn to enamel my teeth; go on with chalk and white lead to lighten my brow and cheeks; use ochre or, in times of need, the lees of wine to redden my lips; and darken my eyebrows with ashes or, in flush times, powdered antimony.

My mirror is only made of copper but it gives me a good look. I don't need much reflection, though; Publia is prettier than me, a fact long settled but a score never quite resolved. She said it was too easy,falling in love with Balthazar. I think she meant because they were equally beautiful. Our relationship is more complicated.

I have the edge when it comes to hairdos though, these days, I do my own. I haven't had a hairdresser since I was Venus' nun; it seems vain to have one now. But even living on the outskirts of Jerusalem, Publia manages to find an *ornatrix* to fix her hair in the styles of empire.

Piled high as a tower, with tiers and terraces, plaited and latticed and crimped to crispy curls; the last time I saw her, nearly a year ago, she looked great but dated. Here in Tyre, I'm closer to the source of fashion, the frills and fancies of Juno herself, conveyed to these shores on boats straight from Rome.

I am sure my hairdo will be trendier than my sister's. Though our natural colour is brown, I'm sporting some streaks of blond; false hair, dyed with a blend of goat fat and beech ash. They're pinned in place, probably not as neatly as her hairdresser could; but Pubi has been on the road for nearly a month now, and may not be so stylish.

They don't arrive till dusk. I have been on tenterhooks all day, but she's been on a donkey, so we're all dishevelled as they clatter up to Abibaal's *domus* with a toppling pack and pair of dusty boys. The slaves are sent to stables in the next street while our host leads Balthazar and Publia inside his house. They rush to the fountain tinkling in his atrium, and splash their dry mouths and dirty feet with recycled Tyre water.

"Thank Mercury we made it in time," Publia cries. "I could not have stood another night in that tent."

"I thought you stayed in inns?" I'm hugging and kissing her but not really listening yet.

"Mostly, but we got caught out when there were no rooms. It is very busy around Capernaum."

"Well, you're here now."

We spit out platitudes with the kisses till we are ready to stand back and behold each other. I was right about the hair. Publia notices my blonde streaks straight away.

"You must lend me your *ornatrix*," she says.

"I haven't got one." I see my modest shrug reflected in the pool behind her. "But don't worry, we'll go to the baths tomorrow. Tyre is brimful of fashion and beauty, and it overflows there."

Publia cups another handful of water to wash her brow and her breast. Abibaal's gaze now lays solely on her.

"By all that's bounteous, I would have sworn you'd be big with baby, now," he shrills, "or even have a little one in arms already. It's a year since your wedding and that olive mount you've settled on must be fertile ground."

Her face is washed of blood suddenly and she sways close to the *impluvium*'s edge. Balthazar rushes to stop her falling in, his arms dark as hers are light, his balance for both of them.

"We should go to rest," he says, "the same room as always?"

"Yes, the best," Abi bows deeply now, "let me get someone to show you."

"I know the way," Bal smiles at his brother. "Left at the statue of Priapus."

I go back to my own flat; dead ahead at the sign of Venus.

In my dream that night, Publia appears to be painted on the wall of Abibaal's best guest room; and I am on the opposite one, silently screaming. She's white as chalk, I'm black as gall; the third sister, Tertia, I try not to go there, even in nightmares. We're daubed in rich detail, brighter than life. But between us; shadows.

I wake feeling like my face has come off on the bed sheet; the eye-liner, the lip-tint, cried and sighed into cloth, though their darkness stay on my skin. Nothing gets me clean.

Publia wants to go to the baths as soon as they open in the morning. The men set off for the docks but we go where the water is not so fishy. Through an archway like the parting in Neptune's mosaic beard, my sister hurries; paying the attendant an *as* to hang her tunic, cloak and bag on a peg shaped like the sea-god's trident. She grabs her scented oil and slips into the *tepidarium* with a sigh of relief.

When only her face is out of the water, she starts to relax. Wallowing in the warm pool, russet dust billows out of her long dark hair; the grime of Galilee comes off her in rings. She hasn't bathed since the river Jordan. To a Roman, that's forever. Laughing, she tells me that Abibaal still looks at her admiringly, though she's so dirty and smelly. Then, she says;

"How do you think I look?"

Her smile is crooked, her gaze is straight.

"Well, you are very pale," I say. "But... "

"... Not very pregnant."

"No. So..."

"I bleed all the time," she says.

With a blink, at first I think she means from her hands or feet.

"Have you seen a doctor?"

"What good will that do?" Her mouth is pretty much the only part out of the water now: "Physicians can't cure women's ills."

So then I see what the issue is; moon-blood that flows all month long. "Seek some specialist help," I splutter. "The midwife?"

"Inappropriate," she says.

"The oracle?"

"Unavailable."

"There must be herbalists in Bethany?"

"There is one healer I have heard of... My neighbour told me."

Publia closes her eyes, lashes moist on her cheeks, and looks like she might float away, privately, in the public baths. I wait for her to finish but then, with a whoosh, she gets out. Rising pink-skinned from the pool, she trips down a warm stone step to get her towel then hot-foots it along the colonnades to the *caldarium*. I run after her, dripping.

In the hot room we stand panting as the drips turn into big droplets of sweat, running down our legs then lower ourselves slowly, slowly into the steaming water. Publia sits closer to me and blows me a story in the bubbles:

"In Bethany, our garden backs onto this lady's; she is Greek but I get her. She's blessed with lots of children and loads of pomegranate trees. Five kids, naturally skint, but she makes extra money by flogging her freshly-squeezed juice in Jerusalem. The trees grow on our land, too, and the buxom fruit is so plentiful I sold her a couple of sacks-full."

"Sold?" I say.

"She makes a big profit in the city. So, I like her just fine. She speaks a little Latin and I speak a little Greek, and we talk sometimes at the crumbling garden wall. Her name is Alethea, her husband is an olive dealer; she's very dark, but comely and coy. However, she is lame. Born with a club foot, she walks with a limp but she's fast and strong."

"Does she tread the pomegranate seed like grapes?" I ask. "With that bad foot?"

"Don't know," Publia sniffs, "I think it's a press, though I've never been to see. Anyway, we are fine ones to talk, treaders of snails; stained to the knees, at least, with dirty purple."

I laugh so loud a lady looks round. The hot bath is getting full and this is a good time to sit on the side, taking it in turns to oil and strigil each other's backs. The slick of unguents and the snick of blunt metal accompany my sister's story, as if it were strummed on a lyre instead of our spines.

"She sells at the baths of Bethesda. It's by the sheep gate, if you ever do business that way, with five porticoes. The pool has magical properties; when the waters start to churn, the first person in gets cured of their ailments. The Jews say an angel comes down and stirs the pond so the place is permanently packed with the dying and deformed and their salacious spectators."

"Have you actually been there?" I ask.

"I never would. Baths should be like this; indoors and heated. So, listen, Alethea set up her drinks stall and called to the suffering crowd: ruby juice, fruit medicine... She can't sing the stock off the shelves like you can, sister."

Publia was the first one who noticed my voice; *pater* was too loud, *mater* too la-la to hear a soft, still song around the villa when I came along. Only Pubi applauded me; the only one, too, when my audience got bigger, who never bought anything off me. Probably the only person in the world I trust, she passes me her *strigilis* for a long job; her back, her shoulders, her arms, her story.

Her next door neighbour was pimping some freshly-squeezed blood-seed, that's how to sing the sale, at Bethesda Baths:

"She usually went on a Tuesday," Publia says, "but this was the Sabbath, which annoys the locals. People of Judah don't sell but they do buy on that day, though, so Alethea would sometimes go. And every time, she saw a man there who couldn't move at all.

"He was lying on a foul mat, at the foot of the steps, unsheltered by the splendid porches from sun and rain. He always lay there, one step from the healing waters. Yet, when the moment came and waves started peaking in the pool, he could not move any closer; and somebody else always got in first.

"She told me that he haunted her as she walked among the customers who sat in the shade, higher up the steps. Beneath fine arches, she sold pomegranate juice to people with no arms, no legs, no eyes, no minds; but whole enough to make a purchase, or accompanied by family and friends.

"It was a hot day and the juice had a healthy sparkle; Alethea said she was raking the cash in. But she couldn't get the paralytic off her mind. As the sun edged across the stone steps, so she edged closer to him; a jug of her life-giving liquid in hand. Perhaps he needed it most, of everybody there. Certainly he could afford it least. She knew he had no money. And even if it were stashed somewhere about his skin-and-bones, he could not hand it over.

"Still, Alethea ended up standing next to him, at the edge of the water, preparing to pour out a cup. Her thoughts trickled loud as the juice into the beaker; 'I cannot pour him a full measure for I can't afford to give so much away. But I cannot leave his cup empty for I do have something to spare. I will give him exactly half a cup; a half measure for my faith in the gods of these waters, a half measure held back in case'.

"Then suddenly it seemed as if she had spoken aloud and someone had heard her, for she saw bare feet approaching along the edge of Bethesda bath; coming slowly, as if their owner had been watching her for a long time, from further away, and had seen what she was doing and had something to say.

"When Alethea looked up to check this guy out, though, she thought it was Apollo! At first sight, against the lengthening sunlight, in long white robes; long, wavy hair too, pointed beard, the most beautiful man she had ever seen, in Athens, in Jerusalem or her dreams.

"When he spoke, at first, it was not to her. He bent down to the paralysed man on the mat. She heard him say something in Aramaic, which she knows a little; 'will you be well?'

"Without looking at Alethea, without turning his face from the man, this god reached out his hand for the cup she was holding. She gave it, trembling, and he took it cleanly. She knew he knew it was a half-measure, poured half-heartedly. But he tipped the begrudged liquid over the cripple's legs; and said 'stand up'."

"How rude," I say, finishing off by oiling her forearms and strigiling down to her fingers. "Mind you," I go on, "the cripple's faith was great; for if he was first in the waves, and it didn't heal his aches and pains, he would sink to the bottom and surely drown."

"No. Alethea swears, and I believe her, that the man got off the mat. He slowly clambered to his feet. The crowd saw him standing up and quickly closed in, then... shh, listen... The god turned to my friend and tipped the cup over her toes and there was still some juice left. He handed back the cup and said, in Greek; 'There will always be enough, even for you.'

"Then he looked over her shoulder, and she glanced round to see that the water was just starting to sparkle, as if he were making it so. The bath was indeed stirred by an angel. And as she looked, she felt a little push; then she was falling. Though she could hardly believe, it felt like he pushed her into the pool."

My sister presses a fingertip to my forehead. "So, always give a full cup, *soror*. I know you always take one, don't you!

"Alethea was first in the water; and when she bobbed up to the surface the crowd who had surrounded the walking man with the mat turned to see who'd been lucky in the bubble bath," she says.

"Stop laughing, Veronica, the naked matrons are looking. I haven't even got to the important part yet. Listen, the point is this. Her foot was fixed. The lifelong deformity, I saw it, was cured. When she came home again, to the bottom of the garden, Alethea showed me a perfect foot. She'd been mended."

Publia puts the stopper firmly in her bottle of oil, and wipes her strigil.

"So was it actually Apollo?" I'm confused.

"No. He was just a man. He was surrounded by the crowd and she didn't see him again. She was mobbed getting out of the bath, with some local lady offering to be her agent, and flog the full cup of fizzy water in her hand to the highest price."

"Did the pomegranate juice cure the paralytic, then?"

"I've drunk it. It didn't heal me. I've rubbed the seeds all over my body. It didn't give me a baby."

I strip the last slick of oil from my shin, forcefully with my *strigilis,* as if I could scrape her bloody loss from my skin. My olive oil is scented with roses. But it is not enough to cleanse me.

All the sights, and sounds, and smells of the *caldarium* take me back to when I was lying face down on the tiles, with a ring of hoary-toenailed, hairy male feet around me.

At the Baths of Agrippa I was gang-raped, during the feast of Venus. I was hardly a virgin before it happened, of course, but I was hardly alive afterwards. Publia does know about this but she doesn't know all the details; I would spare my worst enemy parts of that story, let alone my best friend.

She knows that for ages I couldn't go to the public baths; and she knows that I almost boiled my body in a private bath belonging to a friend of our father, trying to get super clean again.

She knows that if the strigil had a sharper blade, I'd have bled my own hot pool full of pomegranate juice, by now.

When my eyes go far away, as they often do at bath time, Publia knows where I am. When they roll like the eyes of the marble statue in the alcove, here, of a sea nymph chased by the horny Poseidon, she waits for me to return, and she smiles reassuringly.

All the other girls in the *laconicum* are giving and receiving robust massages, bones stretched out on the hot floor, skin slapped and shiny in the steam. My sister and I are both too delicate, mentally and physically, for the full Roman handshake; but we do get warm enough to scream like all the other girls as we jump into the *frigidarium*.

So, here we go, plunging into freezing water, into liquid ice. So cold, it makes the loosest flesh tight; the lady least happy with her looks, perky. Publia and I shriek as we dip and shake.

The female population of Tyre are hot-blooded and warm-hearted but there's an odd specimen fit for a colder home. A fat matron, with skin white as foam, floats in the *frigidarium*, wallowing in the chilly pool alone; while all the other ladies of her neighbourhood huddle in the steam room, bitching and hissing for hours.

I would stay under the water, holding my head below the surface longer, if I could. The colours down there are fascinating for a shade trader; see, in the *tepidarium*, straight off the street, the blue tiles look like splinters of a sunny sky; here, in the cold plunge, the blue is ice shards: in the *caldarium* blue flickers like the hotter part of fire.

Because I am usually drowning in purple, this submersion is like a breath of air. I grab my sister's hand and pull her under the water again, one more gasp before we go. But she bobs back slower than I do, and leaves a trail of blood in the bath. We both see it and so does the whale lady who shouts angrily;

"Plug it up!"

"It soaks through," Publia mutters as we get out.

In the changing room, we stand side by side in front of a dull silver mirror, drying our hair.

"What are you going to do?" I cry. "You can't go on like this forever."

"I don't know. I thought I might try to look for that Apollo man next time I'm in Jerusalem."

"That could be ages. We need to do something now."

"Oh, if you're offering to help..." she sobs.

"Anything..."

"Find me a hairdresser!"

The best one is Haqikah but we can't get her till after work. Publia will be lucky to have any hair left; it's a stressful day on fulfilment, down at the docks where Tyre's seagull chorus always gives us a headache.

She has the paperwork from Jerusalem; a bigger job than ever before. I get the paperwork off a boat just in from Rome, a letter and mega order from our father in the chest with the money. One little coin pays off the slave who guarded it with his life across the Mediterranean Sea.

Unrolling those long papyrus scrolls, in a warehouse filled with the shouts and grunts of Abibaal's labourers, we try to fathom the workload.

It's almost a temple, this giant building at the edge of the earth, the start of the sea. But between its pillars are long rolls of linen, strung up to dry their purple stripes. Bales of cotton are stacked in its caverns, ready to be unfolded, cut and coloured in the nave; by a congregation who sweat and sing like the workers for Venus that I knew before.

Heavy guys for the stock-handling, bald heads and stained loin-cloths; they hoist aloft, and hold fast, and stretch tight the material of this lucrative sale. The tools are held by lighter, brighter worshippers at the warehouse altar; cloth cutters with knives like diamond shards; stitchers with awls sharp as their black eyes and thread fine as their flowing hair.

Everybody in this holy factory has purple hands. People who stir the Tyrian dye-bath, like me, can never get clean. From the old man who scrapes the bottom of clay vats, to the new man who measures the thickness of stripes with a marked-up clay stick; to the lady who packs softness for the most powerful women in the Roman empire. They all have fingers tinted the shade of the sky at twilight.

Only those in the loom room, where Publia and I don't go if we can help it (weaving was our mother's thing), have white fingertips. Ours are slightly pink, as we oversee our father's interest in this place with the lightest touch.

We do have to use our heads and, as we arrive back at the *domus* for the hairdressing appointment, it shows. Haqikah is waiting in Publia's bedroom, the couch spread with tortoiseshell combs and shiny silver hand mirrors. She looks up as we rush in and her nose wrinkles.

"Ladies, have you been dipped in the dying vats and hung up to dry?"

Embarrassed, I run my fingers through my hair. I'm sure there are snail trails in those stiff tresses.

Haqikah may be one of the best beauticians in town but it isn't just due to her skills with brush and blush. She speaks the truth, to customers accustomed to bullshit. As she sits my sister down and wraps a *supparum* round her shoulders, she smiles; but says,

"I am *ornatrix*, not gardener; if you want me to work on this bush, I should have brought a rake."

Like us, Haqikah wasn't born in Tyre, so her accent isn't pure Phoenicia. I think she came as a slave from Egypt, and bought her freedom by hard talking. She is small, round, bronzed; with black teeth.

Publia towers over her, but the feisty stylist still builds an edifice of plaited battlements and crimped crenulations, a castle high on my sister's head. While she works, with the comforting stroke of the comb and cream, or the soothing hiss of the hot irons, I read the letter from my father, calling out to Pubi the parts that concern her.

He tells about a dream he had of seeing her in Bethany with five children (hope he hadn't gone to her next-door neighbour's house by mistake)... He says our sister, Tertia, is keeping snakes in Publia's old bedroom... He advises, on the recommendation of his personal herbalist (not *mater,* who once gave him a mouthful of hemlock) that she should try raspberry leaf tea...

When the hairdresser overhears this, she nods wisely and pins the diadem in her 'do'.

"So. I thought you looked pale," she says gently to my sister. "Try nettles. No, not as pessary! You can get them as pills. And shepherd's purse, know that one? You just pick it, and yarrow, and even parsley's good for bad periods. Then there's this thing that comes in from the east; ginger, seen it? Don't taste it, but that stuff makes a potent healing paste..."

"I thought you said you weren't a gardener," says Publia, ungraciously.

Haqikah tugs on her roots.

"Try the nettles," she says.

When her husband sees the new hairstyle he makes a face like he's tried the nettles. But when she's looking the other way, he eyes her silken fortress with awe and, I think, arousal. I mean to imitate his exact facial expression for her as soon as we are alone together.

In the *triclinium*, Balthazar is lying on the couch, ready for dinner. Publia lies down beside him, hungrily; I make the third. Abibaal reclines on another couch by himself. He is drunk again and laughing loudly at his own ripe jokes, ahead of Bal's trip to the snail suppliers tomorrow.

Shoppers for both Latin purple and Hebrew blue queue at this stinking spring, the source of a million Tyrian *murex*. The same sea-snails go into the pot of traders in stripy togas and into the separate, sacred process of *tekhelet* dyers for the high priest's prayer tassels.

These 'tzitzit' are what Abibaal seems to find so amusing, waggling the word like a silly dog's tail, again and again. He's built with broad shoulders so you can't see his own wiggling tail of long, black hair till he turns sideways, and a big tummy, domed like the top of his bald head.

I hide my smile behind a peacock-feathered *stola* and the same colours shimmer as I pile leafy vegetables high on Publia's plate, though all the nettles and parsley and shepherd's purse in Phoenicia won't help her period problems.

She just picks pomegranate seeds one at a time from a glass dish. I can tell what she's thinking. The juice or the jiggling waters which cured him? The angel or that Apollo guy; her friend heard his real name but she can't remember it now.

She's barely heard a word anybody said all day. Instead, she is picturing the scene so clearly I can see it, too; in her eyes, like shadow figures on the cave wall. A paralysed man got up and walked away.

Balthazar goes on a business trip to the dye works next morning, setting off before the rush hour starts in high-rise Tyre, with two slaves and one donkey. Publia has been tasked with sourcing a second ass for their trip back to Bethany; a big one, for their purple load wobbling in the heat haze all the way up the Megiddo road.

I'm stuck in the shop all day, stock-taking, singing; plying my trade with tales of priests and kings who have worn my product and can endorse its superior quality. Abibaal is mostly at the docks, I believe, humping bales of cotton; or humping between bales of cotton. Somehow, the four of us turn another ten thousand snails into gold.

Three of us are waiting in the *domus* for Balthazar to get back for dinner, again. I'm just hanging out in the atrium while Pubi gets changed and Abibaal shuffles past me, on his way to the dining room. As he goes by, he farts; surprisingly, it's as deep as his voice is high. I frown at him over the scroll I'm reading. And he, the cheeky sod, looks at the statue of Melqart that rules this entrance hall, and makes out that it was the god who farted. With a nod and a wink he blames the main Phoenician deity for his stink.

Then Bal appears, red faced and breathing heavily.

"Where's your sister?" he says.

"In the *cubiculum*. I'll call her." I start running towards her bedroom; but stop and come back quickly. "Why, what is it? I ask him.

"Don't worry, it's good news." Balthazar's teeth are white in his black beard, the smile a crescent moon.

His brother's mouth is bigger, though. Abibaal is shouting out for Publia, so loudly some of the slaves run in from the kitchen, too.

"No, no, it's all good," Bal tries to calm them down.

He takes his wife's hand when she finally appears, fumbling with her *stola*, and kneels before her.

"There is a certain salesman I often see doing business at the snail works; so full of woe a deal lasts half a day but not this time.

"Noam was serene throughout the transaction, which only took an hour. When he nodded goodbye, I asked why he was so happy today. Honey," Balthazar beams, "I think he's met the same man that Alethea saw in Bethany. They call him Yeshua. They say he comes from Nazareth.

"But he is not just a man. He does magic. He makes miracles. He comes from nowhere but people are starting to follow him. Many have left their homes to hear him talk. He took a boat out on the Sea of Galilee, so he could teach without them drowning his voice.

"What man is admired like this in Phoenicia or Rome? If he is a senator, he gets heckled; if he is a general, he gets overthrown; if he is an emperor, he gets arse-licked. Or cock-sucked..."

His wife and his brother lock eyes over his head, then each clap a hand on his shoulder and stand him up.

"Nobody just listens to anybody. But, apparently," Bal goes on, "men are downing tools, shutting up shop and following him. Fishermen, in particular."

"Well, it could be the one, I suppose," says Publia.

"He healed Noam's Mrs." Balthazar is visibly shaking. "She had the same trouble as you. I've known that old sea-snail for years. His wife has always been the bane of his life because she was so bleeding miserable. Then she heard that this Yeshua could heal the sick so she went to Capernaum with some of her synagogue to see for themselves."

"Did he lay hands upon her?"

Bal laughs giddily:

"As the wife of a trader in sacred *tekhelet*, coming face to face with the possible Messiah, it was better to fall to her knees. Sarah reckoned that feeling the rabbinical fringes was as good as kissing his hand.

"She felt the hem of his robe and was healed," Balthazar adds. "The woman's problems were fixed that instant. But this is not even how awesome he is. When she stroked the tassels he stopped walking. The crowd surrounded him in a crush.

"'Who touched me?' he said. 'What, master? Everyone is touching you,' his main men replied. 'Somebody touched the *tzitzit*,' he said; so they bent down and fished bloody Mrs Noam out of the masses.

"She said he was a gorgeous young man, whose beard seemed spun of blackened iron, whose eyes seemed forged of the same. He called her daughter, despite being younger. To plain old Sarah, he said, 'thy faith hath made thee whole'. And Noam swears to god that since then his wife has been sweetness and light."

"That's him," says Publia, "the Bethesda Apollo. Can I be healed, too? Please, husband, let me go to him."

"It is easier still," says Balthazar. "He is coming here. They say he is in the region of Sidon, travelling this way. Purple empress, he's coming to you."

CHAPTER THREE

Balthazar and Publia are only supposed to stay in Tyre for two weeks max, or it's bad for their business. They're away from home nearly two months on this trip, as it is. The next door neighbour is feeding their chickens but it's more complicated than that and they need to head back to Bethany soon.

They take three days choosing a new donkey and are proud of the big jackass, but I think they paid too much for it. To break him in, they go visiting every member of the extended Phoenician family Bal belongs to, and all his friends:

A grandmother with a gold ring in her nose, and lines, deep as cracks in the droughty earth, round her mouth. Aunts, plump and sweating; moustached and musk-odorous, with a gold ring round each wobbling arm. Sisters; big-bellied like Abibaal, broad-chested like Balthazar; ember-eyed like the handsome brother, high-voiced like the other one, with a gold ring round each swollen ankle. Nine times out of ten the women ask why Publia isn't pregnant yet.

A father who's been in the business so long the rings of his eyes are purple, and a gold ring in his ear. Friends, cousins, fellow Tyrians; all mouthy as Mars, cocky as Cupid, rich as Croesus with gold rings on every finger. IX times out of X, the boys ask Balthazar why his woman isn't pregnant yet.

Publia answers every time. Her attitude is positive; she says straight up what the problem is. She adds that there's a healer on his way, (she even tells them his name, while I would keep it to myself), and that she is hoping for a cure.

We don't know who or what to pray to, to bring this about. In Abibaal's house, there is a dedicated shrine to Ba'alshamin, a general purpose Melqart in the atrium, and a little Minerva and the Muses in his *bibliotheca*. We lay flowers and pour libations to all of them, but we're not sure if they're the right deities to address Publia's pleas. Personally, I feel it should be Venus; and as her ex-assistant priestess my fingers are twitching sometimes to make fertility blessings over my sister.

We make the mistake of asking Abibaal which of the gods is responsible for women's health and wellbeing. The son-of-a-bitch says 'Priapus!' and gives a disgusting chuckle. Having seen his statue of Priapus on many occasions I can simply state that this is the god of outsize penises.

But then Abibaal pauses thoughtfully.

"It is Melqart," he says. "In this city, Melqart is responsible for menstruation. And motherhood. He's responsible for milking, metalwork and *murex*. He oversees those who work with wicker and spikenard. He supervises topaz miners. He doesn't deal with locusts but all other plagues and pestilence are sent by his hand."

It is lies, of course, because Abibaal does not know the truth even of his own faith. But the conversation that starts with his nonsense ends with us setting off for the temple, two days later, to a feast and festival for this Melqart, god of cane and nard. When Bal overheard the argument between his wife and brother, his smooth tongue suggested this path; the one we often take, a compromise between religion and reason. Plus, I think he wants to show off the donkey.

Publia and I can both sit comfortably on its broad back, though I find the heat and the smell of the beast alarming, and the constant buzzing of flies around him makes it hard to talk. We are still having the same family argument, though:

This god they call Tyrian Melqart is clearly Hercules. Everyone even slightly Roman in the city knows it. As if one shopkeeper has painted over the signage of his predecessor, so you can still see the old characters through the new; there's an orderly queue of gods and goddesses in this ancient marketplace.

We four (the Phoenician boys and the Latin girls) go through the streets like a shadow puppet show, the sky painted with a sunset behind the downtown turrets and domes. Our fire, a purple sustenance from Abibaal's new wineskin, sipped as we ride. Our script, unbelievably wooden, shouted over the sound of the donkey:

Publia. What if we've been worshipping the wrong one?

Balthazar. Maybe that's why we haven't been blessed with a baby.

Me! You worship different ones; you say Hercules, he says Herakles. Maybe that's why.

Abibaal. But we're all agreed God lives in Tyre, right?

With the animal on a firm leash, Abi walks ahead of us, the sun setting also on his bald dome, with a long dark ponytail swishing beneath.

The temple we're approaching is not the one I usually go to, with the Olympic mosaic forecourt. This is in the heart of Tyre and as old as the city itself, nearly three thousand *anni*; no thanks to Nebuchadnezzar, the king of Babylon, who tried to destroy it five hundred years ago. We can see it on the skyline for ages before we arrive, the massive twin pillars standing like god's legs.

"They are eight cubits high." Balthazar, walking beside his wife on the donkey, sizes them up as if he's going to buy them.

"But they're not identical," Publia says.

Abibaal replies, without turning around;

"One is made of emerald, lit from inside by candles; the other is made of gold. The green one is for Astarte; in a normal temple it would be cypress-wood. The golden one is for Ba'al; traditionally they're made of stone."

"Hmm, Astarte," I murmur, "she's like Venus. That's what you should do, sister, touch the emerald pillar and pray. And you, Bal, touch the golden one at the same time. Maybe that would start a baby..."

"You're not allowed to touch them," Abi says. "Well, not unless you pay the priests a lot of money."

Balthazar looks up at Pubi, wincing as the ass walks, but pretty as Aphrodite.

"She's worth it," he sighs.

Abibaal slows as he comes in sight of the temple gates, his figure slim from behind. The big swell of his belly shows at the sides, but otherwise he has the tall, thin physique of Melqart in a pointy Phrygian cap. No match for the hunky Hercules I've been worshipping all my life.

We clip-clop into the temple forecourt and a trader accidentally lets his box of turtledoves free as we pass his stand. Not quite as bad as the time when a carpenter watching Publia go by, in the *Via Margutta,* sawed off his own hand. As I slip unnoticed from the donkey, there is a beating of white wings and the small flock of birds fly up through the crowd of people waiting to buy them for sacrificial purposes, into the sky.

The brothers park the donkey in a row with others under some palm trees. My sister and I try to plan a route with our eyes through the mass of people in the forecourt and up the temple steps so she and Bal can touch the pillars. It's not easy to plot our course, as the place is seething, but I seem to see a thread of brighter colour, leading in and out, around the groups of Tyrians in their holiday shades of snail juice. As soon as the boys have leashed their new beast to a tree trunk we walk into the carnival scene.

Publia moves a few steps through the people who pave the forecourt like stones themselves; a mosaic of rich businessmen and their glamorous women. Suddenly, she turns her head, with its rigid hairdo turning too, an elaborate shell-like ear, rising above the scarlet caps and dark curls of the crowd.

She shouts over her shoulder to me. "He's here." I don't have to ask who she means. His name seems to spread like a whisper, like a wind through rushes; yes, yes, people seem to be saying, yes, Yeshua. Yeshua.

That's the name we were told by Noam, the name they call him in Nazareth; that's the name thousands chanted by the Sea of Galilee. But that place is so far out of the purple picture, we've never sold a striped toga there. As we struggle to the temple steps and start to climb, the common language among dye-dealers of all colours and traders of all tongues is an aspirational Greek. The way we say his name sounds like this breeze-born wish, Jesus. Jesus.

He is there on the steps, talking like he could topple the temple with words. I can't see him, stuck behind Publia and Balthazar who are on tip-toes, but I can hear the voice. No wonder the crowd whisper; all the air in Tyre has rushed to the throat of this charismatic speaker. His tone resounds with wisdom, yet resonates with wit; unlike any song I've ever heard.

But he is answering the exact question we were asking all the way to the temple today and hundreds of times since my sister married her husband. Which god is real, Hercules or Melqart? Which is the true deity of Tyre? He says:

"All men worship one God, the three-in-one; but one sees him as the God of might, another as the God of thought, another as the God of love. Man names the part of God he sees, and this to him is all of

God; and every nation sees a part of God, and every nation has a name for God." [3]

In front of me, the others shift so I get a glimpse between their bodies; Pubi's dappled green and Bal's mossy cloaks part like valley-sides but I still can't see him, the mountain. Jesus. His name trickles like spring water on the lips of those who say it and pass it on. Or maybe it is more like wine.

Abibaal has been hailed by some fellow from Sidon, a *murex* tycoon we've met before. It turns out that this guy has followed Jesus since he first saw him up the coast a week ago. Abibaal shakes his head in bewilderment as the other man describes how he left his business and just walked away.

"We brought nothing," this Sidonite is saying, "and every night he has fed us and found us somewhere to sleep. Sometimes it's a tax-collector's villa, sometimes it's a stable. He has men who organise the travel and the hospitality."

Abibaal is shaking his bald head and his hairy belly now. "And nobody tries to overthrow this unholy ruler?"

"Listen," the guy says, "I've seen him fix a little girl's face that was so fucked by leprosy her mum could use it as a *koskino*. And everybody here has seen him do something like that, or heard it and believed it. There's this story going round; you'll love it, being in the rag trade.

"When he was a boy, Jesus played a great trick; he threw a bundle of cloths into the dyer's vat and drew them out all different colours. Yes; before the eyes of family and friends, from the same bubbling cauldron, he pulled a blue cloth, a yellow, a red."

"How did he do that?" Balthazar shouts over the crowd.

"It's what we all want to know. Everywhere he goes, people are gasping, or giggling, or weeping with joy. Stand closer. Listen to his words."

"We're trying to but you're in the way." Publia, as ever, not a people-pleaser.

"No, not here, it's too busy. Meet us later; you can come face to face with him."

Abi folds his arms across his formidable gut, but asks, "Where will you be?"

"The necropolis; do you know that place?"

Everybody who grew up in Tyre knows the necropolis, a city of the dead in a city of the living; sepulchre streets and tomb terraces, graves gardened with boxthorn and rockrose, once left for the recently deceased, floral tributes taken root.

Underneath the overgrown stonework are all sorts of secret bowers, hidden nooks for courting couples to use. Cushioned with moss and curtained with ferns, there are many fragrant love nests in the necropolis, much frequented by the young men and women of Tyre.

And the not-so-young; Balthazar took Publia there before they married last year. She told me they'd been 'necking in the necropolis' in such intimate detail I might as well have been there, too, but the thing I remember most clearly from her account is how the slim marble pillars she stared up at were strangled by creeping ivy.

Pale, choking stone; I see her face now, between Bal and Abi's shoulders in the heaving crowd, as Publia realises she has to go to hell to get healed. It's the look of our wall-painted Persephone, done in chalk, with the underworld stretching before her.

In Rome the graves are all along the roadside, reaching way beyond the city gates. It is one thing to be accompanied by the ancestors on our quests for help. It is another, to journey into their darkness to find it.

We go home first to freshen up. At the *domus*, Pubi disappears into her bedroom with a bucket of water. I sing a vigorous burst of worship to the gods in the atrium, then sit and wait anxiously in the library.

I was looking for a scroll I had out earlier but can't find it on the shelf; one of the, frankly illiterate, slaves must have misfiled it. But there is something new to read on the desk. Dad has sent Abibaal the latest collection of old stories, by a singer he loves, a dead poet from Rome. Publius Ovidius Naso; my father was such a big fan he even named his daughter after this star.

I unroll it and start to read, finding a good bit. It's not one of the poems *pater* used to perform at parties, in what was apparently a peerless impression of Ovid himself. No, it's a piece he used to read to me and my sisters, as we waited what seemed like years for *mater* to put her make-up on.

"*Medicamina Faciei Femineae*." I read it aloud, loving the alliteration:

"Although incense is pleasing to the gods and soothes their wrath, it must not be kept exclusively for their altars. A mixture of incense and nitre is good for black-heads. Take four ounces of each. Add an ounce of gum from the bark of a tree, and a little cube of oily myrrh. Crush the whole together and pass through a sieve.

"Pound the first horns that drop from the head of a lusty stag. Then make haste and bake pale lupins and windy beans. Add thereto white lead and the scum of ruddy nitre and Illyrian iris, which must be kneaded by young and sturdy arms. Dry the mixture in the air, and let the whole be ground beneath the mill-stone worked by the patient ass.

"Add twelve narcissus bulbs which have been skinned, and pound the whole together vigorously in a marble mortar. There should also be added two ounces of Tuscan spelt, and nine times as much honey. Any woman who smears her face with this cosmetic will make it brighter than her mirror."

I wish it were true, not a joke but a genuine beauty treatment that really worked. No matter how long it took to weigh and pound and dry and grind, I would do it; for the sake of my looks, tonight. It could not take as long as Publia, naturally beautiful, does to wash and dress again. I think her period is particularly heavy this evening.

Abibaal is almost legless by the time we leave and has been shouting at the servants in the kitchen. Balthazar is sitting at the sky god's shrine, humming and rocking nervously. The weather has turned overcast; it threatens rain in the *peristylum*. We all wear our cloaks. Publia clasps hers around a swollen stomach.

We leave the donkey in the stables, this time, and set off on foot through the streets of Tyre where the ancient and the ultra-modern are hewn from the same stone. Everything is wet; it'll be hard to keep torches alight and there's no moon. It would be easy to go home again; no one would ever know and nothing would ever be said.

But I'm thinking, by Apollo, the neighbour from Bethany swore he was an angel, and half of Sidon seems to be following him instead of feasting with Ba'al. I only heard the wind-chiming voice on the temple steps and tonight I feel that at all costs, and if nothing else, I must surely see his face.

So we make good progress and Abibaal gradually sobers up a bit, but Publia has to piss in a ditch. I concentrate on keeping my shawl out of the mud. It is stitched with peacock feathers around the hem.

There are threads of purple in this trim; I saved up for months. The green and blue silks aren't so dear but sewn by one of Tyre's finest, a wing cost an arm and a leg. They say the peacock is Juno's favourite bird; but the hundred eyes embroidered on mine wink like scales in the mermaid Tyrus' tail as I tighten the shawl round me. I shall not fall easily as she did for Hercules, if it turns out we're about to meet the purple king.

A line of arches like the open-mouthed chorus marks our entranceway to the necropolis. As we go in, Abi and Bal are arguing in loud voices about which historical ruler built this cemetery. They stop talking as we come in sight of a lamp-lit gathering, and a strange camp set up around the damp hearthstones of the grotto.

In the Phoenician boys' sudden silence, another voice calls, from the bodies silhouetted at the edge of the fire, 'The Prince of Peace!'

"This is it," mutters Bal grimly, grabbing Publia by the hand and dragging her towards the rabbi. But now, just a fathom away from her potential saviour, Publia can't go any further. I pull her other hand but she has collapsed to the floor, crying. Abibaal tries to push her from behind, sober now and intoning some sort of spiritual anthem, from mixed snippets of Herculean hymns.

Poor Publia and her posse are causing such a commotion that Apollo himself comes down from the ring of firelight on the higher terrace to talk to us. He speaks in slow, low Greek.

"Why is she crying?"

"Please," Bal says, "She needs your help. We have only been married one year, but it is always her time of the month."

Jesus looks at my sister. Beneath the edifice of hair, her eyes are hidden but her cheeks redden.

"Why do you not ask me for help? Don't you think I can heal you?"

This unleashes a torrent of snot from Pubi.

"I know you can," she sniffs. "We heard of a lady you cured of exactly the same thing. I know you can; I just don't know why you would."

Publia pauses to blow her nose on her shawl. It is embroidered with pomegranates, from the same *plumarius* I got mine, next door to the wine store. She fingers the exquisite stitching of red seed for a moment and seems to take strength from the fruit.

"My neighbour from Bethany," she says bravely, raising her eyes to the rabbi, "she met you at the baths. There was a poor man who couldn't move at all, don't know if you remember? I understand how much demand there must be to make miracles. You can't cure everyone."

Then the god speaks again, and no one who hears his voice will disbelieve it; "I can cure everyone. Stand up now. You shall be healed."

Publia stands and screams; the fringes of her pomegranate shawl shaking. As if he tips a cup of the ruby juice over her, I see this metamorphosis; as if he throws a pot of red paint at her picture, in a scene from Ovid on the wall; the wan nymph transforms to ruddy health.

Her husband raises his voice to the Tyrian stars and Abibaal actually has tears twinkling in his eyes as he kneels at the feet of this Herculean in his turn.

"Thank you, master," he murmurs, who hasn't called anyone master since he was thirteen years old.

Then Jesus turns to look at me. He looks as if he knows who I am. As if he's seen me before. It's not like men look, at the hairdo, the lips, the tits; but at my eyes, the lamps of my spirit, making them flare. He looks as if he loves me more than anyone else in my life has done, even my honoured parents. As if he loved me before I was born.

Smiling, he beckons us all into the bower, where a big gathering of Phoenicians, Romans, Greeks and Jews are mixed in equal measure. It is my gaze he holds (though, afterwards, Publia says he was looking at her,) as this compelling creature tells a tale too simple and too obvious to be true:

"A father gave his sons some pomegranate seeds and said to them; 'he who produces the most fruit shall be my heir.' The three brothers walked away, arguing. 'I will eat mine,' said the eldest, 'while they're fresh and juicy; that's the best way to make them grow, as part of me.' 'That is greedy and selfish,' said the second. 'I'm going to plant mine, in excellent ground, so that there will be plenty of pomegranates growing for all.' 'Noble,' teased the third son, 'but I will eat mine and plant them too.' 'How can you do both?' cried the older boys, but the youngest just slipped quietly into the trees. When he had enjoyed eating the precious seeds he waited patiently by a hole in the earth; then he returned them, as compost, to the roots of his father's orchard."

When Jesus stops speaking there is silence for a moment, then everybody starts talking at once. Wine bags are passed among the crowd as the conversation flows. Some people are saying his story means one thing, some are saying it means another; some are saying it doesn't have a point at all, or perhaps they just don't get it.

There is a lull in the dialogue and, before I can stop myself, I blurt out; "I know a prettier story about pomegranate seeds."

Everybody turns to look at me now.

"Well, it's not actually a story," I add, "it's true."

There is a part of me that came here to sing tonight; to give voice to the purple everyone else in this city works with their hands or their heads. Somehow, I knew I was going to, but I didn't know what. As I belt out the plot, from a time when the god of the underworld stole a virgin from her mother, Earth, and nothing flourished till they were reunited, it seems the only song possible for this gathering:

"Pluto loved spring's child and wanted to keep her
below in the gloom with her groom, the grim reaper
but Ceres, her mother, and serial lover
was grieving a winter of ice and of flint."

I curl my tongue, uncoil my lungs compellingly as I tell how pretty Proserpina was allowed back to the light on one condition, that she had not touched food in the darkness. But though she preferred drinking the girl had plucked without thinking, from a low-hanging branch in death's garden, one pomegranate:

"Its skin was sun-starved where the mother hadn't shone, yet when stripped of the thin, blanching peel, it revealed just as plump seeds that had ever been squished by her teeth. With a sob and a sniff she did five, no, six of its bloody rubies."

It is dramatic, the effect my speech has on the group gathered around Jesus. They are like a pan of mixed spices, sizzling on fires lit in the stone pits of the necropolis. Some of them know that story already, those whose religion is Roman or whose beliefs are Greek. The Tyrians hiss and spit; the tale is familiar to them and the characters have different names but the action is similar.

Then I realise that the god himself is still looking at me. Maybe he hasn't come across Ovidius before, translated on the spot into sales-girl Greek by an ex-temple whore. My voice isn't the sweetest; it's been described as lusty. I think it suits the necropolis by night.

"Consider," Jesus is speaking to me, with forty or more men around him, waiting on his word. "When the rock is rolled from Hades' entrance, how happy Persephone is, to see the light."

"But she was dazzled by jewels in the darkness," I whisper. "Her husband hoards much of the world's wealth under there."

He laughs seriously; this sounds mad but that man can do it. He chuckles soberly and says; "come. Follow me. There are riches that will dazzle you, here, by this fire."

I think he means the people. There are some colourful characters alongside the Phoenician purple of Abibaal and Balthazar, and the Roman red of Publia, like gems in the gloaming. There are many Jews gleaming ochre and gold, crimson and coal black in the firelight; and many Sidonites who've flowed, with this prophet, from along the coast, in cloaks of blue and green. There are merchants and mothers, in stripes, from Galilee; and a mysterious-looking man from far to the east whose white cloth is wound around his head like a cloud crown.

This seems to be aflame as the many tongues around the fireplace declaim His miracles. Everybody there has seen Jesus do something physically impossible. He has supernatural power; he raised a twelve-year-old girl from the dead. The conversation is heated and yet there's no debate. This man is the genuine divine. Brightly lit, not a trickster, he seems to ignite new life in all who enter the glow.

Now and then, as the evening goes on, somebody new stumbles upon the group gathered in these crumbling cloisters by firelight.

Maybe a courting couple have been distracted by our racket; maybe a group of drunken youths have been attracted by our buzz. As the newcomers burst into the circle, challenging its leader, the scene begins again; and Jesus of Nazareth starts with a story, something beguiling but hard to get, like the pomegranate parable he told us.

He acts, I think as I watch in awe, like he knows everyone already; and he picks his words to fit each personally; delicate as lilies, strong as ears of wheat.

If they don't get the weird tale, they just walk away. He sounds bonkers; and this looks like a *bacchanalia*. There is wine, it flows plentifully from somewhere, though our own skins were long since drained; and I am pretty drunk.

Eventually, Balthazar and Publia start saying that we should go home. I'm still sitting cross-legged by the embers listening to him speak and I can't stand up. They get me by the armpits and begin to drag me away, tipsy and giggling, in a comedy exit completely opposite the tragic entrance we made hours earlier, with a weeping Publia dragged by me and Bal. But after all I've heard and seen this evening, I won't go like a paralytic.

I manage to stand and dust myself down then I spot that my peacock feather trim is muddy. How have I not noticed all this time? Veronica Fabia Pictrix doesn't take her eyes off the shawl.

Awkwardly, now, I make a bow to Jesus, some kind of genuflection; though it's not a Roman move, or a Jewish gesture. He's still surrounded by a big crowd of both, and he doesn't know me, so I don't suppose he notices me go. I'm sure he can't tell my heart is screaming, 'when can I see you again?'

Some cheap tart is shouting the same thing at Abibaal as we leave the enchanted grotto and head out of the necropolis. He emerges from an alcove at the sound of our voices, all bald pate and full belly in the moonlight. She follows him, smitten; asking for another chance.

Another chance to feel the degradation? To taste the desperation. To smell the bad breath? How Abi has this effect on women, I don't know. Without a backward glance, he leaves his Dido throwing herself on the funeral pyre, as he farts and departs.

He is courteous to my sister, though, holding out his hand to help her through the cemetery gate.

"How do you feel, dear Publia?" he enquires, as we set off into the dead of night.

"I think the bleeding has stopped," she slurs, "and I'm not in any pain."

"None of us can feel the stones under our feet now," he replies; "but come the morning we will see if the way lies smoothly."

As we stumble along, arm in arm, Publia is singing an ode to her pillow. She compares the silk billows of her cushion to the breast of an ex-boyfriend from Rome, a gladiator type. This upsets Balthazar, especially as he's been so supportive and patient with her problem, and this Brutus guy was a bastard who probably caused it in the first place. So they start to have a blazing row, setting off barking dogs all down the quiet street.

Abibaal tries to change the subject back to the one we came with. "So who did Jesus say was the true god of Tyre in the end?" he asks. "Melqart or Hercules?"

Pubi turns her righteous anger on him instead. "He said: cast in gold or encrusted in jewels, both are just the glimmer on earth of your father in heaven," she shouts.

By the time we arrive back at the *domus*, it feels like I am bleeding from the ears. The curing of her may well be the cursing of me. Still I kiss my sister and her dark kin dutifully at the door, then stagger the last few paces up the street to my shop.

Forcing the shutters just wide enough to squeeze through, I fall inside. My work things are stacked on the counter and shelves waiting for the morning, only an hour or two away now; I knock the abacus off as I crash past. Up the steps to my attic I crawl; my peacock feathers snagging on the bottom stair and slowly falling as I climb. I leave the *palliolum* where it lies and make it to my blessed, unmade bed.

My pillow is the breast of Jesus. I glimpsed that golden skin as he spoke, rippling like the wheat he spoke of, shimmering like the lilies. But as I lay my head on it at last, the pillow feels like fire; and my mind is lit with the words I heard earlier.

One god, loving and forgiving. Like Jupiter, Neptune and Pluto all rolled into one. Like Mars and Mercury combined. He doesn't need bribing with money, milk or meat; but wants us to treat each other like solid gold Ba'als with giant ruby hearts. I think this is what he said. I probably need to hear it again.

CHAPTER FOUR

Golden sand, silver sea, sunrise on the Tyrian shore where the surf spits out empty snail shells; but the foam stays dirty white. I wake up crying. If there is no more Hercules, there is no more purple. He discovered it; at least, his dog did. There can't be a dog, if there's no more god.

Does this mean there are no more magnificent feats, that the mosaics on the temple forecourt are false? He didn't slay the Nemean Lion, capture the Erymanthian Boar, steal the Mares of Diomedes. I lie in my tangled sheets, dyed streaky in the morning light.

Hercules didn't invent Phoenicia, land of the purple; he didn't create Tyre, city of the rich. He didn't carve the coast-line by dog-walking, or swell the sea by mermaid-shagging. Another tear rolls down my cheek, cried streaky in the morning light.

And if there is no more Hercules, then what about his father? Zeus; up in smoke. Alcmena; snuffed out. No more Minerva, war-like but wise; no more Diana, bitchy but brilliant; no more Venus. Time was, that would have meant no more me.

So, if there's only one god, where's the fun; the friends and foes, the frolics and fury? How lonely is the single king of the cosmos; utterly without companionship. I am sobbing on my bed, like I've been left by all the lovers that ever were, all the mothers; like stories are dead and I'll never read any more gossip or hear any more scandal.

There comes a rattling of shutters in the shop. I can tell by the shaft of sunshine on the ceiling that they should be open by now. Pulling the sheet around me, I peep out of my first floor window. Publia is standing in the street below, hopping from foot to foot. I can hear her singing from here; wordless but wonderful.

"Morning," I call down.

"Like the first morning," she beams up at me.

"Are you better?"

"A bit hung over."

"But the bleeding?"

"Veronica, I am standing in the street. Why aren't you open?"

"A bit hung over," I shout. "I'll be down shortly."

"I'll bring you some breakfast." At least, I think this is what she says as she wanders away.

So I try to get ready for the day, splashing water on my face and brushing my teeth with an unhygienic stick and pot of old honey. I can see from the coppery outline in the mirror that my hair is a mess; must splash out on Hakiqah when we go to the baths this afternoon.

I dress in my *peplum*, a tunic the colour of crocuses. I wish I could wear something colourless to mourn the sudden death of purple; but there is only one white item in my clothes chest, a fine linen handkerchief my dad gave me for luck as I set sail from the port of Ostia for my current position. A grown-up gift, a lady's veil; though my hairstyle was too special to cover.

I haven't seen my father since that moment, when our hands touched over the bleach-bright cloth, on the quayside. And though I waved it till he was out of sight that day, and at Publia's wedding as if it could bring him to the celebration; and though I've used it at other times in ways it's better he won't see; the pure *sudarium* is still pristine. So, with one last sniff, I lace my best sandals; calf leather, soft as my own skin, and walk downstairs to the hard world.

The banging on my shutters gets louder. I take a big key to the stiff padlock, my hands shaking. Thank Mercury it's just my sister. I'm in no mood for business. But, man, she is impatient this morning.

"Don't get your pubic hair in a plait!" I shout.

The body that marches onto my premises as soon as the door is open, though, is not Publia's. She must have gone off shopping, leaving her space on the doorstep to one of my most high-up customers.

"Vibius Quintillia Varus," I burst out. "Sorry, I thought you were somebody else."

He burps in my face, wine scented with fennel, I believe. He must have been at a birthday party last night, someone big in the *proconsulate,* and just be coming home. There is a wilted wreath of flowers and ivy round his head; and a whole hedge of celebration herbs stuffed in his girdle. I see bunches of mint and laurel and, yes, they do outweigh the rank smell of a man who has been up all night drinking.

"Was it a good evening?" I ask.

The man sends a mixed message: His smile is wolfish. His stance is bullish.

"I am a *curulis* magistrate, Veronica," he says. "When I dreamed, as a boy, that I would conquer the world, I never imagined this. It's just that..." he clears his throat, comes closer, spice-infused sweat glistening. "I wonder if... you could... make my stripes thicker."

"Your what?"

"The purple stripe on my toga *praetexta*. The width of my importance. Well, I can afford a bit more, I think..."

I fight back the sick feeling. He's not that important; *curulis* just means the folding ivory stool he sits on, as the sign of his office.

"The stripes come in a standard thickness," I say.

"I can afford more."

"Then you need to be promoted to consul." I stare at his face, the full fringed hair-cut, with fair locks brushed forward, making his cheeks look chubby.

"Not that much. Just a little bit thicker than the other *praetors*' stripes; just a tiny bit fatter."

"Why, so they think your dick is bigger than theirs?"

I'm not normally this brisk with my customers, but I can't make his stripes thicker, no matter what time of day it is, or how drunk he appears.

"I just like the colour," he says. And then he starts to get that look in his eye that I've seen in men before; at the very moment I realise they are boys.

"Don't worry, Vibius, dear," I soothe, "soon your nose will be exactly that shade of purple. And then the other seven *propraetors* will know that you can drink more than them, too."

I sang that sale ruder than the silver sea pissing on the golden sand but he makes a purchase of the standard striped cloth and trips out of my shop with the package under his arm when he didn't even need a new toga. Moments later Publia skips in without her *stola* draped over her tunic, the way married women are meant to wear it. Thank Hestia, the goddess of home and hearthside, she waited for the governor to go. She plonks the plate down on the counter.

"Honey cakes for breakfast?"

"It's a feast day!"

"So, you're better?"

"Oh my actual god, Veronica. Can you believe last night? The amazing people there. Bal and I were talking to this couple from Byblos. They'd heard that he could stop the wind and waves. And there was this other guy we chatted with; Tyrian but he's already followed Him to the lake and up a mountain and everywhere they go miracles happen. Why did it take us so long to find Jesus?

"Has the bleeding stopped, then?"

"When he told me to stand up, it was like I left my rotten bottom on the floor of the necropolis. All the old blood had soaked back into the ancestors, it seemed; and I was free to live again."

I'm laughing but it's making me gag. She's brought me two jugs of water; one honey-sweetened, one vinegar-sharpened. I go for the sour. I gulp half the cup. My head starts to clear.

"The thing is, Pubi, you don't want to stop bleeding altogether. Without the blood there is no baby. That is one of the secret tenets at the temple of Venus; believe me, I've chanted it."

She laughs but I speak louder:

"You can't bleed all the time, but you have to bleed sometimes. It's a delicate balance. Don't really want a magician to start messing with your monthly rhythm."

Publia sips the honeyed water serenely.

"Only time will tell," she says, "but I intend to stick around and find out."

"What? Here?"

"No, silly," she says. "We're going to follow Jesus back to Jerusalem. They told us last night he's leaving town tomorrow; and Bal and I will go too."

She sees my face; a honey tear in one eye, a vinegar tear in the other.

"You know we had to go anyway," she says. "But oh my, the purple route will be so much richer, walking next to him."

"There's a huge crowd everywhere he goes," I say. "You won't even get close."

But she boasts that Balthazar has been back to the necropolis already to find out the travel plans before going down to the dock.

He'll be packing the new stock, ready to load onto the donkeys, by now. And she complains that she'll be busy, back at the *domus,* packing their personal belongings until bath time. Then she insists that we'll all have a lovely last night together at Abibaal's, with something special for dinner; saffron chicken?

The tears, bittersweet, have rolled down my cheeks and reached my chin. I tasted yellow, I smelt purple, as they streamed.

A customer comes in behind Publia, a typical consulate wife, hair high as the skyline of *Mons Capitolinus*, bust strapped up in a *milliarium* of sweaty silk, snaking her hips like the river Tiber.

For a long moment, she stands in line; proper Roman behaviour. Then those spidery lashes start batting glances at my sister, who is standing in front, still chatting. From behind, Publia looks like she might be buying something precious; but the real customer soon spots that an idling impostor keeps her from the purchase of purple thread.

It plays out before my eyes. With a look of Minerva, goddess of embroidery as well as war, the matron pushes my sister aside as if she were Arachne; the girl in the story who boasts that her needlecraft could beat the creator's.

My part, the most important, is simple: I turn to serve her.

"*Salve!*" I nod. "What can I do for you, my lady, on this fine day."

"I'll be back at the ninth hour then," Publia says and finally leaves the shop.

I face my customer across the counter and do what I got out of bed for; sell. Only the stuff that's for sale, though. This lady gets carried away by the glamour of my emporium and clearly wants to be me. She ends up bidding for the blonde streaks in my hair, big money for a couple of mangy goat locks that wouldn't even suit her. I say no, get your own from the Latin Quarter. I tell her where to go, exactly. She seems to take it all on board but then, as I'm wrapping her proper shopping, she asks me to throw in the beads around my neck.

I clutch my throat. These teardrops are amethysts. She's already handed over her gold, so I could just tell her to go away now. But I kindly direct her to the street where the jewellery store is, so she can buy a necklace just like mine. Though, choking, I hope she'll save up for some more of my silken *purpura*; it does go to the head of these magisterial wives.

When Publia comes back around three o'clock her hair is tangled and her neck unadorned by jewels. She looks worse, in some ways, than she did on arrival in Tyre but in other ways she looks miles better. Her back is straight, her stomach is flat, her eyes are sparkling.

"Still no blood?" I mutter, as I lock the strong box.

"No."

"No pain?" I sweep the clutter off my desk, into a drawer.

"No."

Now I stop and stand there and stare at her.

"That is impossible," I say. "How did he do it?"

"They said it was the healing power of belief." She picks up her bag and leaves the building. "Come on, let's bathe."

I follow her; I'm pretty sure I've felt the power of belief before. It is, to an assistant priestess, what wood is to a carpenter.

Outside my shop, the street is bustling; so many potential sales, though most punters are heading bathwards now. I can't resist a quick pitch;

"One single strand of my purple thread; you can embroider your cloths with the glory of kings! Phoenix's seamstress herself will be waiting on this shop doorstep when I open in the morning..."

A couple of the ladies and a man in the passing crowd look like they might be tempted. I love how the hexameter, the beat I worked as a temple dancer, can also be powerful in marketing; the song of the city street.

Publia leads me briskly to the baths, bustling like I haven't seen my big sister for years. I can't bear that she's leaving town tomorrow and I won't see her again for another year. She's not particularly aware of my pain, but is tipping the bath attendants generously, tossing an *as* to any slave who so much as hands her a towel. We speed through the strigiling, and then she stretches out on the *laconicum's* warm floor and smiles. She's not looking at me. She seems to be lost in the bliss of her own body. And I don't feel like that about mine.

But then she comes up again with a rush and snatches my hand and runs to the cold plunge. She whoops as she goes into the water, still taking me with her. I gasp and the water goes into me instead. Coughing, I make it to the surface; eyes streaming, blonde hair straggling. My streaks are ruined, the fatty dye leaving a residue in the pool.

"Hey you!" It's the same whale lady we saw on Pubi's first day here, loitering large and pale in the cold bath. She floats closer to us. "No false hair allowed in the water." She looks from me to Publia, and recognises her. "Hey you! No red threads in the blue."

She is clearly mad, but in the conversation that follows, between her and my sister, it is unclear who is madder. Publia says that her flow of blood has been staunched by the lord, that her sickness has been cured by the master. Why is the most powerful woman I know, my veritable mistress, attributing her salvation to a man. The fat lady replies that only demons can cast out evil, insisting repeatedly that a particular devil has attached itself to her house and is turning all the neighbours against her with wicked allegations.

She says it tells lies about her, loudly, in the night. Publia suggests that she should find Jesus, for he would be able to help her with that.

"He's only in Tyre for one more day," she says finally, swimming towards the side. "But he could deliver you for ever." She climbs out of the bath and stands there, looking down at the blubbery breasts and belly of the madwoman, waddling on the water. "He'll love you," she says firmly.

I clamber out of the pool, too, and run after her firmer buttocks to the changing room. Pubi and I together, tan and lithe, still wouldn't fill out that lady's curves. In this nude-painted palace, where looks matter, we get more than double the love from punters we pass in the passage than she would at twice our size.

We're going to glam up for dinner tonight. Hakiqah comes and sorts us both out. My goat locks are ruined; but the *ornatrix* notices how good Publia is looking at once.

"You tried the nettles, no?" she says, as she starts to comb through.

"No. Let me tell you." Publia's hairdo takes a long time, always has done, always will do, and she talks constantly; about how she didn't need to try the nettles because the son of man has magical powers of healing, about how he didn't even need to touch her but just told her to stand up and how, from that moment, she was whole. And how she and her husband Balthazar are now going to follow the Messiah back home to Bethany.

Hakiqah crimps her hair quickly, looking scared.

"Have you heard of this person?" I ask her.

"No, but I heard of magic," she says, "and I prefer the ginger."

Publia tips her handsomely and looks beautiful as we make our way into the last supper with the boys. Abibaal and Balthazar are lying on the dining couches. They have already started on the *mulsum* and are laughing together. They look up as we appear. They both look at Publia first, then Abibaal looks at me.

"The Fabia Pictrix sisters," he says, "looking good."

We lie down and start to nibble the *gustatio*.

"Feeling better, darling?" Balthazar asks Publia.

"Feeling great," she says. "It's like my body has been born again but this time with fire not water in its veins."

"That is how you appear," Abibaal tells her.

"Thank you. Pass us the *garum*."

"You're not supposed to put it on the starters."

She puts it on everything; *garum*, just herbs, fish and a fuck of a lot of salt, left in a barrel in the sun for a month. It is, truly, the sauce equivalent to purple dye; so no surprise Publia loves it.

"Did you see Jesus today?" she asks her husband. "Does he know we're going with him?"

"We can't," shrugs Bal, "he's not going straight back to Jerusalem. They say he might not go back at all. He's on a tour of Galilee, apparently, heading from Bethsaida to Cana.

"We can still go," says Publia.

"We can't, sweetheart. We have to get back to work."

"They don't need to work, the ones who are with him," she says. "Even that guy from Sidon. He left his business and survived."

"But it's not just our business, it's your father's."

"Didn't you hear what he said last night? Our father is in heaven."

"I get it. But what if everyone in the world gave up working, and relied on the kindness of random strangers? What if we were all poor?"

"Didn't you hear what he said last night? The richest are the poorest," Publia states, "and vice versa."

"I believe it," Balthazar says, "but I've got to get back to Bethany..."

Slaves start to come in with the *prima mensa*. I'm distracted for the moment. My favourite dish is there. Lean. Strongly-flavoured. Rare.

I don't know what his name is but we've had sex a few times.

Being gang-banged would probably put most people off fornication for ever. Yet I was not discouraged completely from so-called copulation by this rape of five. It did put me off submission, humiliation and agony. It didn't put me off domination, adoration or ecstasy.

Sex was part of my job as an assistant priestess. The handmaidens of Venus were not supposed to be virgins. We didn't just kneel at the altar; sometimes we lay down. Yes, the dancing and singing could certainly include jiggling and moaning.

But that's not how I do it now. I'm a businesswoman, rich and powerful. I never get underneath anybody. And when I get my kicks, they are not in self-defence. Luckily, I am a patrician lady so there are slaves to deal with that.

I'm afraid I've been using Abibaal's kitchen staff for personal pleasure these last few moons. It is not just a one way transaction, though; I've done him a big favour, too. The slave, I mean. Sinewy and mostly silent, though he speaks the same language as me.

He stands behind my couch, waiting to serve the *seconda mensa* in a while. Slowly, I eat a leg of chicken and throw the bone on the floor by my feet. The slave bends down to pick it up. And I tread on his hand, just as it reaches the chicken bone, I press down with my foot and can feel a grinding together of his fingers and the food; harder, so that I can't tell whether it is human knuckle or fowl gristle.

As I do, my eyes are fixed on his face and, though his features strain and flush, he never looks up to meet my gaze. His eyes remain lowered; the way I like them. In fact, for the three times we've *futuimus*, he has only been allowed to look at me twice.

He has been allowed to touch, only when I say so. I have taken only the parts of him that I can handle, in the only way that I can manage, after my brutal assault at the Roman baths. I don't want his eyes, hands or voice. I wouldn't say no to his skin, smell or raw energy.

I still love the dance, up against clandestine pillars in the dark; I still love the song that is hissed through bitten lips. I still use the skills I learned as assistant priestess, and still achieve Olympic heights of physical bliss.

It never used to matter, then, whether I knew the name of my sexual partner or not. It matters even less now. I did find out the names of the five men who abused me in the *caldarium*, because they kept chanting them, shouting and laughing them, as they competed in my spiritual defeat.

But now the meat is a man, and I am the one who's eating. So, yes, I would describe my sex life as satisfactory, as it stands, this evening. But tonight isn't about me; I bring my attention back to Publia. She has suddenly started screaming:

"We need to go together! What is the good of me being well if you are not there?"

"I will be with you," Balthazar insists. "On the road with our donkeys and slaves; stopping to trade in Philoteria, Scythopolis, Ephraim. Then back at home, feeding the chickens."

"They'll be dead by the time you get there," Abibaal chuckles.

How tactless.

"Dead as this bird that's feeding us tonight."

So hopeless in a tense situation. I try something else:

"By the time you get there, a new life might have started, a miracle baby may be on the way..."

Publia splutters into her wine cup. Her husband shushes her.

"It's only been a day; this whole healing thing could still be a lie." Balthazar's brow is low and dark. "The guy might be an illusionist."

She tips the rest of her wine into his lap as they lay together on the dining couch. A dark red splash in the underbelly of his tunic. Before he can protest, she takes his face firmly in her hand. His black beard curls over the 'mount of Venus' at the base of her purple-stained thumb but we're not lounging under the mists of old Olympus any more...

Publia is talking fast and loud now: "God was there last night at the necropolis. We've been to see shows that look like magic, we've watched performers do amazing tricks but in the morning the audience have gone home. They've paid and clapped and left to go about their ordinary business. So finally, an act worth sticking with, when the performance is over.

"Those booksellers that tailed him from Byblos told us this; thousands followed Jesus last year, hoping that he'd come to free Israel but they all stayed in Galilee when he started freeing the Romans too."

Pubi pulls her poor man's beard to add emphasis to each phrase.

"God has come to walk with us, to talk and sit and eat with us, so why would anyone in the world know where he stood and not stand alongside or where he sat and not sit there too? What have we spent our lives kneeling to worship? Apart from money, Abibaal. And women's breasts."

She throws this over her shoulder to her brother-in-law, lying on the other couch, then turns back to Bal.

"We have lavished our love on statues, poured wine and milk and blood on carved images, spent vast sums of money building and maintaining temples, and for what? Him. That is God. And he doesn't want it."

Balthazar suddenly becomes aware that the slaves are listening. They've just stopped in their tasks and are openly staring. With a snap of his fingers he becomes scary.

"Get back to the kitchen," he shouts, raising his hand to them.

I watch their retreating backsides, and my own personal slave's in particular, which I might actually smack, later.

My sister looks shocked. Bal threw her off as he moved to threaten the servants. Her hand, tugging at his beard seductively in the fight; that hand is hurt, a bit.

He gets up from the table and stands in front of her. His words are harsh, his manner hostile, but I guess it's what any modern, married man-about-Tyre would say:

"You will not follow Jesus without me. I healed you." The red wine stain in the lap of his shirt shows like a weird echo of Publia's disease, as he says: "I am your husband. You will go with me."

As it happens, they all go together. As the sun rises over the ancient city next morning, a horde of followers accompanies Jesus of Nazareth through the gates, on their way back to Galilee.

I do not see him, at all. Not a glimpse of the dawn lit skin, the head or shoulders I saw before, nor the god-like feet and shins I sat at, listening to his talk. I can still picture those parts in my mind but, with all the other bodies crowding round that sacred place completely, I can't even see the ring of light that shone around him as I watched from the fireside.

In the cloud of dust drifting slowly down the long, narrow road, built to join the island of Tyre to the Phoenician mainland, Balthazar and Publia are following the procession. They are still arguing. They bickered all night and squabbled this morning. As we breakfasted at the *domus*, and loaded the mules, and ordered the slaves, and locked the *ostium,* Pubi was still trying to persuade Bal to be born again with her in the lord. And he was still insisting on business as usual.

Two donkeys and two strapping boys loaded high with the purple dye; they will follow the trade route back up to Bethany, by the Jordan river that is running with gold. Coughing in the dust kicked up by the fans of Jesus, my sister disappears, trying desperately to convert her husband before the turn in the road to Damascus.

She turns to wave me goodbye where she's stopped before by an olive tree with its boughs outstretched in a cross. I have never been down this road. I haven't left Tyre that way since I arrived by sea from Rome. But I've bid farewell to Publia three times in that lonely place and now I've waved god off down that road, too.

No. I'm going to find him in the temple. God is still in Tyre. His calves and thighs are still made of gold and I can still lie at his feet, licking the salty stone, sipping the sacred wine from a chalice cut from the same crystal as his toenails. And when I'm through with civilized worship, I can walk home; across a mosaic pavement that clearly demonstrates exactly who, what and how Herculean god is. And then I can sit in my flat and admire the divine objects on my private altar.

God would never ask me to leave those worldly goods and go with him. Would he? As soon as Publia's purple dust has settled on the causeway, I turn back into town and hurry to my usual temple. It's quiet on the forecourt but there's a dove seller and I buy one. With the money in my purse, I could have bought the whole basket, and I wonder why I didn't. Let them all go: a shout to heaven, not a whisper. But I just clutch the one, and run up the steps with it and through the cedarwood doors, tall as when they were growing in a forest.

The priest is at the altar already; he sees me coming with the turtledove and smiles tenderly. I'm fighting the urge to panic, like the bird in my hands, repressed flapping. He takes it from me with one well-practised pluck and puts it on the altar-stone, his fingers a cage, crooning a hymn to the temple ceiling.

Through a curtain below comes his assistant, summoned by this song; not with a feather duster this time, with a sharp, shiny knife. She does the self-conscious walk of someone who has suddenly been called upon to perform a public duty. We have eye contact for a moment but this is frowned on and she quickly looks away. She kneels to offer the sacrificial blade to the priest.

I'm dancing, as he holds the beating bird with one hand and cuts its throat with the other, as he aims the stream of blood into the silver dish and pours it steadily over the toes of Hercules. Both soft and hard, slow and fast; we praise our gods in various ways.

The one who said there is only one God has gone his separate way. Publia asked 'why would anyone know where he was and not be there, too?'

She went. I stayed. Though we are soulmates, she said yes, I said no. I never answered why I wouldn't go when she was still here but I do know. Because, why would anyone leave home and hearth, riches and reputation, with nothing but the parting shot of a *homo vagus*?

Because, I need to be where my stuff is. The heart of my personal empire, in Tyre.

CHAPTER FIVE

Singing, dancing, now acting; it's like I'm still a priestess, after all. Half drunk when I turn up at Abibaal's *domus* tonight, though I seem to be completely sober, I come panicking about my lost shawl.

"I think I left it at the necropolis," I plead. "It's very precious; peacock feathers, embroidered with purple, remember, and fringed like the bird's wing?"

"I thought you wore it home," says Abibaal. "Half hanging off."

He always looks as though my clothes are barely there, except when Publia is. But now she's not here, I feel as if my *palliolum* really is missing.

With a chill around my shoulders, a lonely shiver down my spine, I step closer to my landlord and business partner.

"It's dark out there. Do you mind if I take one of your slaves?" I whine. "He won't be long."

Abibaal isn't really listening. He's sitting at the table in the atrium, trying to play himself at *duodecim scripta*. He must be missing his brother as much as I'm missing my sister.

"Fine," he sighs. "Take a kitchen boy. They're not doing much at the moment."

This time of the evening, dinner over, no guests to entertain, it's pretty quiet in the *culina*. Two slaves, not mine, are cleaning the wooden table and the metal utensils with soapwort and scouring bushes. Another, not mine either, is sweeping out the oven with a bunch of blackened twigs.

When they see me they nod nervously and carry on working, quicker but clumsier.

"Where's the other guy?" I say and gesture to signify him, tall and skinny. It's a rude translation but they know who I mean.

"On a break," says one.

"On the roof," says another.

The third simply jerks his head upwards.

Slaves. Who knows what they're thinking? How can I be sure he hasn't told them everything.

See, I've been up on the roof before. My body still behaves like I'm an assistant to Venus, goddess of beauty and fertility; making me want to commit these acts of worship. Two times I have climbed the four flights of stairs, with the slave in question, and twice I've come down again without him. He stayed on the pile of itchy, discoloured sacks he calls a bed; sleeping like Mars after our war.

There's a beautiful view from the top of the *insula*. All of ancient Tyre, battle-scarred and trouble-worn, was laid out beneath me at dawn and dusk; but in the dark, it was like being on the surgeon's table, lit by the stars, under the closest scrutiny of the gods. Yes, sex with my slave elevated me almost to heaven.

They run a reeking cesspit up there, though. All the bondsmen from the neighbourhood seem to sleep, eat and shit in that communal dorm. Each has his own space, by the means of broken brick and stones, carried up from the floor of the real city below.

How men mark their territory, even when teetering on the edge of a chasm, tickles me. So while my slave peed off the parapet at the top of Abibaal's building, I took a look around his turf. He'd made a cabinet in the wall by his bed by pulling out *cementum* and brick and putting back a fascia. Both the priestess and the businesswoman in me instantly noticed his locked safe. I picked it and peered inside while he still peed. Long stream; a promising sign in a sexual conquest.

It seemed, as I stared into the dark recess, that this was a high altar. Hidden in the secret gloom, gleaming in a sacred line-up; ivory carvings of the sphinx. Hand made by local craftswoman Urbana, I think. Stolen from her shop by a thin thief, I believe.

First time there were five. Second time I looked again, while the slave lay in a post-disciplinary daze; only three. I wonder how many are left up there now but I just can't be bothered to climb the four flights of steps again to find out.

"Fetch him here," I say. "Don't just stand there like effigies."

They can't refuse. By some system of ranking I don't understand, one of the lowly looks at another who looks at the other, and he is the one who goes. I hear him shouting on the landing. It's Latin but they're not words I would use.

I haven't said anything to anyone about the stolen goods stashed up those stairs. Haven't told the tribunes or mentioned it to a magistrate. Why? Well, I'm not without sin myself, searching in the rubble of my sex slave's hovel. I was never going to find anything good.

Why hasn't he told about me? Even in the gutter, men like to boast but there's no lewd looks from the other guys as he hurries into the kitchen. In his haste he meets my gaze; only for a moment and then we do not have eye contact again. His look in that split second is dark but bright. There will be life in the necropolis tonight.

We walk through the city in single file, naturally. His eyes may be on my rear the whole way, or lowered subserviently; I don't turn around to find out. We don't speak. The streets are noisy enough with dogs and drunks and crying babies, with women shrieking and men shouting from every lamp-lit window. Makes me glad not to be in a normal relationship.

The moon is full but it's cloudy so the reassuring face of Phoebe comes and goes. I can feel her pull, though, from behind the clouds, urging me toward the necropolis; a tugging of the nether regions. Cold stone, my lust and love are twin columns, choked by the creepers that twine around them. Even when I came with my sister and her husband this place turned me on. Now I arrive at the entrance again, and I think the slave is still behind me. The ivy rustles in the archway after I've passed. He is following.

I have him on a big tomb, blindfolded with my handkerchief. Without touching any other part of his body, I enshroud him: with, pretty much, the only part of my body that wants to touch. I don't use my hands for this. Being a priestess of Venus gave me great muscle tone around the hips and thighs.

I do use my hands to smack his face, though, three times in total. Once is for my father, who bossed me around endlessly; once is for the men in the Roman baths, who abused me mercilessly; once is for the master, who made me love him and left without me. All the rage and regret leave my body on the third slap.

Just the pleasure remains. At its climax, we are breast to chest, mine pink-tipped like my dye-seller's fingers but more sensitive. Our bodies touch though my face is turned firmly away from his. I tell him when to finish, like I told him when to start; I suppose he must like it really or else he wouldn't be able to.

We come together but I climb off the moment it's over, staying close to the slave on the tombstone because it's dangerous around here in the dark. No cuddling, I huddle round the dying embers of my own inner fire, cloaked in woad shadow while he slumbers behind.

The ledge where I sit is on the shelves of Tyre's dead, untidily stacked. This grave edge overlooks the place I sat (was it only three nights ago?) when Jesus was here.

His followers didn't leave a mess in the grotto but there are hearth-marks, cleanly swept, and breaks in the fern curtains where the large crowd came and went. There are small mounds of stones someone moved out of his way, with a pair of sparrow feathers stuck in the top of the closest one. A wooden cup, a sandal strap, a scrap of papyrus lie on the ground. And then I see, incredibly, another souvenir in the dust; a peacock feather, where I knelt at his feet.

If Jesus were here now I wouldn't be cold or crying. I wouldn't have done something so sordid or stupid. No woe, if I could be listening to his wise words again: 'When making oaths to God, don't swear by Heaven, it is his throne; don't swear on Earth, it is his footstool; don't swear at all, just say yes or no, and do what you say.' [4] Does that mean he still loves me for refusing to follow, and sticking to it?

I remember another moment; the fire was blazing then and the red wine flowing. Somebody asked him how God feels about tax-collectors. Silly question so he gave a silly answer: 'The sun shines on the good and the bad people of the land. The rain falls on both the do-gooder and the sinner.' [5]

Now the moon comes out from behind Tyre's purple clouds and shines fiercely on both me and the slave on the white marble gravestone. Two dark shapes, one in ragged tunic, one in quality drapes, illuminated in every crease and crack by graceful moonlight. Those blue rays don't cast judgement on who is good or bad, here; plebeian, patrician, man, woman, enslaved, free. The moon beams on us equally.

Its finger of light points down the terrace of tombstones, stepped like a rocky hillside. I jump to where I saw the glimmer on the grotto floor. In a ring of dust lie the filaments of bluey-green, looking at me like an eye.

I pick the feather up and blow on it, astonished to find this real one while faking the search for my peacock embroidery. On that outbreath comes a wordless song, a wow of iridescence, a glow of greeny-blue light.

Can Jesus commune with everyone he sees, whether their eyes beam on him or not; moonshine even through the clouds? Does he really stay in contact with all who come to him, in touch with anybody who reaches out? Can it possibly be that he has left a message here for me; an object with unique appeal, just like the wooden cup and the sandal strap will have for another follower, clear as words written on the papyrus scrap.

I tuck the feather into my girdle and climb back up the tombstone terrace to the ledge where the slave is still lying. Kicking him gently makes him jump up quickly, then he leans over the ledge and spits.

The moon goes in as the slave spit drops to the necropolis floor. In the tense pause that follows, pictures from my old villa walls flash before my eyes; the story with a peacock. How that gorgeous bird went to Juno, queen of Heaven, to complain; why couldn't he sing like the nightingale? But it's obvious, isn't it. Same reason my gobby slave can't talk like Ovid to me. Beauty, brains, brawn; nobody gets them all.

I walk out of the necropolis with shivers up my spine and ivy rustling in the arches as we pass through. Surely we have offended the spirits of the dead whose stone-cold bed we just got in for angry sex... Spooked, I run up the street with the slave's footsteps behind me, threatening to go either way, friend or foe. I'm not paying him, so there's no reason he should see me safely home.

He doesn't know I know he did the ivory job at Urbana's; I've got no hold over him. Maybe he's too dumb to do anything but follow me. At least he's too docile to take advantage of me; which, by Venus, would be very easy.

As soon as Abibaal's back staircase is in sight, I slow down to a fast walk. All the lights are out in the *domus* so most of the labour must be off-duty on the roof. At the bottom stair I mutter '*vale*' and keep walking.

It seems to take ages to undo my padlock and get into my shop. Before I'm inside, there's a burst of laughter from the roof of the neighbouring *insula*. Has my slave got to the top already? Cheeks purple, I rattle my shutters closed. The whole underclass must be laughing at me from up there.

In the bedroom, I unwind my girdle and the peacock feather comes loose. It falls on the bed next to my feather-stitched shawl which was, of course, here all along. Both are lit by the moon shining in through my open window.

Soon it will cloud over again, though, so I act while I can still see; opening my *alabastrotheca*, selecting a particular little bottle, uncorking it, smelling it, wrinkling my nose; reaching for wad of sheep's wool, washed. I soak the small white ball in vinegar then, leaning back on the bed, open my legs and push the contraceptive sponge inside.

As far as it will go: for an ex-assistant priestess, that's a long way. I used *silphium* for this blessing, in Rome, but can't seem to get it here. So I lay in the stink of my foreign bedding for a while, wondering which is worth more; the real peacock feather (broken) or the embroidered fake? Wondering what Jesus would say.

A whole moon passes before I think about the slave again. Then, it is only in passing, when Tanis in the wine shop tells me one evening that the silversmith in the next street was broken into and ten bracelets were taken.

"Not last night but the night before," she intones darkly. "Some people think it was the same villain done Urbana's. Surprised you haven't heard about this."

"I've been busy at work."

She gives my change in Tyrian currency, the shekels with Melqart wreathed in laurel like a Roman emperor.

"So what makes people think the same guy did both robberies?"

"Broke in the same way. Picked their iron padlocks with lamb fat on a *terebinth* spike."

"Gods, it sounds disgusting," I say.

"Double your security, Veronica," the wine-seller replies, "Use a bronze barrel lock, too. And don't sleep alone."

"I can't help it." She knows this.

"Don't need a forever bedfellow," she shrugs. "Do as I do."

"A new man every night?"

Another customer comes into her shop, at this point, so we stop the dirty talk; but, turning round, I realise it's Abibaal, so we finish the dirty laugh. He wants to know what we've been saying. The combination of his big body and little voice gets me laughing harder; but he's been kind to me, since our brother and sister left, and I don't want to hurt his feelings.

Instead, I smooth them with song. "It's about the burglary at the silversmith's," I explain, before chanting a tale as if I had it for sale in my own shop. Shiny *argentum*, cool and seducing, flows as I sing of the smithy. And the bracelets, charming trinkets now, that were shackles originally, the jangling bondage of slavery. I hymn a thin thief, dark as the night, slinky as the store shutters he can squeeze through. Not hungry for food, exactly; but for beauty.

Abibaal's eyes go from mine to my wine bag, wondering how much I've drunk already. It's firmly stoppered and full. It's not my first today, however. There was some left in a jug in the sun in my window when I came in from work.

He offers to walk me home and it's hard to refuse as we have to go the same way up the gold-stoned street. There are still a lot of people rushing past and he manages to put his arm around me protectively without actually touching my body. So gallant, yet so gormless, it gets me giggling again. But now he asks a serious question;

"Do you know who did it?"

"No. Of course not."

"Why did you sing about that young man, then?"

"All songs are about young men." We reach my shop front and I start rattling my single key. "And gods."

Abibaal finally seems to have accepted the fact that I will never go to his house if he asks me like that; but now he keeps trying to get into mine.

"Shall I come up?" he says, in a male voice that couldn't get any higher. "Fancy a bit of company?" he's tried on several occasions and once I even got: "will I pop in and check your figures?"

That time, I burst into tears.

He knows about the rape, since Publia told Balthazar who blurted it out to his brother. So he is gentle with me but he still keeps trying to enter my premises. And I still keep saying no. Because Abibaal coming to my flat would be like a brick-laden ass clomping up the steps to the temple of Venus.

If I want a man physically close to me there are slaves for that. And still it's another moon before I feel any need. My work keeps me satisfied, or just shattered. It's hard to hold the position all day: sell, sell, sell. I've been a thrusting businesswoman since dawn so at dusk I need to pull back. I have spent many evenings upstairs, polishing my ornaments.

Then, all my dreams are about young men, their outlines fine as my Roman pottery; or gods, their contours smoky as my glass vases. As for my antique sword hilt, well, let's just say it doesn't always stay on the display table at bedtime.

So one morning, weeks after we last met, I decide that I have to see the slave again. I'm down at the docks where my ship has just come in, watching them unload the cargo. Red urns of olive oil, the size of a man with broad shoulders and narrow hips, are rolled off the boat, while my consignment of purple-striped togas is stacked in crates on the quay side, ready to replace the imported pots in the hold.

This is Tyre as it appeared on the wall of my father's study; freshly painted in seagull shit, sailor spit and snail slime. The smell is a slap in my face with a wet paintbrush. Thanks to the Fabius Pictor daughters, the other end of the business, our high-class shop is all silk threads on ivory spools and purple-hemmed luxuries, and only smells as strongly of the evil dye as is absolutely essential.

I think the best way to satisfy my slave-need will be to invite myself to Abibaal's for dinner tonight and get him so drunk he falls asleep early. I might even put him to bed then call his boy to serve my third course in the *triclinium*. A sort of theft, not for beauty but for hunger; I'm still planning the details of this date as I walk back to my shop.

In the street outside, a familiar figure is shuffling in faded shoes, trying to see through my shutters. It's the flax dealer from Sepphoris but we don't have any outstanding business so I wonder what she wants.

"Can I help you?" I call as I come closer.

The travelling saleswoman looks like she's been far and wide; the jackal hide slippers I admired last time are scuffed and torn now.

"Other way round." She reaches into her bag. "I bring a message from your sister."

Out of a hairy pack, strapped to her donkey's back, she pulls a papyrus scroll. I don't understand how she has a letter from Publia. I don't hold out my hand to take it. I'm scratching my head.

"You... you've seen her?" I wonder. "Where? Have you been in Bethany?" But I didn't think she traded there.

She doesn't and neither does my sister:

"I saw her in Capernaum," the woman says. (I think her name is Chava.) "There's a whole army of them, following that blinding Nazarene."

"Hasn't she gone back to Bethany?" I gape. "Was Balthazar with her?"

"Didn't see him," Chava says. (I can't pronounce her name the way she would, with a cough for the ch.) "Anyway, where are you getting your flax from, these days?"

I had actually started sourcing my linen from someone slightly cheaper. Now I feel obliged to put my trade her way. So, much as I want to unroll the scroll and read what Publia has written, I have to discuss terms and conditions with the lady from Sepphoris again.

It takes ages and, at times like this, I wish there were a better way to trade and transport our purple. If there were a special recipe to preserve the dye, or rush it to the destination faster, or convey its essence only, in tiny containers of Herculean dog spit, packing the secret ingredient for people to apply themselves to any length of fabric; I wouldn't need to rely on common suppliers if we could package the ejaculate of Tyre.

As soon as the linen lady leaves my shop, I open the papyrus scroll. Seeing Publia's handwriting appear on the page makes me smell her, too; rosewater strong as if she were really here. Leaning on my counter, wagging her finger, saying:

'Dear Veronica, you know that I have always been a true and kind sister to you. Even when I was too bossy or big-headed, you know I was always your best friend. Trust me now. There is love if you want it. Not like our father's measured stripes; an unlimited supply from the father who drenches us all over.

'I have been following Jesus since we left you; to Galilee where we gathered by the lake to hear him speak. The whole neighbourhood came and I saw him lay hands on hundreds of sick people; I promise, my little sidekick, I saw the blind walk away seeing.

'The most incredible thing he did there, nobody even noticed at first; he fed us all, four thousand, they reckoned, with a few loaves and fishes from one little boy's basket. I now think, no matter how many sat with him on that remote hillside, they would not go hungry. Though my logical Roman mind (not as lyrical as yours) finds no evidence for this proposal, my living flesh is the proof.

'I have become friends with one of the men who works for him. Not just me; there is a group of us, staying with his family in Capernaum. I'm afraid that Balthazar and I went separate ways when it came to the turning in the Damascus road; but I've promised to go back to Bethany, when Jesus gets to Jerusalem, and I will beg Bal's forgiveness for splitting then.

'Sweetness, it's like this: recently his men were talking about the coins they'd need for temple tax and he suddenly said, 'go fish; and in the mouth of the first one you catch, there will be a four drachma coin, enough to pay for us all.'

'We are witnessing miracles; life is not the mundane comedy or tragedy we thought it was, but magical realism. As your older sister and wiser advisor, I tell you, Veronica: you cannot miss it. I'll be at the address below for eight days then we are going up to Jerusalem, in glory.'

I wait in my shop for a long time when I've read this, at the counter where the customers stand, not behind it, where I serve from. I don't assume my usual position. I pause, my eyes on the words, 'Love, Publia'. Her kiss. I don't read the whole letter again. I just think about what it says.

I wouldn't believe it from anyone else. But strong as I can smell roses, I know my sister doesn't lie to me. She gives plain truths, abrupt facts; the sidekick of reality. Though it's hard, I need to go her way on the road to Damascus. Though it's crazy, I must heed her calling. After all we've been through, I'd follow her to Hades, and this can't be worse.

My mind is set but my body still has a will of its own. After a bath, I dress basically, accessorise with amethysts, and go to Abibaal's. He's not in. It is a bit early and I have to wait, sitting in the empty atrium. After a few minutes a slave passes through, a new one, I think; I haven't seen him before.

"Excuse me," I call. "Is a certain person in the kitchen? Tall, thin..." I do the gesture that nails my slave's sinewy form. This guy gets it. He looks confused; why would the wealthy business lady be asking for a particular *servus*?

Then his eye brightens.

"Oh. You are viewing the jewellery." He raises his own rough, brown arm and shakes it so I can almost see what he means; ten silver bracelets, shiny and jingling, stolen from my fellow shopkeeper in the next street.

"Yes," I say, pleased with the way it's going, "take me to the jewellery."

We pass through the quiet kitchen and out of the side door and up the back stairs to the roof. Not so quiet here; six slaves are leaning on the balustrade, shouting as they watch an *insula*, half way across the city, rumble into rubble, a loud cloud of dust. One of them is calling on Ba'al to stop it falling.

But I reckon Ba'al rules the ruins, too. That's God: of the going up and the coming down. My own slave isn't at the parapet. He's lying on his bed. That's it: whatever unholy blood was up, in me, has come down. I start berating him, all of them.

"I don't know why we call you slaves," I shout, "because it isn't what you do. I should name you 'sleepy'," I say to him, "and you lot 'lazy'." But I dread to think what I'd be called, in this *nominalia*.

He lays there looking up at me. I see his eyes flick to the safe in the wall and he kicks the door shut.

"I know what's in there," I say.

He climbs to his feet then I see him wake up, eyes flicking from me to the group of men at the ledge, realising they could easily throw me over the edge, if I threaten to tell.

Really, though, I'm approaching him as a priestess, not a businesswoman. Not coveting his booty, hunting his bounty, he knows that much. But he doesn't know this: I'm looking at him as a priestess of Jesus, not Venus, a purveyor of spirit not flesh. A convert from Mount Olympus.

I'm probably not the first there's been, and hopefully I won't be the last, to quietly commit to a new kingdom, pledged by a silent heart. How sad if I fell to my death before anyone noticed I'd submitted to heaven. I've been using my body as a twisted temple, and now it seems that building has crumpled too. There is no further to fall.

Anyway, he lowers his gaze. Though he could single-handedly toss me off that tower-block, he's a true slave after all. But I act like a natural woman, backing away too, turning to go downstairs.

"*Mane*. Wait!" He runs after me, trying to catch up in Latin, though that's clearly not where he comes from. "Veronica!" He is saying my name with such a strong accent that I mishear it as separate steps: *Vera. Icon.* True. Picture. (That's the way my father used to make it sound sometimes. A pun in our illustrated villa, where every wall told a true story, and anagrams were key to getting any kind of mixed-up loving.)

He is holding out a silver bracelet. I pause on the stair and, as it jingles in the air rushing from the roof top, place my hand in its lock. He still holds it so that suddenly I am his slave. The pretty trinket is my manacle.

Slowly I pop it off and hand it back.

"Yes," I say, "you should give it away. But not to me. Give it to someone who hasn't got anything."

I've got eight days to catch up with Publia. Four have passed already. I must head that way, fast. Feet racing down the stairs, my plan falls into place. I go back to my flat and get a bag and put everything precious into it.

I wrap the glass vases up in my sheets, nut-gall black and knobbly. I put them on top of the gorgon's head, nestling in the ivory bust. The sword hilt slides down the side. Its jewels stick out uncomfortably but this won't be for long. I shoulder the hold-all and set off for the antique dealer, just up the road.

I know what I need to get for this stuff. I'm planning to buy something from myself; and I'm aware how much it costs. So I do get the price I ask of the old Persian who buys and sells objects of art. Two of my pieces came from him in the first place.

But if I were my old self, I'd have bid for a higher price. I'd have bargained, using the skills I learned as a temple dancer. It wouldn't have been hard. Tonight, just as he's about to shut up shop, though, the Babylonian gets a bargain and I'm happy for him. I have all that I need.

I take the empty table with me, the three-legged *mensula* with lion's feet, when I go back to Abibaal's. It is only one hour later but my life has changed completely.

He's home now, sitting in the atrium and, horrible habit, paddling his feet in the pool. I sit down next to him, hands folded neatly in my lap, ready for the hardest conversation I've ever had.

"They said you were here," he starts. "What's happened?"

And I tell him. Jesus is actually God. God is real and only three day's walk away. We could be with God, right next to him, close up, in the flesh. And why would anyone in the world know where he stood and not stand alongside or where he sat and not sit there too?

Then I ask him:

"Abibaal, will you look after the business while I follow him? Just to Jerusalem, with my sister, and a thousand others. Please will you keep the turnover going and not let my dad know I've gone? I've brought you this."

I put the display table down in front of him. In itself it's worth at least seventy silver shekels. But he knows how much it means to me.

"I've traded all my ornaments in," I say.

My business partner, and brother-in-law, is aghast. If he does say anything his voice is too high for me to hear it. Whatever else has he said to me that I haven't registered properly? Perhaps, our relationship lives in the spaces between his silly speeches and our love is alive in the silences between his farts.

"I want you to keep this," I say. "Abibaal, promise me you'll hold the fort."

Tyre has fallen many times before; the old city has been razed and raised again. The causeway I have to cross was built of the rubble of the Tyre that fell to Alexander, the king of Greece, who tried to destroy it three hundred years ago. They fought him in the water, each block of this passage laid at the cost of lives on both sides. I make my way, as the sun comes up, across to the mainland for the first time; at the cost of my previous life.

Maybe a million dawns have pinked the Phoenician coastline; I'm not sure how big the numbers can go, though I've been dealing in the biggest numbers I know. The last thing I did before leaving town was a business transaction. I cashed in everything I owned and brought the most expensive thing I could sell. Something that's been in Abibaal's safe since I've known him and no one has been able to afford.

I can, if it means I have nothing but the clothes on my back. So now, I am wearing a tunic of pure purple; solid colour, not stripes, in raw silk. This should be embroidered in gold for an emperor's wife. But as it stands, naked, heavenly, it is fit only for a nymph; Tyrus, mythical princess and nagging girlfriend of Hercules, finally gets her purple dress.

I've given everything for it. Wearing my entire fortune on my shoulders, I cross the golden sand, silver sea from New Tyre to Old. The only other things I'm taking are stuffed into my animal skin bag with legs crossed and tied for handles: my peacock feather shawl and the real peacock feather I found at the necropolis, with the clothes and jewels I was wearing when I went to buy the purple. Oh, and my white linen handkerchief.

The hardest thing to leave? My *alabastrotheca*. I love that make-up case and will never be beautiful without it. I locked it in the shop. I think I will come back. But I don't think I'll ever need beauty so badly, again.

Looking like Tyrus, the half-girl a half-god loved, I walk slowly out of sight of the city. Turning back for the last time, I can still see the little silhouette of Abibaal standing on the ruins of a fortification. Funny, the outline of his fat tummy and his pointed cap; he looks like a Phrygian idol. But I wave once more and turn away because I'm the half-girl going off to love God.

CHAPTER SIX

I have traded my own voice for a purple dress and now I'm not singing any more. Previously, I would be selling this landscape to the highest bidder as I went along. Blue sky, palm trees and rush-stitched river banks. Flat roofs, domes and pinnacles pricked through the olive groves; with the hills of Galilee gradually growing in the distance.

I had not figured how far it was. I'm worried about my hair. When I left the city, my head was city-shaped. It was a construction, built up and held in place by bronze-pin scaffolding. Now I'll be walking across this plain for three days, my hairstyle is going to fall flat.

My voice could probably still be raised: 'blue sky, green trees, richest woman in Galilee'. All I've got to sell now is myself. And with Jesus, my plan is to give it away. But it would be rash to advertise this to the people I pass on my day's journey, the first of three, while I'm wearing my wares.

I haven't planned this trip properly. Presuming there'd be a Roman road, I've worn the wrong kind of shoes. I've got no travelling rug and hardly any food. I did remember to bring some drink but, guess what; it's not water, it's wine.

I worked out that I was in trouble after the first hour of walking. Almost as soon, in fact, as Abibaal's outline faded behind me. Then I started to think about what he'd been shouting: 'It's not the bloody *Via Appia*, Veronica. You need to carry enough supplies to survive on. And you must have a weapon.'

Silly me; I thought at the time, my voice is my weapon, I can always sing. But here on the plains of Acco, birdsong is so sweet I can't compete. Silence is so complete I can't break it. Without my song, I'm pretty impotent and in a bit of a predicament. As I waved goodbye to Abibaal, I made-believe he was waving happily back; but his after-image is shaking its fists at my foolishness.

The men I see on the way, and they are all men, are working; with their animals, in their fields and trees, or as travelling traders (though I am not sure this is the right route for me). All I know is to head for the hills and probably best not to sing, even if I could. No sales pitches or religious snatches, I walk silently and try to not have eye contact with anyone I pass. Their heads are covered but they're clearly staring at me. I should have worn a veil.

I stop to pass water in an olive grove. Normally, I love to *mingo* in the woods, with the tinkle of Pan's pipes and the wink of eyes from tree trunks. But if it's not the dryads peeping at me, who: Jesus? Is he somehow watching people's lives as lushly painted scenes on a garden-room wall?

I tiptoe through the stand of gnarled trees, creeping through the leafy shade. If I wanted to wake the primitive spirits of these woodlands, I'd suggest a sing-song. But I hope they stay asleep, at least until I've found a safe place to rest.

There's a khan, exactly one day's walk from Tyre, on the edge of a small town called Beth-Anath. Many of my friends and customers have told me about it, in passing, over the years; in more than one language. From an inn to a caravanserai, this setting for famous stories of touring and touting is so familiar I'll see it a mile away. But for miles and miles, today, I see nothing but hills and trees and sky, with lowering clouds and cowering settlements; grim and gritty, like a stick-scratched map of a holy land.

The rope of my sandals has bitten into my ankles by the time I hear beasts lowing in a big stable yard off the main street into the town. I suppose I should celebrate being here by nightfall but, honestly, I'd just as soon sit under a rock all night on the starlit plain than at the noisy manger of a Galilean travel lodge.

It's hard to pass through these gates without a camel or an ox. The gap is herd-wide, the ground dung-paved. It makes me feel less human, walking in here without an animal. The attendant is another man in a headdress who stares. His price is a pittance. The facilities are simply a floor.

Around the big courtyard where cattle are tied, the rooms are on four sides with stone archways open to the square. Everybody can see inside my alcove. Not that they'll see me doing anything, as there is nothing to do. No stool to sit on, nor a hearth to warm my hands by or cook food, if I had a morsel.

I've planned this trip very ill. Don't even have a mat to lie on, all night long. Won't be able to sleep, anyway. I'm being stared at by men in scarves.

I'm not sure how many; it's hard to separate them in the shadows of the khan. At least one must have seen me come in because it would be hard to separate me now from the purple shadows leaning against the back wall of my *leewan*.

Squatting there for a long time, nothing happens except I get pins and needles, and the urge to pee. This grows, more than the time does. Like a water clock, I gradually fill up. I've only drunk wine, today, but it seems to turn to water all the same.

There are three possible ways to piss. I could walk out of my cubicle and find somewhere to go in the courtyard. It's full of horseshit already so I'm not concerned with hygiene. It's just that, with hooded men watching, bare-arsed in the moonlight might be a challenging pose.

Or, I piss where I sit. That would be much easier, probably not too inconvenient; but I don't want to get my dress wet.

Eventually, the third thing occurs. The men come closer. A man finally comes in. His brutal attack is merciful; I mean it. He raises his hand. That's the last thing I remember. Then I wake up lying on the cold stone floor. A lot worse things could have happened than getting a headache.

Merciful, I lie there thinking. Not like at the Roman baths. One whack *vs* five consulate wankers is no contest. But then I start to feel my body. My naked body. Well, I'm still wearing underwear but, oh my god, this is worse than being skinned. The purple dress has gone.

That was my fortune. However that's counted, it was worth my weight in gold. It was my future, to cash in when we reached Jerusalem. I was going to be just as rich there as in Tyre. Now, I am worth nothing.

And the floor is wet. My silk undergarments are damp. I haven't been raped again, simply emptied a bladder full of old wine when the darkness struck.

It is light now; the animals are starting to low. Even the most broken-down donkey in that stable yard has someone to attend it this morning. Someone to put out food and water, to offer a pat, to load with riches and ride away.

It is my own fault; every aspect of the sorry fate that brings me here is, no doubt, of my own making. I shouldn't have come on my own. But it was a merciful attack. No bones snapped, no membranes ripped. My bag is intact, sitting in the darkest corner. I can get dressed in my spare tunic and leg it out of here, as soon as I can stand up. But where shall I go then?

Slowly, slowly, I rise from my knees to my feet like a priestess getting up from a long prayer. And in the lowest voice possible, I sing a response. My chant is back, though it's hard to catch:

'Veronica Fabia Pictrix. True picture: just a story. This is my plan. It is one day's walk back home. I can be in Tyre tonight. I can knock at the door of Abibaal's *domus*. He will take me in.

'He'll believe I changed my mind about going to Jerusalem. He'll help me get the story straight. We'll send an urgent scroll to Rome, informing my father I've been robbed. My entire proceeds taken, by the same thief who's done a couple of other jobs in the neighbourhood. Ivory. Silver. Purple.'

Wrapped tightly in my cheap woad cloak, I will run out of here and hope they've had all they want from me. Within a few paces, I'll be back on the main street, heading for the sea, away from the hills of Galilee. I guess I was never meant to climb them. Not in these sandals, anyway.

It's a good thing now that I don't have an animal to untether but can just gallop away. Head down, halfway through the gate, I heed a cry.

"Lady!"

I look round.

It's a man in a headscarf.

I sigh. "What?"

"Don't go without breakfast. I have ewe's milk and nutty bread, kneaded by my bountiful Avishag."

"But I was robbed here last night."

He sits up straighter on his stool by the gatepost.

"Not on my watch. I was in bed with my beautiful Avishag. This is a fresh day now, take it."

He hands me a flagon and a flat bread. Both have the same odour, how shall I say; body of Avishag. He licks his lips while I drink and eat, then speaks again.

"How much did you lose?"

The bigger the quote, the more stupid I'll sound for carrying it on me.

"Everything," I settle for.

"Where are you going?" the gatekeeper asks. Scarf-shadowed, his eyes could be cruel but his voice seems kind.

"Home now, I reckon." I hand back the empty milk jar.

"Avishag would never have ventured abroad at all. What were you doing, out of doors without a man?"

I start to walk on.

"I was following Jesus ..." I mutter but it's not my job to tell a blind watchman about the light of the world.

"He is more than a man. So many travellers who pass through this place swear on his beautiful words, his bountiful deeds."

I pause as the threshold guardian says:

"But he is not meant for women. With your curves, you will never fit through the entranceway to heaven. Like my Avishag, be satisfied with men of earth."

I think he's upset by my parting verse, shouted through a red mist, about how easy it must be for him, on the other hand, to fit his tiny manhood between the great gates of paradise.

With this, he kicks me out of the khan.

There is a crossroads at the edge of town. The sun is still blinking in the eastern sky as I arrive. A goat is standing there already. She and I both dither, in the dawn, whether to go hither, thither or yon. If I went with her, I could at least get milk (though I'm terrible at milking) but eventually she goes one way and I go the other.

The goat heads back towards Tyre. I head for the hills. When that doorman said it wasn't for women, I remembered Publia. Much better to throw myself on the mercy of my big sister than our big-bellied Phoenician millionaire. Plus she's married to his brother, so Abibaal will still have to help me on that account.

I'll go and tell Publia that I've had all my purple ripped off, and she will take me to Jesus. I face the smallish and friendly-looking mountains of Galilee. If it wasn't for the gatekeeper's bread, though, I don't know how I would have crawled from the crossroads. Did he know who took my clothes? Every time I step with the right foot, sandal re-tied to miss yesterday's blisters, I question this. But when I step with the left, I answer; if he did know, he would never tell me.

Ten miles I march into the mountains, terrified to look back on that eye closing behind me in the Western sky; and only me, as far as the eye can see. No more shadowy farmers, no more shady travellers; the most alone I've ever been. (Oh, except when I was with the five men in the *caldarium*, that time.) But I've got my voice back. Swapped it for the purple dress. Now I can sing as I go:

'Nothing to sell, I've got nothing to trade with, nothing to deal in, nothing to bargain for; what can I offer Him? Songs of purple, stories of gold; skin of ivory, eyes of silver.'

As I walk, on every right step the hooded figures from last night accompany me. Rough characters from the inn but one of them is rich now: more than one, if they choreographed the crime and split my silk booty up strictly between themselves. For every right foot step, five of them pace alongside the body they stripped last night.

And every time I step on the left, the boys from the Roman baths are strutting in my head, a synchronised pro-consulate with a series of rude responses. Who fancies Veronica's chances of bringing those thieving bastards to justice? What will they do with ten talents worth of purple toga in a crap village, anyway? Where will they go, to sell on the length of pure purpura worth more gold than their whole cow byre town?

Ergo, they can't return to Tyre, which is full of suppliers of such luxury fabric in fresher conditions. So they must be hustling onward, along the same track as me, to deal with the richest traders in Galilee. Maybe they'll find beauty's trappings will trip them up, slow them down, perhaps they'll be robbed in turn.

Ten imaginary men, ten very real miles, this lyric goes round in my mind. 'Nothing to sell, I've got nothing to trade with, nothing to deal in, nothing to bargain for; what can I offer Him? Lies of ivory, spin like silver; stories of purple, songs for gold.'

The chant keeps me in a trance until it is starting to get dark and I look about in alarm. I say out loud in my fright, 'I will actually die if there isn't a miracle in these mountains tonight.'

Is that my real voice? It sounds different, the tone neither a pitch nor a bitch; its source not the tits nor the teeth with which Venus empowers her priestesses. Over the clamour of men-memories on either side, my backstory chorus line, this speech seems to come from my heart.

And the moment it is off my lips, I see a person in the distance; a light, bright figure moving quickly towards me. The last of the day's rays are reflecting off his white headwear, a crown of clouds.

I sit on a rock and watch him come closer. He seems to be heading straight for me. Friend or foe, I don't know, but I've walked so far, I can't run now.

Cross legged on a big stone (which I don't believe can move, or else I'd think it was approaching him), I watch the figure in a turban getting bigger. I've seen him before. He was at the necropolis the night I met Jesus.

We didn't speak but we did meet each other's gaze, twice. The first was when I, stupidly, sang Persephone and the pomegranate seeds in Greek, in the hope that most of the gathering would get it. Embarrassingly, I stared at him later, when he said... well, never mind what, he's nearly here now, but at least I know we can speak the same language.

He won't remember me, though. My most notable aspect was the peacock feather shawl and he doesn't seem the kind of man to be swayed by embroidery. Or maybe my enormous nose, perhaps he'll recall that. As soon as we are in earshot, though, my fears are dispelled by a single word.

"Veronica!"

He keeps coming and he calls my name again. Who fancies Veronica's chances of finally seeing an angel? His white robe swirls around the ankles as he flies swiftly over the stony ground, his staff glowing in the sunset. He carries a large bag which I hope has food inside because I've walked two days on a bite of nutty bread. I sway on this rock which feels as if it's been flung towards him, too.

My eyes roll back in my head as the thought hits; somebody will save me. My silk dress must have been found empty and traumatised, alerting his emergency services. Did the robbers stupidly try to sell it on to the friends and family who have gone before me and would wonder urgently where I had fallen out?

With a judder of relief I fall off the rock... and come round in the rolling hills of Galilee at dusk, where Kaspar has erected a billowing tent, circles and stars silk-stitched on its fabric. He is Persian, and we talk in a mix of street Greek and schoolroom Latin.

He gives me a blanket first, then water, and bathes my wounds. A cut I didn't even know I had, to the head. Blisters, oozing yellow blood, to the feet. Some other scratches and bites (though neither of man nor goat) in between.

The next thing he says is, it's better to drink water than wine on a long walk like this. He passes me a waterbag again and bids me glug. But my throat is too shy; I have to sip.

Kaspar conjures a fire, right there on the stones where I fell, the earth's hearth. He cooks a chunky vegetable dish and when I'm full he settles me on a fringed mat which the flames seem to lick comfortingly in the dark. I manage to thank him, saying I feel safer out here on the hillside than I did at the inn. He's aware I've been robbed but I haven't said how much.

My eyes are stinging, smoky tears; I need to close them soon. Kaspar sits on the other side of the fire, still burning strong. I realise that my first thought when I saw him tonight must have been wrong; nobody from that group knew I was coming in purple, so couldn't possibly have traced any stolen goods to me.

"Were you sent by Publia?" I ask tentatively.

"No, not her," the Persian says. "I know your sister but she didn't send me. Jesus did. He saved you."

In what kind of language did Jesus say that Veronica is on her way? How did he put it; she's got herself in deep shit/*stercore*/*σκατά*...? Why do they care about a brown-haired, big-nosed Roman girl, anyway?

Is this the true picture? Did he see me leaving Tyre? Did he know I was coming? If so, how; how could he observe me from so far away?

Does he look with the eyes of the whole wide world, or the blindly-beating heart in the darkness within every single person? Because it would have been obvious, then, that I was going to get into trouble, hiking to Galilee solo, in a highly desirable dress.

If he did watch me walking across that causeway, or weeing in those woods, I can only say: never before, in a temple of Hercules, or at the altar of Venus, never at shrines to Melqart or Astarte, have I ever seen anything that defies explanation. Smoke and shine, money and meat; it's all done by penance and performance.

Never, in my years of service to the gods, have I seen anything that could be described as supernatural. But many times, as an assistant priestess, I have produced the special effects. I've wafted, whispered, waved things about. Nothing has ever moved by itself, though. No-one, no matter how visionary, has seen something that wasn't actually there.

So I started this walk still thinking I was divinity. First night, I slept like the dead, second night I sleep like a baby. I strode off on the journey as if I were its creator; and am about to end it, now, with my feet falling humbly after the servant of the servant.

Kaspar does not talk much as he leads me along a winding path through the mountains. At this conclusion to my three day journey, I do not require conversation; just somebody who knows the way to Capernaum. I'd never be able to find it myself. (As we come over the top there's another town visible first, Chorazin; I'd have gone there.)

My guide is simply walking the way he came. I study the back of him. The turban is pleated like a Roman matron's hair: goodness only knows how long when unplaited. His robe is dazzlingly white. But his arms, his ankles are darker than almost anyone's I've seen.

The way he walks is different too. Like, he's thinking with his feet, not his head. My thoughts fly upwards, so I often stumble over small stones on the path. He is sure footed; his soul is in his soles. I don't see him trip all day.

We're trying to beat the night, walking fast against the falling dusk. While the outlines of mountains can still be seen against the darkening sky, the flat roofs of Capernaum come, in counterpoint; a dark stone. Black rocks of the blacksmith god, Vulcan, I think before remembering; I follow the fire now.

As the daylight fades, nightjars sing louder, trilling an accompaniment to our descent into town. Once we realise we'll make it there by dark, we both relax and enjoy the scene. The town is nothing like Tyre. There are no tower blocks, no battlements, no giant statues. It's by water but the very nature of the sea seems different here. Fish soup, slightly salted; unlike the boiling snail stew of Phoenicia.

Purple: the beauty of pain. Or the pain of beauty. That's what it was, that's what he said, that night at the necropolis. Someone had asked the lord, which were the professions closest to God's heart? Jesus had replied that trades were closer, starting with the purest of all; carpentry. The conversation turned, as it would with all the Sidonites there, to the rag trade: how holy were the dyers?

Kaspar had answered instead: the poetry of purple. Or purple poetry. I'd looked at him because I wasn't sure what he meant; was dyeing a good or a bad thing? I looked at him twice because I had mixed feelings about it. And while I was distracted, I think Jesus said: 'Blessed are dyers; they witness the transformation.'

As the mountain top becomes hillside, I ask Kaspar questions about himself and his relationship with Jesus. The long walk and timely arrival, the peaceful setting and sharp appetite, all seem to whet the edge of our talk now;

"So, how did you meet?" I say.

From behind, I can see he's smiling.

"He came to learn from my teacher, but he taught us more."

"Who was your teacher?"

"The Arch Magi of Persia." My guide slows down so I can walk alongside. He says: "When Yeshua was born, the wise man read it in the stars. Hafed knew that this was a king, the king of heaven itself, and went to worship him. Later, when his parents were living in Egypt, they sent Jesus to study with Hafed. I was there already, a boy from the ruins of Nineveh, come to train with the great astrologer."

"You were school friends?"

"Yes, but even then he was the master."

The town of Capernaum comes closer as we talk; I can hear doors slamming, voices shouting, sawing and hee-hawing. Smoke is rising, meat is cooking.

I have never walked into a new place without money to spend. I could not feel more vulnerable if I were walking in naked. Clothed in cash, I've flashed my wealth around Tyre, easy as smiling; now I wear a worried frown. Where is my power if not in a purse?

I hold on to the one thing:

"He's really here?"

"Staying at the house of a man called Peter. I'll be there, too. We'll go first to your sister. She's at Nathaniel's Aunt's. But tomorrow or the next day, everyone's moving on."

The way he says it, a wave of excitement hits me, as if it had swelled from the streets of the seaside town. We're on the outskirts now, well-trodden tracks; and the view isn't spread before us anymore, we're within it.

I focus in on the one thing:

"It's hard to imagine him as a schoolboy."

Kaspar laughs.

"He was never young. Yet he was always the most childlike."

"What did you learn?"

"Reading. The stars. To see what is happening far away, what will happen next. Hafed taught us the art of prophesy."

"And Jesus taught you more than that?"

"He told us why. How. When. He told us who. We didn't know God, for all we marvelled at his work, till Jesus showed his hands."

We have come over the mountains in silence but our conversation reaches its peak on a busy street down to the centre of town, surrounded by people for the first time in three days.

They don't look Tyrian. It's headscarves and beards again, all roughly the same, not the range of men you get in Tyre. I can see Romans here, though: we rule. Across the street, a pair of soldiers; hurrying round the corner, a tax collector. Hardly any women.

It smells of fish like my town smells of steaming *murex*. I start to wonder where my sister is. Who did he say she was with; a man's name...? We're walking past shops and workshops, houses and temples. Everything looks different from Tyre; blacker, flatter, smaller, newer. Yet the people are doing the same things they'd be doing back home, now: eating, fighting, sleeping, washing up, standing in the doorway, looking at the stars. No brighter, no smaller, no newer.

"Not far now," Kaspar says.

The street is earth rather than stone. The marble pebbles we get underfoot in Tyre are salty clods, here. I kick one, which becomes more. Busy looking down at the gutter, I miss the lady standing in the doorway, looking at the stars. I look up when I hear a familiar scream.

"Oh, Veronica!"

Even when I'm looking right at her, I don't quite recognise Publia. Her hair is hanging down, dead straight, with a centre parting; at least, the bit you can see of it, disappearing under a massive headscarf, a shawl the size of Galilee.

Her face changes as she looks back at me. Am I crying? Probably, yes, and dirty where the tears don't run; perhaps even bruised and bloody.

"What's happened?" she says. "Did you walk here like that? Did you come on your own? Have you been attacked?"

I collapse in her arms. It has sleeves, her garment, strong linen striped in earthy shades. I'd like to explain to her: robbed, not raped. Somehow, she might find that comforting. But when I think about what I've lost on the way here, it makes me cry harder.

Soon, she's giving me the classic Publia pep talk.

"I'm not taking you inside till you shut up. This is the house of Nathaniel's aunt, who has kindly been letting a set of random strangers live on her roof. You can sleep in my bed tonight but only if you're quiet."

"Who is Nathaniel?" I gulp.

"He's a guy who follows Jesus really closely. Come on."

Up one step and through an arch in the dark stone wall, she leads me into a room that is open to the skies. The centre of the house is a courtyard; its hearth is blazing and a group of people encircle it. The firelight flickers and the smell of food I've been following all the way from the mountains seems to come from a big black pot that sits on its flames.

One of the figures at the fireplace looks up as we walk in. Her face is lit in gold for a moment then she gets up and says to Publia:

"Is that really her?"

She walks towards us.

"Veronica? Is it really you?"

I'm just standing there like a *malum*, so my sister speaks first;

"This is Emeshmoon," she says. "Remember? From Byblos. We met her at the necropolis."

"Oh, yes," I blurt now, "but we didn't get to speak…" As soon as I heard Jesus talking, that night in Tyre, there was no time for small talk with anyone else. But there was lots of eye contact around the fire, everybody looking golden between the gravestones, then; and I do recall her ash-painted eyelashes.

"Call me Emesh," she says.

A second woman stands beside the hot stones, slower because she's older than the first, with a bigger spoon because she's more important.

"Aunt Naomi," says Publia.

The lady holds out her hands as she comes closer but stops short of a hug. Instead she waves chicken-winged blessings at both our faces.

"You look almost identical," she says to my sister. "Her eyes are smaller, her ears are bigger, your nose is smaller, your lips are bigger."

I glance at Pubi; this aunt has nailed the reasons why she's always been more beautiful than me.

But Naomi is now hugging me.

"*Salve*, Veronica," she says.

A Jewish person has never greeted me quite like this before. I embrace it.

"Shalom," I say; and she leads me to the fire, and the food.

CHAPTER SEVEN

"Even your name sounds like a story." The book-selling girl from Byblos stares at me. "Fabia Pictrix. What does it truly mean?"

Publia rubs her eyes before she replies, how the Fabius clan may be as old as Hercules, or it may be a kind of bean. She goes on about great-grandfather Pictor being a painter, and how women have to take sexier versions of their men's *nomen* and *cognomen*.

I'm just going 'nom nom', eating a plate of food that couldn't be more different from the dinner I'd have had in Tyre, or Rome, while still being essentially the same; vegetables, grain, spices and oil. It was hot and it was given freely, without taking anything off the plates of other people. I don't know where my next meal will come from, so I eat slowly, the best beans I've ever had.

Publia is saying how she was also named after Ovidius, the greatest poet in Latin. Now Aunt Naomi stares.

"Oh, he's naughty. Ooh, it's saucy." she says. "To be at a public dinner with my husband, and know that the smooth-chinned, bare-shouldered hunk sitting, no, lying opposite is secretly in love with me."

"Yes," I swallow quickly, "and he's planning to make you come, under the table, with his toes."

I may have misjudged quite how Roman this middle-aged lady from Capernaum is, because she doesn't laugh as loudly as I do; it's more of a shrug than a smile.

Emeshmoon, from Byblos, and her husband, Farzan, remain straight faced, though he raises a single eyebrow. A second man positively bellows; I'd guessed he was from Roma. Publia tries to paint things over.

"Naomi, your passion for all things Latin, led by the centurions' legs that pass by your doorway every day, is pleasing. If Ovid were here now, I'm sure he'd adore you."

The hostess is still looking at me, though:

"She says you are a great singer. You can wake me up in the morning with a song. After the cock crows. "

The Roman guy, I think they call him Marcus Manlius, is doodle-doodle-doing, now; but it's all a bit too soon for me.

"My sister needs to sleep," Pubi helps me to my feet. "She's had a risibly long walk in a ridiculously short outfit." She leads me towards a ladder against one of the courtyard walls. "She'll sing tomorrow."

I look back at the group round the fireplace, trying to smile. There are some sons, or servants, I'm not sure which, of Aunt Naomi there as well, all dark and golden-eyed.

I turn back to Publia with a loud whisper.

"Which one is Nathaniel?"

"Ssh."

She pushes me up the steps through a gap in the thatch, a squeeze through the eaves, but her rooftop view is worth it when we get there.

The moon is shining on the Sea of Galilee and the lights of the night fishermen add their magic to the water. Moonlight is splintering off every wall and flat roof of the city, and at a hundred little windows the lamps are lit like stars. Capernaum is still and silent.

As we stand there, Publia says:

"Nathaniel is from Cana. But his father grew up here, in this house, with his sister, Naomi. About three years ago, Nathaniel's friend Philip went to a wedding. There, a man turned water into wine."

I give a thirsty cheer.

"Literally," she says. "Philip saw it. He drank of it. Since that night he's been with Jesus. And the next day, he introduced Nathaniel to the lord."

"Where is he now, then?"

"They all sleep at Peter's house. But you'll see him in the morning. Luckily, his aunt loves him and Yeshua and all the Romano-Phoenician disciples, and is happy to have her half-empty *domus* filled with his followers. "

"So, turning water to wine was awesome, but how did he kick open the door to Nathaniel's heart?" I wonder.

"He said that Jesus already knew him..."

"I felt that way, as well."

"And he said that Jesus saw what he'd been doing, before they met..."

"Isn't that what your friend from the baths thought, too?"

"Yes," she says patiently. "He knows us. All. He even knows our names."

I turn to her, on the edge of the roof, and I feel like my eyes must be sparkling like the fishermen's lights on the water.

"He knew I was coming. He could tell, somehow, when I left Tyre. He sent Kaspar to meet me. It's an invisible miracle. Nothing changed, but if it hadn't happened, I'd probably be dead now."

She looks solemnly back at me, her eyes shining more like lamps on the windowsills of the fisher-wives and mothers. Slowly, she nods her head. That sleek centre parting makes her look very wise. I wait for a respectable moment, then say:

"Publia, have we actually got any wine?"

She shakes her Hebrew hairdo, now.

"Only water up here, and I'm not going back down again. Come on."

Under a canopy is a little bedroom she's made her own. There's a covered bowl with a splash of cool water to wash in. Then we sit on some pillows, with sheets round our shoulders, getting dry. Publia is pointing out that the acacia wood bedframe was made from an old cart. It's a short respite from her questions about my journey; still, basically, 'What's happened? Did you walk here like that? Did you come on your own? Have you been attacked?'

I seize a moment to think as she shows me her bedside storage in the wheel arch with a matching one on my side too. My story has unrolled back to the place where I lost the purple. I don't want to tell her that everything has gone, yet, but I need to say something, just to free my *murex* pricked spine, my snail fleshed heart.

Those pricks. They've driven me to Hades in a hand cart just like the one we're sitting in. This bumpy, stripped-down trip is so uncomfortable; I just hope I'll see them round the next corner, and somehow get my birth right, my family blood, my global business, the invested dress back.

"It's a bit insecure, only having one small bag, isn't it," I stutter. "No change of clothes. Only a saffron-yellow tunic that goes see-through when wet and a dusky-blue *palla* I can never get clean."

"Jesus will say throw that away," Publia answers at once. "Honestly, it's not a problem. I've only had one outfit since I left my husband at Hazor."

"It's... just..." I try again, "so naked, only one layer of protection. What if it suddenly rips in half?"

My sister stifles a yawn and lies down on the bed. "What else is in your bag?"

"Hardly anything," I whisper, lying stiffly beside her. "My white linen handkerchief. A peacock feather shawl, you know, like your pomegranate one, we got from the *plumarius* in Tyre, the day we struck a deal with our first *praetor*. And one real peacock feather, worth practically nothing."

I should say it now. That I was wearing my entire fortune in purple silk and had it stripped from me, first night out of town, easy as pulling a petal off a violet.

"I'm sure you could cover your modesty with those," Publia murmurs. She's falling asleep; I can hear her thoughts turn dream-like, see her strewing the flowers in tassels and a hanky.

I try to follow her to that happy state. But as I relax, I remember; sleeping on a rooftop in a makeshift bed. Last time I did that, it was with my slave, Abibaal's kitchen boy, on the flat roof of his *insula*, four floors above the back door.

His skin felt hard next to mine and smelt of olive oil and sawdust. Publia is a softer bed-mate and smells more like lavender oil and wood smoke. He was peppery, she is papery; I know who I'd rather tell that I've lost the purple, though.

Just as I am nodding off, the couple from Byblos come onto the roof, and squeeze past our bed with a quiet rustle. They said, tonight, that they're in the paper trade; exporting papyrus to Rome by much the same route I used to send my product. It's huge; a luxury item the Empire suddenly relies on.

I give them a nod as they go. I will probably need a job, after we've been to Jerusalem.

Red sand, purple sea; as my dreams course away in the morning, I recall Publia's condition. She is sitting up next to me in bed already. Soon as my eyes are open, I ask her.

"How is your bleeding?"

She turns and smiles at me in the ruddy dawn.

"Better. Much better," she says. "I wax and wane with the moon."

"And not a spot in between?"

She shakes her head and stands up, stretching.

"Couldn't have travelled like this if I wasn't healed," she says. Looking back down at me: "How are you? I think we're on the road today."

I need to get used to it. Being nowhere. Having nothing. Going with Jesus.

"Fine," I say.

We breakfast with the rest of the household, the second meal I've had from Aunt Naomi without paying. Could the milk be more silky if I wasn't skint, would the bread be less fresh if my heart wasn't heavier than my purse?

I chew this over, sourly, while Publia and the other guests get ready to go out, until Naomi sits down at her loom to start working, when I almost spit it out.

I am afraid of the shuttle. It makes me wince for a slap, and my sister, too. We avoid the warp and the weft, wherever possible. *Mater* was the hand behind a pretty claustrophobic web, at home. But the fabric Nathaniel's aunt is weaving has layers like the hills of Galilee, lighter shades overlapping the darker levels, a pattern repeated to the horizon. The way she moves is lovely, too, creating the earthen stripes with a shake of her shuttle.

I lean against the doorpost and let my eyes linger on the moving lines of time, the patience of Naomi's art. A woman can tell the whole story of her house, her family, recording the years in sediment at her loom. The designs my mother wove, in the villa at Rome, got progressively weirder. So I never go near weaving if I can help it but, if I did, I would definitely do an experiment. Can't be too difficult to put a signature in the cloth, picked out in purple.

I don't realise that my finger is moving till it feels something strange on the doorpost. As if I've carved the glyphs I was thinking of in the stone; curly, snakelike letters. So different from the chiselled *XL* lines of Latin. I'm still tracing it with my finger when Publia arrives.

"What is this?" I say.

"That? They call it the *Shema,* I think. It's on all doors, sometimes on scrolls; a reminder to praise God as you enter or leave the building."

"We should have done that in Tyre. The only words I had written above my door were a reminder to buy and sell..." I stop before the P-word. If I say it, my sister might sense, from the emptiness of my tone, that I've lost it.

She leads me out onto the street. There's a smell of fish on the wind and the men sitting on their doorsteps are mending nets. As we walk past them, I wonder if their knots tell the same story as women weave in layers like Naomi indoors, or whether their handiwork takes harder lines, outside.

I see Publia pull her headdress low over her eyes. It seems to be the colour of the sea breeze itself, making her almost invisible.

"What happened to your pomegranate shawl?" I ask casually. "That was so pretty."

"Bal took it. When we parted. Clung to it. Ripped a bit. I let him have it." Hardly moving her lips, she wraps the oversized local scarf right under her chin and around her neck.

We hurry along, a group of five, a V formation; the Roman guy leads, with the Byblos couple and the Fabia sisters fanning out behind.

"Is there a bath, here?" I whisper to Publia. We are turning a few heads and I feel completely filthy.

"Nothing public," she replies, "but I can get us a private one later."

Our companions cannot agree what the plan is; leaving today, tomorrow, at dawn, at noon. They bicker about the itinerary: a short tour of Galilee or the long haul to Jerusalem? There's even a concern we might have missed it altogether, so everyone is walking quickly.

We turn a corner and Marcus gives a shout. This is the busy main street but his voice rings out like an actor's in a hushed auditorium. He shouts a foreign name and strides into the crowd. Farzan rushes after him.

"It's Matthew."

My sister and Emeshmoon share a satisfied nod.

"They're still here, then."

"He'll know what's happening."

They both speak together then laugh excitedly.

I look past them, through the morning throng, down to the water's edge where the waves of Galilee beat like blood against the sea wall. Are those men here, the ones who stole my life-cloth, scouting for the wealthiest buyers in town? Are they dealing purple in the shadows or trading it in broad daylight on the quayside. Selling in Latin, hawking in Hebrew.

This place makes me realise how bad home smells. Here, in the commercial centre of Capernaum, the whiff of fish is mild; gull-breath instead of the hell-reeking snails of Tyre. That might mean there's nobody rich enough, no one rotten or corrupt enough, to stump up the cash for my Tyrian toga, though.

It's not long to wait in this pleasant air, straining to hear 'Purpura!' in the seagull chorus of vendors, before Marcus and Farzan come back.

"It's sorted," they say, steering us toward the seafront. "We meet tonight to hear his plan."

"Then set off tomorrow morning."

Marcus lets out a huge sigh. "Matthaeus, I adore him. When we were talking," he says, "I could see Jesus in his eyes."

"So, who is this dude?" I ask.

"There are twelve of them, specially chosen, his closest followers and personal favourites," Marcus explains. "Matthew is one. Nathaniel is another, much easier for us to get an audience with, normally. We're going to meet him next, by the water."

As he falls into step beside me, I look down at his feet, noticing the silver tips to his sandal laces.

"How do you come to be following Jesus?" I ask him. "It couldn't have been from Rome; Yeshua hasn't gone there. Yet, anyway."

"I met him in Scythopolis," Marcus says. "I was working there, building a new theatre."

"Oh, I do love the theatre," I don't mind admitting. "I was taught by a Thespian."

"I know, Publia's told me all about your dad. She thinks you saw an old production of Plautus I was in at the Theatre of Pompey."

"Darling, I was there every week," I gasp. "Rome's first and finest theatre has a temple to Venus Victrix built into the roof, doesn't it? I was one of a chorus of assistant priestesses, come to service that chapel."

We would have been there at the same time but both wearing masks. It's not surprising we don't recognise each other. I was clad in myrtle; he, Marcus Manlius Nerva, to give his complete *tria nomina*, was wreathed in laurel. Here, we've come out from under the bushes.

Arriving on the Galilean shoreline in the sunshine, we swap stories; mine the 'rape to riches'; his, the 'actor to theatre impresario'. Having conquered the Roman stage, his skills were sought by the city of Scythopolis to build their own great auditorium. The glamour and the glory of this work overseas was like his own purple trade route.

"So what was your favourite part?" I ask him.

"Thousands of people staring at me, rows of faces, stacked up to the gods. I loved all the attention. Theatre was hard to leave till I realised; the show was only ever between me and God..."

"I meant, what about the parts you played?"

"Oh, that," he laughs. He'd swept out his arms to encompass the amphitheatre of Galilean hills but now his stance is more speculative. "They were all the same in the end. The young hero; every play has an *adolescens* and that was me for a long time. But I was starting to take on the old man's role, *senex,* when I got head-hunted to build the new theatre. Since then, I've sometimes played the cunning slave."

On that natural stage, next to such an experienced actor, I consider my roles, old and new, too.

Twelve disciples, he said. Could the Prince of Peace possibly have use for an assistant priestess? I am wondering, as we pause dramatically dock-side, if there were ever any chance of being disciple number thirteen.

Standing at the sea wall, looking across a little ocean in the hills, our group is quiet and contemplative. There's time to spare now before we travel on. I wait, while thirteen waves wash onto the basalt quay, then decide.

These are the reasons why I should sing; I said I would, I could pitch for a livelihood, and confess to my destitution at the same time.

When the next wave comes in, I catch its flow. My voice ebbs gently into the scene:

"This is a song that could sell you your own soul, by she who used to trade in Roman Venus, by she who used to market Tyrian Purple. It's a tune whistled by Melqart, once; hummed by King Phoenix. Originally sung by Hercules, it tests her skill in the highs and lows, who made her fortune with this powerful and persuasive voice. She sold the world to men, could still do it now, but there is a problem;

"Disguised as sea-nymph Tyrus, whose half-divine beauty begot our great city, she set off to find the true God but was stripped of her riches on the first night out of town. As a mermaid her wealth was all in the costume, a beautiful purple gown."

I see Publia's ears prick up at this point and she starts to look at me suspiciously. The others are looking charmed by my embroidered tale:

"Un-armed Tyrus, bare-legged and sore-footed; the sea-nymph limps to her night at an inn. In the hills, in the dark, in the animal pen; they don't hurt her. They just peel off her skin. It is worth more than gold, already sold by the time she wakes up again."

Audience shifting uncomfortably now, I come to a swift climax:

"But the sea is purple, so she'll swim dressed and the glittering fish will be her jewellery. No robber can take what comes free. And a net, for all it can catch, lets some fishes go."

I stop singing and sit on the sea wall, looking away modestly as the small crowd applaud. When I look back again, I realise there is one more. The famous Nathaniel has caught the tail end of my show. I'm as sure it's him as if I'd actually seen his aunt Naomi weaving those smouldering eyes and charcoal brows from the cloth of her own loom.

Marcus is spluttering: "Well, darling, it's lucky that ladies can't be actors, because I couldn't compete with that. Half the *virgos* I know would be out of work, if you were selling those wares on the Roman stage."

"Why can't ladies be actors?" Nathaniel poses back guilelessly.

Marcus looks like he's forgotten his lines. "They just can't," he stutters. "They never have. They don't know how to..."

"They're not allowed to," Publia nudges him.

"They don't want to." I jump off the wall and start walking toward the beach.

Heads are swivelling now, at Marcus, my sister and me, strutting and fretting along the quay. I turn my face away from the town, with its bustling waterfront. I don't like being crowded when I'm dirty. Fiddling with my hair, the towering style of Tyre fallen, I shudder at the thought of how it must look in Capernaum.

"You will need to cover your head," Publia calls after me, "when we're on the road. All women do, they have to, they want to, they're allowed to..."

I'm heading for the scurf-line, the grubby sand, grimy sea; and I so badly need to bathe my plan is just to walk right in. Publia grabs me by the hand as my feet get wet.

"What the hell was that song?" she hisses. "Where is the purple?"

"Like I said, I was wearing it. I stayed at an inn. I was robbed of it. Like I said, it wasn't a rape, this time. I thought you'd be pleased about that, at least."

"Gown?" she says. Harking back to my recent performance, she's hooking me out of the water. "What the fuck do you mean?"

I describe the sheet of purple silk. She has seen it, several times, folded in protective covers in Abibaal's safe. We have both fingered it. Together and, no doubt, separately. But never, to my knowledge, had it been unfolded and held up to the sunlight, and draped around the female form, till the moment I brought it.

"That," she says, "is probably worth its weight in gold."

"It was all legit." I tell her. "I sold everything for it."

"Not your pottery? Not your glassware? Not your ugly ivory bust?"

We tussle, to and fro, at the edge of the foam.

"I don't care about them," I say. "Didn't you hear the last verse; I swim in a sea of glass. Sshh!"

The others are starting to come towards us, crunching on the shingle, shattering our wave-whispered mood.

"I do care about *pater*'s business," I swear. "I gave Abibaal my display table and begged him to keep trading."

"He will," says Publia. "And Balthazar better do right by us both when we get to Bethany."

"He won't have to marry me. I can still work," my voice is getting louder. "You know I can out-labour Hercules."

There's a sudden silence on the beach as if the stones pause and the sea holds its breath. Everyone stops in their tracks. It feels like we're walking on mosaics in a temple forecourt, aqua *tesserae* representing holy water.

"You can certainly out-sing the angels," Nathaniel says. He steps towards me, somehow drawing me away from the rest of the group, and we walk on a pace or two before the shingle seems to move again.

"Stripped of your skin?" He means in my song.

I smile politely. "I've previously been gutted, so it wasn't the worst fate that could befall me. This was a risky trip to take, and I'm lucky to be here alive, though I didn't sing it like that to my sister."

Nathaniel says, "Jesus saved you."

"I think he saw me leaving Tyre though he'd already gone."

I glance back at the others, none in earshot, boys throwing stones, girls finding shells. I have some serious questions to ask this disciple and I hope they're not too rude.

"I have heard that the master saw you," I mutter awkwardly, "before you'd actually met? Publia said there was proof he knew what you were doing without really seeing it..."

Nathaniel's voice has an echo as if we are in a temple instead of on the seashore.

"Rabboni saw me praying," he says, "in a particular way. Nobody else could have known it."

We're walking faster, getting further from the group, but he doesn't confide any more. I'm dying to know in what peculiar manner he prayed, but I do understand why he can't tell me. I'm nowhere near the thirteenth disciple.

So with nothing to lose, well, I've lost it already, I blurt out another embarrassing query.

"Who is his richest follower? Which of the fishermen's friends has cash?"

"Why?"

"Some men are looking to sell a *toga picta*," I pant. "That skin of mine, pure purple silk, a garment worth a king's gold and fit only for the lord."

"You know where it is?"

"I'm a saleswoman. The world's a marketplace. I know, I should just let it go. But, not for me, for Jesus; if there is a buyer, I would source it." I am a Fabia Pictrix and will fight, sing or scream, till I get the colour back.

Then out of the blue, or perhaps in reply to my purple, he answers the first question. Gennesaret only has a gentle swell but even that mild tide waits as he delivers this jaw-dropping gen:

"Ever since I was a small boy, I've seen angels. Every size and shape of angel and some I couldn't even measure. Angels in a chorus and on their own; angels that looked like men, and angels that looked like snakes; angels that had lion's heads and eagle's wings, that were made of fire, that were spinning like wheels. Angels that could sit on a leaf or stand as high as the tree."

Everything seems to stop again except Nathaniel's confession, his words so vivid I can see them fixed like mosaic in the beach pebbles, pictures on a temple forecourt.

"Nobody I knew ever saw them too. Aunt Naomi, my sister, the odd friend like Philip; they listened as I told of my visions, though, and sometimes acted on the advice I'd been given.

"There was a special place I went to talk to this particular angel. He was the biggest one I'd encountered and always seemed to come when I sat in this spot, between two ancient fig trees at the foot of a mountain. My most searching questions were answered when this brilliant *angelus* opened his book of light."

He pauses for breath and the sea breeze starts to blow again, the pebbles to chatter at our heels. My sister and friends are catching up.

"I wasn't at the wedding in Cana." Nathaniel's story speeds on, as he's surely reeled off this witness statement before. "My mate was one of the musicians and his cousin was related to the bridegroom. The veil was lifted from Philip's eyes that night. When I saw him, rubbing them, in the morning, he said Jesus wanted to meet me. 'How does he know you?' Philip kept asking me. 'He is the anointed one and you're just a local greaser.'"

I laugh and let him lead me further along the shore with wet shingle getting into my sandals.

"I didn't know how this prophet knew me either but, the moment we met, I knew who he was. All the angels I'd ever seen were with him, though no one else saw them," Nathaniel smiles. "The towering archangel beside him said 'this is the king of heaven' then they all sang it, in a chord that made every hair on my head stand and sing, too. And Jesus knew that I knew they were there. He said three names to me, Metatron, Elijah and Enoch..." the rest of the group are approaching so he finishes hurriedly; "...beaming introductions into empty air. And that is where I remain, transfixed".

Standing on the sand in the shade of a giant stone, I greet my sister with mouth agape. All the characters in that man's story could fly in at this moment and I would do nothing to close it. Oh, if I could sing in their harmonies having thus inhaled.

"Pardon?" Publia looks back at me, though I didn't speak. I suppose I start trying to say that angels are all around us, but am saved from doing so by Nathaniel, who gathers the group together in the bosom of cool stone and leads them in a prayer.

They must have done this many times before. They speak as one, facing inward, focussing on the words, effortlessly making them resonate. Standing in their circle I hear snippets, hallowed be thy name, on earth as it is in heaven, between my own musings.

I'm thinking about Hercules, about Venus, about Apollo. Gods are real. We have seen them. But what if men first saw Olympians and thought they were Seraphim; rings of fire, what if Jews and gentiles both envisaged the same heavenly beings? There could still be a Hercules. I don't have to give him up. He could still invent purple and make another cloak and send it, by winged Hermes, to my King.

"Amen," Nathaniel says, and the group murmur in agreement.

It might be too soon after that I pull Pubi aside and softly coo; "you know Hercules."

She nods suspiciously.

"Do you think he is actually an angel?"

"I think you're talking *stercus bovis*."

I can understand her calling it bullshit; last thing she knew I was devoutly minding Jesus. But the other guys are looking again, more amazed; these Fabia Pictrix sisters, if they're not rapping, they're snapping.

Everyone shakes the sand off their hems, and the stones from their sandals as we walk back the way we came, the beach gently turning into the sandy streets of Capernaum. I pause though before the tide of this scene turns completely.

"Publia," I declare, "If I can't bath now I'm just going to jump in the sea."

"No," she says, "wait. We're going to Artorius."

"He's expecting us at the tenth hour. It'll be our last bath," Marcus says. "He will be sad."

I'm ecstatic at the thought of immersing myself in hot water and watching the steam rise. Not being able to wash for many days has finally cured my fear of the public baths; but this, apparently, will be a private one.

We go back to Aunt Naomi's till then. I trace the snaking shapes on her doorpost, and I touch the twisting threads on her loom, shivering at the thought of wrapping myself up in a towel. Publia goes upstairs to pack. I haven't got anything, now, that isn't in my bag already. A shawl, pretty but impractical; a large linen handkerchief, still pristine; a lucky peacock feather. Can tell just by feeling, it's full enough.

I don't miss my snake-haired statue or the set of drinking glasses that were empty and unhandled. I don't miss the glittering sword hilt of Hercules. It couldn't do anything I can't do with my finger. If I had all those things again, I'd sell them all again. I could do with the cash. Because I don't need prettiness, but I don't like pennilessness.

Emeshmoon fires up the hearth and brews her smoky Phoenician infusion. She tears off pieces of this morning's flatbread to toast and spread with some melting herbal butter. She passes it around freely and I partake, marvelling at how much I can eat without paying. The price has not yet been set.

I chat to her and her husband, Farzan. They are good company, like theatrical Marcus Manlius. Our small talk about the passing of time leads to bigger details; they tell me their city was founded by Cronus. Old as *tempus* itself, Byblos holds the secret to the best record keeping system, in the world, ever: paper. The couple work in the page-turning business and, as the surface appeal of purple has faded somewhat, I'm ready for a job that's deeper and more meaningful. After we've been to Jerusalem with Jesus.

Just before the tenth hour, Marcus comes down from the roof where he's been sleeping and joins in the conversation again. He tells us that the biggest cult in Byblos is still Adonis and he does a dance in honour of this demi-god. It's brilliant, funny, sexy; if I knew the words, I'd definitely be singing.

But then he says: "You like the song? Listen on. I'll unscroll my hymnsheet inches further..."

Marcus strikes a pose that makes Aunt Naomi drop her spindle. They are both screeching as she rolls about on the floor trying to catch it. My sister jumps up and gets our mother-figure back to her feet, and the day on track by steering talk back to the man whose private baths we're going to be washing in shortly.

"He is Spurius Artorius Pavo," she tells me.

I squawk.

"Knew she'd like it," Pubi says, handing the spindle back to Naomi. "Pavo means peacock and that bird is her mascot."

He is not one of those," Aunt Naomi says. "No. Though he collects beauty, he is plain black: a jackdaw, if the man must be a bird, already."

"Why don't you come with us?" my sister asks her.

"The Israelites do not bathe with Romans," insists our hostess, "though I would certainly like to see his mosaics."

"Seriously? What's he got?" I turn to Pubi.

"Come and see." She gives me a wink and starts to leave. "Anyway, I didn't mean come bathing," Publia turns back to Naomi, who has bent to light the fire for dinner. "I meant come to Jerusalem. Be a stone in the mosaic of Jesus."

We have to get clean first. The bath of Artorius is in the next street. This Roman Consul to Capernaum has built a shrine to Neptune beside the Sea of Galilee. As we walk through the archway and down the steps I am transported through the plumbing of old Roma to the empire's womb.

It is the most exquisite little baths, inlaid with precious stones, polished till they gleam. On every surface, save the water's, faces of gods and goddesses appear; made, apparently, by an artist who previously tiled at Herculaneum. Even under the water, god-like bodies are waving from the floor and the walls of the pool.

If I'd seen this place before my rape I would have been thrilled. If I'd seen it before I knew Jesus I would have been awed. Now I just want to scrape the dirt from my skin: the shit I've been carrying since I left Tyre, the crap I took at the inn; muck from the mountains, bits off the beach, the almost holy smoke of Aunt Naomi's hearth.

There are three small pools, the six of us can fit in each: if Spurius Artorius Pavo sits very, very close to Marcus, dripping consulate sweat onto show-biz muscles. Spurius is one of those men who defy every law of manhood and still manage to be a perfect brute.

In between his attention to M. Manlius Nerva's ribs and nipples and pecs, Pavo regales me with his personal details. He has worked in every city I've ever heard of. He has signed forms and ticked boxes and wax-stamped across the Roman Empire. There are names dropping like the beads of bathwater from the tip of his nose but they are famous administrators we may, or may not, have heard of so they don't make much of a splash.

It's a bit better in the hot bath. He gets very excited talking about theatre; his face one moment a comic mask, the next tragic as he recounts the plays he has seen and the actors he has met. But it's the lover's role he's playing for Marcus, who he's never seen in action but has certainly heard of.

This is why I don't go mixed bathing, if it can be helped. That, and the other thing men do, as Farzan is now; simply staring at all the breasts bobbing on the water. At Publia's and mine (hers are bigger, mine are less pointy, etc.) as well as his wife's, in no particular order. Then we get out of the hot tub and sit on the side, my sister and I; oiling and strigiling each other much more vigorously than we were able to previously.

She is very robust with me and as I open my eyes from a wince, I see Farzan staring, open mouthed. Some wives would be jealous of this look but Emesh is cool, even in the hot water. She's kind of staring at Publia and me too. She gets out next but Farzan stays submerged; eyes wider still as his missus sits between the Fabia Pictrix sisters and gets oiled and strigiled too.

Artorius and Marcus don't even look up but the book dealer from Byblos looks like it will never go down.

The three girls have been in the *frigidarium* long enough for the goose-pimples to subside by the time the men jump in. I just want to say thank you to our hissing host quickly and jump out. I try not to be too brisk, though:

"You have given us a little hint of heaven today," I say.

The three boys glance down at themselves at the word 'little', like an involuntary toot on the piccolo. The cold water works better for the ladies. My floating bosoms seem fuller and firmer now.

Artorius Pavo bigs himself up.

"Mine are the best private baths this side of Sparta," he says. "I'll have you know, my mosaics could compete with the finest in Roma."

I'm still trying not to be rude but I had a collection, too.

"As a serious dealer in fine art," I smile, "I can appreciate its worth."

"I fear you cannot, young woman," he says, "because it is priceless."

"A hundred Tyrian Shekels for a set of *Terra Sigillata*; a hundred for my glassware; ninety shekels for a bronze bust of Bacchus and eighty for a Gorgon's head in ivory. As for my jewelled sword hilt, long and thick as Hercules' thing; personally I thought that was priceless but it fetched a hundred and twenty silver pieces. That's what I paid to get here. In purple dye which, as you know, is worth more than gold."

"Veronica," Publia hisses, "stop pissing in Spurius' water."

But he likes me better now. He likes Publia because she deals in purple, and now he knows her sister does too.

"Is that how much it cost you to come?" asks Marcus.

I remember the counting stones on my desk in the shop at Tyre, the Babylonian abacus in the drawer, how high the numbers could go.

"No," I say, "it cost me much, much more."

"For Jesus?" Artorius looks at me as he asks this; but then his gaze goes round all the others too, in no particular order, as they are all here for the same reason.

Marcus speaks. "There was a prophet in the wilderness called John, the Baptist. When people went to him, he washed them of their sins. It was to prepare for the day of judgement."

"I know," tuts Artorius. "Many people went to him. Jordan way. There were tax implications."

"One day," says Marcus, who knows how to speak dramatically, "a man called Jesus from Nazareth went to him. Now, you might think nothing good can come out of Nazareth but when John the Baptist saw him coming he said to his disciples: I have baptised you in water but here is the one who will baptise you in the holy spirit."

"How does it work? I've asked you before," Artorius says.

"And I've told you before. But now I can show you."

Marcus stands in the cold water, his breast the best of any of ours. To Pavo's thrill he suddenly takes his shoulder; "God will make you clean and new, Artorius; without the vanity, the jealousy, the petty-mindedness."

Then he dunks him under. He doesn't hold him down for long and yet, when Spurius bounces back again, he seems to have shut up. He gives a baby cry but doesn't speak.

I'm more in need of a baptism than him being competitive, superficial, judgemental.

"Do me too," I say to Marcus. There is a true tear in my eye, not a drop of Pavo's bathwater.

And Marcus is such a great actor he can actually make it real. He grabs my shoulder and says; "You will be re-born, Veronica. Without the ghastly blonde streaks or the pride or the rage or the greed.

I go under the water, eyes wide. Though I've only just met Marcus, I trust him with the fashion-tips, at least. I willingly reach up and pull the streaks out of my hair. Goat-grease, the false locks are easy to find underwater, heavier clumps in the floating strands. I guess it's just something you can feel.

As for the pride and the greed; do I let that go? How will I know when to: have I even been tried yet? And maybe I should be proud, for the example I set is not so much competitive as motivational. Perhaps its fine to be judgemental if well-informed, and superficial can certainly be resilient. I run my fingers through these epithets along with the bristly hair extensions, and try to let the balsam soak in.

I thought that nothing would get me clean; my skin still had a bruise-tint from those original Roman baths, till this. Like it was an actor's painted mask, after a show, Marcus took it off.

In the end, everyone has a mini-baptism in the unlikely but engaging arms of Manlius Nerva. He prays slightly differently every time so this is definitely not a script. Fit for the kingdom, we all climb out of the chilly water and run for our towels.

Publia and I are laughing as we dry our hair, looking in a silver mirror the shape of a sea-shell. Naked, I have nothing; washed clean, I am nothing; I have never felt more secure. When I wrap myself in clothes, shaken and steamed while we bathed, the dress feels silky on my skin, though it doesn't look it.

The consul walks us out to the street, still damp. He is beaming, eyes locked onto Marcus, who clamps a hand on his shoulder as if to dunk him another time. But was that the kind of wash we only get once in our lives?

"You'll come again?" Artorius is crying, eyes like his lapis lazuli tiles.

"No. You," says Emeshmoon, leaning in to smooth a fold in his toga. "You come to Jerusalem. Be a stone in the bath of... What did you say, Fabia Pictrix; be a drop in the water of Jesus?"

CHAPTER EIGHT

Everyone who is going in the morning (or who says they will tonight) meets at Capernaum quay as the setting sun makes a golden mirror of Galilee. There is a sea of headscarves at the dockside and my hairstyle no longer stands out like the Coliseum. It lies sleek, combed through with my fingers as it dried, and covered by my shawl.

The little group I spent the last day with, led by Nathaniel, disperses like a dye slick in the ocean. I stay close to Publia, though; the tassels of our scarves touch reassuringly. Then I see a tall white turban, its folds the high columns of a heavenly kingdom, rising above the other heads in front of us.

"Kaspar," I shout, "I never said thank you for helping me."

He turns around and sees me, jumping up and down in the crowd.

"Do you know what's happening now?" I scream excitedly.

"He is going to speak," Kaspar nods. "Look."

Publia and me are tiny next to the fishermen of Galilee and the matrons of Israel. We can't see over the people in front of us, even if we jump, but we can hear Jesus talking.

He tells us he is going to Jerusalem. He asks us to come with him. But he says not to stay together. Journey in pairs and talk to everyone we meet on the way, flocking out from the group to enter every home, walk through every market place, drink at every well, sit in every temple along his path. [6]

The instructions sound like he's singing, a quiet chant on the evening breeze, though I slowly realise that the whispering is of my own heart. His voice comes in so easily at my ears, his ideas settle so comfortably on my mind, that I wish for him in my vision too.

Grabbing hold of Publia's hand, I back out of the crowd, away from the action, bowing through the bodies till we're in the last row: at the sea wall where I sang earlier today. Now I climb on that dark stone and pull Pubi up beside me: standing we can see perfectly, over the whole congregation to Jesus.

As we suddenly appear above the sea of stripy headgear, he looks at us. From across the quay, with the setting sun behind him and the

Roman sisters dressed very differently to how we were before, both Publia and I are convinced by his mere blink that he knows it is us.

I have to listen harder to what he is saying, now that I can see his face, and when I get the point, I punch the air. Pubi grabs my wrist and turns my fist into something more modest.

"He's saying to only take one set of clothes," I protest: "and we've already done that."

"Sure," she concedes. "This is not the start of our spiritual journey."

It has long begun for everyone on that leg but we're the only ones in the crowd who have to be careful not to step backwards or we'll fall off the sea wall with a splash. So, my urge is to kneel down. To kneel like I did as a temple dancer to Venus, when faced with a manly seeker after grace, to whom I would offer oracle sex.

In my old religion, spirit was physical, lust could be prayerful. Worship may have been by succumbing to, as much as by overcoming, temptation. The trouble is, there's a long, long queue to get to him. Fishermen three deep and, fighting with them for his attention, two kinds of Israelite lady; the motherly and the would-be wife.

Maybe that's mean and there are other kinds of women in between; but the main thing is, they are all between me and Jesus. And Publia loves him too. The way that I have previously worshipped will be hard to do, without stepping on any toes.

We climb down from the wall when the talk is over, when we've been blessed and told to go in peace. He is our shepherd, Jesus said, but we mustn't follow him like sheep. Going two by two, through the villages of Galilee and by the river Jordan, is how to fish for men.

On the way back to Aunt Naomi's we walk into Marcus Manlius, with Emeshmoon and Farzan again. We all hail each other as sisters and brothers. I've only known them for one day.

"Where is Nathaniel?" asks Publia.

"Sleeping at Peter's," says Marcus. "He'll call for us at sunrise."

A thrill of excitement and fear is running through me.

"I'm feeling the sunrise now," I giggle as if Aurora were tickling me intimately.

The actor walks quicker to keep up, laughing too: "I mentally cast you as a *virgo* first," he says, "but now I know you can play the *meretrix*."

He will need to know me longer before finding out which of the masks I wear have my heart in, for any friend will see that I'd never play the prostitute again. As we carry on with this first scene together, though, I ask him how he met Nathaniel; was that in Scythopolis too?

"No, it was on the road," Marcus says, "on the way back here. I was following the master for the first time, all clenched and uncertain. We went through a field of giant daisies and this chap walked up behind me. I thought '*clementia!*' His words to me clinched the deal."

"Did you unclench?" I smile.

"Completely," says Marcus.

"Was that Nathaniel?" I ask him. "What did he say?"

"He said there was an angel flying next to me, a guardian who never left my side. He described her dress in the colours of dawn edged with silver and her gorgeous wings etched in gold. He outlined her flaming hair and warm eyes, her statuesque nose, and told me she was smiling over my shoulder."

"Oh. That's nice," I say.

"It wasn't nice, it was my mother," says Marcus. "She died the year before. I was bereft but suddenly: saved. The message of eternal life was delivered in person by my heavenly *mater*. I've been at peace ever since."

"You still seem unstable to me," I murmur.

"You can talk, V. Fabia Pictrix," he replies, pushing me through the archway. "Now, get in the house and put on a show."

I was planning an early night; but Aunt Naomi hasn't heard me sing yet, and I get another supper for free, so I do lay on a little song or two. The hostess loves Ovid and I'm happy to start with him; she gets her kicks from the illicit sex scenes and I'm willing to oblige.

"cum tibi succurret Veneris lascivia nostrae,
purpureas tenero pollice tange genas.
siquid erit, de me tacita quod mente queraris,
pendeat extrema mollis ab aure manus." [7]

The language sounds ruder than it really is, sung in my saucy warble. Then they ask me to sing the thing from earlier, at the beach this afternoon, with the nymph stripped of her purple raiment but swimming in the Phoenician water.

"I can't remember that," I protest. "My songs only come one time."

"Which is exactly why books were invented," says Emeshmoon. "Write it down once, remember it for ever."

The page is the last place I'd put my words. With that tune, the low notes were carved in the Capernaum sea wall and the high ones were the colour of the breeze. Singing ink is invisible but tonight I have to invoke Rome's laureate, Ovidius Naso, and recite one I penned previously:

"This is a song that could catch you a man, by she who used to work for the goddess of marriage, by she who weaves wedding veils with holes big as fishing nets.

"Disguised as a purple dye seller, she sold beauty to the world, could still do it now but there is a problem. As a woman her riches were all in the costume, a stolen gown of silk. Now she swims naked in Galilee, casting her net broadly, catching fish for the kingdom.

"A sea-nymph from Tyre, who made her fortune with this powerful and persuasive voice. What couldn't she sell in the marketplace?"

When the evening is over, I lie in bed next to Publia, letting the silence sink in. I can hear three different people snoring before long and the rhythm evokes my chant again. Basically, I think the first version was better; the one I sang this afternoon. The fish were glittering jewels, then.

They swim in my mind; amethysts. Suddenly, I gasp in the dark and sit up, groping for my bag beside me. I find it, pick it up, shake it: didn't I put a set of jewellery in here, just before I left town? If it wasn't robbed with my purple robe, those precious stones should still be there.

But I've popped my hand in a few times and haven't felt them. I feel again, now. This is a good bag. It's made of pigskin but it has a silky lining. Out slips the peacock feather shawl and the white linen handkerchief. Out comes the actual feather, which weighs almost nothing. The bag still feels heavy and it rattles.

Careful not to wake Publia, I turn it upside down. An amethyst earring falls onto the pillow, glinting in the moonlight. I run my fingers round the bag's rim; there, a split in the seam, the other earring poking through. I pick it out and probe further; yes, a rip in the lining and the silver necklace and bracelet, studded with night-coloured gems, drop onto the bed.

I'd thought my bag was empty, that I was naked and swimming freely in Galilee: it turns out that I'm still anchored by a weighty chain to Rome. I wrap my riches in the hanky and put everything safely back in my bag. I'm worth something now but, as I lie down to sleep again, I feel more worried than before.

'Walk the way, believe the truth, live the life!'

We are woken before the sun rises by the voice of Nathaniel, singing in the courtyard of Aunt Naomi's house. I open my eyes to the first grey light and look down from the flat roof to see him lighting a small fire at the hearthstones. He straightens up and sings again:

'Walk the way, believe the truth, live the life!'

I sit up in bed and see the rose wings of dawn, edged with gold, in the sky. Publia sits beside me.

"*Soror*," she says. "It is happening now. We're going to Jerusalem in glory."

Then I remember the jewellery in my bag. And though it should make me feel safer, like our passage will be smooth and our stay comfortable, my heart seems to sink with the heaviness of the stones.

Downstairs, Emesh is brewing herbal tea and toasting old bread, spreading Nathaniel's with something she calls *zaatar zejd*; a paste of olive oil, thyme and sesame seeds. Farzan is handing out water skins for us each to fill. I put wine in mine. Nobody notices; it's still dark in the corner where the water urns and wine jars jostle together, stood in the cooling sand. But it seems to me that, if I didn't have my secret stash of gemstones to keep, I would have chosen the clear water.

We sit and eat till the sky above the fireplace is flaming, too, then Nathaniel says it's time to go.

"*Carissima* Aunt Naomi," says Marcus, kissing her.

"Are you sure you won't come with us?" Emesh whispers.

The lady shakes her head.

"They need me here," she says.

"Thank you so much for your hospitality," Publia hugs her.

We have come to the doorstep of her house. The others step through into a street paved with pink; it's quiet but we can hear the sound of many voices from around the corner at the harbour side.

"Come on," Farzan sets off at a run.

I hold back, under the archway, one hand tracing the prayer carved in Naomi's doorpost, one hand in my bag, feeling for something I still want to say.

I bring out an amethyst earring and put it in her hand.

"Thank you for having me," I say quickly and start to walk away.

She looks at the gemstone. For a moment her eyes gleam. She knows the price of this unexpected item. Then she looks up at me.

"I didn't want paying," she says.

"Sorry..."

"Pay is made of heavy clay; we deal in the currency of heaven, hey?"

"Ovid would kiss your ass, Aunt Naomi," I say, before her lips purse as if he really has!

From the end of the street Publia is shouting at me to hurry up. I had thought my days as a businesswoman were done, but we've just made a transaction here.

Naomi turns and shouts at one of her sons or servants inside the house.

"Catch!" She throws the jewel at him. "That'll keep you till I come back..."

Then she picks up her peasant skirts and runs after Nathaniel.

"Wait!" she cries, "I'm coming with..."

When I catch up, the crowd at the seafront is starting to move off. Veronica Fabia Pictrix is probably the last person to follow Jesus out of Capernaum. I can't see him, as usual. The flesh is packed tight around the spirit; he walks at the heart of this body.

I do see Spurius Artorius, standing at the door of his baths, watching us go past. Marcus has spotted him, too.

"*Salve!*" he cries, "this way salvation lies."

Spurius tuts.

"Join us," enjoins Farzan. "We're following him to Jerusalem."

Spurius shakes his head. Then Aunt Naomi stops in front of him. She looks him up and down, the way she looks at all the Roman men, with their shoulders and legs on display.

"Come on, Pavo," she says.

Now the peacock stiffens.

"Haven't you heard what they did to his friend John, the Baptist?" he says.

With an angry flounce, Artorius goes inside to his warm bath tiled with the figures from a childish faith. I picture him hanging his toga on a trident and slipping into the private clam shell of Neptune with a sigh.

We don't know where or when we'll get our next bath. For Romans that is a bit like facing starvation. Publia and I hold hands as we walk. All our souls are clenched as we reach the edge of town.

"What did happen to John, then?" I ask the others.

I do not think the gift of an amethyst earring would have made Spurius change his mind and follow us. He would have kept it, no doubt. He would have cemented it into his baths, a sea nymph's tear.

Imprisoned by Herod for dissing his wife/sister. Beheaded in a drunken promise to her daughter. Diced on a plate; that's what happened to the Baptist. Pavo will never risk being dipped in the piss of death though he may weep for us who do.

Everybody in my group will wish we stayed in Capernaum's safe *caldarium* many times before we get to Bethany. This walk will take over a week, without a civilized dip. By the first evening, the dust of the foothills has settled so thick on my skin, it feels like no water will ever wash it off.

We weren't allowed to stop in Nazareth. Apparently, Jesus has sworn never to go there again. I still can't see him in the crowd that skirts mount Tabor, streaming round its rocky curves, but I don't picture him unmoving as the mountain.

I can't see him as we mob the town of Tiberias for lunch. Farzan calls this funny little place 'Rome-by-the-Sea' where the Empire beat Israel to the best bit of Galilee. The food is fabulous: Pubi and I find *savillum*, a cheesecake dressed with bay leaves like we used to get in the Via Vitella. Anyway, I don't see what Jesus is doing now, or later as we walk on to Philoteria. This town is named by the Greeks, obviously; it's the plug hole where the 'Sea of G' drains into the river Jordan.

It all goes downhill from this point. We arrive too late to go knocking on doors, as the lord would have us do. Only those followers with friends and family here go confidently into the dark street to find a safe floor to sleep on.

Our rag-tag group (actually we're smart as a *toga picta*) end up lying in a couple of boats, tied up at the harbour. The warm wooden berths are comfortable, the stars above are comforting, but the motion is rather too rocky for me. Nathaniel has led us here. He doesn't know whose boat this is but he knows boats. (I just know about sea-sickness on the trip to Tyre from Rome.)

In murmurs lower than the waves, Emeshmoon and Farzan are asking him what happened when Jesus walked on the water.

"I wasn't there," Nathaniel said. "I know it came to pass but I didn't see it. The thing I saw was when he stopped the storm."

"How?" Publia sits up.

I see the heads of Marcus and Aunt Naomi pop up from the other boat, nearly obscured by Pubi's bosom.

"We were sailing one night, back from some talk he'd given, in Bethsaida, maybe. He was sleeping and a storm blew up. He was snoring. But it was a big storm and we were scared. I think James woke him, in the end.

"Jesus laughed. He opened his eyes to a flash of lightning and crash of sea spray, and those eyes were sparkly. But then he looked at our faces. And he stood up in the boat. And what I saw then was, like, he was the mast. Still. Powerful. The deck steady beneath him. He raised his arms, sleeves billowing like sails, but his hands were not moved by the wind. His hands made the wind stop moving. I saw him somehow calm the sea..."

Nathaniel is gazing north into the dark Galilean. It moves silkily, under and around us, pressing to be the river that will flow south to Judea.

"Like laying a cloth on a table," Nathaniel says, "like laying a sheet on a bed. He smoothed down the storm and it stopped."

Dimly, I see him doing the movement as I look up from the floor of our own bobbing boat.

"What did everyone do then?" asks Publia.

"They said 'wow, master, that was cool, we were scared and you saved us from the mean wind. How do you do such things?'"

He makes the disciples sound like sheep. They must have felt stupid when: "Jesus lay down again and went back to sleep, with one sorrowful look at us men," Nathaniel sighs. "'You could do such things, too', he said and the next thing we knew he was snoring."

Now we have Marcus trying to stop their craft moving with the sea, standing in the tiny prow, doing the sign of peace. Then Naomi is on her feet, the tablecloth or sheet-smoothing very Jewish in her hands. Publia's laugh must be carrying across the water into Philoteria. Somebody will come and bust us off these boats if she doesn't shhh.

I lie with my eyes shut, trying to will them all into stillness. Jesus said we could do it too. But how? How? After a while, the voices stop and the human hustle and bustle ceases. As I quietly breathe, it feels like the wind drops a bit, too. But to actually stop the waves? I give it all the unseen power in my possession, imagining myself suddenly singing 'stop' at the top of my voice, at the top of the scale, in a tone that would shatter the temple Hercules made of solid gold. I picture this note, could hear it if I wanted to wake the whole town up; but would it cause the sea to miss a beat, could it make the ceaseless rhythm stop?

For a long time I lie there trying to still the waters; I'm sure the others have fallen asleep before I realise that I'm bursting for a piss and that really will be tricky.

The next morning starts abruptly with some angry fishermen kicking us off their boats into thigh-deep water. We wade with tunics held high and handbags aloft to the shore.

"I saw a beautiful moon last night," says Marcus, flopping on the sand. "Almost full it was."

"Couldn't have been," Emesh says firmly, "it's waning."

"This one was weeing." He winks slyly at me.

An unmarried woman, sticking my butt over the side to pee, virtually in the face of Marcus Manlius lying in the next boat; my position was compromising. It took stomach muscles trained in the temple of Venus to hold that pose and still *minxi*.

If it had been Publia, a married woman on her way to meet her husband, although by a very long road, the scandal would not be as great. But this semi-famous actor we're walking with is unbothered. He's hardly a stalker, waiting to pounce on inappropriate ladies. The dear boy mainly potters along with Aunt Naomi, both watching the backsides of the men in front.

The path ahead curves into the mountains, further away from the river Jordan, which I thought was going to lead us straight to Jerusalem like a vessel of purple blood. Instead we swerve a route, missing Nazareth but hitting some other places where Christ has been before.

At the last town in Galilee, we stop. There are shouts echoing round the rocky outskirts. A rant coming from the cliff calls out the son of God, the holy one.

When he starts to walk toward the stone wall, it is the first time I've seen Jesus since leaving Capernaum. He steps away from his followers, off the track, onto a barely beaten path to some caves. The man that appears before him is naked, crouching in the dark mouth. Someone in the crowd beside me says he's the local crazy; they dress him but he rends his garb, they chain him but he breaks them.

I step closer. Or else I'd run in the other direction. But Jesus is between us: and even with my mustard-seed faith, I know that means a mountain. Nothing bad can happen to me with him there.

The village psycho is big-built and smeared with shit. His beard and claws grow wild, yet he does not look all animal. In his eyes is some too-bright knowing; an overflow of wisdom.

"They said you were coming," he cries. "I heard them in their hundreds, walking to the well, waiting at the temple gate, calling from their houses. I heard them before that; when I walked to the well, or waited at the temple gate, or stayed in my house. I heard them say you were coming. And I heard them before that, when I dreamt of an angel in a wheel of fire. I knew you were coming, then."

"Peace be with you. I am here."

Jesus slowly approaches the mad man. Out of the corner of my eye, I see a few men from the crowd following him. And there's another woman, emerging from between his wannabe wives and mothers. But Publia is hanging on my woad cloak to hold me back.

"I have seen the beast and it was beautiful." The wild shout resounds in the wilderness. Foaming at the mouth, the madman squats in the cave entrance, spitting at the master: "So I am bedevilled. So I am demonised. So I am gone to the dark side."

Then, with an insane cry, he rises and raises his right hand with a weapon lifted from the cave floor. A big, sharp stone that could smash somebody's skull open.

"Lord of Heaven and Earth," he cries, "but not Hell. You don't rule my darkness. You don't rule my pain."

Leaping from his rocky platform to Jesus, stone dagger ready, he seems to stop in mid-air. Some of the fishermen have rushed forward to save their master, strong fists lifted, but the Rabbi handles the saving. He holds his hands out to the foaming *rabiosus* and helps him down.

One of the disciples said just now that this man's name was Jephthah. But Jesus calls him something else.

"Lucifer, you were my friend. Why did you forsake me?"

The man growls: "You forsook me first. You watched my fall." His eyes are rolling back in his head. "Up there you were a ring of light, down here I can still see the halo."

This is being translated, of course, from the lunatic's own tongue; Aramaic, I think. Farzan has taken on the job of simultaneous translator for me, Publia and Marcus Manlius; hopefully for the whole trip. We all speak Latin and Greek, Pubi and I know some Phoenician, Marcus some Egyptian. But none of us are well versed in any others, so I'm not sure how accurately the bookseller from Byblos is translating the loony talk.

He says, in the voice of Jesus:

"They think I tell devils to go. 'Begone,' sayeth the lord, 'get hence'. But no. I say come. Come with me. If you are mad because I left you, then come with me."

As he speaks, Lucifer has fallen to his knees at Jesus' feet on the rocky floor. The lord places his hand on Jephthah's head and I stare till the air moves like a heat haze shimmering around them. We are all licked with fire just looking at it, whatever he says.

"Be clean of your sin. God has forgiven," Farzan reckons it is. That works for me. I am so bedevilled, too. There were many evil men inside me. Five from the Roman baths, maybe more, possessed me. They were legion.

Falling to my knees at the front of the crowd, I feel my demons come and go, too. Drained onto the Nain stone, the last of the Roman bathwater.

I wait, down there, till the crowd have moved. Embarrassed but euphoric: that purge left me legless. It felt like five men got up and walked away from my body. Now I don't know what is left.

Light as a feather, I'm floating near the ground, face covered by my peacock shawl, heart pounding. Publia is still waiting for me and I hear Emeshmoon and Marcus coming back to ask her what's up.

She reckons I just reacted badly to the exorcism but I feel much better now. Slowly I stand. The masses are moving toward the town gate with Jesus walking near the back. He probably wasn't waiting for me to get on my feet with little purple toe-nails. He can't possibly see the jewels hidden in my bag, but he might notice their shadows in my eyes.

I know he didn't actually touch me: but I don't feel untouched by him. So I have to give those gemstones away now, because the only thing glittering in my temple will be Jesus. I know it wasn't me who was healed but I do feel whole. Though Pavo's bath washed me on the outside, this cleansed within. So as we make our way up the Jordan to Jerusalem, my river of amethysts will be unstrung, one by one.

I won't hand the beads out carelessly. I gave to Naomi but not Artorius. I didn't think it would make a difference to his life. I didn't give to Jephthah but I give to the next person we meet, when we go knocking at doors in Nain.

This is the hardest part so far. I would rather go back to the khan than turn up on some stranger's doorstep in Galilee. It feels too dangerous for Pubi and I, a pair of Roman girls who don't speak the language or have a silver piece between us to buy our way out of trouble. Our friends stay pretty close; on the other side of the street Marcus and Aunt Naomi are talking their way in to a house, and next door Emeshmoon and Farzan are trying the same thing. They all have one language in common, but we are limited to a bit of business Greek. I could sell a *homer* of purple dye to the old girl who answers our call, but that doesn't seem to be what she's in the market for.

First the mad man. Then the crazy lady. She chastises us but we can't understand why.

In fact, we can; Yeshua, Yeshua, Yeshua. She clearly knows who he is and that we are with him. She's very angry about something: I recognise the Hebrew way of saying King Herod repeated a lot, too. Publia and I listen politely but we don't give the right responses in the right places and the lady gets angrier.

Farzan and Emesh aren't having any luck next door either and, as they back away from a hostile archway, I beckon them over.

"What is she saying?" we hiss at Farzan.

With one foot on her doorstep, he starts to translate:

"Everybody is talking about Jesus, the super saviour, the humble healer, Christ; he killed my baby.

"Yes, that's right. I'm not lying. As a young mother I lived in Bethlehem and it was the time of King Herod, then. And one day he decreed, though he didn't say why, that all the boys under two had to die.

"Herod was afraid of them but what was he scared of? He was king, a big, powerful man afraid of a baby, a rich man afraid of all the poor babies, all the baby boys in Bethlehem under the age of two.

"The soldiers were from Herodium, his paranoid fortress, and they came right down our street without a word of warning until I heard my neighbour (nice lady, her son the same age as mine) screaming. All the baby boys in Bethlehem under the age of two.

"She was screaming, though the soldiers had left her house and were walking towards mine; with just a flurry of straw and sawdust in the street, with our husbands out in the fields at work and the dogs barking uselessly. The soldiers didn't give us a chance to get our baby boys out of Bethlehem."

"Did this really happen?" Emesh asks, out of the side of her mouth. But the Pictrix sisters only shrug silently. It is stronger than wall paintings, the story our hostess tells.

"Strapping men in smelly leather came into my house. They saw me backing away with my son in my arms. One of them stepped forward, armour rattling like a child's toy.

"What was Herod scared of? The soldier snatched my baby and ripped off the nappy to see if it was a boy or girl. Not roughly, he didn't cry; all was silent as a nod went round the helmet heads.

"When the soldier threw him in the air, my baby smiled because he played this game with Daddy. And the soldier threw him gently; maybe he played this game with his sons when they were under two. He threw Joses into the air and caught him on the point of a sword.

"His body was pierced, his heart, and mine, arrested instantly: not because of who he was but for who he might have been. A new-born King of the Jews, that's what Herod was afraid of, they said. His arrival had been prophesised by wise men asking to see the Messiah."

This much we know is true; Kaspar taught me previously. The history is written already in mystic schoolbooks from the East. But it seems the story is older than we thought and Mother Time has been mourning all the while. She says:

"Years later, I learned this: Jesus was not even in Bethlehem that day. An angel had warned his parents of danger in a dream but why didn't one warn me? My baby was good, too, and golden in my eyes."

The lady is crying on her doorstep.

"Ask her if we can come in," says Publia to Farzan.

Emesh and I don't really want to.

"We need to explain," Pubi says firmly, "to tell her what we've seen him do. It may bring her some peace."

Farzan is the mouth of the group, that night; all the talking is done through him. Each of us give examples of the miracles we've seen, which he gifts to the grieving matriarch at her hearth. He translates the parables and the prayers. We actually pray, kneeling closer to her fire with Farzan whispering a simultaneous translation. 'Abba' father means the same, in both our languages.

Publia and Emesh tell how they'd travelled with thousands of others to a remote mountainside to hear him speak. They were far from civilisation and nobody had brought any food so a huge body of hungry Galileans were starting to grumble. But the disciples of Jesus took round baskets full of bread and fish, offering morsels of fresh loaves and cooked flesh, again and again.

When the girls talked to their friend Nathaniel, from the group of twelve disciples, he said it had all come from one small boy with a single bag of lunch. But Jesus had unpacked it and his servings were bottomless.

After she hears this, translated by Farzan's flagging tongue, the lady of the house fetches out some figs and walnuts and goat's cheese for us and pours some wine. I think we may have overspent the sympathy; this is probably her whole month's supply.

We all sleep, utterly sated, by the embers of Raizel's hearth. (We learned that her name means 'rose' during the night's long and deep conversation.) I think, at some point near dawn, Farzan half sits and spits into the cold fireplace.

At sunrise we all sit up, stiff but surprised to find we can lie on God's bare earth, no burrow, no nest, sleep well and wake up refreshed. I feel alive for a while but soon feel dizzy; wine for breakfast, while the others have Emeshmoon's makeshift tea, with herbs she gathered along the way yesterday.

I gather; regaining my senses to say a proper thank you to Raizel, our purple rose, of rich insights and uncommon perspectives. Her last words arch through the doorway as we leave:

"Remember, my baby died for Jesus."

With a sigh of relief, Farzan, who voiced both sides of the conversation (if not a conversion), moves into the morning sun.

I seize my moment. The amethyst is already in my hand. With a final bow, I seize her hand and press the petal in. Walking away fast, from a women who's already paid the highest price of our faith, I glance back to see her smiling at it like a child at its toy; more at the simple beauty of the earring than what it cost.

Now, hidden in my handbag and my heart are an amethyst necklace and bracelet. 'A methustus' is Greek for 'not intoxicated'. In Rome, we even had wine cups made from it to prevent drunkenness. There's a story about how the purple stone was created and I sing it, slightly tipsy, as we walk:

"This is a song that could stop you from dancing; a chase of the chaste, on the Olympian hillside. God of wine, Dionysus, was in red pursuit; after a virgin nymph, Amethystos, who was running in white. She gasped prayers to the gods, to help her stay pure, while he tried to get her sloshed.

"The virgin's pleas were heard by Artemis, galloping up behind, and this is what she did. Of all the ways to save a girl's innocence, the huntress turned her hard and cold; her fleeing form crystalline, her frozen shape ice-white. Amethystos was transformed to the core into quartz. Granted purity by the goddess and guaranteed impenetrable by a god.

"In awe of her self-sacrifice, in honour of her chastity, Dionysus tipped his cup over the girl; wine poured down her body and turned the crystal purple. So this is how amethyst gets its name..."

I'm singing it but I'm not believing it. Was it always like this? Did I ever believe in my sales pitches? Some of the people walking in the crowd can hear me. They turn their heads; customers or critics?

"Amethystos, dyeing not selling. Beauty is closed for business."

I twiddle the necklace as I sing, hidden in my handbag. Gems the colour of nymph's ink are set in silver and linked to jingle. It seems absurd to think I wore them in the Tyrian street, what, a week ago? Just another mindless display of wealth on a pretty neck.

As we walk on, into the mountains of Samaria, I try to picture my shop front. The hanging baskets from which tumbled well-watered tendrils of hyssop. The sign, painted bright but not too brash: 'PURPURA', decorated with spiked *murex* shells. I try to see it with the shutters up, a customer coming out of the door, and Abibaal in opulent dress and proprietorial air about to enter.

There are many fine details of the scene that I recall as if it were wall-painted. The cracks in the terracotta flowerpots that, one day, will open with a shower of dirt, roots and shards on an unsuspecting shopper (or proprietor). The signature of the sign writer curled in his best painted sea-snail. Afternoon sunlight slicing through the doorway at such an angle it hits the necklace and bracelets of the businesswoman trading inside and shines them back through the shop window in rainbow slices. The rows of silver stitching on Abibaal's jacket, making his back gleam like fish scales.

My memories place the multi-coloured tiles in a mosaic of Tyre. My mission is placing one purple stone after another, as we walk into Samaria. There are ankle-scratching herbs of the same heathery hue, growing along our path. When trodden, they release a healthy fragrance. Sun-warmed, they're collected by Emeshmoon for tomorrow's tea.

Across the plain of Jezreel, over the river Kishron, round mount Gilboa; we pluck our route in handfuls of thyme. We hardly speak today, Publia and I, Emesh and Farzan, hoarse from the long conversation of the night before, in which we told the whole story, so far, to the woman who shared her own revelation; the good news we bring might not be so great for everybody.

Our group gets nearer the front of the crowd that sit with Jesus as evening falls. For once, we're not standing at the back but are close enough to see and hear fully. The way the words come out of his mouth, where his eyes move to, what his hands do. Even the gentle sway of his long hair as he speaks and the stillness of his bare feet beneath the hem of his robe. I know he is the Messiah but I can tell, tonight, that he is a man, too.

This is what he says: "God makes Ten Commitments to you. You shall know that you have taken the path to God, and you shall know that you have found God, by these signs, these changes in you [8]:

"First, you will love no other God but me; you will not worship sex or fame, any longer, nor money and power. You will give those up, like a child outgrows his toys, and you will put them aside; not because you have to, because you want to.

Second, you will not use the name of God in vain. You'll realise it is impossible to call and not be answered. When you say God's name, you'll know he's already listening..."

He goes on listing but I am also looking. Eye lashes, knuckles, breastbone; the next commitment I hear is number six.

"You know you've found God when you will not murder. Because you understand life is eternal and cannot be taken. Because life is sacred, you won't even kill a spider.

"Seven. You won't commit adultery. I promise you, God will send this sign when you are on the right path. You shall not lie to love. Nor will you lie down with lust.

"Eight. When you have found God, you will not steal. There'll be no need. You own everything there is."

I clutch my bag convulsively when he says this. If I were Publia, sitting next to me, I'd wonder why; but she doesn't seem to notice. The jewellery suddenly feels like a dirty secret and I'm clutching it for guilt rather than guile.

Jesus goes on, numbering the ten commitments: like, your neighbour's goods, your neighbour's spouse. You can have anything you want but, when you've got God, you won't need anything else.

I have been feeling this freedom, lately. As an assistant priestess I did kill (only animals, for sacrificial purposes), I committed any number of adulteries, and I stole. I stole from the worshippers even as I danced for them and I stole from the temple repositories. We all did. It was for eye-liner, wine and abortions.

But now? Well, I would still have sex for religious purposes. I wouldn't kill, even if it was someone I hated, though I wouldn't hate. And I wouldn't steal; in fact, I'm looking to do the opposite. I'll give away my jewels to Jews for the love of their son.

I'm going to leave a trail of purple stones from here to Herod's temple. The poorer I get the richer I shall be. Jesus tells me this and I believe what he says because I can see the line of his jaw; and the blind man, the leper, the one with the withered hand who are standing at his shoulders, cured.

CHAPTER NINE

Dusty sand, dry sea; we spend another night in another village on another stranger's floor and by morning we are talked raw. It's hard to tell the story from scratch every time we want to sleep.

"We need parables," I croak to Publia, as we set off from Salim at the back of the small horde, loosely following the lord, in the cool dawn.

"You should sing them," she says.

"We could write them down," adds Emeshmoon.

But I choke a plume of nonsense, with only a puff or two of pithy verse, on the long leg of our journey today. The sun comes up in Decapolis, blazes overhead at Mount Ebal and is just starting to set across the Plain of Sharon, when we hear a voice from back down the track.

A woman's voice, dreamily in the dusk, calling my name; 'Veronica!' followed by my sister's; 'Publia!' We stop walking, turn and stare along the rocky pass. No angel in white turban hailing me this time. No woman, either; the outline is quickly coming into view. A tall red cap and silvery jacket straining over a belly not quite as fat as before.

It can't be. Abibaal. Unbelievable.

"Fabia Pictrix!" He can see us now; we've stopped moving and the crowd are carrying on.

We don't look much like we used to, though. I hardly recognise my own shadow on the ground without the towering hairdo and the tugged-in waist. It looks like Abibaal has lost weight, too. As he limps closer, there's a hole in his hat and a rip in his jerkin. The jewelled shoes he always wore don't shine any more, the precious stones gone and the sole torn.

We wait for him to be with us, a long while. The sound he's making reaches us first. I can't tell whether he's laughing or crying. Publia starts shushing him when he's too far away to hear her.

He comes so slowly that, in the end, Pubi and I walk towards him, though our Roman sandals hurt worse than his Phoenician flip-flops.

Stumbling along the stony road behind us come Emesh and Farzan; and it's a good thing the booksellers from Byblos are with us for, when we finally meet Abibaal, he doesn't seem to know Latin or Greek anymore. Publia can speak his language pretty well, being married to his brother but, in his agony, Abibaal hardly knows his own tongue.

"The bugs, they bit him," he greets us. "The dogs, they barked at him." His voice is lower and slower than before. (Farzan whispers that he's using some very arcane grammar.)

Publia gives him her bottle of water. Emeshmoon does the whole "is that really him? Abibaal, is it really you?" thing. And then Farzan relieves my old business partner of his backpack and hand bags. I pass him my bottle of wine.

As we all shuffle after Jesus, again, following the main crowd into the Shechem dusk, Abibaal brightens up. His ancient Phoenician quickens, and he throws in clues for me and my sister in Latin.

"The birds, they swooped at him, screeching over his hat. Many times it was knocked off the head. The hard ground, he laid on it. The dark nights, he was lost in them.

"I want my house, please. I want my oil lamps and my *triclinium* and my well-stocked library. I want my bath and my padded bed. *Luxuriosa emere cupio*."

None of that means anything now. Even when both Publia and Farzan have translated, Abibaal doesn't make sense.

"I need to contemplate a marble bust. It is so difficult here in, where are we? I must shop for luxury items."

He indicates the bags. "I've done pretty well so far."

"What have you got?" Publia and I say it together at the same time. We haven't quite left the material world behind yet.

"Some of that stripy cloth from Capernaum: for couch cushions, I'm thinking. A nice, leather-cutting knife, from Cana; could take a man's eye out neat as peeling a lychee. Oh, and some cheese from Gischala. Did you try it; you should, it's famous. Rock hard, really tastes of goat..."

He is surprised how hungry we are. The Fabia Pictrix sisters and even Emesh and Farzan are suddenly clamouring for a taste of his goat's cheese. As our group join the main body, we are chewing and swallowing, quickly and quietly, the supplies that if we had offered to Jesus, no doubt everyone would get to try.

It gives me indigestion and I'm looking around for mint leaves, on the edge of the followers, as we enter Shechem.

It is harder for Publia and I to find somewhere to stay in this town with Abibaal alongside. People tend to take one look at his pointed red hat and turn us away.

But his bald head, bare in the sunshine, would be redder.

Now it is nearly dark and we are still homeless, sitting under a huge old olive tree in the village square. One by one, we've watched the twosomes disappear into welcoming houses; Emesh and Farzan will be sitting at someone's hearth, already, and Marcus and Naomi will be supping a warm stew. As a threesome, we are currently unhoused in this pilgrim town. Tired, cold and hungry, Publia finally snaps at Abibaal.

"So why exactly are you here, then? My sister said she left you in charge of the business. What has become of the shop and the stock? How did you leave it?"

He pauses before giving an answer and an olive leaf floats to the ground nearby. Now it is clear he is crying, not laughing; crying, though Abibaal is always light-toned.

"I was there, too, that night at the necropolis. But I was too busy, for a while, to realise what had happened. I was the boss, Mr Big," he sobs. "This domed head was full of my own worship. This domed belly was full of my own sacrifices. No way on purple soil would another man be king of me.

"When Veronica walked across the causeway, Tyre seemed to fall silent. I could hear no fighting; no clash of pikes, no gush of blood. I stood in her shop; buying only forgiveness, selling only peace. I sat in my house and would have turned into a statue, then. My bronze Melqart, my marble Ba'alshamin. I was empty and full. I was frozen and fired. My life finished there and I saw only one way forward, one future. I had to follow you two."

Pubi rests her head on his shoulder, her face half-hidden by her fringed shawl.

"You did the right thing," she sighs.

"Hang on," I say, on the other side of him. "What about the business? What about my shop? What about the Numerius Fabius Pictor inheritance?"

"We might have to let that go, now," Publia murmurs.

"What on earth will Dad say?" I'm crying too. "Luckily, we may never know."

This makes my sister weep as well. She kneels up in front of us and the scarf falls off her head.

"Our father in heaven, remember," she says. "Let's pray. *Abba* father..." and she goes through the prayer Nathaniel taught us on the beach at Capernaum, that we've taught about ten people on our travels so far, and which Abibaal is hearing for the first time.

He seems to enjoy it, watching eagerly as Publia and I come to a climax: 'for thine is the kingdom, the power and the glory, for ever and ever.' But we're all still sniffing, hopelessly. Snivelling, love-struck fans of the king, our passion has made us homeless.

Before another leaf falls from the old olive tree at this small town's heart, Abibaal grabs his bag and says, "Sod it, I'm still loaded. There's no way I'm sleeping on the ground tonight. Come on, girls, let's buy ourselves a bed."

The pointy red hat doesn't look as threatening when the wearer promises to pay a silver piece for B&B for three. Abibaal as rich Tyrian trader works better on the doorstep than Abibaal as a penniless follower of Jesus of Nazareth. I'd never heard of it before but no one we meet seems to have a good word to say about that place.

So we blow one of Abi's purple shekels on an easy night and a slap-up breakfast before rejoining the flock somewhat sheepishly. It feels like our white wool, the simple wrap of discipleship, has been Tyre-dyed overnight and everyone can see the streaks. No one gives a funny look, though, as we follow the group the next morning.

The feast of Tabernacles is approaching, or we are approaching it, I'm not sure which. It's a strange festival for casual passers-by to get, eating in a tent. I saw it a few times in Tyre, not so much in Rome.

Now, we are trying to get to Jericho before it starts; confusing as, surely, the feast is about being on the road. Still, one good long hard day's walking and we'll be where people can pitch their tents on rooftops and courtyards and gardens instead of in the wilderness.

Sometimes singing, sometimes silent, we walk; sometimes falling asleep on our feet. I'm lucky today; all the way I can watch the heels of Jesus. I can see the swish of his *tzitzit*. In the dusty sunlit spaces between his apostles, I witness the ankles and the hem.

After one good long hot meditation, I turn to Abibaal and say:

"You know, Nathaniel said the others saw him actually walking on water."

A long time passes then Abi replies:

"Do you think he can swim through land?"

We walk for another *C* paces along a mountain road before I answer:

"He does fish for men."

Then we are quiet again and I catch glimpses of his feet, shoulders, long damp locks of dark hair in shimmering light. The crowd is thick around him on the road down to Jericho, with the streak of river Jordan deep in the distance. As we walk, I am weighing the jewels in my hand, hidden in the soft folds of my bag like some secret testicles.

It feels like Abibaal's sudden appearance is a sign, the baggage I'm carrying from Tyre is holding on. I saw myself laying a jewel trail to Jerusalem. Spurting an amethyst river, I imagined. But links of metal are still a chain.

Shuffling on, Abi says;

"Do they have slaves to put the tents up?"

"They don't have slaves for anything," I puff. "The only slaves here have already been set free."

"Yes, I'm starting to think there'd be less trouble that way," he says. "I had to have one of mine executed, before I came."

I don't speak.

I would ask, who? Which slave? But I seem to already know.

He carries on saying it, anyway.

"Tall, tough, rather attractive. You remember that one? Thief."

I think I'll remember his arms most; strong and scarred. They were almost black, story-lined with new pink and old white scabs.

"I caught him with an alabaster Venus he should not have been handling," says Abibaal; "taking her up the back stairs."

We are walking the Samarian mountainscape through Shiloh to Jericho, stepping down God's own staircase to Judea, each tiny footfall wearing the dip in another giant rock-hewn stair.

We stop for lunch in a sun-baked town. A big crowd follows Yeshua to the temple. Another group goes to find food but the hungry crew don't have much cash and the market traders won't give anything away, not even a fig.

I step in. If this were Tyre, I'd sing, too, as I do the deal. Cleaning up the food stalls for a couple of small amethysts, bitten off my bracelet. Then I'd sing as I gave out the grub to my travelling companions. Some drum-beat bread, piping fruit, whistling fish. But today, I work silently. I bargain, I buy and I bequeath the goods with just a wink and a nod. And silently, I smile when I see Jesus and the others come back to join us and someone whispering to him that his flock has been fed.

Inside, I'm singing. 'City girl, slick and cynical; it's not all a competition. The last can win and the least come first. Sick girl, piping and whistling; it's all about survival now and that means working together. Silly girl, no longer number one.'

The song stays inside me, sitting closely packed in the crowd, with Publia, Emesh and Farzan chatting happily together. But then my mood changes as Abibaal speaks:

"She's nice. Who is she?"

We all look where he's looking, still city-slick enough for a quick glance at a pretty face. It is the one I spotted before, always closest to him. There are several women who look after him, not all maternal types, some of the right age and race to be his wife. But this one is the most beautiful, though mostly hidden under a shawl.

He still has need of an assistant priestess, doesn't he? The lunch I bartered, for the sparkling jewel of my previous soul, sits heavy on my stomach now. It is hard to concentrate on what Farzan is saying:

"She's called Maria. They are all called Maria. He picked her up in Magdala years ago. She was a prostitute; Jesus saved her."

"A temple dancer?" I try to understand.

"A *meretrix*. A whore," he translates.

I think that my lips move but no sound comes out.

"The other women are mothers or sisters of the disciples, mostly," Farzan says. High brow bone-dry, the bookseller is still in his comfort zone, flicking between tongues fluently. "But one is the wife of King Herod's head of staff, I believe. Proper palace piece."

"Ssh," says Publia, in any language.

Abibaal is open-mouthed. He is still staring at the Magdalene but what can he see beyond her fringed shawl and fringed eyelashes? She's lit up, smiling in the face of the lord, a holy mirror in a human frame.

We walk down to Jericho that afternoon. The Dead Sea is a gleam in the distance. The Jordan winds broadly across the scene. And then, so exciting that I actually run at the front of the crowd; it's an aqueduct. A *splendida* Roman build. Approaching it indecorously, with Publia and me, is Marcus Manlius, our actor friend. We indulge in a Latin moment, awestruck by the size and scale of our empire, of its dramatic scenes and practical schemes.

We study the stonework at the aqueduct's feet, the unerring curves of its structure, and we talk like it's a famous athlete we're watching at the *stadium domitiani*. I already thought Marcus was more of a man-watcher and now he praises the broad shoulders, the muscular legs, the rippling pecs of this architecture.

Yet he doesn't love every man.

"Abibaal is awful," he declares as we wander in the arching shade of the aqueduct. "Why is he with you?"

"He's family," I laugh. "Publia's brother-in-law."

"His voice is so high," Marcus says, "but his belly is so low."

"He looks better than he used to."

"And what's with the horse-tail of hair, while he is bald on top."

"It's a traditional Phoenician hairdo," I say. "I think we are meant to love our neighbours."

He leans against the stone support and sighs.

"I know," he says. "But the years spent backstage bitching wore some mean grooves in my script."

"The water washes them all away now," I murmur like the *aquaeductus* in his ear. "If Christ's best girl is a fallen angel, I'm sure an ex-actor can be his baptist. It would be good if you could do Abibaal like you did Artorius, one day..."

I hush when Publia reappears from behind a column where she's been to piss.

"You should go, too," she says to us. "We'll be arriving in town soon."

"The place is full of palm trees," Marcus replies, but he goes between the legs of the aqueduct anyway, and we hear his water run.

"Have you got a rag?" my sister asks quickly and quietly. Her once screaming period has started with a whisper.

"I've got my white linen handkerchief," I say, opening my bag.

"No, I'm not using that," she says. "It's immaculate. You waved it at my wedding. Let's catch up with Aunt Naomi, if we can. She'll have something I can get dirty."

In six different languages, Farzan says that Jericho is older than Rome, that it's the oldest town anyone knows. It's on top of a small hill, quite a steep little climb, even after the mountain passes; and he says that it's built on the ruins and remains of all the previous Jerichos. A heap of broken pots from the past, that's what's under these urban streets.

We arrive at the feast of Tabernacles; the townspeople are erecting special tents on their roofs and in their yards. It's a good time to be homeless, if there ever was one, and a soulful welcome to the place. Still, slightly awkward to be standing around on the temple forecourt, watching all the activity and not having anything to do or anywhere to go.

Happily, we find Naomi there, too. She fits right in to the heart of that crowd, closer to its centre, because she's blood-related to one of the chosen twelve. But she treats Publia and Marcus, Emesh and Farzan like family and proudly introduces them to two ladies who look just like her. One's called Mary, of course, mother of one of the disciples, James; the younger one. The other lady is Salome, the wife of somebody we're supposed to have heard of, I think she said Zebedee; and she's the mother of the other James.

Theirs is a warm welcome though we can't see their faces for veils. I think they might even hug us but they're holding armfuls of reeds and giant leaves already. They tell us that they're going to make a *sukkah* for the lord. They ask if we want to help.

Publia and I go shopping. Nowhere is open. Everybody is on holiday in their tents, preparing for a party. The muse of marketing is with me, though, so we manage to get the ingredients for our feast, paid for with an amethyst and a song.

At first, Publia thinks we only have songs to pay with. In fact, she thinks she'll have to sing too. The gods, I mean God, has been generous: to Publia, the gift of beauty; to Veronica, a beautiful voice. Pubi can't sing to save her life so, at this point, I reveal my secret stash of jewellery.

"I forgot I had them in my handbag," I say. "And when I remembered, it felt wrong to horde them. I'd already let those babies go… Now, I'm giving them away again."

This is the real beauty of my sister. Never mind the big eyes and small nose, the alabaster ears and bronze breasts. No matter how complicated the figures, when we speak it's simple: she sums it up.

"Let's have a look, then," she tuts. "It had to be the amethysts. Honestly, sis, are you made of purple?"

If so, I'm spitting it out. I'd prefer to be made of song; shit, I get so carried away, someone listening actually thinks I'm from Zion. Anyway, Publia tells me what each stone in my stash would fetch, from a silver *as* to a bronze talent to a Tyrian shekel such as they pay in the temple. But in the backstreets and the forecourts, we do a spiritually-sound trade off with the cooks of Jericho, and the Fabius Pictor sisters triumphantly return to the *sukkah*. It's the biggest one we've seen, with mighty acacia poles draped in cubits of linen, decorated with fruits and flowers.

We hand over the goods to Naomi who sings our praises till her hands are full and she can no longer laud us. Then with a loud amen on her lips, she turns to take the stuff inside.

"He'll be back soon," she says, "so stay close by."

Emeshmoon and Farzan are lying on a patch of grass in the late-sloping sunshine. She opens one eye when I lie down beside her. There's a pause while I watch a cloud scroll past us. She's not looking at the sky.

"Veronica," she says, "if I got hold of some paper and a pen would you mind if, next time you sang, I wrote it down?"

That would be strange; I see the songs as birds that just fly out of my mouth and disappear. What would a song look like when it had flown; a picture of a bird, I suppose.

"Hmm," I say.

"What does that mean?"

"Shall I sing now, just to make you flap?"

"I've been trying to recall the Amethystos one," Emesh sits up and scans the crowd around the tent. "But since we started the business, my memory has suffered. You know, I can't see Marcus anywhere. I wonder where he is."

Publia is people-watching on the other side of her.

"I haven't seen Abibaal for ages, either," she says. "They can't be together, though."

Still with my eyes closed, I finger Emesh's shawl, where it fringes on the grass. "Why does business make your memory bad?" I mutter. "It improved mine. Was it all the worry?"

"No, it was all the papyrus," she laughs, "I just wrote everything down. If you never have to memorise you can't remember how."

"Memory looks like roman numerals tooled in stone," I say. "Not the notes of a birdsong on fluttering paper."

"Yet..." she says. Then, "Oh, look, there's Marcus. And, oh, Abibaal. Together. Well, in quick succession."

Our Phoenician friend comes first.

"I have been baptised in a drinking trough in the town square," Abi declares breathlessly. "He grabbed me from behind, sneered a prayer in my ear and thrust me under the manger water."

He falls to his knees beside me, grabs a corner of my woad-dyed cloak, and wipes his lips with it.

"I drunk animal spit," he splutters.

"But have you been washed of your sins?"

"Didn't have any. I am see-through, girls, you know; I cast no shadow."

Publia is listening in.

"Abibaal, you are stuffed with secrets and varnished with lies," she smiles; "we can't see your soul for the purple padding."

"You can see it," he pleads with me, "can't you?"

Marcus sits on the grass as far away as it's possible to be from Abi and still in the group. "I could hear your asshole. When I shoved you under the water, it spoke."

"Sshh," Emeshmoon whispers, "Yeshua is coming."

He leaves the synagogue, followed by the twelve men closest to him, with many others behind them. Ragged to rich, some have come up from Galilee, some have turned up on the way; some treat him as the Messiah, some curse him as Satan.

The accusers have the tallest hats, the longest beards, the biggest tassels, the most books strapped to their bodies. The more religious a man, the less he likes Jesus, it seems. The top scholars in Jericho are running after him, asking questions on the scriptures, giving their own answers.

He will not bring them back to the booth his women have made but turns to face the men on the synagogue steps. We can't hear what he says but, see; the way his shoulders flex beneath his white robe, the way his hair moves in the evening breeze, the way he raises a finger to the main Pharisee and it's almost like there is light streaming from it.

Everybody by the tent is staring, too. The team of old ladies shaped like pepper pots have stopped laying the table and are looking on. The younger ones, curvy serving dishes, start walking towards the action.

Then it really kicks off. The Scribes are taking issue with something Jesus says. It's a scourging by scroll as they literally hit him with the word of the law. His supporters rush to surround him; Marcus and Publia are in this scrum, answering shouts from the back. Farzan goes forward, translating the Hebrew accusations and the Latin insults into Aramaic then Phoenician, for anybody who doesn't fully understand the argument.

I stay on the grass in the shadow cast by our tent's festive lights, watching the fight. Emeshmoon is there, too, pale in the gloom.

"I don't like it when they shout," she says.

I hardly hear it. I can see Jesus from here and the sight of him always makes sound disappear, till I seem to be in silence, watching his lips move. Can't tell from his face what he's telling those who face him but clearly it's the same for the ragged and the rich. He pours out his retribution equally.

And the pillars of Jericho are slightly shaken as the purple-fringed establishment goes back into the synagogue. Jesus comes down to the tent. I don't see him enter it, though; Publia is suddenly in my face.

"That freaking Pharisee called me a proselyte," she says. "What does it even mean?"

Farzan shrugs. "It wasn't a Pharisee, it was a Sadducee. They support Rome, ultimately."

Beside me Emeshmoon sighs. She must be torn between trying to remember and forget the raised voices. Singing will stop people shouting, I think, but my song has turned melancholy:

"This is where purple goes when it has run like a thread from the sea, call it Mediterranean red, it wants blood, it is fiercer than Hercules' dog; it is sharper than Murex shell spikes, they look fluffy, those fringes, those *tzitzit*, that *tekhelet*, but it kills in thousands and could kill the one..."

Emesh has her head in her hands. All the others are clapping grimly. Aunt Naomi calls over the top; we are to sit down at the table. Our band of Roman actors, fallen businesswomen and Phoenician literati have been invited to the feast.

'Finally,' I think. 'I'm starving.' Then I politely lead the way to the very bottom of the long, long table.

"Pssst, sit higher," Abi hisses, but he can't split from us without making a scene.

"Listen," Publia whispers as they sit at the bottom, "we can work our way up. And, look, it's several different tables, pushed together, not just one; some are just logs resting on stones."

They still can't see what I can: being at the very bottom gives an uninterrupted view of the lord, at the very top. I am indeed resting on a log, leaning on a stone, but this is the best night of my life so far, maybe ever.

There is loads of wine. It comes round time and again, the jug always feeling full. The matrons labour till they sweat, along the length of the table. They're serving the ultimate 'finger food', fit to eat in a sukkah on the run, heart-beat fresh and ingeniously neat: apples filled with pomegranate seeds, red peppers stuffed with meat, dough folded with nuts and honey.

Between first and second courses, Emeshmoon writes on the palm leaf platter with walnut juice. She cuts letters and presses nut skin into the wounds, staining words there. Later, I catch her scratching on an earthenware plate with a bone. I think she is trying to record the lyrics of my song, notching Phoenician letters into anything her knife will nick. Is she hooked on paperwork like I still have my head turned by purple? Or does she need writing like I need wine?

The jug comes round again: after a top-up I give Emesh a piece of my mind.

"Forget what I'm singing. It's the sayings of Jesus you should be trying to record."

"Some men are doing that already," she says. "There's one called Thomas. I always see him scribing away obsessively."

The jug comes round again. More torches are lit. In the tent a drummer starts to play; his beat so subtle, at first, it could be anybody's heart beating. But then it gets louder, so that everybody hears it, and it must be the drumming heart of Jesus.

Other musicians strike up inside the *sukkah*; a lyre, a harp. They are instruments of joy. The disciples start laughing, and getting up, and pushing the tables away. The ladies come out with timbrels: leading the group slowly into two circles, with their tinkling cymbals, then snaking outside to dance in the rough grass.

The men dance with their hands on each other's shoulders, kicking and calling in riotous concord. Righteous, too; the lord is dancing in that circle. There are so many of them there's a second circle and, of course, Farzan, Marcus and Abibaal are in the outer ring. I see a Phoenician shirt fly past or the rare, bare shoulder of Manlius Nerva in his toga.

There is no touching in the women's round, and no shouting. We have far fewer dancers in the ladies circle. It gives us all a chance to shine. Aunt Naomi, and the clay-jar mothers of men, can really move. They've been walking and working and haven't slept well for a week but the spirit is shaking their bones and filling their wrinkled skin with ecstasy. It reminds me very much of my old temple of

Venus days. To shimmy within a ring of sisters in a trance was commonplace, then.

But we are not all friends here. Some of the younger women, roughly the same age as Emesh, Publia and Me, don't like us. Even when we're all travelling, a diaspora, on the move, lines are still drawn around our territory. Even though we're in the same circle, there's still some competition for the sun and moon, for the waning and waxing.

The jug comes round again, or we go round it and, after another revolution, the men and women's circles are no longer separate. Everybody is dancing together, spinning and jumping, kicking and clapping. At the centre of it is Jesus. I can't see him but I know he is there. This couldn't be happening otherwise. At the heart of the dancing is stillness, light and love; it flows effortlessly through the crowd, signalled by the ringing of hand bells and stamping of feet; from his very cousins, who dance with arms linked at the core, to the couples and friends and family groups who sing and spin in rings around them.

On the edge of the dance, just beyond the torchlight, just behind the tent, men stand watching; the scribes have just come back from the synagogue, to keep their own log.

I go further in, to the altar of this worship, where I belong as an ex-priestess. To the place in the dance that is pure and perfect. Then I can see Jesus.

He dances like he's fishing. Summoning the shoal out of the sea by raising his hand. They cling to him and it's as if he's glistening, when people come, one by one, and he swings them in a circle.

I watch him with that woman, uncloaked now. Dark hair, dark eyes, don't we all have; and if she's the prettiest, perhaps it's because she's closest to the source. I hope the Sadducees can see this. I hope they can't; it's nearly my turn. I'm close to the front of the queue for communion.

One swing, that's what everybody gets; but I'm sure Mary from Magdala went round twice. I'm sure he looked at her differently from the tax-collector guy and the ex-leper chap that are swung round before he gets to...

Me. It's my turn, my chance to dance with the lord. To touch his hand. He holds mine and I feel his power; I almost see it move up my arm and over my eyes.

On my way here, I paused by the Sea of Galilee and saw light trip off the water. On my way here, I was caught in a storm on the mountainside and saw light strike off rock. On my way here, I sat by firesides and saw light burn off leaves. But I've never seen light coming from a man's hand before.

Did I see it or not? Like the green *phosphoro*, the white lightning, the red-hot flames: it was there, then gone, then there again. On my way here, I've stared at stars, eyes, baths, wine cups; I've never seen shine come from a man's skin before.

Is it there or not? Is the colour of gold glimmering on his forearms where most men have curly black hair?

On my way here, I sat one night by a hearth and saw flames not as something there, but something that wasn't. Flickering gaps in the darkness, crackling splits in the dullness; I saw an opening into brilliance, fire as a doorway.

It feels like his hands could pull me through it as we dance. Through a rip in the cheap, un-dyed fabric of life; with a lining of flame-coloured silk, like a wedding veil, glimpsed behind. They are dancing in the kingdom of heaven, too, as its king spins me round.

But the move that looked so fast when everyone else at the party did it with him, is a slow dance. In fact, it stops. This is the still, unmoving point at the heart of the whirl, at the centre of the story. We don't spin; the world spins once around me and I am a silver pin, with an amethyst head, stuck in the map at Jericho. I look into Jesus' eyes and the earth moves.

This is the song of long eras and eons, both Jewish and Roman, both ancient and modern I see in his look. Behind my big-nosed reflection in his gaze, there is something the shape of the moon, turning slowly, swirling with cloud; now light, now dark. There is something the shape of the sun, only water-coloured. Orbs revolve when I look into Jesus' eyes, though he holds my gaze steadily.

I have gone all the way round in a ring and am supposed to pass on, now. The next person is waiting for their turn. I cannot let go of his hands, though. The lightning is my lifeline. I hold tighter and give him the look I used, on high days and holidays, in Venus temple. It's the look of worship and can only mean one thing.

He speaks to me. Though the crowd is noisy, I can hear him clearly.

'The bridegroom belongs to everybody. Not only the pretty maidens, Veronica,' he says, 'but also the sturdy matrons and the stout fishermen.'

Then he reaches for one of those and I reel off into the sea of bodies again. How he slipped through my net, I'm not sure; but am not feeling too upset because he called me by my name.

The first person I bump into is Publia.

"He knows me," I stutter. "He remembers my name."

"What?" she shouts. Wine makes her angry.

"Jesus knows my name," I say in her ear as we swish past each other.

"Have you danced with him?" Now she's furious.

The whole night goes up in flames. A small fire starts in some rushes on the roof of the *sukkah*. There are torches lit at each corner of the makeshift tent and sparks are flying. A few followers pour on water, sparingly to conserve our supplies, on the rocky road to Zion.

I wish I'd been wearing purple to dance with the lord. A whoosh of silk in the colour of kings and emperors was apt for that occasion. In the tassel-shaking Tyrian sheath, I would have seemed a worthier dance partner for him. But if the item were still in my possession I would have taken it off and donated it to the cause of our journey. Wine makes me generous.

How can I make those thieves pay for taking my chance to shine away? A single revolution at the centre of the story, one moment of sheer crime and I'm in a spare, bag-creased tunic. I blame those beasts from the khan. I hope Christ knows my soul is really purple. If he can see the true me, will I also be able to discover who the robbers of my dance dress are, surely no more than one step ahead on our approach to the kingdom?

Though this booth was built for our leader, it's the followers who end up sleeping in it, long into the evening of the feast, slumped in drunken rows. In the morning, word is the lord knelt all night on the synagogue steps in prayer.

I had already fallen, again, and further this time. If my night hadn't gone wrong when I stupidly flirted with the Messiah, it went downhill, easily done in Jericho, when I tried to sleep with Abibaal.

I didn't mean to; God knows I don't fancy the fat magnate. But I fell on top of him, trying to lie down in the tent. It's possible that I was slightly tipsy. He was completely pissed, grabbing my hips, thrusting his.

"'Oh, Veronica," he trilled; the drunker he gets the higher his voice goes. "I've waited so long."

I fell again, further; my breasts bumping on his hairy chest, my hands sliding along his outstretched arms. My lips smacking softly on his sparse moustache.

Then I remembered. The last time I lay like this: with the slave, on the gravestone, where we met Jesus at the necropolis. He was blindfolded with my white linen handkerchief, because I didn't want him to see my true face.

I still wonder how the slave, still don't know his name, died. Now I ask: *in vino veritas*. Abibaal can't see me for the pointy red hat covering his eyes. He says:

"Crucified, of course."

That slave's skin touched mine; I'm not bone-hard, it moves me. His heart, for a few beats, synchronised with mine; I'm not soulless, it's sad, even though he was a *servus*.

I jump off Abibaal abruptly. But, from his point of view, thieving slaves are executed outside Tyre every day. If he knew I was still thinking about *this* dead slave, his damaged flesh, he'd have pushed me off quick enough.

And I still need his support, even though we're not in business together any more. Publia and I both need him because we are going to make it to Bethany tomorrow and he can help beg Balthazar to take us in.

CHAPTER TEN

The last leg of this journey is eighteen miles uphill through the wilderness of Judea. At one point, I'm actually dripping jewels of sweat in the rough grass as I sing a prayer; please let us be nearly there.

Like arriving at Capernaum, with Kaspar, the closer we get the more we talk. Publia is loquacious today, in other words she goes on and on, all the way:

"Sometimes Jericho to Bethany takes two days, you know. It's not always possible to get there in one go. Last time it rained, I think; we had to shelter prematurely. So we might not make it today, after all, it may be tomorrow. I can't believe I'll see Balthazar tonight. No, we just can't do it; all the signs are against us, look at those ominous clouds.

"What should I say when I see my husband? Bal, I'm sorry; but I'm not. This is the way, the truth, the life; I'd be lying if I said otherwise.

"What if he's got another woman? How long has it been? Three months? And before that our marriage was blighted by my unmoonly bloodflow. Sure as the river Jordan runs below us and Mount Zion rises above, he could have had a smoother love."

The rest of us are just stumbling along the stony road between the endless bosoms of Judea, in tired silence. Publia's monologue is the only thing that's keeping us going now:

"Should I go straight home? Is it still my house? You'll laugh at how un-Roman it is. Never mind a *compluvium*, the whole atrium has no roof. How long has it been since I was there? Six months? I'd left chickens scratching for my bread crumbs and *kaneh-bosem* growing in a row of terracotta pots by the south wall.

"I'd left an unmade bed that might have still smelled of us when Balthazar got back but who will it smell of now?"

She pauses for breath. Abibaal puffs beside her.

"Bal's very farts smell of *purpura*," he says.

The sun is setting behind the Mount of Olives when we see the first roofs of Bethany appear. The little town nestles in the mountain's cleavage and our road curves up and at it. We are hungry, scrumping for figs at everblasted tree that leans across the rocky path. There's some commotion in the front; apparently the lord is cursing the lack of fruit. [9]

I have found a few figs, as many as there are stones left on my silver bracelet. They are like warm, squashy amethysts, slightly furry on the outside and full of juicy crystals. Biting into them as we stand under the tree, I feel I should pay for them with a jewel.

It's a good little tree, far back from the path where the others are gathered round some blighted stump. Eating a fig with one hand, purple juice running down my chin, I pull the smallest gem off the silver links, hidden in my bag.

As Emeshmoon turns to go back to the main group, I bend down quickly and pop the precious stone into the earth, where the roots run into the soil so hard and dry that both seem to be made of mountain rock.

"What was that?" Emesh turns back. "What did you do? What did you put there?"

I should have remembered that my book-selling friend takes note of every detail. She picks up the stone, easily seen glinting in the disturbed dust at our feet. She brushes it off, looks closely, licks her finger and makes it shine.

"Amethyst?" she says.

"From a bracelet."

"A trinket of Tyre? It's pretty."

"It's paying for the food now," I say, stoically. "There's a necklace, too; but when that's gone..."

"You don't need to buy fruit from the tree." She tries to hand it back to me.

"Leave it there. Jesus would say so. Come on: it's hard enough to let go." I watch her pop the crystal back in a slot between the roots.

"Easy," she says, "though this fig would rather be paid in pee."

She stays squatting but I can see Nathaniel looking towards us, beckoning us forward again, bringing us back to the main group, who are starting to move on.

"*Non mingo*," I whisper, "we're going."

Bethany sees us coming. A big crowd starts running towards Jesus when we're still half a mile away. Headscarves flapping, sandals slapping, half the town seems to be coming up the hill toward us.

They stop, of course, when they get to him. He's way out in front, white robe glowing in the Judean dusk, and then he is surrounded by a screaming, laughing, shouting, praying, crying crowd. We don't see him after that. There is just one man who keeps running, past the hugging hordes, up the road from town, past the rows of disciples slowly following the lord down. He seems to be looking for one in particular.

Balthazar and Publia catch sight of each other at the same time, in a clearing on the path. They stop. Everyone does; everything does. They look at each other for a long, long moment. I'm holding my breath, right behind her; Abibaal is there too, beside me, with the rest of the Romano-Phoenician team.

Publia said she wasn't going to apologise. She'd decided not to feel guilty. She was planning to be loud and proud, to act unashamed.

What she does is better than that. None of us could ever see it coming. After standing eye to eye in silence awhile, she kneels at Balthazar's feet. She gets to her knees before him and bends her head.

My sister is a beautiful woman, even after a week on the road. Her tunic is still looking good, too; it slips into elegant folds as she falls to the floor and settles like it's sculpted in ivory. When she is down, Balthazar sees me standing behind her, and his beloved brother: eyes starting to twinkle he also takes in old friends Farzan and Emeshmoon.

It was exactly as she'd said. Publia would come back to Bethany, safe in the company of some booksellers from Byblos. She would be following Jesus to Jerusalem; not lost, dead, remarried, wandered off never to be seen or heard of again. It was right and meet to follow her heart.

He grasps his wife by the shoulders, raises her to her feet, and plants a smacking kiss on her cheek. Then, with us all looking on from behind, he smacks her on the arse.

We enter Bethany, house of alms, in high spirits. Balthazar leads the way, with Publia tucked firmly under one arm, and the other round his brother.

"What are you doing here?" were his first words to Abibaal, and Abi replied with a high-pitched whine:

"The bugs, they bit him. The dogs, they chased him. The birds, they swooped at his hat. I did want my *triclinium*. Now, I will just settle for a sit down and a bite to eat."

He rubs his stomach, smaller still. Once he'd have added details of his dream snack, growing into a full-blown meal, narrated salivating. But now:

"I believe in the bread of heaven, see. I have been fed on manna." Abi gives his brother a slap on the back.

Eyes popping out, I can see Bal thinking, if the big boy fears hunger no more, he's welcome to my home.

The crowd is slowing down as we enter the town centre. I walk closely behind Publia.

"Don't worry, you're staying with us," she says to me over her shoulder. "You won't have to give the true picture of events to complete strangers for a bed tonight."

I tweak her cloak gratefully.

"There's plenty of room," she says, "and for you two."

Emeshmoon and Farzan whoop with joy. Suddenly, it feels like a holiday.

The little town of Bethany, on the second day of Tabernacles, is in party mood. Music and the smell of fried food hang in the air, so all senses are enchanted by the festive scene.

We mingle with the crowd for a while. The tall white turban of Kaspar appears and, on tip-toe, I let him know I'm still here. Every time I've entered a town since Capernaum, I've remembered how good it felt to get there, thanks to his care. We beam at each other in the fading light.

"Has your sister been happily reunited with her husband?" he asks.

"Oh, yes, thank you." I'm surprised he follows the lowliest followers' love-lives. "We'll all be staying at their place tonight. Well, me and the Phoenicians."

When I get back to them, Aunt Naomi is meeting Balthazar. He is quickly finding out all about Nathaniel, and the house in Galilee, and how Marcus and Publia have become like family to her.

"Who is Marcus?"

"Like a brother to Publia," she emphasises. Then Aunt Naomi wags her finger in Balthazar's face. "You can trust your wife. She's a good girl and you know it."

He is pleased with this and a boyish grin appears in his bushy black beard. The lamps have only just been lit around the square but he's clearly keen to take his wife home for the night.

"Come on, then," he says. "All of you."

"Nathaniel has somewhere for Marcus and me," says Aunt Naomi. "We'll see you in the morning. It won't be crack of dawn. We're only two miles from Jerusalem now."

Down the side-street that leads to Balthazar and Publia's house, it is so quiet we can barely believe it's that close to the city.

"I wasn't sure if you were coming," says Balthazar, "so I didn't tidy up."

The house is on the edge of town and in complete darkness. We have to wait on the doorstep while he goes inside to light some lamps. This seems to take ages. I feel the posts for the *Shema* prayer, if the place is as authentic as Pubi says, but don't find any carving.

I can feel her shaking as we stand there together, with Farzan and Emeshmoon huddled alongside. It's not the middle of nowhere, there are houses on each side, but we can hear hyenas on the hillslopes behind.

At last Balthazar returns, holding four little lamps in his two large hands; mismatched pottery dishes full of olive oil, with flaxen wicks aflame in each curling lip. He gives them out, I get a sweet one, pointed like a *murex* shell; and he leads us inside.

Basically, he's been living in a purple dye store. As the hearth flickers to life, we peer around his emporium, at vats and racks and safes and stacks of cloth and rows of cotton reels

"Where do we sleep?" I say in a small voice.

Publia gets the measure of the situation, as surely as if it were a length of dyed linen, and quickly begins to delegate tasks. Emeshmoon is to rule the cooking fire, Farzan to procure the food and fuel. It turns out that Balthazar does have plenty to eat and drink in the kitchen, if he can get past the piles of bones and peelings and empty bottles that litter every surface.

My sister and I attend to the sleeping arrangements. I'm sore all over and can hardly wait to lie down. There's a row of bedrooms off the central courtyard; we rapidly allocate them as singles and doubles, with mattresses, sheets and water jugs for the night.

"If I'd known you were coming, I'd have provided a vase of flowers, and a peg to hang your cloak," she sighs.

"This is fine," I assure her. "Silence and darkness are all I need now."

But we also have a hot meal, thanks to Emeshmoon putting everything Farzan found in the kitchen into a pot. There is wine and, miraculously, I end up having a good time.

Emesh hasn't had a chance to do her 'Balthazar, is it really you?' thing. She does it now. Then, as the overtures go on, it turns out that Balthazar thinks his brother and I came all the way from Tyre, together.

I tell him, "We started our journey three days apart."

"But I caught them up," Abibaal adds.

"With dog bites. And a hole in your sole," Publia smiles sweetly.

So then, bless Balthazar, he wants to know all about my solo journey to Capernaum. I tell him a bit but I really need to sing it, and I don't feel like that tonight. When I say so, Emeshmoon agrees:

"No, don't sing, yet," she says.

She always is the keenest for me to start chanting so this is strange. But when I show her to her *cubiculum* soon after, she reveals why. In the olive-oil lamplight, she puts her arm around me softly.

"Veronica," she wheedles, "would it perhaps be possible for me to have, well borrow, a teeny-tiny little amethyst from your bracelet for a really, really good cause?"

"What," I say more loudly, "what is your good cause?"

"Posterity," she whispers. "I need papyrus. We should be writing this down."

"Is that why you didn't want the travel song?"

"Not till I've got a pen. Please, Veronica," she says.

This is simple. "Only if," I say, "you also record the words and deeds of Jesus. That is what we've come for, after all."

"Fine," she says.

"I haven't got my bag with me. It's by my pillow, where my head should be. I'll give you the jewel in the morning."

Luckily the contents of Publia's linen box survived her absence, the bedding clean and crisp, layered with lavender. A decent homecoming, it makes me cry as I crawl stiffly between my sister's sheets.

After a few deep breaths, I remember where I always lay my head these days; on Jesus' breast, on his holy and heavenly bosom. Even the night we slept on the boat, that was my pillow. I wonder if Mary of Magdala lies there for real.

But then the sounds of my sister and brother-in-law re-consummat-ing their marriage start; and I put the covers over my ears and try to block it all out.

In the morning my sheet is red-stained. I'll enjoy pounding with stones the blood that accounts for my bad mood. I have never wanted a bath more in my life. Just dipping my fingertips in the water jug by my bed makes my whole body long for submersion.

The others all got drunk last night, I think, and are sleeping in this morning. There is a great snoring coming from Abibaal's room and deep, deep peace from Balthazar and Publia's.

I roam around the premises at dawn, looking for anything remotely like a bath: being a dye trader's place, I find it. There's one particular butt of water, just outside the back door. Not a vat of snail sauce, of course, nor a tub of bleaching urine, painstakingly collected by family and friends alike; this is pure, old rain. I cannot resist.

In the drear morning light I peel off my tunic and pop into the tank of water. Ooh, *frigidarium*. It's physically shocking but mentally I was brought up to bathe every day, so this feels right and proper, even though there is sludge between my toes.

I don't fancy dipping my head under this water. I splash my face and tip my chin up so my hair gets wet instead. To baptise oneself in a water butt; it can't be done. But I do think about Jesus when I'm in there, and not like I wanted to dance with him but like I want him to cleanse me of sin.

I believe he already cleansed me of the sins of others when he sent Satan out of the madman at Nain. Five Roman demons went out of me then, too. But my own evils; I am still swimming in them. This water would be bright red if it told the whole story but it just washes the dust of a week's walk to Judea off my skin. Dirty as I am the water remains transparent.

The sun comes up on this chilly morning and I see it through closed lids, a red gem shimmering. Sometimes, I still catch myself thinking of Apollo driving his fiery chariot when I see the sun. And surely Jesus is like the sun god, driven down to earth; I've seen charioteers at the *Circus Maximus*. I've seen them crash.

With a shiver I stand up in the tub, rivers of colour from muddy to bloody running off me. I step out of the water and shake to dry before wrapping my cloak round my shoulders.

Then I open my eyes and see why gloom has fallen on me, doom is standing in front of me. A man, one of Balthazar's dye slaves, looks like he owns the drying lines and the *solium*. No co-incidence this Latin has two meanings, bath-tub and throne; but I am not the queen of him and he's not indentured to Bal, either, I presume.

I smile nervously but the look he gives is furious:

"We cannot use that for business now. You had better tip it over."

Even wheeler-dealer dye-traders need a tank of spiritual fuel to convey their product to the temple. And though the secular thread of purple flogged to local senators could survive being sullied by my nude infusion, such rudeness would drive this man's more discerning clients away, even if it is a waste of good water.

"Our women could be stoned for this," he says.

I stick my considerable nose in the air.

"If I were stoned, they would be rubies," I reply though it's probably not my most sensible lyric ever. "Tip it away yourself, if you must."

He tuts, a small sound for such a big glare, each eye having its own agenda, annoyance and upset, in this incensed stare.

"It is a religious festival. *Sukkot*," he says. "How can you be following Jesus and not know that?"

Then I walk out; well, walk in because that water butt was outside the back door of Bal's house. As I turn to go, he kicks it over; the vat turns on its side and water rushes everywhere. I don't turn so fast I miss the extraordinary play of his agony, in the moment before he lays into the urn, as the poor guy decides that dirty dye-water is worse than him having to get the mop out on the third day of Tabernacles.

Slamming the door behind me, I stand, shaking, in the courtyard. There's no real difference between inside and outside as the water races through this portal. I stand in a big puddle, arms folded across my chest, feet planted firmly apart, bottom lip wobbling.

Whether I feel it slip or hear it splash, I'm not sure, but I look down at the water and a drop of blood, a liquid jewel, has dripped in to that pool. My trail continues, my hard travels from trader to soul, Tyre to Jerusalem; this step of the journey is marked by my menstruation.

Then Publia starts wailing. She's still in her bedroom. She's just woken up. I knew this would happen. Last night, with the soft lamp light, the house looked romantic: this morning, and not even my rosy dawn but a cold daylight now, the place looks ruined.

There is more than one dead rat in the marital *cubiculum* and an autumn sunbeam coming through the hole where they get in. There is (I later learn) a pile of old excrement in the corner of their bedroom; not rat shit, much bigger than that. She doesn't know what would be worse poo, Balthazar's or whose?

Rushing out into the courtyard where weeds are coming through the holes in disused dye machinery, she sees me standing in a pond, still crying.

"It wasn't like this when I left," she says. "There were chickens and vegetables, and I swept it and kept everything dry."

I'm still thinking about what being stoned actually means. I have seen it, back in Rome. I could not believe that the people who brought civilization to the world, who built circuses and coliseums, who invented the viaduct, would actually do that. The rough edges to their chiselling; I can't imagine what it would feel like to have stones thrown, in the same way that man in the back yard threw sharp words at me.

Pubi and I slowly make our way together across the devastation caused by Balthazar's bad housekeeping. By then I know what to say to her; it's what Jesus would say, hopefully.

"Sister, don't judge him on the surface clutter. I'll help you clear up."

"It'll take ages," she sobs.

"You've been away nearly half a year," I say, "Nature's fingers get a hold. Don't you love to fight back?"

Balthazar appears from the bedroom. Slightly moody under a floppy fringe, he knows those cries had his name written all over them and has come to face their music. But Publia is calmer now, and she'll probably be doing things the Fabius Pictor way; in our parents' marriage, most issues are never mentioned again.

So I tell him about the man outside the back door. I don't describe in detail how this guy judged me on my background, while ignoring my naked body (the very opposite to how an assistant priestess is generally treated). Bal knows immediately who I mean, though. He says:

"If you think you know purple, he knew it first: born into the dye bath at the heart of the Hebrew faith. A *tekhelet* thread is his birth-cord and he would sooner hang himself with it than disrespect the *tzitzit*.

"But he works with me not for me. Hod is his name. Not a slave, Veronica; a free man with a family, and a business hauling the Tyrian purple over the hills to Judea."

The purple of King David comes from the same sea-snail as the purple of Emperor Tiberius, though the way they squeeze the lifeblood differs; and Hebrew and Roman dyers deal in separate marketplaces so I might never come face to face with him again. But, as Balthazar goes on talking, it seems that Hod is still in the picture.

"It's what they describe as a joint venture, two heroes, one quest; how to get heavenly purple here faster," Bal says. "We're working on ways to package it and new kinds of additives to bring the dye here cheaper; not as a toppling stack of pre-striped togas, not as a sploshing vat of rapidly spoiling *murex* stew, but as the dried spice of itself, ready to be mixed with water far away from the coast. We could make so much more money, shifting so much more shade..."

There's an awkward pause as no one else is thinking about making money, only about shifting it. But everyone is fascinated by his experiment to drain, distil or draw the essence of *purpura* into a box or a bag.

"Between hundred mile dye-runs, the boys are keenly watching and waiting on my inventions. Because, if we discover a way to make senators' stripes go further, then priests could grow longer tassels, too."

"They would never do that," Publia decrees. "Every single inch of the manufacturing process is sacred."

"Every snail is sacred." Bal's mansplanation is only beginning.

I don't feel ready to enter Jerusalem yet. We're just two miles outside and Jesus will get to the temple today. But we won't be able to go in with him, anyway.

The Fabia Pictrix are coming to the same conclusion. Because we're women, gentiles, unclean; Jerusalem is not running to meet us with open arms.

We go to find the master at the fifth hour. His disciples look unduly relaxed. Jesus has said he is not going, he's told them it's not yet his time to enter the city. Apparently, he has family friends here that he loves staying with, the other side of the village from us in olive grove gardens, so the twelve are just doing a day trip to the city and will be back in Bethany tonight.

It's when we're talking to Nathaniel that my sister and I start to realise; we can stay and tidy her house today. Farzan and Emeshmoon are fired up to follow the fishermen all the way: that's fine, they can come back and fill us in on the exciting details this evening. Marcus Manlius is going on, as he should because he's been with Jesus for the longest of any of us.

When Abibaal hears that Publia and I are staying at home today, he immediately decides to stay too.

"I will help you clean up my brother's do-do," he says.

He says that but, in fact, he sleeps in his room while we slave from the hearthstones of the household out; pulling weeds from the courtyard, dusting cobwebs from the archways, sweeping rubbish from the corners of the rooms.

We find a forgotten silver shekel and bring it back to the folds of Publia's purse. It reminds us of a story Jesus told us on the way here.

We bake bread and roast meat and Publia takes me through that back door again, to an overgrown hedge of wild herbs on the hillside. We grab a couple of handfuls of greenery for the pot. While we cook, we chat.

"So who are the people he lives with in Bethany?" I wonder.

"Girls."

"Really? What a surprise."

"There's a brother, too, apparently. They're like cousins," she adds. "This is what Marcus told me this morning. He saw them."

"Pretty?"

"Not by his reckoning. But then, I've never seen him look at a lady."

"Abi will check them out for us," I say.

"He thinks all women are beautiful."

"Better than thinking we're all dirt..."

"Nobody does that; God, you're glum when you're on the rag."

"That guy this morning. You missed him, luckily. He thought I was scum."

But one knows one is destitute when even rags are hard to come by. Publia finds me a supply as we clean the bedrooms. We leave Abibaal's well alone, the plague of dead rats his punishment for laziness. But the other rooms are tidied up and wiped down and, finally, we arrange the jugs of wild flowers that my sister proposed to accessorise with, ever since she got a guest room.

Then we sit in the late afternoon sun that matches with the cooking fire to warm us. I am mending a small hole in my tunic with a needle but the camel-coloured thread doesn't quite match my yellow dress...

"I'm bored now," says Publia. "We should have gone with them."

But that might be the last quiet moment ever because then they come through the front door. Balthazar first, bringing somebody famous, the one who started this whole story, for Publia and thus for me.

Darker than us, shorter, plumper, with bushier eyebrows and sweatier lip; yet she is luscious and sweet. In the curving shadows of her, several children cling. Behind her knee, at her hip, breast and shoulder, little faces appear, all more or less the image of hers.

Laughing and nearly crying, my sister leaps to her feet to greet them. She kisses Alethea on each cheek and tries to eat the children, exclaiming hungrily how big they've grown. It takes me a moment to realise she is talking in Greek.

So this is the lady who lives at the bottom of her garden, with surplus pomegranate juice she sells in Jerusalem to the sick and afflicted. She was giving half measures when she met Jesus, but he cured her, and the complete cripple she was with. Her cup of red juice was tipped over his stony bones and they were both made whole. (Is it me, or does that sound a bit like Amethystos, in the myth I sing?)

Publia always says that I speak Greek like an actor, even when I'm trying to be natural. So I'm waiting as long as I can before I have to deliver my first line. It was, in fact, an actor who taught us to speak Greek; the Thespian friend of our father's. We both learned together, over a couple of golden summers when we were girls. Never went to Thespies, the seat of drama, though. She entered business and I entered religion: and Pubi got to practise the language of global trade, while I got to sing obsolete hymns.

The child at Alethea's shoulder height is responding politely to Publia's questions. I think she says yes, they have built a seasonal booth in the garden, in honour of the local custom, and it looks so cosy. But the kid at hip height might have actually bitten Alethea, the way they're both wriggling.

"And how is your husband?" Publia calmly carries on.

"We never see him, he's always working," the neighbour says (if I understand her correctly). She is groping behind her back, grappling with the second smallest child. "But tell me, how went it with Jesus?"

"We walked with him from Tyre," says Publia, "where he made me well. You know, I was bleeding constantly; well, after one touch, in fact, he didn't even touch me, my body was re-set, like a water clock but flowing red. I've followed him for more than four moons, now, and seen him morning, noon and night; and even though I've been homeless and practically penniless, this is the most regular I've ever been. I hope now for a miracle of my own..."

She reaches past Alethea to the littlest child and pats its curly head.

"Lady come see tent?" the baby says.

"Tomorrow," Publia promises, "it's nearly bedtime now. Lady spent all day cleaning house and ...

"I knew it looked better," Balthazar bursts out, "but I wasn't sure why. I thought it was just because you were here."

"No," says Publia, "it was because we were here and spent ten hours scrubbing and sweeping. How did you not notice the dead rats were gone?"

"There were dead rats?" he gasps.

"And the miracles?" Alethea's voice is timid. "I saw a paralysed man walk away. And I, who limped into the baths, was healed and walked away, too. You who went with him by the Jordan, and the Sea of Galilee; did you see him do a miracle?"

"More," says Publia, "every single soul who meets him, if they want to, will be transformed. Everybody gets a spiritual uplift. Marcus Manlius; more than a man. He's not here at the moment but you'll meet him later. Farzan and Emeshmoon, too; personal make-overs by the master. Veronica; not so much. She's just miraculously unscathed by the journey that could have undone her..."

"No." Here I go now, with the Greek; have to, because Pubi is telling me wrong. "The night we met, the way he listened to me. I sung the sleazy Persephone; underworld theft, virgin seduction. That tale I hummed was all mother-mania and husband-melancholy, only just sweetened by the pomegranate seeds.

"The way he looked at me. The way he listened. The way he turned his head to face me. The way, the truth, the life. The light in his eyes rolled the rock away from the mouth of Hades where I had been hiding in darkness."

There's more but I don't know if my grasp of the language is firm enough:

"There were demons in me. He cast them out."

"What?" It's news to Abibaal, too. "When?"

"Oh, when he was healing this madman at Nain. We got caught up in the exorcism."

Alethea decides it's time to take the children home, now.

"I like the one about Persephone," she only half-smiles at me. "At least, I used to..."

She goes out the back way and we walk with her into the overgrown garden where the children run through the purple broom, popping the seed pods as they pass.

"I don't know whether to tell them stories like that anymore."

"You should take them to see Jesus," says Publia. "He gives little ones the biggest blessings. And…" she is picking her way through a field of straggly herbs "… I've heard him tell the fishermen not to keep children away."

As we struggle though the famous Jerusalem sage, all three women are breaking off the choice stems for their savour in our stews and their succour on our skin.

And there is a camomile patch in the hillside garden, beneath the tumbledown wall to Alethea's land. Grabbing an armful, I think that Emeshmoon's next cup of tea will be the best she's brewed yet. (I might even drink it.)

Promising to visit them in their tent tomorrow, Publia bids the family goodbye. The knee-high child is nodding off on its mother's shoulder as the taller ones leap the fallen stone wall to home.

Then we turn to go back to Pubi's, which is my tent too, now; offloading our garden gatherings on Abibaal who's waiting half way up the wild hillside. We sweep indoors with hands free, which is helpful because Emesh and Farzan have arrived and we can shake them.

"Tell us everything that happened," Publia shouts.

"I got paper! Look," a grinning Emeshmoon unrolls a new papyrus scroll.

I think I just saw the plant that this comes from in the garden. We could probably make our own.

"I got ink!" Her eyes are gleaming but her grammar, as she greets us in our own language, is slacker than my Greek… "Proper *atramentum* like you gets in Roma."

"Ooh, let's see!" My sister and I still are suckers for dark dye. It comes in a little brass well and there's a pen made of wood with a metal nib. The scroll is as yet unwritten on.

"So, what did Jesus say today?" I prompt.

Emeshmoon's face falls:

"There was shouting. I don't like it when they shout."

"It's the scribes," Farzan says. "They're very picky about the word of the law."

He takes a deep breath and becomes three or four men arguing passionately in Hebrew. Different voices clamour at once and his face seems many-sided; that handsome profile fractured, the fine cheekbone showing more facets, the chin making several points.

We're all laughing now as one side of Farzan's body tries to beat up the other. His impression is so powerful it's as if the very clothes he's wearing look longer, shorter, shinier, shabbier on the right and left, as if his tunic is parti-coloured and his cloak patched.

Did they actually come to blows on the temple steps? Were the factions really fighting over Jesus in Jerusalem today? Emeshmoon says there was no physical contact, that it was all done by the book, by the word but not by the body.

"What happened was, he went in secret but got found out when a Pharisee spotted him at prayer," she says. "A huge crowd gathered around them."

"Apparently, his disciples started shouting at Jesus, too, for not telling them he was there," adds Farzan. "They thought he'd lied about his whereabouts. It was quite a commotion. Nathaniel came out and told us to go shopping. We'll see them tomorrow to find out the rest."

So we settle down for the evening by Balthazar's fire, at Publia's hearth, in the house of bread. I pick up my needle and thread again; Emeshmoon her pen and ink. Stitching and bitching, I sew, she writes; me mending a hole, her making a mark. The men whittle with Abibaal's new knife, drinking and talking; part purple business, part Jesus.

I wish my stitches were words embroidered in the silk of my stolen garb. A long night that would be, to fill its whole length with embroidery. I fear it must be ripped into patchwork pieces by now, torn into strips, and sold as relics. Unless it reaches Jerusalem whole there's nobody but me, surely, who'd give nearly everything they had for the entire gown.

To patch the prayer shawl of a small-town rabbi, the loin cloth of a wilderness prophet, the handkerchief of a senator's wife; my dress could conceal holes across Judea's fabric but, even though I'm trying to move on, I am still a Fabia Pictrix and will fight, sing or scream, till I get the colour back.

CHAPTER ELEVEN

In the morning, when the fire is out, there's no centre of attention in the house. I come from my *cubiculum* first, yawning in the courtyard where we crowded last night. Now there are only cold stones at the hearth, and black ash wet with dew, there's no direction to look in. No face to pray to.

A Romano-Phoenician couple really need his and hers shrines. Back home, there'd be a Hercules for Pubi and a Melqart for Bal. In every alcove, the image of a different deity. Yes, it was confusing sometimes; but at least it helped us focus.

I need to kneel, to give praise like we did when we were with Jesus. I need to fall to my knees as if we were at his feet again. Imagine; a statue of him in marble. Odd, now we've seen him in the flesh, unlike one of our old gods.

A shrine but with what sign? His hands are empty; he holds no bow, thunderbolt, or trident. If anything, he holds a fishing net. He's asked us all to catch men. How can we build a temple for that?

Whatever it looks like I'd serve at the altar, I think as I sweep the damp hearthstones with Publia's broom, its twigs tied Jewish, not Roman, style. I almost start to sing, then, some swish hymn to the king of Galilee. But as I open my mouth, the sound of breaking wind startles me.

Abibaal is up, surprisingly early. Being the only single man in the house is making him sleepless; and, as the only single lady, it would be much safer for me in a double bedroom, right now. But not with him! He farts and there's no marble statue to blame it on in this *atrium*.

"Good morning, Veronica," the swaggering soprano arrives at my clean hearth. "Shall I light your fire?" he says.

I do need it lit and I'm not good at that. Alone, I'd stay cold and eat raw; so long as there was red wine on fire in my belly. But otherwise, yes, Abi can go down on his knees and blow.

By the time the kettle's boiled, Emeshmoon is up too and making the best tea we've had on our whole journey. I sip a little. It tastes of flowers, whereas I prefer the *gustus* of grapes.

Farzan appears next. He grabs a cuppa and goes back to bed, saying that Jesus won't be out of the synagogue till the ninth hour. When Publia arrives soon after we decide to go visiting the neighbours first.

"Is Bal having a nice lie-in?" I ask her.

"No, dear, he's working," she says. "Somebody has to feed our five thousand."

We have toast for breakfast, then Emesh, Pubi and I wander up the wild garden, and Abibaal comes too. Leaping the wall we saw those kids scramble over last night, we arrive in the greener, lusher and fruitier garden of the next door neighbours.

First thing I see is a naked slave, swinging an axe at a tree. There's a worker's butt crack in full view, like the gash he's making in the tree trunk. There's thick black hair all over his body, much stockier than a city slave. He must be very well fed.

When he sees us coming from behind, he stretches up for his *pallium,* hung on a branch, and slips it on in a slow and sensuous arc. I gasp at the cloak's quality; raw silk, cut with great skill and dyed at great expense. Not a slave, again; Publia is holding her oily hand out to an olive tycoon.

He is the top importer of Greek olives to Jerusalem, I remember her telling me now. It's strange that Alethea said she never sees her husband, but we saw him bare all, the moment we got there.

We're all shaking hands as Publia makes gushing introductions. His name is Anastasios, though everybody calls him Tassos, and obviously he has heard of us. Alethea must have seen him last night, must have said: Veronica is the single sister, Emeshmoon is the married woman, Abibaal is the creepy brother-in-law. Because that's the way he treats us. Fair play, for the way I looked at him first time was specially reserved for slaves.

But while the hairy Hellenic hubby of my sister's next-door neighbour looks me up and down lustfully, the brother-in-law is thrusting his belly at us, as if he were my husband. Neither approach will claim me, of course; my head, my heart, my feet are full of Jesus, just beating the time till I can see him again.

The dance we did, I'm still doing it; a slow, slow circle. Not one sided, that's the sort of partnership for me, now. Even if it has to be with the man for all women, for all people.

Alethea appears in the distance, running towards us on a path between the pomegranate trees. She looks like the sun coming closer, her headband a brilliant yellow. A plump chariot, wheels rolling evenly, decorated with gold; and full of little passengers, driving hard or hanging off the sides.

"Yes, you are right to follow this healer from Nazareth," Tassos is watching his wife approach. "She could not walk straight before he poured our own juice on her bent foot."

The first time I heard about Jesus, that miracle at the baths, it sounded like a story. But now, here I am standing nearly where it happened with the one whose toes were healed. And Publia, the one whose womb was healed. She is all about the children today.

"Look, five!" she says to me, arranging them in height order.

Alethea's oldest son is taller than her, Timotheo. A proud moment that must be for a mother, when her boy outgrows the body that bore him. Shy as the hairs in his beard, he still stands behind her, though. Athens would be a better backdrop for his fresco-fine profile than this Judean hillside.

Two girls come next, with a head's difference in height between them. Maybe a year apart, closer than Publia and I; not beauties, bless them, but even so they'll probably still have the same 'bigger nose, smaller eyes, bigger mouth, smaller ears' thing going on, as they try to work out who is cuter. They both look a lot like Tassos, as does the boy who comes next; this one at home on the hill, a goat-haired apprentice. Then comes the final child, an olive-skinned little princess.

None of them notice me. They direct all their fun and games at Publia. It doesn't bother Abi and Emesh who are talking to the adults but it makes me, the big-nosed *soror*, feel a bit left out.

Then we get to their tent and, for a twisted moment, I'm triumphant over my more popular sister. While she's playing with the children, the men are fighting over me. As if this makeshift tabernacle were the highest altar of Venus, two worshippers are competing for the sexual attention of the assistant priestess.

This is probably what Alethea was complaining about. Her hirsute Greek is horned like an old-time god. But Abibaal has also been blessed by Priapus (and has the statue to prove it). As they square up to each other in the kids' *sukkah* the sheets flap and the leafy boughs sway alarmingly.

I step outside and Alethea's waiting, as if she thinks I might covet her husband and steal his love-seed, perhaps through a chink in that boundary wall. So I compliment her on the brightly-coloured headdress.

"Know what the dye is?" she says begrudgingly. "Pomegranate."

"How strange," I say. "It's yellow but the seeds are so red."

"The colour is in the skin. It's tough before the fruit ripens and vibrant when it's gone past its best..."

"Are they like sea-snails: two hundred lives lost for a pinch of the dye?" I ask.

"Far fewer than that," she shrugs.

"And they don't cry when you peel them?"

I'm talking to myself but she hears me. She can't answer this, of course, but in her eyes the score is settled. Drunk ex-priestess to a sex goddess, yes; threat to her marriage, no. That's how she sees me now.

Can't she tell that I'm in love with Jesus? That my only care is when we'll see him again? That I wouldn't cry if she peeled me. That I wouldn't beg if she squeezed me. That I wouldn't scream if she dunked me. I don't even wear make-up anymore, so I'm not that hard-eyed. I don't fear death since he showed me its kingdom.

When Abibaal bursts out of the tent, all the others follow; Tassos with a laugh like a battle cry, Pubi and Emesh giggling like the children and the five kids running a race that the eldest will always win, back to the garden wall. The teenage boy goes like it's Marathon town he has come from.

As we walk, I suddenly sing to Alethea: 'Yours was the story that started this whole thing, it got the blind seeing, it got the lame walking, it led me away from a paralyzed life, out of the purple and into the light; but I would give anything to jump in Bethesda Baths now...'

Just trilling the word 'bath' makes my mouth water and my body long for the splash. But the ground beneath me is still solid though the wall crumbles as our large party climb over again. Alethea promises she'll come with us after noon to meet the lord on the temple forecourt.

My sister kisses all the children on their bristly little brows and says she'll see them soon. The men grunt goodbye and then we're spilling over into the garden of Balthazar, steeper and sparser.

"Did you know, the bright yellow is pomegranate dye," I tell Publia, as we go. "Let's learn how to make that. It doesn't scream."

"How many times, Veronica," she tuts: "sea snails don't scream."

"Ink does," Emeshmoon teases me, "it's virtually blood."

We run down the hill trailing this nonsense behind us. Abibaal, running after, is shrieking like a eunuch, trying to mop our spills. The sun is behind the clouds but I feel as if we've suddenly run into a deeper shadow.

Looking round, I see him, looking back; the one who saw me at dawn, behaving badly outside the back door. The zealot who, as Bal said, would rather hang himself from the purple thread than see it disrespected. Now he's there again and I have to get past him on the path to the house.

I've been ignored by men, enjoyed by men and abused by men but I've never been entirely hated by a man before. As we pass him, Publia tries to be pleasant. I think she says, though my ears are ringing; 'Good morning, Hod.'

He doesn't reply but his look is convincing: it's not himself he'd kill for the purple. It's me.

To Emeshmoon he is just another man in a headscarf. "Why does he hate us so much?" she whispers as we hurry away.

His gaze is fringed, those eyes in deep shade, but Publia knows, for once, that a guy is looking at me rather than her.

"Why does he hate *you* so much?" she asks, as we get back to the house.

"He saw me in the bath," I say.

"We don't have a bath."

"Exactly..." He saw me in, what I now realise is, a dye bath. The *urna infectoria*. He saw me naked. His wife, sisters, daughters do not leave the house with the beautiful black hair on their heads uncovered, even. "I made an error of judgement."

Now the day is nearly at its peak, even Publia would be horrified if she knew how I stripped off and sat in a dye vat full of sacred rainwater at dawn.

After a long and liquid lunch we all feel calmer. It's nearly the seventh hour and Alethea will call for us on the way to the temple. We can't go in, of course, but we can meet our master outside.

I need to enter that building like I need a bath; a physical craving for the spiritual. This feeling boiled in me till I mentioned the idea of making a shrine in the house and everybody seemed to like it. We've decided where. Opposite the front door, so it can be seen as soon as we step into the courtyard, on the wall facing Jerusalem. Now we must think what to raise on that spot.

I pull my peacock feather shawl low over my eyes as we leave the house. This habit of head covering has come surprisingly easy to me, for a Roman lady, I believe; though if I still wore my Tyrian dress, perhaps my hairdo would be piled high and my stride proud. Sometimes when I walk it seems the silk swishes round my ankles. Always, my eyes swivel for the trail of those bloody *purpura* thieves who took my true outfit away.

The worst that will befall me today is to awkwardly bump into Hod again but I try to leave that naked fear on the doorstep. I am not against his powerful, heartfelt beliefs; can feel their beat woven through the streets, their colours dyed in the houses and hillside, on our pilgrimage through Bethany.

Alethea has brought her son, the big one. Publia and Emeshmoon and also their husbands are keen to walk next to this tall, handsome boy; so I end up walking with his mum again. I'm not sure if we're talking in Latin or Greek, must be a bit of both, and a lot of body language. She is showing me how she used to look with a bad foot, demonstrating the lame gait as we come into town, and stopping suddenly when she realises they can see her from the synagogue steps.

We come as we are, across the square at Bethany; a familiar little group of Romans, Phoenicians and Greeks who love Judea and adore Jesus. We must look serious because a couple of the locals smile as they welcome us, then move up so we can crowd on.

Sunlight strikes the steps and sharpens my vision. There is a flash of purple in a fisherman's belt, then I see it's the sheen of his blade for gutting or scaling. There is a glimpse of purple lining to a seamstress' sleeve, then I see it's the gleam of a cheap bangle.

I seem to find my lost material in every look, a violet uprising as we climb the next stair to the throne of our teacher. Dazed, I almost think he's gowned in my old dress. Could another one of his rich friends have bought it from a dark market and gifted it to the lord of the light? Then I realise it's just a heat haze and remember that all of our king's real friends have already spent their riches. And me, if I still had it, would strip off the heliotrope colour now and carpet these steps with it.

Closing my eyes, I kneel in front of him. Peace streams from his body. The musk of men is like incense from him. I'm so close it knocks me out. Slowly I sink lower so that my spinning head is level with his feet. There I can feel the buzz without losing my balance. I can cope with the vertigo, lying flat before him.

Abibaal can't bend so low but that doesn't mean he's not into it. He and Balthazar both are changed men: pages to the Prince of Peace.

It wasn't precisely like he was waiting for us, to start; Jesus is at the end of the prayer, now, explaining what Amen means in many languages. Let it be, make it so, mote it be, so be it. But he did seem to pause as we arrived and in that moment, afterwards, Alethea and Tim both said he saw them personally and knew them; the mother he had met before and the son he hadn't.

My eyes are closed so I don't know, my forehead pressed to the cool stone close to the feet of Jesus. I listen to the teaching; is he speaking Greek for us? His voice is a deep rumble from the belly of God:

"But what do you think? A man had two sons, and he came to the first and said, 'Son, go, work today in my vineyard.' He answered and said, 'I will not,' but afterward he regretted it and went. Then he came to the second and said likewise. And he answered and said, 'I go, sir,' but he did not go. Which of the two did the will of his father?" [10]

Somebody in the crowd says, "the first." Jesus replies; "And that is why harlots and tax collectors may enter the kingdom of God before Pharisees. For the way in is not with words but thoughts and deeds."

We stay on the temple steps till its lengthening shadow stretches all the way across the square then people stand and stretch and rub their bellies, but I feel well fed. And though I get up with the others, and go home with my family and friends, hidden under a peacock feather fringe, my shadow is satisfied and stays there, still kneeling on the holy stone.

That night, I put my true peacock feather on the new shrine at Publia's, the one I found at the necropolis in Tyre. It signifies a lot of things; Spurius Pavo, our last bath at Capernaum, silence versus singing, and life after death.

But to me it means Jesus knows I am still with him. I haven't fallen by the wayside on this long journey. I have transformed almost beyond recognition but the threads in my feathered shawl tie the start to its finish. Can I still catch the end of the full purple dress and reel that identity back to me triumphantly, the most beautiful Veronica I've ever been, the best self I can achieve, on this same trip?

The next day we go and sit with him again. Why would anyone in the world know where he stood and not stand alongside or where he sat and not sit there too? More than a hundred people come to the synagogue steps.

We find Marcus there, bare-shouldered though it's nearly winter now; and Naomi is close behind, his broad back her gladiator's shield in the crush. It seems crowded to me but they were with five thousand back in the day, before I found them and Publia in Galilee. All those people who stayed on the seashore, who didn't follow him; the fish, not the fishermen, have they forgotten?

Nathaniel walks us home at sundown past the well with a view of the Mount of Olives where he says Jesus likes to pray. We stare in awe as the rays strike bloody fire at its peak and his disciple starts to speak from the heart:

"He went in prayer to another mountain once, with Peter, James and John; who told me not to tell anyone. They saw him transformed, his robes shining brighter than snow, his hair a glowing halo. In a trance, they heard him talk with Moses and Elijah..." He looks at Farzan first, to Abi and Bal in the middle, then Pubi and me last. "If you believe in my angels, you can believe in these."

We take Nathaniel home to see our shrine, that night, with a flask of well water. Showing him the makeshift altar I suddenly wish for my three-legged display table, suitable for such treasure. But this disciple kneels when he sees where we pray, the way Jesus is teaching us.

Publia lights the fire, Emeshmoon puts the water on for an evening brew, Abibaal cuts some bread, Farzan pours some wine. I sweep the stones for Bal to sit with our visitors, desperate not to catch the eye of Alethea or Tim who have popped in on their way home.

We are all trying not to laugh. Because the first sacred object on the shrine, placed there by us previously but invisible to Nathaniel's eye, is a toenail. A crescent moon-shape clipped from the foot of our next-door neighbour; an iridescent cutting from Alethea's miraculously healed toes. Timotheo suggested it go there but now the relic seems as rude as Aphrodite's pubic hair. The poor boy is blushing red as his mother's pomegranate juice.

Balthazar manages to ask for sober suggestions as to what we could put on this altar and Nathaniel thinks again, closing his eyes and inclining his head as if to hear a small voice more clearly.

"This is what he said yesterday, to the teachers that were troubling him: 'Woe to you, Scribes and Pharisees, oh blind guides; for you pay the tithes on mint, anise and cumin; but neglect the much weightier matters of justice, mercy and faith.' What about a display of herbs," Nathaniel asks us enthusiastically. "As a sign of His warning..."

We have that stuff strewn over the floor as room fresheners, already. Publia looks at me and I know what she's thinking. Sometimes she even uses the big mint leaves for intimate wiping.

Luckily, Nathaniel moves on, saying that he needs to get back to the others soon. Jesus is planning a trip to Bethphage early in the morning. He invites us along, it's only a few miles and only for a few hours.

But we have to work, too. Emeshmoon and Farzan, Abi and I have to earn our keep at the house of Balthazar and Publia. We've all given up our proper jobs but hope to survive in Judea till spring, planning to get through the colder months by pulling our weight around the home and supporting Bal's purple dye business, all that's left at the end of our empire.

I put my amethyst necklace on our new found altar. Positioning it carefully, like I used to line up my possessions in Tyre, I promise myself: if we get really skint, if we're starving, I'll give this up. But I'm not sure we would dismantle our Christine shrine for dinner.

So I fix on a new line of colour to trade in; the yellow dye Alethea has made from pomegranate skin. I start from the roots, stalking the field on our side of the wall and hers, seeing how the trees grow. Then I attend to ours like an *ornatrix*; trimming, combing, brushing off the fallen leaves. The voice of Hakiqah comes to me on the breeze from far Phoenicia; 'these tangles need a rake!'

I feed the fruit trees with chickenshit from the coop that Abibaal has started to run again. This was meant to be one of Emeshmoon's tasks, in the new family business we've set up, but she didn't like the clucking so they swapped jobs.

Abibaal was originally given the role of goat keeper, in our new goal of countryside survival. The trio of goats, previously under Publia's rule, were living with Alethea's flock and she gladly sent them back. But Abibaal did not like handling those girls at milking time. No, he said in a high voice, it un-manned him, squeezing the dugs of a goat and 'it puts me off feeling the breasts of women'. (Not that I think he has the chance in Bethany though, of course, we can never be sure.) So he didn't like the pumping and Emeshmoon couldn't stand the pecking so they switched roles in the rural idyll we're crafting here.

Then I ask Alethea to teach me how to make that brilliant yellow from a skin I've always thought of as red. In my imagination the ruby pips were trodden like grapes. In fact, it takes a smallish dyer's vat in the corner of the courtyard, near the doorway to my bedroom, and I don't get so much as my toes wet. The labour is simple and not strenuous; my main challenge to stay clear of Hod and the big purple experiments in the backyard.

In the season since we all arrived in the house, the heavy vessels full of strong-smelling liquid have been moved out to a stable behind the main building. Farzan has set up a desk by the old manger and is keeping the books there. In his spare time, I think he's also developing a side line; he and Emesh reckon they could grow and make papyrus here. At lunchtimes and early evenings I see him in the boggy area, breaking new ground, preparing to plant the paper.

How long does it take to grow from seed to scroll? I'll dye fifty bright yellow *peplum* with a single harvest, ladies' tunics more brilliant than my old one dyed with crocuses. But Farzan looks like he's planning to hang around outside Jerusalem for years. How long does it take to go from craze to crazy? I just can't see Jesus lasting in that city.

Eventually, Publia and I have to face it. One Sabbath day, when the Christ and his apostles are going to the temple, we walk behind them, over Olivet, following the sun. Nathaniel kindly shines on us, as always, walking with Marcus and me one moment, Publia and Emeshmoon the next; through an olive grove with the three Phoenician fellows, across a rocky outcrop with Alethea and her son.

He tells us what they've been doing since last time we met; our talk is full of wonder. The way Nathaniel describes the kingdom of heaven, we can almost see it shimmering in front of us. But in fact, from the top of the hill, we can finally see Jerusalem.

For a Roman businesswoman, if that's what I still am, it glints with the promise of commerce. There's a needy populace there with many requirements, some mundane, some exotic. I always thought that, if I ever came to Jerusalem, it would be at the luxury end of the market; in short, I'd be selling the best thing they'd heard of. Purple.

The sacred thread runs through their religion like blood-veins through their hands. *Tekhelet* goes deeper in that tradition than the toga hems of Tyre and Rome. The Semite tassels are more complex, a cluster of sensitive endings, than the smooth edges of a senator's clothing. Yes, some bit of me is still a businesswoman, for my fingers itch as we walk; to deal dye, to feel cloth, to count proceeds.

The path winds downhill between a couple of palm trees to the city, so beautiful I see it through tears. Nature gleams but the real spectacle round here is the work of man: inspired, or terrified, by his maker.

It is all walls, Jerusalem; whether they are keeping a monster out, or in. The tallest wall protects the giant house of Herod, girdles all the houses towering over the plain. A spiritual fortress; a defensive temple. It is probably the most graceful city I've ever seen. Rome is brutal, Tyre is cheap, compared with this.

The closer we get to its majesty, the more its power tempts me; I find myself, even before the shadow is fully cast over our advancing army, planning how to make it mine, to take back the purple silk, to own my robes again. Whether the men who robbed me are hiding, or blatantly pumping their wares through the veins of these streets, I will find them.

We walk down the hill towards it, then we have to cross the level while it rises up above us; it stays on top of us, way over our heads, and we are overwhelmed. We're not even through the gate when the trouble starts. I think, but I'm not sure because I can't see properly, he heals somebody and we get chased by Pharisees because it is the Sabbath. There is a lot of shouting but we're standing too far away to hear what they're saying. Even Farzan can't manage to translate anything from where we are.

But we can see a man in the crowd who is writing it all down. He's got one arm crooked around a scroll, the other hand scribbling in straight rows; now he looks from face to face of the speakers, now he looks down at his handwritten record. The words unroll in real time on his paper, so nobody will ever forget anything; the page will remember the age.

I think it's Thomas, who Emesh told of, when she was trying to save my outpourings instead of our master's, that night at the feast of tabernacles, ages ago; I haven't sung since Hod shushed me over some dirty dye bathwater.

But in Jerusalem I feel written on all over. It's like a whole new story is starting here. I keep my headscarf on and my eyes low but still it feels like I have been scribed upon; my scrolling drapery signed off by many hands. When Alethea suggests we slip away to see Bethesda Baths, I'm eager to go. She leads us along backstreets to the sheep market then through an arch or two to the legendary water. I've never wanted to jump in a bath more. It would wash all the writing off my skin, that is for sure.

"This is where the cripple lay," Alethea is saying, "and this is where Jesus cured him."

Publia and the Phoenicians are laughing again; they've been on a guided tour like this in Tyre, the very spot where Queen Dido threw herself on Aeneas' funeral pyre. Still, my sister prizes up one of the pebbles that Jesus' foot would have touched, and washes it in the holy bathwater. She takes it home with us, for a spot at the household shrine.

Nobody is watching. The porticoes are packed. Between these ancient columns where the legless and dumb lay, there's a lot of wheeler dealing going on. Somebody is still selling pomegranate juice, there's bread and wine for sale, there's salves and inhalations. This is the perfect place to set my honey trap.

Contriving to fall behind the others, leaving Bethesda baths, I stand in the archway and bellow a song in my best voice ever. Like the most tempting sales pitch but even better: I'm offering to pay.

"This is a song that is buying not selling, the voice of a customer, seeking your goods; she will purchase at any price, that which she longs for, like a Tyrian mermaid who can't get enough of your sheet of pure purple, dyed with a million little murex deaths..."

Some people turn to look and I actually blush. Because I do remember how I first heard about this place, the advertisement of Alethea's miracle healing, by Publia as we bobbed naked in the baths. If Jesus were looking at me now, would my greedy song seem a half measure, a selfish portion of juice like she poured out for the invalid that day, too?

Anyway, my commercial has been posted and I hurry from the colonnade as it seems I might have some keen customers already, though they don't look the type to be in possession of a firkin of *purpura*.

Then, from the sullied water of that Jerusalem sheep dip, he leads us next to the purer source where we finally get to wash clean. We go down to the Jordan with him, near to the spot where John the Baptist taught. We sit down at the edge of the water, in the bulrushes, and Jesus teaches us.

On that trip, there are five of his disciples, including Nathaniel; about twenty of his new followers, including a guy who was a leper when we met him in Samaria; about twenty of his older followers from Galilee, and our small group of wrangling wordsmiths, with Balthazar and Farzan missing. They're doing a big deal in the city having decided they can best support the cause by shifting more purple than the Pharisees.

Marcus is present, and Abibaal, of course, but it seems to me that there are more women than men there, that day. Yes, there are as many, if not more, women than men following him down to the river. We are not the five thousand fans that sat with him beside the sea, hoping he'd come to overthrow the gentiles: no, we are fifty and not all sons of David.

As he speaks, we let the headscarves slip and sit bare-haired in the winter sunshine. Later, when we bathe, it is with tunics on; but God, it's good to get wet. Some people there are only paddling but us Romans seize the day and get drenched from head to toe. Publia and I used to run and jump into the bath hand-in-hand. Now we move downstream to get water up to our armpits. Away from the main group we shriek and dip, shake and duck, and completely miss the conversation.

Abibaal stops splashing first, perhaps because he splashed most. His tail of hair flips a rainbow of sparkles at every turn. Now he draws us back through the water, his bald patch a stone in the stream as we swim reluctantly after him. Half way, we meet Aunt Naomi, who has waded in up to the knees of her long black skirts, to tell us what was said:

"Susanna asked if he would baptise her; others joined in the clamour. The lord just splashed his own face with the water. When we followed him back to the shore, he turned and said; 'John baptised with water. I will baptise you with the holy spirit.'"

We come out of the current, wallowing again in Jordan's shallows, feeling ashamed of ourselves. Like the oil and strigil, our cleansing only goes skin-deep. We have rinsed bodies not souls, here.

Jesus stands at the water's edge, talking in quiet ripples, smiling like the gentle waves; telling us about Heaven as if we might find it round the next bend in this river.

Suddenly, Abibaal starts to speak. His voice leaps like a silvery fish from the mid-stream, startling the Fabia Pictrix sisters on either side of him.

"Where is this kingdom?" Abi pleads. "How do I get in?"

And Jesus says, "This kingdom is not far away, but you can't see it with your eyes. Why? Because it is inside you; its capital city is the heart."

"So where is the king?" Abibaal is on his knees before him, in the water.

"Don't seek him in the river, on the bank or in the cloudy sky; he is nowhere to be seen. And yet he is everywhere," Jesus says thoughtfully. "And yet he is here." To our surprise, he bends down and picks something up from the river bed near his feet. He puts it in Abi's hand.

Then he says: "The gateway to heaven is not high. All who wish to enter must bow down low. The gate is not wide; no one can carry baggage through. The body must be transformed into spirit, must be washed in living streams of purity. [11] The king does the cleaning."

Abibaal pipes up again, despite the burly fishermen chortling at his high pitch: "Can I become his subject?"

And Jesus answers, "You are yourself a king and can enter through the gate to be a subject of the king of kings. But you cannot take your silver, your gemstones..." He is looking at me and Publia as well as our Phoenician business partner and brother-in-law. "... your *purpura*, your peacock feathers, your pomegranate stitches. You cannot take them."

We know. We all know what we must still give up. And yet we take it home with us; the stone that Jesus picked off the river bed. It is purple, heart-shaped, and we add it to our increasingly loaded altar.

Alongside the amethysts and this water-rock is the stone Publia picked out of the earth at Bethesda. And now, Balthazar decides, we need fire. We require the sacred smoke of our previous deities, incense from altars we've knelt at before.

Bal appears one evening with an armful of dried sage, the woody legs of long-bolted bushes, to burn fast and fragrantly as we pray. And to that smoky note, we add bellows, when Emeshmoon asks me to sing. We're sitting around the hearth in the ember gloaming after dinner. Above our heads the courtyard walls are sewn to a sunset sky glowing with amber clouds.

The burnt-out stars of the fire and the first bright twinkles in the sky are speaking to each other, as surely as if they were halves of the same black coals; twins split by an almighty hammer blow at the forging of the world. With this picture in my mind, the song that comes out of my mouth is a pounding ode to Vulcan, the blacksmith god:

'Husband of Venus, you struck with precision the solid erection of ignorance, arrogance and utter nonsense that stood in the way of love. God of volcanoes, you spurted a mixture of beauty and wisdom and watched it destroy the world as it was. Let your lava flow, oh lord...'

"Wrong! Stop," Publia interrupts me. "Better not worship false gods, Veronica. Best not to sing at all."

With a sigh Emeshmoon stops writing, too. She wants a scroll to display on the altar but isn't getting very far with the words.

Next afternoon, as we squat on the temple steps, listening to the teaching of Jesus, I see her watching the guy called Thomas, who takes it all down. Not on a long roll of papyrus, this time, but on old tax collector's notepaper; he's using shorthand to keep up with the fiery flow. He sits near us in today's small crowd, maybe three or four steps below our master and to the left. Just another man in a headscarf, he and I, and the wider public, can hardly keep our eyes off the lord's face.

My Vulcan looks like Jesus. He has the features, the physique, of Hercules, too. Those gods were all a kind of Christ, so I see Zeus in his hairline, Apollo in his jaw; maybe Dionysus in his wrists.

My sister is right. I'd sooner not sing again than defame Jesus of Nazareth with an old Roman name. When I was in the wilderness, walking three days solo from Tyre to Galilee, I was silent then: there was nobody to hear me. While there is an audience near my body, the hymn should go on.

I give Emeshmoon what she wants. A devoted outpouring, a besotted sing-along that brings a tear to my eye, sometimes, with its poignancy (and sometimes because I am pissed).

I give song with a pure heart. Perhaps for the first time, as I was always trying to sell something when I sang before. Now I buy it, completely:

'Lord of the sky, I see you
Lord of the water, I feel you
Lord of fire, I breathe you
Lord of the earth, I die in you
Lord of the dance, I join you'

I don't sing the whole scroll in one go. It unrolls over several weeks. At the same time, I'm learning how to make and use Alethea's yellow dye from some wizened pomegranates. The coarse skin is so tough, its complexion rough but, when the colour is ready, I transform a length of Publia's old wedding *stola* into an altar cloth for the family shrine.

Then I sing the last verse:

'Be still, for he sees you
Be strong, for he feels you
Be fast, for he gets you
Be free, for he lets you
Be ready, for whatever he wants you to do'

We lay the yellow silk across the altar and rearrange our sacred objects on top; the peacock feather, the amethyst necklace, the Bethesda bath stone, the Jordan river rock, the sage incense holder, the holy well water. Alethea's toe-nail is still there, too. Apart from my gemstones, this stuff is not worth a shekel to the world; but we are rendering our currency to Jesus.

Abi and Pubi wait while Emeshmoon blows on her black ink and dries my final words, then they place the scroll ceremoniously on the shrine. We stand there in silence for a moment, a few plumes of grey smoke curling around our heads.

Suddenly we hear a commotion in the street, a clattering in the doorway, and Balthazar and Farzan appear. One is red, one is pale, one is silent, one shouts:

"He is gone into Gilead. They've all gone over the river, and nobody knows when he'll be back."

CHAPTER TWELVE

The chickens are loose in Publia's house. The coop has been abandoned, its gate wide open while Abibaal curls up on the straw inside, crying; not cockadoodle-do any more.

The conversation went like this, a chorus of voices straight out of a tragedy on some suburban stage:

Balthazar. They have all gone. Nathaniel, Naomi, Marcus.

Publia. Why didn't they tell us?

Farzan. It was early, apparently. The master decided at dawn and his men only had time to gather those living close by.

Emeshmoon. They could have called on the way. Nathaniel has been to this house.

Bal. It was the other route out of town, by the Jordan road, they took.

Abibaal. But Naomi's hardly been able to hobble since we got here.

Me! There's a hunky Roman actor to carry her.

Publia. And Jesus Christ, the son of God, our saviour, to heal her.

Farzan. What do we do now? Follow on behind? We'll never find him.

Emeshmoon. There is only one way to walk.

Bal. And we still need to work: this makes it clear. We have to provide for ourselves.

Abibaal. If we were walking with him now - nay, if it were through the desert - we would not go hungry.

Farzan. They say he will be back for the Passover.

Publia. Passover? When the fuck's that?

Bal. Halfway through the month they call *Nisan*.

Farzan. Just before what you call *Floralia*.

Bal. About three moons hence. He will return, dearest. Friends are here, closer than family: he's certain to bring more followers from Capernaum.

Emeshmoon. He's going all the way back there?

Me. It is no distance, when you think how far we have come.

Publia. (To her husband.) How do you know this? Who did you speak to?

Bal. The cheesemaker. That round lady, wrapped in dairy-stained linen, looks like she's been left in the sun to dry. She lives next door to Lazarus.

Publia. Who?

Bal. He's a cousin of Jesus, or something...

Emeshmoon. With the beautiful sisters.

Me. One is. One isn't.

Publia. Oh, them.

It's unthinkable but this tragedy has touches of comedy. As we act out the feelings behind our words, serious as they are, silly things happen. Abibaal lies down in the chicken run and pretends to be dead.

Balthazar tries to move him on with a broom, a bit roughly, and Publia clings onto the broomstick with arms and legs; first to try and stop the fight but finally for something to hug.

I go out into the garden and climb a pomegranate tree. There's no fruit to pick but in desperation I go as high as I can then come crashing back down through the branches. My hair is untied and the locks are full of twigs; yes, Hakiqah would need a rake to comb it now. But when I get to the top bough, it's not to look back at Tyre. I'm looking for Jesus.

We are all looking for him. Farzan is actually walking the road out of town; to and fro, along the Jordan way, a good two miles, up and down, muttering all the time about how long it would take to catch up and how lost he should get.

I can see him, a solitary figure sweeping back and forth, as I sit in the tree. And when I return to the house, his wife is sitting alone in silence, writing in the firelight. This is so strange, I stand and stare: Emesh only takes dictation, normally, or transcribes conversation or song. To see her pen moving though no words are spoken makes me shiver. What voice can she be drawing out of thin air?

She doesn't ask me to sing this evening. We watch Publia going to bed still clutching the broom. No sign of Balthazar but his brother is lying in the hen coop. I run my fingers through my tangled hair and turn in early, too.

Then I find myself doing something I used to do, long ago, but haven't done for ages. In bed, at night, I tie myself up, tight as I'm able. Once it was for excitement; now it's for comfort.

I can bind my wrists so the blood almost stops flowing with my own hanky. It's still white; I tug the ends of it with my teeth, delicately so not to spit, firmly so not to split. I tie myself into one complete sensation, breath-taking and spine-tingling. I rip a smile, I repress a sigh. My hands are tied in front so they're handy for pressing needs but I wish I could tie them behind my back.

Bound, I dream freely. The road out of Bethany unrolls in front of me like a handkerchief, lined with stones. I'm running barefoot along it, as this road leads me to the lord. I see the unfolding linen-length blend into and become the hem of his garment. Still racing, in this dream, I rush up the white lines of Jesus' robe; and all the little rocks that were lying in the road are flung at me, striking my face and shoulders and thighs.

Bound, I feel this dream stoning. At a snail's pace but with the force of a bull, I witness the pelting, throwing up my hands to catch the pellets but, tied together, they are helpless. As the dream ends, Jesus is untying my hands. Yes, I know I am asleep and, even awake, I am a complete fantasist. The image races off, like the linen road, but I catch him rubbing my wrists to start the blood flow.

Pale songstress to the highest priest, I can't even sing how happy I am when I wake to find the real bindings have held. Perhaps I'm starting to master myself.

In the morning, the bread is burnt. Finally pulling the loaf out of the oven, Emesh looks at the blackened crust as if for a message written in charred letters, and bursts into tears. When she brews the herbal tea, it is to read missives left in the leaves.

Farzan doesn't get up for a cuppa; she takes one in. I never heard him come home last night but his road must have ended here. Eventually, he makes it to the manger, where Bal's business accounts are stored. Work is going on as usual in the outhouses; the Phoenicians are building a new emporium.

Balthazar has had sacks of snails hauled from the coast for these experiments. He's brought brine in a wine carrier, to discover if the purple blood of Tyre can be reconstituted miles inland. Away from the ancient source, without the authorised salts, will the dye be deep enough? How much of the Mediterranean sun and sea needs to be in it, for the colour to suit buyers across the empire?

At sunset on the third day since Jesus went away, Balthazar literally spills a vat of the stuff all over himself. A talent's worth of Tyrian ingredients splashed across the factory, staining people, equipment and paperwork.

The sludge of Hercules; slowly and silently it must have dripped off faces and pages and slid down the sides of vats. Hod might have stood there looking in disbelief at Bal as another wave crashed between their material and spiritual interests.

Bal walks slowly into the house, covered in the shade more valuable than his lifeblood. The man-made dye doesn't look right, though; and what's worse, it doesn't smell wrong. With nowhere near as dreadful a whiff as the real thing makes, this stuff doesn't stink bad enough to be the true purple. Still, it's a glorious sight as he comes up to us at the hearthside.

Publia drops the broom.

"Good evening, honoured friends," Balthazar addresses his houseguests. We are all still there; Abibaal covered in chicken feathers, Emesh burned, me bloody and bruised from the tree. Farzan is dusty and dehydrated. Publia is thin as a stick. But we're all still there.

"I think I've just been baptised in the holy spirit," says Bal. "How could we doubt him for a single moment. Nobody said Jesus was staying in Bethany for ever. Of course he still needs to gather more supporters. It doesn't mean we don't count anymore. I have never seen him turn a soul away. Putrid sores, shocking deformity, raging insanity; he hasn't put one person off. No matter how sordid, how unsightly they are, his smile beams as brightly, his arms open as wide. There's no way we should feel abandoned by him, whose miracles we have seen, and whose stories we have heard. Instead let's whisper our prayers and assume he hears them."

"I agree," says his brother. "We're not babies. We can walk in his footsteps without holding his hands." Abibaal, who has lain three days in the hen house, has a surprising ratio of feathers to crap. Enough fluff for a nice pair of wings and no chicken shit.

It is he who leads us, more than anyone, in the three moons till our lord returns to town. We all made our own decisions to stay faithful in his absence, choosing this path individually. When Farzan stopped pacing, Emesh stopped penning, Publia put down the broom; when I climbed down from the pomegranate tree, we all decided then. And separately we all agreed with Balthazar that the Jesus we loved and believed in would come back again; and independently we all concurred with Abibaal that we could trust Him. Nobody made anyone do anything they didn't want to.

Though our conversion happens alone, our conversation happens in a group, and this grows bigger and louder. We start to meet in Bethany again, every day at the seventh hour, sitting on the synagogue steps. Not as high up as we were when we sat at the feet of our Rabbi; nearer the beggars than the money-changers in the climb to the temple court. The six of us work a rota so that there's always three or four there; Alethea and Tim come most days and bring family and friends from the Greek oil stream. Gold and purple carpets the worn stone steps in the afternoon sunlight.

Lots of locals start to turn up and sit with us, their headscarves striped in muted shades, bent intently to our words. People want to hear our stories again; the Bethesda Baths, the issue of blood, the madman of Nain. Again, they want to hear the blind man seeing; the leper made clean; the paralytic pick up his mat and walk. Again, they want the five thousand fed, the walking on water, a coin in the mouth of a fish. And they want his words again, too, spat by a fat Phoenician with a high voice: stories of workers in vineyards, of fathers and favoured sons, of wheat and chaff, of soil and seeds. They want it translated by Farzan into bookseller's Hebrew; and transcribed by Emeshmoon, who copies down everything she hears, except the bits we all know off by heart, now, like the lord's prayer.

Publia's on a rota to lead the small crowd as, at the end of our daily meeting, we pray it. When I say the 'our father' with everyone else I find myself wondering how long would we go on saying it, if he never came back: a thousand years, two thousand years, till 'thy kingdom come'? And would the crowd go on growing?

We want his peace but make a loud noise getting it. The group chant 'forgive us our trespasses' quietly but it sets up a strong resonance on the synagogue steps. The Scribe, on his way inside, stops to look disapprovingly.

It isn't just the praying. Things start happening like they did around Jesus. One day, when Abibaal is selling eggs to an old lady at the alms house (for he now makes a killing from the *ova* like that wily

Tyrian can from anything he pleases) he manages to cure her of a horrible deformity.

He'd hawked eggs at the door of this hunched creature before. He told us (when we found him back on our doorstep in delayed shock) that previously he recoiled from the hag but this time his hands boiled with an urge to touch her. Suddenly he felt sure he could straighten that crooked spine with a single, hot finger that had been dipped in the golden rays we'd seen outlined around Jesus.

"A voice came out of me, deeper than my body. You should have heard me booming," Abi says in his usual high-pitched tone, "from the bottom of my soul. 'Be healed,' I beckoned her; 'your sins are forgiven, stand tall.'

He laid his hands upon that old lady, and she stood up straight as a stone column. Collapsed against a wonky Bethany doorpost, he stammered out this account, then she came to the temple steps where we were all sitting later and showed herself. All the locals knew she'd been bent double for decades and were amazed.

We go on cross-examining Abibaal long into the night: was it the voice or the finger that did it? Did he feel possessed by the Christ and completely out of control; or was it just like hearing the Muses murmuring ideas in his ears?

I guess those nine goddesses we saw, painted on our villa walls in ancient Rome, were really angels; though we never knew their background, blue and gold, was the kingdom of heaven in those days. Our new setting is far from Olympus.

The next day the Scribe comes with Pharisees, and they stand on the steps for ages, watching us closely and whispering between themselves; glyph-stitched robes rustling.

It isn't just the praying. I sing, sometimes; the hymns I first came out with in the quiet of our hearth, the friendly silence of our shrine. Because Emeshmoon caught those sighs of praise on paper, I can re-sing them. After the first few times, everyone else joins in with 'Be Still for the Lord of the Dance', or something.

There are little groups of local men in prayer shawls passing in and out of the synagogue with the Scribe and Pharisees. Some still don't seem to notice us, but those that do look puzzled or pleased or stare at us crossly as they hurry up the steps; and talk about us loudly as they walk back down. Then they stop with the polite distance and start to hustle.

It isn't just that we're women, and foreign, and were disabled, once. It's because we love Jesus. We are his harvest. The priestly fringes are quivering like a field of wheat with a storm coming.

It breaks over Bethany in the night and when we wake up in the morning, the darkness is dyed in. Bal's labourers don't come from the town to get their pay but when we go down they're waiting. Standing on the synagogue steps where we usually sit, a menacing band of men.

While it's just me and Publia, and our Phoenician friends, we do not go and take the steps. We wouldn't be so bold to provoke the children of Israel without Jesus there, especially when he doesn't seem to think they're worth fighting. But I don't suppose they'd actually touch us; we're as prickly as *murex* shells, and they say we smell.

Then the rest of our congregation turn up, from the other side of the market place. This group has been growing for a few weeks among the local *populus*. There are some who live and breathe the lord. Among them is the cheesemaker who lives next door to Lazarus, with her daughter, the cream to her curds, and the bent old lady Abibaal cured. They are oddities but there are lots of them; Bethany's eccentrics but they were born within its boundaries and by the right of blood and bones can sit on the synagogue steps.

The Romano-Phoenicians walk across the square to join them. Alethea and Tim are there, too. Although it's uncomfortable with, what seems like, half the Sanhedrin staring at us, we have our service as usual; the joyful greetings, the true stories, the rousing songs, the thoughtful prayers.

It's the praying they can't stand. When we all whisper the same words together, polished now and smooth as our purple stone, it rumbles like the law. Not as in the books their scribes read from. The living word thundering. We are the sign Jesus is coming back.

They don't talk to us, or touch us, or throw things at us that day but the mood is dangerous and we start to use signs ourselves, to be sure we know who is safe to talk to. Timid behaviour for those he termed 'fishers of men', but we trace the outline of fish in the sand, in the dust, in the ashes as a secret test of faith when we meet new people around the village.

And back at the shrine, I shape the amethyst stones of my necklace into the same outline of a fish. Those purple crystals don't seem to be guarding me from drunkenness, I think; putting my goblet down on the altar cloth with a clunk and clumsily fingering the gems into place. I hear a splash and start looking for the wine stain; it's dark by the courtyard wall with everybody else huddled round the fire. Then I spot not wine but blood on the floor.

I go to my room for my menstrual rags, musing as I do that Publia always has her period before me, but this moon she doesn't seem to have; and I can always tell when she's on.

As an ex-priestess to Venus, and high-class temple whore, I know how to do a pregnancy test. The woman must wee on seeds of barley or wheat. The wisdom says, if the barley grows, it's a boy, if the wheat germinates, it's a girl. If neither is sprouting, you're barren, baby!

Publia squats to pee over the seeds of barley and wheat. I watch for a moment, in prayerful stance, then wink at her and say; "You could sort the wheat from the chaff in that position."

She laughs and her stream of urine spurts and scatters my carefully placed seeds in this sacred act of piss prophesy.

We have to wait for the results, possibly a week, during which time a letter comes from our father. Addressed to Publia in a tone of distress, it makes an urgent enquiry. He has heard that Veronica's shop and Abibaal's premises are all boarded up. He's been told we've ceased trading and nobody in Tyre knows where we moved to.

This devastating news, I'm uplifted by; there's a great sense of freedom now my earthly father doesn't know where I am. As the letter goes on, it's the whereabouts of the money he is concerned with; the stock and profits. Then my feeling of freedom becomes one of emptiness.

After breakfast, we borrow pen and ink from Emeshmoon and try to reply.

Publia writes: 'Dearest *pater*. Hope this finds you well.' She stops and wrinkles her paper brow.

Once we would have asked the Muses what to write, our opening lines an invocation to the nine goddesses of creativity from Mount Helicon, where they rule the Hippocrene spring which poets drink from for inspiration. But Pubi is abstaining from the source and the words aren't flowing: 'Veronica has met a man.' She stops. 'So has Abibaal.' Stop. 'So have Balthazar and I.' She stops again.

“You try,” she says. “The smell of ink is making me feel sick.”

Don’t think we’ll need to wait for the wheat seed she peed on to grow, to know. She doesn’t like writing, neither of us do (there was another teacher), we both prefer numbers to letters; but ink has never made her feel sick before, so she probably is pregnant.

She gives the pen and the page to me. I take them with one hand, grab my cup with the other. I, too, was sick, last night, probably from excess wine. Felt bad this morning but better now I’ve breakfasted on just one cup. Perhaps if this goblet were actually made of amethyst I wouldn’t keep getting sloshed but it’s plain old pottery; and my last anti-drunk device, the necklace of purple worry beads, is lying on the shrine.

I pause for ages with pen in hand, trying to recall all nine of the muses. There’s Calliope, the first and foremost, mistress of epic poetry. Clio, who wields her pen more nimbly than most women hold a needle, spinner of history and the heroic. Erato for the sex, Terpsichore for the dancing. There is gay Thalia and gloomy Melpomene, for comedy and tragedy. There’s Euterpe for music and Polyhymnia for prayer. There is Urania for the supernatural, the stories from the stars.

I finish my drink and pour another one before I’ve written anything. It’s no good, I’ll have to do it as a song, shout it out to the whole house, then write it down quickly before we forget it. Emeshmoon has gone to take her goats’ milk to the cheesemaker or else she’d copy my lyrics as quick as I can spit them.

Telling Publia the plan, I knock back another *vinum*. She gives me a sour look.

“Can you only sing when you’re drinking?”

At least I can sing when I’m drinking. That’s the way I look at it.

‘*Carus* Father, this is a letter to tell you the truth, from the awful to the awesome, which is at the sober heart of our story. We are following the son of God; he has shown us the way.

‘Jesus first came into our lives in Tyre, though we’d heard of him already; three times we were told of his healing powers and his holy presence before we saw his face. At times he’s been followed by five thousand. At times, just fifty to a hundred. Currently, he’s travelling in Transjordania while we are busy rebuilding the business at Jerusalem.

‘Sadly, Veronica was robbed of all she was worth; don’t worry, she’s not badly hurt, but her vast earnings are gone. She was bravely defended by Abibaal, who boldly executed the slave that ripped her off: the same one who ruined Abi too.

‘Enough about money. We have witnessed the miracles done by Jesus; we have seen lepers restored. That disease is impossible to cure, as you know, but we have seen people with it touched by his hand and made whole again. He fixes twisted feet and weeping wombs. He knows everybody’s names and loves sinners better than saints.

‘A lot of the locals have a problem with him, the priests, the law men and the hired boys. The atmosphere is getting tense and doing business here is becoming more difficult. We’re all working on other ways of making money in case the purple dye vat explodes. V is developing a nice yellow pigment from pomegranate skin and others in our group are growing papyrus. Abibaal sells eggs, from a coop of chickens that are in love with him, and lay like fuck to please the silly clucker...’

I don’t write that last bit down, drawing the line at ‘papyrus’. Dad would never picture his smooth, rich Phoenician dye tycoon reaching into warm straw for shitty eggs...

Publia is sick in the cooking fire. I turn my pen to the accounts, instead, transcribing numbers from the tablets used by Farzan to reckon our gains. I write out the sums for our father, showing him how our fortune stands.

Trying to invoke my sister’s voice, in this letter, I say; ‘Don’t rely so heavily on your wealth though, Daddio. You can’t take it with you when you go. Heavenly currency is the lightness of your heart; ill-gotten gold will only weigh you down.’

Then I pause, and chew the end of her pen.

“Shall we tell him about the baby?” I say.

The wheat seed is growing. The old me would all-hail Ceres, goddess of the seasons and mother of the spring, for the gift of Publia’s pregnancy. We rejoice, as she blooms, in the prospect of seeing a pretty little Fabia Pictrix face. Balthazar is permanently beaming.

For the new me, every day the fruitful belly swells is one step closer to the feast of the unleavened bread, one day sooner to see

Jesus. God of the seasons and father of the spring, everybody is now waiting for him to return.

We found out from the lady who turns Emeshmoon's goat milk into cheese. She's teaching her how to make it, too. Golda can't believe that there are three grown women in Publia's house and none of them can churn. Does it count that we are high-powered businesswomen, and an ex-assistant priestess? Does it matter that we can make dye? This, at least, should impress her, my pomegranate yellow in particular. Sunshine from an urn of old skin, and it doesn't scream.

We all idolise her, but Emeshmoon actually goes to Golda's house a couple of times a week. It's across town and down a lane where the brick walls look like they're built of bread loaves, cemented with honey. The home of Martha and Mary is there, the sisters of Lazarus, the great friend of Jesus. She passes it every week on her way to the cheese lady. And she hears weekly updates on the famous family because Golda is their milk lady, too.

We already knew they hadn't gone on the road with the lord. We'd heard their plans; he would be at their place for the Passover. Now there is a new thing. Lazarus is ill. A gradual illness, the cheesemaker says, though other marketplace sources say sudden. He is stiff all over, they say, though Golda asserts he is floppy. He is boiling hot; or ice cold. Everybody agrees there is a red rash and he doesn't recognise his sisters. It seems he is getting worse.

Emeshmoon updates us one night as we sit round the fire. Some are listening more keenly than others; Balthazar and Farzan don't really care that a man is sick but Abibaal's concern is pricked for Jesus' sake.

Publia is starry-eyed about how 'this is the house He stayed in, the path He walked on, the gate He went through', *et cetera*. On our way here we did sometimes see sparks in his footsteps, scorch-marks where he'd touched wood, and I want to see what trace he's left in Bethany.

We could go and call on Golda: I think she'd like to know about the yellow, in exchange for teaching cheese skills. I decide to take the brilliant cloth from our shrine to show her... but I accidentally break the sacred egg, which symbolises Abibaal's healing power, as I put the things back on top of the table.

When he finds out, Abi only laughs and brings another one. Then he sees me folding the golden altar cloth and tucking it into my tunic and the second egg breaks in his fist.

"Where are you taking it?" he asks.

"Downtown. I want to get a look at Lazarus' house. And I hope to trade with the cheese lady."

Abibaal beats his chest with a hand full of broken egg.

"It's dangerous out there, now. Veronica, this is like you leaving Tyre in a purple tunic all over again. The bigger our group gets on the synagogue steps, the less safe we are at large in Bethany..."

It's a sunny morning in the middle of winter. The Feast of Dedication kept the neighbours up late last night and the street looks empty. I shrug Abi off and walk out; and yes, it is like leaving Tyre all over again. He cries a high-pitched warning, which fades into the distance with his dancing figure, as I disappear down to the village.

I pull my peacock feathers very low over my Roman brow. Despite the increased tension of my Phoenician brother-in-law, I don't feel any more threatened than I did before; scared of one man only. Hod.

I don't see him. He still does grudging business with Balthazar, so could be coming up our street but I get to the centre and through it and out the other side of Bethany without meeting him. Then I'm walking past Lazarus' house and looking through the trees at doorways and windows and roofs where Jesus lived and hopefully will again. I dawdle by, filling my eyes with the wintry garden. This is the lawn he trod upon. Silvery olive trees shiver like they're living souls, though I don't see anybody.

But when I come back again, after a good hour exchanging tips and tricks with their cheesemaker, one of the sisters is outside, talking to a passer-by in the street. With my shawl pulled low, I can't see their faces but I walk slowly and listen hard.

Their conversation goes something like this:

Lazarus' Sister. We don't understand why he doesn't come. Our message was sent over a week ago and soon it may be too late.

Neighbour. Perhaps he didn't receive it.

Lazarus' Sister. He did, for certain: the messenger returned to claim his pay. We have since sent another as our brother's condition worsened. But our friend will surely sense when Laz is dying.

Neighbour. How do you know?

Lazarus' Sister. Since I was small, I saw them playing together, this game: my brother would take an object from the house and hide it in the linen box in our mother's bedroom and Jesus always knew what was hidden. Soon as I was big enough to bring things to the secret chest, I helped them play. Put two items in; an egg and a pomegranate, for example. He always guessed right.

Lazarus' Other Sister. (Shouting from the sickroom window.) When you've finished with the public appearances there's some private business for us to clear up, in here.

They are called Mary and Martha but I don't know which one is which.

I walk past their house again the next day. It is silent and still; no doubt when Jesus turns up his entourage will fill it but today the place looks lonely as a grave. On the way back home afterwards, I pass the cemetery behind the synagogue. I've seen it several times from the outside but never been in; now, in sombre mood, I do go inside.

Wandering among the gravestones I remember the necropolis at Tyre. That place made death seem like an old city far away; glorious but faded. I remember the last time I was there, astride a slave in the darkness on a slab of white marble. When I think of somebody sexually now all that comes to mind is Abibaal; reminding me, as he brought the grain for my morning grind, that he is the voice of our group because he has the biggest *mentula.*

When I think of my slave now all that comes to mind is Abibaal, killing him or causing him to be killed, for crimes of hunger and other natural passions. When I think of the slave, I wonder how we even had slaves; how anyone thought that slavery was okay, now. What would Jesus say, who talks urgently of workers and wages in his scheme of heaven?

I'm lost in thought for a long while and find myself again nearly home. It looks welcoming in the dusk, the friendly glow from the hearth lighting up my family as I arrive. Tired but satisfied I go into my room to get ready for dinner. I tip dusty water into a bowl to wash, and wipe dry on one of Publia's lavender-scented towels. I untie my sandals, and loosen my girdle, and sit down on the bed with a sigh of relief. Then I go to unwind my peacock feather shawl from around my head, mindful of the fringe as I'm about to light a lamp, but it is not there.

With a wild toss of my hair I look behind me on the bed then stand to shake the creases of my tunic and folds of my cloak, and kneel to feel all over the floor in the darkness, but it is not there.

I have lost one of my last possessions, my final reminders of the days in Tyre when I was a rich businesswoman with style. How did I not feel it slip from my shoulders, its silk comfort from my throat, its feathered caress from my brow? How did I not realise that I could suddenly see; and that I was walking across Bethany with my head bare and my big nose on display. One of my last luxuries, leaving me unprotected, and Jesus is not here to see it.

My fingers used to love the feel of that shawl, its silky fringes and tactile stitches would sooth me in the night. I lie down on my bed, trying not to cry, winding the anonymous guest-room sheets round my fists.

I can hear the others talking outside my door, their voices echoing in the open courtyard. Publia is fired up; she has found a Roman bath in Bethany. Some ex-senator runs a nice little set-up just off the market square. Not pretty to look at, apparently; but warm, hot and cold in turns, and the perfect depth in every case. She says he doesn't allow mixed bathing: "He told me he'd die if he saw me naked," she boasts.

I wait till it's nearly dark before going out to the hearth. My face feels raw as I scuttle across to my sister and squat beside her, chin down so she can't see I've been crying. How far I've come, from Tyre where my hair was piled high and Rome where it was piled higher. I wouldn't recognise myself, even if the light was brighter.

We have been so close to heaven, on this trip, that the angels' breath has blown our hairstyles down. But their healing puff has not yet changed my mind, still feeling unbearably bare without my purple sheath and fixed on getting it back. That's why I didn't notice, I know now, when the peacock feather shawl fell from my head. This must be a sign.

When Publia passes me a plate of food, I hold onto her hand. In a whimper, trying to stop my lip wobbling, I tell her about my lost *stola*.

"Can you come with me to find it, first thing in the morning?" I say.

Before that, she turns night into day in the darkest recesses of linen chest and laundry basket, dripping an oil lamp into the deepest shadows of her bedroom, store cupboards and storage crates, to offer me a replacement: her old pomegranate shawl. The two were like sisters, embroidered by the same seamstress, scored from the same *Plumarius* in the same celebration of commercial success back in ancient Tyre.

Publia lost hers previously. She's told me already; it was ripped from her body during the dramatic parting from Bal on the road to salvation when she went wilfully one way, and he stubbornly the other. It was even then blood-stained and mud-splattered. He may have bundled it in one of the hairy ass packs or used it to wrap or strap his load. Transported back to Bethany, the pomegranate shawl must have remained, slowly rotting in the dye-dealers' den.

Publia finally finds it tonight. At the back of a dark shelf, in a dusty kitchen corner, wrapping a bundle of dried beans, Bal would have bought on his solo route home. She brings it to me, eyelashes like its greasy fringes. The sight of this nostalgic rag just makes her weep harder for the loss of mine.

Balthazar is not impressed. He prevents her leaving the building on a fingertip search at midnight and reluctantly lets her go out on foot with me at dawn. He attempts to come with us but it's so early he is fobbed off easily with promises that we will be fine and he should just crawl back to his nice, warm bed. I shivered in mine all night without the embroidered peacock tail, and squint in the cold light as we set off down the lane. I don't expect to see my shawl this close to home. I think it must have fallen in the graveyard. My eyes, a hundred-fold, watching everywhere for the sneak thieves, like the faithful Argus, were closed then.

Now they're lowered as we walk but Publia's are scanning our surroundings as if she'll see my curtain hanging at somebody's window or fringe hiding somebody's guilt. We don't see a single person, though, all the way through town and down the lane that leads to the cheesemaker's.

It is quiet at Lazarus' house but there are two men sitting on the pavement outside. Ragged, dirty, vacant-eyed; they are quiet too. I think they must be waiting for Jesus.

"Any news?" I ask them, hopefully.

They don't reply but I spoke in Latin. I try Greek. I think I know how to say it in Aramaic and try that too but they make no answer. I can say it in Phoenician but somehow don't think that would work either. If I thought the two random men knew when Jesus was coming, I'd sing it out of them. I could so make them speak with a song. They don't know when he's coming but they believe he is.

My peacock shawl is gone. It's not in the graveyard, snagged on stone or snatched by tree. It's not lying on the path, of course, it's not tied to a pillar of the temple.

Our congregation are starting to appear on the synagogue steps by the time we stop searching. We walk through the busy market place with Publia saying fiercely, "If I catch anybody wearing it, I'll strangle them with it." But she stops at a stall selling headscarves and buys me one, like all the others, in the colours of Judean soil; out of her own money as I haven't got any.

As we join the group, the cheese lady calls, "did you find it?" We'd called on her earlier, though I kept trying to tell my sister that I didn't leave it there for sure. I was pleased to see she'd started setting up a dyer's vat already; and now, when she sees my sad face and the drab new headscarf she says, "I'll make you a bright yellow one, hey?"

Also there today is the man with a bath, and Publia introduces me, Emeshmoon and Alethea, to the old *semicaper*. He invites us all for a dip, insisting that he will be a million miles away when we come.

Then I realise that, over his shoulder, Hod is standing, staring hard at us. Behind the old Roman guy who would politely die if he saw me naked, is the young Jew who would kill me, because he saw me naked.

It isn't just the nakedness. He sees the whole thing, Hod, and a load of local zealots. They stand outside the synagogue and watch our ceremony. They hear us asserting that Jesus will return to join in with it, too. They hear the words of the hymns and the stories and the prayers. They listen to the whole service, nearly; but it's the seeing they can't stand.

Just as we are coming to the climax of the lord's prayer, I don't know why, I open my eyes; and my gaze somehow meets Hod's. My mouth stops on the word 'heaven' but my eyes stay on him; I guess I'm agape, watching as he bends down to the earth. There are some stones where the temple step is crumbling, a couple of other men seem to be collecting the rubble, talking sharper over the rumble, stepping closer to us.

The air between flicks like the brisk shake of a linen cloth, like in my dream, with the handkerchief road lined with little rocks, flung in my face as I woke again.

Today I don't take a hit. I fling my scarf over my face and fly out the back of our friendly crowd, grabbing Publia's hand and only thinking about family. Bal's not there, or I'm sure he'd feature in this graceless retreat. Abibaal is hit twice, in the belly both times, no real harm done: he backs away quickly, too, and we start down the side street to home. But then we realise who is shouting from the steps now. Those voices are women's and children's.

We all stop at the same time. The three of us look at each other and see at once, we can't just save our own skins. A reluctant turn on a footfall and we're running back up towards cries we recognise, loved ones screaming. The loudest we hear is Alethea.

Covered with blood so we don't know whether it's hers or her son's, lying in her arms. She bends over a grief surely greater than the pains of childbirth. A mother's howl makes my blood run colder than the tears on Tim's cheeks must be; then he moves.

So, not dead, but gravely injured; the handsome young man covers his face with his hands. Hit by a stone flung with fury, his eye is pierced. Marble white, the eyeball cracks. Oozing purple and yellow between his fingers, Timotheus is blinded.

He who threw the stone is nowhere to be seen. Our attackers have disappeared inside the temple already, to sacrifice turtledoves and be forgiven for their sins.

CHAPTER THIRTEEN

The chickens are loose in Bethany. Squawking from the rooftops, clucking on the street corners, scratching for news in the square. The hens in Abibaal's coop go unfed and nobody collects any eggs.

After a day, it becomes clear that Tim's eye is lost forever; he will be white-blind. Alethea comes to tell us, running down the back garden, hidden under her darkest cloak, no more sunshine yellow.

She says that she is leaving Jesus. She will no longer be his follower or gather to praise him or openly declare her love.

"I can't risk my children's lives for this," she sobs, "for there is no happiness greater than theirs and no peace as sweet."

Pubi, Emesh and I hug her, sobbing too. There is some consolation; Tim can still see out of the other eye. But his beauty will be gone; he's been scarred by hate. None of us can ever say that Hod's stone did this damage but it is his face we'll see, layered in a snarl over the boy's smile.

When Alethea has gone home, we see Bal standing at the shrine, staring angrily at the place he usually prays.

"What are you looking for?" Publia asks him.

"The toenail," he shouts. "Her fucking holy toenail. I cannot believe she has caved in. That woman witnessed miracles, she has seen the honest truth at Jesus' hands, yet at the first sign of trouble she chickens out."

"I think the toenail was lost when I wiped the broken egg off," I say helpfully.

"No, it's still there." Publia walks over to the shrine, bends down, looks and points. Balthazar is staring at her backside. "Nothing has changed," she adds, then stands up and turns around, putting her baby bump between them. "If our child was threatened, we'd do the same thing."

"It won't come to that," he soothes.

"I would die to save Jesus," my sister kisses her husband and walks away. She comes to where I'm kneeling by the fire and sits down; not looking at me, doesn't even know I'm here. She contemplates the flames, the future, her hand on her belly. "But I would kill to save my child."

Everybody is looking at her. Emeshmoon has tears in her eyes.

"I agree that Jesus is God," Publia whispers. "I agree that God has given us this baby. But if I had to sacrifice a hair on its head, then we might have a little disagreement."

"It won't come to that," Balthazar says again.

"They are stoning kids in Bethany," she replies. "What will they do in Jerusalem?"

After two days, Abibaal ventures down the street, where he meets our ex-business partner, leading his flashy ass. Abi keeps his head down and tries to walk straight past but Hod says:

"Why don't you heal the boy, if you're so good."

Abi tells us what happens next with an apologetic shrug:

"I was bad. I had my knife on me, you know, the blade I scored from Cana. And when the purple mist cleared from my eyes, I saw that nice new knife was plunged into the right eyeball of my foe."

An eye for an eye, as I think Hod would say. But I hear Abibaal crying through the mud wall between our bedrooms, that night, his sobs lower than his usual high-pitched tones. He sounds more manly when he's weeping. Should I upset him more often? But maybe I find causing him pain too easy, and too addictive. Or maybe he's still the only man who can resist my sting. It's not all 'I, I, I' tonight, though. His tears, though horrible to hear, are welling from a new and wonderful spring; true remorse, deep regret, that just make me like the sissy better yet.

After three days, some of us creep out, but only to keep our date with the ancient Roman baths we've discovered in a backstreet not far from here. There is green algae all over the tiles of the *tepidarium* and the *caldarium* is in complete darkness but the *frigidarium* is fine. We are rejuvenated as we dry off and wrap our damp hair in the homespun headscarves of Judaea.

Our host is not a million miles away. In fact, we rather suspect him of having peep-holes in the walls but he's waiting in full view as we emerge from his mildewed changing rooms, squawking and clucking in a proper Roman panic.

"I have news, terrible to tell," he announces. "Lazarus is dead. Jesus hasn't come and Lazarus is dead. Jesus is too late."

The chickens are quiet in Bethany. The whole village seems to draw a disappointed sigh and is still. Life goes on but silently. Market is open but trade is hushed. We rush quickly home from shopping. Most of our time is spent, now, huddled by the hearth, cold and sad.

"Shall we even say it?" Publia asks, eventually.

It's the seventh hour, when we sat on the synagogue steps, a while ago, praying. That group is not together any more. Balthazar and Farzan have gone to the city, working hard to build up a new clientele. Abibaal is, I believe, stretched out snoozing in the hen coop. Emeshmoon is in her own room; who knows what she's doing. It is soundless.

The whole village seems to hold its breath. There'd be goats bleating in the back yard, ordinarily; a dog barking next door. In the hush, we're finding it hard to speak. But if we don't, now it's just two of us, the things we said when there were two thousand mean nothing.

"Our father," I whisper.

"Our father," Publia joins in. Then we pause. Both of us are thinking of *pater*. This never used to be a problem. In that big group our father was everyone's not just ours.

"Who art in heaven, hallowed be thy name." I can speak easier with my eyes closed. It's still not dark inside me, though the day is gloomy; the fire glows behind my eyelids, too. He has given us bread, daily, since I ran out of cash; but also the temptation of freely-poured wine. So I keep them shut tight till we whisper the Amen. I'm listening.

There is a slight buzz in Bethany; I'm sure that, where there was silence before, there is a distant murmuring, a distinct rumbling. Publia hears it too. We're so convinced, we get up and go out into the street, squinting down the lane towards the village square, as if we could see the muffled sound from here.

And then he appears, running up the street towards us, panting and calling our names. Long flowing hair, fine but firm features, a toga still slipped off one shoulder even in midwinter. Our actor friend is declaiming our names loudly as he comes;

"Publia! Veronica! Fabia Pictrix!"

"Marcus Manlius!" We run to him.

"Why didn't you tell us you were going!" Pubi grasps fistfuls of his tunic and hauls herself up to the neckline. "Where have you been? How are Naomi's feet?"

"Never mind that." I'm clinging on at the back. "What about Jesus? Is he here too? Is he in Bethany?"

Nerva nods and smiles, his full beam fit for a giant auditorium, rather than a back street off the broadway. His olive skin turns pink from neck to Roman nose; and that flush of joy touches our bosoms, too (even though he wouldn't ever). Pubi and I start shouting for Emeshmoon and Abibaal to come. Her face appears at the front door.

"He's back," we shout. "Jesus has come!"

We all seem to run in a circle, till Publia cries, "Alethea needs to see this." Then she hitches up her tunic and hurries off, round the side of the house and up the hill behind it.

"Hang on," calls Emesh, "I'll go instead." Publia is starting to look pregnant now and any good friend would step in at this point. They swap places by the back door and we take Marcus inside for a drink of water. Abibaal hurriedly feeds his chickens. Then we wind scarves firmly around heads, plain stripes now, no more peacock feathers.

Emeshmoon reappears without Alethea.

"She wouldn't come," the bookmaker puffs.

"I bet I could have made her." Publia just doesn't care who she upsets.

We set off the way Marcus came, hearing a new shout behind us now. Tassos, the super-slick olive oil tycoon, is chasing us down the lane. He's coming, instead of Alethea, or else Timothy's tragedy happened in vain. He must see this vision that caused his son's blindness.

His cloak is bright yellow, his wife's brilliant dye; Publia and I each hold out a hand to him, and so we march onward.

There is a huge crowd at the cemetery. Its old walls can't be seen, or the gate or any of the graves; the avenue between serried ranks of headstones is blocked. When I walked here, a week ago, it was the loneliest place in the world. Now people are stacked deep as the dead in these stone rows, and as quiet too. Breath is held and even heartbeats seem hushed, as they stare at something we can't see, near some big family tombs on the far side.

Suddenly a gasp goes up, all together, a great in-breath is heard. Then, after a short pause, come the screams. Not the same screams as the temple steps in a stoning; more like a groaning.

They start backing away, people stream past us, stumbling over their feet and ours. The crowd thins out considerably but doesn't disperse completely; we still don't get a good look at what they're running from. But now I can see something I recognise, something reassuring, rising above the chaos like a cloud of peace.

"It's Kaspar!" I call to Publia, pointing at the tall white turban. "I'm going to talk to him..." I struggle to where he is standing with his back to me. Moving between the gravestones like this, I think, must be like being dead; so slow and awkward and unseen. I have to tap the astrologer on the shoulder three times before he feels my touch and turns to face me. Then he blinks and smiles. I resist the urge to hug him; it's been a long time since we stood so close.

"What just happened?" I ask.

He only nods serenely.

"What?" I say. "Why is everybody running away?"

"Lazarus lives. He walks," says Kaspar. "He breathes."

"No," I'm shaking my head. "Lazarus is dead."

"He lives," the wise man insists.

"He died four days ago."

Now Kaspar hugs me and says, "He just came out of the tomb."

In a corner of the graveyard, the really resting peacefully place, there are houses for the finest families' deceased. It keeps up with the pillared sepulchres of Tyre, this area of the Jewish cemetery. The crowd is still packed, probably five deep, there, and I can't see what's buried in the middle.

On the outskirts, I see big burly Tassos trying to squeeze through, with Abibaal behind him, belly after brawn. I see Publia and Emeshmoon holding up Golda who has rent her rennet-coloured garments. She has seen her neighbour, four days dead, rise again and unwind the shrouds of the tomb. She is telling my sister in a hysterical shriek. I want to go and hear it too.

Kissing Kaspar on his crinkled star-map cheek, I slip through the crowd to catch the cheesemaker's story.

"... And he was weeping. He looked at Mary and Martha, and all the family and friends of Lazarus who were crying. That's what did it. Jesus wept; and I heard one of his men, close beside him, say to another that they'd never seen him weep before."

"When you love everyone but still have a best friend..." Pubi starts to say, but Golda interrupts:

"I saw him walk."

"Did you see his face?" Emesh; always the gruesome details. "Did you see his eyes?"

Golda whispers, "I heard what he said." She doesn't tell us now, though; she is swooning. Her daughter comes through the crowd behind her, whey-faced too, and helps her stagger off home. They will have to go past Lazarus' house to get there; so best to be ahead of the furore that will follow shortly. The house must be tomb-still for now.

We set off for home in the opposite direction. The crowd is too tightly packed around the risen local to let a loose band of Romans, Greeks and Phoenicians through. The girls want to be back when their husbands return from business, anyway, so we slip away from the miracle scene.

"It's a shame we didn't actually see it," says Publia.

"Don't you remember," I reply. "That first night at the necropolis, they told us he'd raised a twelve-year old girl from the dead. If we believed once we can believe forever and we don't even need to see it to know that it's true."

Emeshmoon brews a herbal tea and we sit hugging our cups by the fire, hoping Bal and Farzan will be back from Jerusalem soon. There's a disturbance at the door; we jump up eagerly but it's not them, it's Nathaniel and Marcus, who've hurried after us from the graveyard.

"Is it true?" Publia demands, before she even pours them a cuppa. "Is Lazarus alive?"

They say he's gone home with his sisters, that the crowds are breaking up but lots of followers need beds.

"I don't know how anyone will be able to lie down tonight, who saw a four-day old corpse come out of its tomb this afternoon," I murmur.

Marcus grins cheerfully. "Can I sleep here?" he asks.

We're happy to have him and, when Nathaniel wonders if we could squeeze a couple more in, Publia says, of course.

I don't want to share my bedroom with anyone. It's big enough for a family but I love my own space. Dark and quiet, with a single lamp flickering and a vase of wild flowers or foliage, this winter season; just enough nature to know that it's all under control. I like when there's nobody to look at my big nose or big bum or hear the breath coming out of my big lungs, at bedtime; I don't mind so much during the day.

But since I've only had one tunic, one cloak, no purple shawl, it's felt so naked. Only one layer of protection. What if I suddenly rip in half. It still only takes one person wanting to pop in and check my figures to make me fear the threat of five, again, trying to enter my premises.

Marcus stays, and Nathaniel leaves, saying he may bring some people back later, then Balthazar and Farzan arrive, and are filled in until their eyes pop out. They're both agog and I think Bal is physically sick as their wives, and mistresses of their sane minds, tell them what happened in Bethany today.

But Publia can't persuade Bal to believe the impossible.

"He couldn't have been really dead. Must have been sleeping deeply. Maybe it was just a death-like pallor, perhaps it was painted on, like in a play," Balthazar keeps insisting. "He could have been pretending."

Abi is the one who eventually makes his brother see sense, grabbing him by the shoulder to hiss: "we've seen him rebuild an entire body, with all the bits and pieces he's fixed in our time, from blind eyes to backward feet. So starting a simple heartbeat must be easy."

We all really want to see Jesus. After a dinner of my hastily cooked *primavera*, we'd go out and try to find him; but it's dark and he's, no doubt, indoors now having walked his dead friend Lazarus home.

As Abibaal is washing the dirty cooking pots, and I'm standing them to dry, Nathaniel turns up again with a flaming torch held aloft, lighting his gentle face as he comes in from the night street. Huddled behind their angelic guide are Aunt Naomi and two old ladies who look just like her. Small, dressed in black and shaped like pepper pots; we danced with them in Jericho.

One is one of the many Marys. The other is called Salome. We walked with them from Capernaum but they have come further. Their sons are among the apostles, so their journey goes all the way.

They're tired, now, but their eyes light up when they see us waiting at the hearth of our respectable establishment. The place looks so much better than it did when Publia and I got here. Our cookware is gleaming in the embers, with brimful jugs of water and wine standing on the well-swept hearthstone. Around the edges of this hub, large cushions and small stools sit companionably side-by-side, with blankets folded neatly, for the cool of the evening.

It's a warm welcome for the mothers; hugs and kisses all round with the happy revelation of Pubi's pregnancy. The others didn't know about her previous issues, so Naomi fills them in, the full details of blood flow and ebb, as Mary and Salome settle themselves down by the fire.

Then we serve them a feast of leftovers and standbys that makes us realise, again, how far we have come since we settled here. Abibaal's eggs, Emeshmoon's goats cheese, good bread and passable veg, pickled at the tail end of the season, soon as we knew we were staying. I made a pomegranate seed preserve, with the bits I didn't use for the dying process; a step up from the first meal we were served by Balthazar, a bachelor's soup in a cup, tapped from the industrial dyer's vat in his kitchen.

Aunt Naomi wipes the juices from her shining plate with a crust of bread.

"So, you have a lovely home. Very well appointed. Beautifully clean," she speaks between bites. "But where's your loom?"

"Oh, I haven't got one," says Publia. "We don't really do much weaving."

"All women must weave," she insists, "or else they'd be naked."

"We buy the fabric ready-made," my sister replies.

Time to distract Naomi, I think: "You must see our new colour," I say, "it's better by daylight, but still looks brilliant in candle flame. Our business is dyeing, you see," I explain to Mary and Salome, "and we've brought it back to life. Now, what to show you?"

First I make Emeshmoon model a tunic I turned yellow for her recently. Then I take them across to the shrine. I ask Abibaal to hold a flaming torch up so they can see.

Our so-called 'altar cloth' was my trial run for pomegranate yellow but, to appreciate this, the ladies have to get past the burnt sage, the stones and the egg on our shrine to Christ. We don't point out the toe-nail.

They all like the amethysts, of course, and Aunt Naomi tells her sisters, with a tear glistening, how it was my generous gift of a matching earring that persuaded her to leave Capernaum. Encouraged by this, I show her how the unclasped necklace is arranged in the shape of a fish, tracing it with my finger. They are all delighted with this symbolism though they haven't yet used the sign to tell who is friend or foe on the dusty Judean roads.

Then I explain how the fish's eye is a stone Jesus plucked out of the water, when he was teaching us on the bank of the river Jordan. They were there too that day. Then Publia says about the stone she picked up, the one his foot must have touched, as he cured Alethea at Bethesda Baths.

So they want to know about the egg, and Abibaal reveals his miraculous healing power. Balthazar lights the incense, I smudge the smoke with the peacock feather, and Emeshmoon unrolls the holy scroll to show wisps of words in ash black ink.

This is far out of the comfort zone of Salome and the other Mary, the *piperatoria*. The way we worship is strictly Roman, or purely Phoenician for the boys; but they are the mothers of men whose master turned the tables of their religion over, therefore some gentile shrine can hardly upset them.

They cheerfully go and plonk themselves back down on the cushions again, by the fire. And then they start to sing. I have heard them singing before, when we were on the road; I think they called them songs of David. I think they said Jesus was descended from him. They're in Hebrew and virtually sung through the nostrils, so I've never understood what they're about before. But now, Farzan says the words; a fourth voice in the chorus, none of the melody, all of the meaning:

"Oh lord, you have searched me and know me! You know when I sit down and rise up. You perceive my thoughts from afar."

He intones it in his native language and the ladies nod appreciatively, though they don't know if he's got it right. They speak Aramaic mostly, with Hebrew for the spiritual life and Greek for shopping. Aunt Naomi speaks pretty good Latin, considering she learnt it looking at Centurions' legs.

But conversation with Mary and Salome had been a bit stilted, so it's great that they can sing. Just the sound of their harping soothes me, and now the words translated by Farzan, thrill, too:

"For you formed my inmost parts, you knitted me together in my mother's womb. I praise you, for I am fearfully and wonderfully made...My frame was not hidden from you when I was being made in secret, intricately woven in the depths of the earth."

No wonder they have a thing about looms, I smile to myself, if God is a weaver. Next thing, though, he is a writer as they go on:

"Your eyes saw my unformed substance. All the days ordained for me were written in your book before one of them came to be." [12]

Emeshmoon gleefully gets pen and paper at this point. I get pissed. She copies down Farzan's version of the psalm, which is good because otherwise I wouldn't remember it in the morning.

When people eventually start yawning, Publia appears with an armful of spare blankets. The perfect hostess but her next words fill me with horror.

"So," she says, "how about the ladies go in with Veronica, the single girls' room? And Marcus with Abibaal; the single men? All happy to share like that?"

Marcus isn't; I distantly hear him exclaiming that he'd rather sleep on the roof.

"Nothing personal," he purrs at Abi, "but I prefer the fresh air."

"It's cold," says Publia.

"I like it that way," Marcus insists. "And it would be good to have someone on guard; it's getting dangerous out there."

Abibaal is still holding the torch in one hand and a pile of blankets in the other. He must be looking at me because nobody else notices, specially not my sister; rooming with three old ladies is the most shocking prospect I could face. I don't like sharing my private space; for the old fear of being tricked when I'm sleepy, or robbed or raped. I don't want to lose my peaceful place, but I've been homeless before, like Naomi, Mary and Salome are tonight, and there's no way I can refuse to share my bedroom.

I try to smile but it's like tearing a sheet. My face is ripping linen. The women stand up, slowly; silhouetted against the dead fire as mountains between me and my silent sleep.

Then Abibaal speaks:

"You're right, Marcus, the roof is the best place for men like us to lay our heads, on constant watch through the long night, braced by the open air. I'll join you up there and our guests can move into my room. It's super-Spartan for them; Veronica has so much stuff. Come on!"

He grabs all the cushions from round the fire and carries them quickly into his *cubiculum*. We hear him sweeping and beating for a few moments, humming the song that the ladies were just singing.

They are now discussing the lavatorial arrangements with Emeshmoon, who has offered to show them the facilities in the dark. I still sit by the cool fire, my white cheeks flushed red now, thinking that Abibaal has saved me. He's fat and smelly and has a silly voice but he's been a hero tonight.

CHAPTER FOURTEEN

Abibaal acts like a clown in the small hours of the morning. Everybody is woken up by the sound of that *fossor* falling off the roof. Whether we lie in solitary confines, like me, or in the married quarters, or the old ladies' dormitory, the shout penetrates our bedroom walls.

The soft Phoenician bounces in the courtyard and comes to rest in the chicken coop. In the morning it transpires he was kicked out by Marcus for snoring.

This day, my main aim is to find out what Lazarus said when he came back to life in the graveyard. I feel it could make a good song. I know that Golda heard it, so I decide to try her first, plus we can get goat's cheese. And I want her to meet Naomi, who is pleased to come along with the promise of seeing a great loom and a new domestic dyeing plant in Zion.

We walk through Bethany where the crowds thronged yesterday. It's strange to see the empty graveyard; I go past slowly, trying to decide if it looks any different. There are lots of broken branches, laurel and olive, strewn about, some woven through the bars of the gate, some trodden in the muddy walkway. A torn cloak is hanging from the gatepost. Nobody wants to go inside. Three different people had nightmares in our house last night, I counted the shouts, about the walking dead.

Three of us have come this morning, Naomi, Emeshmoon and I, to do cheese and dye business with somebody who is traumatised. Golda knew Lazarus well, saw him grow up, mourned his loss. Then she watched him walk out of his tomb, when he'd lain for four days, with the bandages still on. Apparently he unwound them with hands that barely worked.

We sit in silence for a while beside her unstrung loom, thinking about this. Then I force myself to ask her: what did he say?

Slowly, slowly, she replies; "That? That wasn't so bad. Lazarus said he'd been brought back by an angel, said he could still see it standing beside Jesus. They had been friends from boyhood and though he loved him like a brother, and treated him like a master, Laz'd never called him lord, like Mary and Martha. But now, Lazarus told us, he'd seen heaven and knew that Jesus was king."

"Alleluia," sighs Naomi.

Emeshmoon is shaking her head. She can't get past the part where Laz came out of the tomb. "I saw a man who'd been dead for three days, once," she says in dismay. "He could not have walked or talked if lightning struck his crown."

"Did he say what heaven was like?" I ask Golda.

Now she shakes her head, too. But the cheesemaker's daughter is standing at her shoulder, Zissel, by name; and she is the double cream. Only a year or two younger than us; she is way prettier than Emesh and me, and even pregnant Publia looks overblown beside this bud.

She was close to the grave mouth, too, but doesn't seem to be breathed on like her mother by this, the darkest of all the miracles we've seen. Surely the lord preaches from inside the tomb if that's where to find heaven.

"I heard his answers to all the men's questions," Zissel says. "*Ima* had gone, but I lingered. He said there was a long, dark tunnel and his long dead parents were waiting in the light at the end of it. They spoke to him without using words and explained many incredible things that he couldn't remember now. The only knowledge he retained was this: he had come back to help Jesus. He had a new point, a purpose in this awful world."

"He said all that?" Emeshmoon is feeling her jaw, gingerly as if she's been dead for four days, now. Whoever the stiff she saw was, they weren't pretty, and probably not in one piece.

"He was still talking," this girl laughs grimly, "when I went after my mother. And singing; he'd heard music in heaven and was trying in vain to hum the tune." She makes us giggle, now, with her impression of the divine song but I do recall the melody later.

The cheese deal goes smoothly and we all leave Golda's small house at the end of Lazarus' lane together, happy and excited. It's the seventh hour and Jesus will be out of the synagogue; surely he will gather his flock on the steps to hear him speak, as he did before in Bethany.

There are a lot of people standing outside Lazarus' house. I can see those two crazy guys that were here before, and a lot more lunatic-looking tourists, as well as some perfectly sane ones. Two Roman centurions are at the gate, leaning awkwardly, not certain whether they're posted there to intimidate or protect. Aunt Naomi gets a good look at their legs as we go past.

There's a crowd outside the cemetery too, now; loads more people than actually live in Bethany. Half of Jerusalem has come sightseeing, it seems. There's the sound of a bustling marketplace in the village graveyard.

And when we get to the steps, well, we don't know when we've got to the steps because we can't see them. It reminds me of the very first time we walked into a crowd around Jesus, at the temple to Melqart at Tyre, nearly half a year ago. The masses on the forecourt seemed to rise into the air between the columns, obscuring every glimpse of the stone stairs, so their ascent looked magical.

As we cross the square, a group of local women wrapped in homespun stripes, we see the rest of our family coming the other way. Publia is causing a stir with her head uncovered and a Phoenician man at every hand. They flank her, Bal, Abi and Farzan looking their most exotic. And she has a train of followers: Marcus Manlius Nerva is bare-shouldered behind her, with Mary and Salome on either arm.

We Fabia Pictrix are not sisters of the Roman Empire for nothing, though. Breaking formation, barking a swift litany of orders at the boys, Pubi and I pair up and press through the ranks of Jesus' army till we can actually see his face. Our men meet with more resistance, foreign and somewhat effeminate-looking; big enough to just barge through anyway.

But Publia and I get to the heart of the crowd first. I go in front of her, hands held behind me, helping to protect her bump in the bustling. I crouch low and listen for the stillest point, the quietest place in this seething mass which must be at its core. Creeping between bodies which all seem to grow in the same direction, like bushes toward the sun, we soon find the one they are definitely calling the Messiah, now. We hear his voice:

"The Scribes and the Pharisees: all their works they do to be seen by men. They make their phylacteries broad and enlarge the borders of their garments. They love the best places at the feasts, the best seats at the synagogue, greetings in the marketplaces, and to be called by men 'Rabbi, Rabbi!'

"But you, do not call anyone on earth your father; for One is your Father, He who is in heaven. And do not be called teachers; for One is your Teacher, the Christ. But he who is greatest among you shall be your servant." [13]

By the end of this speech, Publia and I have got where we can see his lips moving. I can view the full beard, fine cheekbones. There's a muscle twitching in his neck, and a smear of blood on his brow. Or it could be mud, darkly encrusted.

Because I picture his face every night at bedtime, each morning as I rise, in most pools and puddles, in smoke, and hillsides, and every time I see a shepherd with sheep; because I prayed when I couldn't see him, the face doesn't seem quite real now. It glows. Like the first time we saw him, in the city of the dead, beside the fire; but I see now the fire's inside him.

Publia gets that feeling, too, and Emeshmoon who has squeezed through with us. On the edges of the crowd, fights are beginning to break out, though. I fear that one was kicked off by the away team from Tyre. It is so dangerous round here now both sides have lost an eye.

When the jostling gets so bad we lose sight of Jesus, us civilised ladies back out of the picture. We know where he's staying and promise ourselves, as we slip home for a *somnus*, that we'll find him again later.

At the tenth hour, we wander back down to the little town. The square is empty now, the synagogue steps deserted but for two figures; and one of them is Abibaal. Obvious a mile off, he's still standing there, gesticulating like he used to do when he gave the sermons before Jesus came back. Low punches and slashes, Abi's body language is much deeper than his voice.

One person is left listening. I recognise her, too; it's Zissel the cheesemaker's daughter. She's sitting three steps up from him, so they are almost face to face. Have to hand it to him, she's good-looking. Publia shouts across the courtyard at them but I might never speak to him again.

We go down Lazarus' lane. There is a big crowd outside the house. This time, though, there are two fishermen guarding the gates, and they recognise us and let us through. The son of Salome; it's good that a little old lady can create such a burly young man. Small and weak becomes big and strong: this is life the way Jesus lives it.

They actually let us see him. The Fabia Pictrix march in, but most of the disciples know Aunt Naomi which eases our passage greatly. We're shown through a kitchen where Mary or Martha sits, trying to smile. The place is full of men.

I don't think Jesus will recognise me when he sees me without my peacock feather shawl. Unless I can sing in front of him, all my colour comes from dye. But then, I'm shakily kneeling before him; a brown eyed, brown haired girl in a brown headscarf.

I meet his eyes and they sparkle at me; pomegranate juice that's been fermenting since the start of this story. Publia later says he does the same thing to her, holding her look through a pink fizz. Luckily, we don't see Lazarus; sorry, but his gaze would be wormwood.

He is in the next room, lying down, apparently sleeping; the other sister is standing guard and appears regularly in the doorway.

"How fares he?" one big man or another asks her.

"Still sleeping," she says.

"And breathing?"

She nods, her eyes on Jesus. (Afterwards, at home, our Mary says that's their Mary.)

The master is talking to Nathaniel. I listen, barely breathing myself. His voice does not have the beauty of human song; it surpasses that faulty instrument. The pure note of a pipe, blown by the breath of God; Jesus' laughter is a flute.

I know what I hear them say but can't repeat it, like I know there's an angel in the air between them but can't see it. Afterwards, at home, our Emeshmoon says that she wrote it all down, like this:

"Master, what is the truth?" asked Nathaniel.

And Jesus said, "Truth is the only thing that changes not. In the world there are two things; one is truth and one is falsehood; truth is that which always is and falsehood is that which sometimes seems to be."

"Then, master," said Nathaniel, "which is man?"

"Man is the truth made flesh, so lies are conjoined with him. But a wise man can divine the true picture." [14]

Laz's living room is turning into a temple. The crowd is bigger as we leave, so getting out is harder than going in. The old ladies come home with us again and we celebrate something, we're not sure what; working together on a special dinner, with almonds and figs baked in egg-enriched bread, and a honeyed wine drunk warm at sundown.

The men go round lighting all the lamps and the women sing. At least, Naomi, Mary and Salome give another of their ancient psalms; but when Publia asks me to do a new song, I have to remain silent, looking at Emesh who looks guiltily back at me.

Somehow, I haven't been able to sing one since she wrote down my final shrine song. Perhaps she stole the words forever: all elicited by her illicit literary act. Or perhaps they were perfect, never to have sequels. We haven't quite worked it out between ourselves, yet.

The winter stars are reflecting in Balthazar's best silver wine cups, as the company drink their final cheers of the evening. Wrapped in Publia's lavender-flecked blankets, Aunt Naomi and the mothers make their way into Abibaal's bedroom for a second night.

"Yes, darlings, you have a lovely home," Naomi calls as she goes. "Shame you've got to leave it!"

They all speak together, roughly, Bal and Abi and Pubi: "What? What do you mean?" They go after her. "Why are we leaving?"

It's obvious to her, who has been on the road since she left her house in Capernaum, with no sign of returning.

"Well, the lord's not going to sit at Laz's forever, is he?" says Naomi. "We'll be off again in a day or two, and this time you all need to come. No point being a follower of Jesus if you don't follow him."

Stunned, the rest of us go to bed, too. Publia and Balthazar, Emeshmoon and Farzan, into their double rooms; me in my beloved single. It strikes me, as I walk through the doorway (no wood, just a hole in the wall) that this is the best *cubiculum* I've ever had. When I was a baby, my bedroom walls were painted with pictures: Venus and Cupid, Pegasus and the Muses. Then Dad had them painted over with Apollo and Daphne turning into a laurel tree as I grew up.

Those gods were on the surface, I slept with them superficially; here, in a mud house outside Jerusalem, I've been sleeping more deeply and soundly in the face of God, who I now know in person.

Suddenly, the house feels like a shell; it is certain we will leave it. And nothing will be lost but convenience, nothing left behind but routine. Comfort will come with us, though not in bags on our backs; I'm more slug than snail now.

So, I turn back at the door of my room, trying to say something nice to Abibaal, who is preparing to bed down with the chickens again. Marcus has made it very clear that the roof belongs to him; Nerva needs his space, no matter that it doesn't have any walls or a ceiling. I don't want to be that cagey, so I say: "If you need to, you know, change, or something, you can use my room. But not when I am in it, okay?"

"Thank you, sister," he says.

I hold back a shudder, swivel on my heel, and disappear inside my bedroom. There, I hide between the sheets, imprinting my darkest thoughts on the night, where nobody can see.

In the morning, the sun pokes a cold finger through the mud-punched window, and I gather my laundry with a view to packing up and moving on.

Naomi says at breakfast that the lord's travel plans will be revealed at the well, when we collect the morning water, and we finish our chores early so we can be the first to arrive there. I'm ready before the others. Abi is fussing over his chickens; Publia is looking wistfully at the row of *kaneh bosm* in terracotta pots on her patio, immature now; she'll probably miss the flowering like she did the last lot. [15]

We hurry to the well, the one Nathaniel took us to, on the low slopes of Olivet. It was a quiet, reflective place when we went there before; but nowhere is like that in Bethany any more. We hear the buzz before we see it, a crowd round the source of the spring, sitting on the mountainside to listen to Jesus.

We run to join this group before he starts to speak. As we sit, in a row near the back, he stands by the well-side to address us. There must be about *LXX* people there. Many of them, I've seen with him since Capernaum; many were in Tyre, too; but many are new, joining him in Jericho, signing up in Samaria, bonding in Bethany. In fact, it's bad timing but I feel a song starting for the first time in ages, as I sit in that gathering.

I have to keep my mouth shut and sing with the heart only, as Jesus is speaking: but, to my joy, he does the only thing worth not singing for. He tells us a story.

"There was a farmer who had just one field, and the soil was poor, dry and rocky. He worked hard to make anything grow, toiling all day in the sun to pick out the stones and pull out the weeds; and still the crops struggled and failed.

"Then, one day, a miner was passing by, a man who had spent much time in the East, digging the earth's seam for gold and gemstones. Purple, red and green, he'd unburied gleaming beauty from deep below the crust; and he knew that such riches were hidden in this place, too.

"Leaning on the fence, he tried to persuade the farmer to dig deeper but, hot and tired, the man still ploughed the surface, desperate to provide a meal for his family. Eventually, the miner's stories of coloured stones worth hundreds of silver pieces inspired the farmer and, just for one hour, he dug down. Deep under the rocky field he'd laboured to cultivate; hard, hard digging into the rock itself.

"And then he found the treasure. Riches beyond his wildest imaginings, once he went below the stony surface of his land." [16]

I think Jesus just used me as an analogy. He said my signature stones, amethysts, were like the glory of heaven; the grace of the holy spirit in the shape of purple gems, gleaming secretly in rocky ground.

As we walk home, I whisper to Emeshmoon that I nearly spat the words of a song, sitting on that hillside, and would have belted out a whopping number if our master hadn't been talking already. She is glad to hear it but I think she's gone off singing like she went off shouting.

Yes, Emesh has got quieter and quieter lately, as if she isn't quite here. And then I notice that Abibaal isn't with us at all. Balthazar and Publia are walking in front with Farzan, Marcus and the old ladies behind, but there's no sign of our big-bellied brother-in-law. He must have stayed at home this morning.

I've forgotten all about him, again, by the time we get back to the house. We called in at Alethea's on the way past; since her son was blinded, she won't be seen out with us, but she wants to hear where we've been. She knows Lazarus was raised from the dead and we keep telling her to take Tim there, but she fears worse reprisals: "the whole thing will end in tears," she tells us, crying already.

We come back down through the garden, where Emesh stays to deal with her goats, and the men go into the outbuilding to do a bit of business. Publia follows them; she's still trying to clean up the purple patches after Bal's big spill, though his home-made stuff dries to a basic black. I think she likes shouting at him as she scrubs.

So I'm the only one who arrives home, quietly by the back door, carefully carrying two full jugs of water, stoppered with fresh leaves. I put them down in the corner and stop to check my pomegranate dye vat: I've started to do a little trading again, too, using the brilliant yellow stew.

As I stand there, peering into my golden brew, I can still hear the noises; is it Alethea weeping? Is it Emeshmoon's hairy pets bleating, or Publia yelling? It sounds like all and none of these cries, and seems to be coming from inside the house. I look around the courtyard; nothing stirs, the hearth is cold. The chickens are in their coop. But there are animal murmurs and they're coming from... my bedroom?

I peep inside. It has been made-over as a shrine to Venus; the highest order, a super shrine, for even my goddess-worship wasn't this extreme. I never prayed to her in the way I catch Abibaal doing now, with Zissel, the cheesemaker's daughter.

By lamplight, their bodies are linked in a kiss but it's not the lips on her pretty face he's kissing. He's kneeling at her feet, she's standing in front of him with her dress lifted. At the doors of a celestial dairy, he prays to the whey.

This is probably the sickest thing I've ever seen him do but, though he used to make me squirm in a bad way, now the squirming feels good. The light is too dim to see any cheesy details but their bare outlines, slicked with the oil lamp's shine.

The way Abi is kneeling makes me want to kneel too; all his curves are manly from this angle, carved in dark marble like a statue of Mars, turned from fighter to lover by the one beauty who can win him. But the way Zissel is standing makes me want to stand, too; the swooning sex goddess, supported only by the strong tongue of her heavenly consort. Her hands are clutching at the hair on his head one moment and her own Venusian tresses the next as she moans softly.

And, oh gods, forgive me; the only other thing I'd want, in her position, is for him to have trussed my hands behind my back, so I would leave the hair unmessed and be moaning hard. At this thought, I fall through the doorway. They both hear me tumble into the room.

Wiping his mouth on his sleeve, Abibaal comes towards me quickly. He looks like a man who has done that hundreds of times, and been caught in the act more than once.

"Veronica, I'm sorry," he says, as he gently helps me up.

All the cunnilingus must be what makes his voice so high.

"I have desecrated your bedroom. I'd never have done that if you were in here."

It looks like I'm about to cry, lip trembling, watery eye, but I burst out laughing. I'm as nervous as the cheesemaker's daughter, who can still be seen over his shoulder, tying her cloak on. I laugh at Abibaal because of how I'll get my revenge for pissing me off. Every night from now on, and often during the day, I will picture myself in the exact position I just saw Zissel assume, with him kneeling between my feet.

And at the moment of climax, it won't be kindly milk; I will release a torrent of bitter dye. I'll wash Abibaal's unfaithful face in the golden stream. But he'll never know. Because all I say, in a matter-of-fact way, is this:

"We've just seen the lord and he wants us to go on tour with him. We're leaving in two days."

Then I rush at Zissel, who is still fishing around under my bed for her sandal, screaming at her to get out. Even as an ex-priestess I can be threatened by a girl who is younger and prettier than me. When she goes from my bedroom, hotly preceded by Abibaal, I'm in a frenzy, trying to find my *alabastrotheca.* I know it's not really here, of course; I left my make-up box in Tyre. But what I wouldn't give right now for all the little pots and flasks and alabaster jars that I needed to be me.

What I find instead is my white linen handkerchief, probably the only thing I'll pack when we go on the road the day after tomorrow. I might need to blow my nose in Jericho or wipe my brow at Jeshanah. Who am I fooling; I need it to clean the make-up off my face. For though I have no powdered antimony, my eyes are still black with jealousy. And though I have no ochre my cheeks are still red with lust. And though I have no white lead my face is pale, because I am weak and sick. I am a clown and an alcoholic.

I only tell Publia some of this, when she comes in shortly afterwards. The bit about Abibaal tongue-churning the cheesemaker's daughter. She tells everybody else in the house. As we pack our things and prepare to leave it, our voices echo in the roofless courtyard, as if it were some suburban amphitheatre:

Publia. Abibaal, you utter twat.

Abibaal. She said I could use her room if I needed to change.

Balthazar. That wasn't changing. That was staying the same.

Publia. So what would you sacrifice for Jesus? What would you actually give up? Wine or women?

Abibaal. Easy. I'd give up wine every time.

Me. And drink cheese instead.

Abibaal. Pardon?

Me. I would prefer to give up men for wine. In fact... *(laughing),* I already have.

Abibaal. You need to give up wine for water, darling.

A miracle, backwards; wine into water? The last thing I do, before we leave Publia's house at Bethany, is pick up the amethyst necklace from the shrine. The purple gemstones, currently worth about thirty denarii, are wrapped in my pristine linen handkerchief. Truly, this is the purest thing I can see with my eyes, apart from Jesus, who we are going to see every day until we die. It is all I carry now, in my animal skin bag.

CHAPTER FIFTEEN

I say every day till we die, but some disciples are saying he's going to die first. He told Mary of Magdalene, who told Mary and Martha, who told our Mary and Salome. And we've all seen the sinister way the lesser Sanhedrin look at him.

It's best to live on the road, staying one step ahead of any threat. The way Jesus travels, though, is not like running away. He doesn't leave Bethany because he's scared of the big city; no, it seems to us that he's drumming up a bigger crowd ever to watch him run bang into Jerusalem.

First we go to Jericho. People line the streets to see him, grown men climb trees to catch a glimpse of his face. He shines it upon those who show most faith, and graces them with his company for the night, and honours them with his posse of hungry fisherman.

The hard core takes care of us too, especially since Publia is pregnant. Nathaniel and Kaspar normally bed down in the host's house with the lord but they always make sure lodgings are found for the Fabia Pictrix, Abibaal and Balthazar. Often Marcus and Naomi go with the elder ladies, and sometimes sleep close to the Magdalene Mary.

I haven't even spoken to her but I've stared; she looks like a picture of Pandora on the wall of the atrium in my father's villa. Her box was painted purple and gold but I've never seen that Maria holding a single possession except, perhaps, the purple and gold heart of Jesus.

Everywhere he walks, men gather round, calling to him in all manner of ways. Some are silent but some speak to him, asking questions, offering information, beseeching forgiveness for their sins; and some actually touch him. The fishermen do form a protective ring around him, though they too are basking in a peaceful glow.

But lots of people stand near the back and argue with each other in voices that are angry, or scared or incredulous. That's why it's best for us to be closer to the centre of the crowd, nearer to Jesus, safer for everyone, quieter for Emeshmoon.

We see him very nearly, every day now. Always from the back! As we travel, it's the new faces that he comes face to face with, like we did in Tyre. Our group are behind him, constant and close, seeing his shoulders, his hair, his heels; seeing these things as our sunrise and sunset. The leader is in our eyes, so that we almost see as he sees, as we travel through the early spring, not quite as far as Galilee.

And every day, he does what the sun doesn't; he turns his face upon us, personally, by turning around and talking to his tight band of followers intimately, in between meeting hundreds of new fans. He tells us a tale, in one of these asides, that makes his sunlight crystallise:

A vineyard boss employs a group of guys first thing in the morning and promises to pay them a denarius for the day. At the third hour, he scouts the marketplace again and picks up a few more workers. Then that vineyard owner comes across a group of unemployed men on a street corner; it's the sixth hour but he sends them to tend the vines. Come the ninth hour, as he's heading home, he stumbles into a den of undesirables and he employs them too, promising to pay what is due. Even at the eleventh hour, he hears a drunkard passing in the street; and the boss sends him to pick grapes, too, at sundown.

When they all finish work at the end of the day this guy is first in the queue to receive his earnings. One denarius, handed over readily. The ne'er-do-wells are next in line; a denarius apiece for a good day's work. Those who clocked on when the sun was highest; this generous landowner pays them the full day's wage too. And as for those who'd started first thing in the morning and laboured from dawn till dusk, a denarius each for working all day.

When they complain, the boss says; "but this is what I promised you. A denarius is what you did it for. No cut has been taken from your pay: so why do you begrudge God for his great generosity?"

This isn't word for word the way Jesus said it. That was in a different language for a start. He told the story in quiet Aramaic as we rested by a mountain roadside in Samaria. Farzan muttered it in a Phoenician tongue, so just Emeshmoon, Publia and I could hear it. Then we walked on and I sang it back to them in Latin. It was good to sing again after so long; being on the move has shifted something from my heart, something that felt like one of our altar stones.

When we stop that evening, Emeshmoon writes those song words down on a new scroll she brought with goat milk money. She was drinking a lot of that stuff in Bethany, and looks thinner since we've been away. With Farzan's help she turns my Latin back into a language she can spell, translating the lyrics into her own lingo.

We're sitting at an inn in Ephraim, a rough old sleepover that reminds me of the khan I stayed in on the way to Capernaum. The song I sang then was thin; the travel rug we kneel on now is thick. Glorious glyphs, woven in colourful rows: Farzan reads the latest story aloud by firelight, the flames flickering dangerously close to the page.

"If you translated it back into Aramaic again," I ask him, "would it be exactly what Jesus said?"

"No," he laughs, "the two versions are as different as the vineyard workers; but the pay-out is the same."

As we bed down for the night, I think about the slaves in this parable. I think about my slave, my old, dead slave; and I think about being a slave myself. I think about Abibaal, executing my slave. And I think about Jesus, who would not have a slave. He pays everyone equally, whatever work they do and why ever they do it. In fact, he is our unpaid servant. I've even heard him say this, and not in a sarcastic way.

In the old days, in Rome, I never gave slaves a second thought. Hercules would simply agree, of the conflict between Abi and his *servus*, the freeman is always right. Abba father says, instead, that the last come first, and the poorest are rich. But in the secret temple of my soul, I'm starting to prefer Abibaal to the enigmatic Latin slave; strong and silent was sexy but so is a man with a loose tongue.

Anyway, he is sharing a *leewan* with Balthazar and Publia tonight, and I'm with Farzan and Emeshmoon. Our sleeping arrangements were quickly and cheaply made, and it was best to go in threes.

At least, on this trip, there are bedding rolls and blankets provided, even for those who are not pregnant. As Emeshmoon and I lie side by side, by torchlight, with the voices of our menfolk coming softly from the stableyard just outside, I ask her something that I've wondered for a long time but haven't wanted to say.

"Emesh, why don't you get pregnant?"

She is silent, for a long time. Till I think she's asleep and turn to look at her and see that she isn't.

"Don't you want a baby? Can't you have one? He could heal you, like Publia, you know..." I falter.

She turns to me then. Emeshmoon, bookseller of Byblos, I can actually read her face like a book. Bless her, she is plain as a page of paper, but has the most beautiful expressions. Right now, she is about to tell me her deepest secret though she really doesn't want anyone to know.

Her eyes gleam with trust, two bronze discs in the torchlight. "There is nothing wrong with me," she says. Then she gets her bag and slowly takes something out of it. Sombrely, she gives me a coin. I peer at it closely, turning it over in my palm.

"What's this?"

"It," she whispers, "is my contraceptive coin."

I've heard of them. As a fertility goddess's assistant priestess, I know such things exist but have never used one. I hand it back quickly now I know where it's been.

Then I say, forcefully;

"That is *how* you don't have a baby. Not *why* you don't."

Emeshmoon sighs and I hear tears in it, like tasting rain in the *Februlis* wind. She holds onto the coin but grabs my finger and makes me feel the image on the old metal, words and a picture worn smooth with unimaginable usage.

"This," she whispers again, "is why. Why I do not want a baby. Why I'll never be a mother.

"Mine is an old Phoenician family, who came back to Canaan from Carthage in my great-great-great-grandmother's day. They still spoke of this god and goddess, Ba'al Hammon and Tanit. See; his likeness faintly on the front of the coin and his wife still just visible on the back. In Byblos she was called Ba'alat Gebal..."

"I know her," I say, "she's a Venus."

"She is not. She's like no goddess of matrimony or maternity should ever be. At her temple in the town is a secret altar. What I saw there, when I was just a child, made me decide never to have children of my own..."

She is interrupted again, this time by shouting outside in the yard. Farzan, Abi and Bal are there, taking the evening air; we can hear their bellowed answers to questions from further away.

"He's not here!" Farzan calls to some Roman guards. (I reckon that's what they are.)

"Yes, we're with him," Abibaal pipes up, in response to the next query, "but he's not staying at this inn!"

"He's the King of Heaven; he doesn't sleep in a cattle shed," Bal adds.

Emesh and I clutch each other's hands in horror. Surely their cheek will be the end of our menfolk. But after a long pause, the soldiers seem to have accepted these rude replies and moved on; we hear feet marching into the distance and our boys' long-running argument about whether they should have brought the ass resumes.

As we held hands, Emeshmoon's contraceptive coin fell on the floor between our crude bedrolls. I can see the bronze face now; Cronus as he looked in Carthage. She picks it up again and puts it in her bag.

"I was always told that coins didn't work well as *anteceptio*," I say.

"Well, this one works for me," she says.

She's weeping now, quite loudly; Farzan will hear and come in any moment. I have to be quick if I want to know, what happened in Byblos' ancient temple to stop her wanting babies. I ask her again, more gently but more urgently. She knows that I've suffered abuse in the name of a deity, too.

"There is a bronze statue of this goddess, palms outstretched, stood above a fire pit." Emesh blurts it out. "The flames lick her metal wrists till the fingers tip downwards. But the priests lay babies, and put young children that can walk and talk, into this great mother's hands; so they roll off and fall into the fire."

"What?"

"I saw it happen lots of times. Families we knew. There'd be drums and whistles but you could still hear the screaming. A mum fainted and fell into the fire with her child, once. That was when I promised myself..."

"Why?" I'm crying too, now. "Why did they do that?"

"If there was something wrong with the kid, they'd offer it up to get a new one. But often they were gorgeous babies; Syrian toddlers are the cutest I've seen. Perfect children thrown on the pyre.

"I don't know why, Veronica," she sobs. "I don't know why they killed their own innocents."

I think about pregnant Publia in the room next door. She said she'd die for her religion but she'd kill for her baby. What would she do, if forced to murder her baby for the faith?

"Syro-Phoenicians are really bad," Emesh is sniffing. "Don't tell Jesus."

We follow as close to him as we can get, behind the apostles, and their mothers and sisters, and the Magdalene, when we move on next day. And when we stop to rest, if I keep my feet still and lay flat on the floor, the farthest stretch of my fingertips would touch Jesus. If I fell prostrate I could reach him, at any time, over the next few days.

And often, he'll look round to where we are standing, a mixed bag of gentiles he picked up in Tyre, who've pretty much lost their purple now and just look brown like the rest of the crowd.

People laugh and cry in their groups for a long time after he has passed by. Women swoon, and sometimes I see men who I think are just going to stand in the spot where they saw him, whether they heard a parable or witnessed a miracle, for the rest of their lives; scratching or shaking their heads.

In the middle of nowhere, a mountainside in Samaria, we meet a group of ten lepers, nine men and a woman, decimated by it. He just says, go and show yourselves to the priest, and we know that by the time they get to the temple, their leprosy will be gone. It's impossible but we've seen it happen before: sores and lesions, scars and deformations, He can make those people clean. He can cure all ills, he can heal all wounds.

This is the version of the story I sing, again; to Emeshmoon, as we trudge along, trying to cheer her up. And she writes it down the next evening, unrolling the scroll as we travel an unwinding road.

She pens a bit more the next week, when one of the Lepers turns up again in Sychar, as a whole man, to give him thanks and praise. Only one out of ten; the lord looks back at his close-knit twelve and broader net of men and women, brothers like James and John, sisters like me and Pubi, mothers and sons and daughters and uncles, his whole family defying the odds, with a twinkle.

And another week, I sing another verse, for a sweet guy we meet in Megiddo. As Jesus is making his way to the temple, a rich young man runs up to him; from his fine clothes, his fabulous manner and the long train of servants that attend him, all lovely-looking too, he's the ruler around here.

"How do I get eternal life?" he asks and we all step closer to hear the answer.

"Keep the commandments," Jesus says, and he lists them: don't commit murder or adultery, don't lie or defraud, honour your father and mother. Nothing about drunkenness, thank God.

"I've done all that," says the young prince, "since I was a boy."

"There's one more thing," says our king. "Give away your money. Sell all your possessions and donate your wealth to charity. Then come, and follow me."

I know that men don't cry, not like my friend Emesh did, or like I do each time the moon is full. But this boy, so handsome, so wholesome, so horny if the adoring slaves watching his ass are anything to go by; this boy sobs. We see the look on his face from our places behind the Christ as they meet each others' gaze. He turns and walks away weeping; wealthy and powerful, rich and successful, totally locked out of heaven.

As we wander slowly on, I sing in his honour: "A set of glass vases, all sexy and smoky, an ivory bust and a snakehead in bronze; a collection of fine Roman pottery, a jewelled sword hilt like Hercules' dick. These are the things I have given away.

"My business, my bedroom, my income, my hairdo, my *alabastrotheca*, loaded with make-up, my friend in the wine shop, a bath every day. These are the things I have given away."

Emeshmoon walks with me. She's smiling and nodding and I know she'll be writing this later.

"We've given up Byblos, Tyre, Bethany; we've given up Hercules, Melqart, Venus; we've given up goat's milk and eggs; we've given up yellow and purple."

"But I haven't quite given up paper," she says, as we sit that night, on the roof of somebody's house in Aenon who has taken us in. It's starting to get warm again in the evenings with the early scent of spring in the air as we stay up late talking. Publia's there with us but tends to fall asleep fast and starts snoring straight away. The men are lying around in various states of consciousness and undress.

"And I haven't quite given up purple." My bag is my pillow and I can feel the last string of amethysts in it, hard against my temple. Formerly the fish sign from our shrine, I didn't leave this behind when we left Bethany.

"Or singing," says Farzan.

"You're not supposed to give up everything," says Abibaal, "only the bad stuff. For example, I haven't given up women."

"I haven't given up on the donkey." Balthazar's voice comes from the other side of Publia, though we can't see him.

Everybody lies here looking up at the stars. Down below, our host family can't believe how casually we sleep; men and women mixed together and not all married. The couples are closely bedded and I'm between them, with a girl on either side so Bal and Farzan are further away from me. Abibaal is beyond his brother, a distant mountain, half hidden by the bump of my sister.

Though I can't see him, I know he's there. I can identify his breathing, aside from the other four. It is the breath I imagine, blowing on me where I saw him kiss the cheese girl. The fire I envisage pissing out. My hands are tied but my power is untouched, in this picture. And the stream is purple.

Most mornings now I'm woken by Publia clambering heavily over me to go for a wee; suddenly it's not the moon that tells us how time waxes, it's her fat belly. I still have recourse to the rag and two rough times pass, on the road, before we finally get back to Bethany.

As we walk up the mountain path towards the pretty village, it is so quiet that all seventy of us can clearly hear his voice.

"Now the curtain parts and we will step beyond the veil into the secret courts of God. All that will happen has been written in books, on earth and in heaven. Every thought and word and deed of man is recorded in the book of God's remembrance."

He stops walking and turns slowly so we can all see his face. A glorious sunset halos him. Speaking more softly, he insists these things may never be written down by us; they are the still, small messages of silence. Afterwards Nathaniel tells us that, while Jesus was speaking, the angels themselves were silent, and the courts of heaven spoke with baited breath. [17]

We walk back into Bethany like that, cross the village square in whispers and climb the lane to Balthazar and Publia's in quiet conversation. We are taking Naomi, Mary and Salome home with us; and they are telling us that the lord keeps saying he's going to die soon. They say he's sent for his mother from Nazareth. It's hard to picture the mother of Christ.

"What's her name?" Publia asks.

"Mary," says Mary.

We say no more.

The house is full of chicken shit when we go in. Alethea agreed to feed them, they pay her in eggs, but there was no arrangement made for the cleaning. Apart from feathers and dust, our rooms are how we left them, and the dye factory could run again. The goats are still in the garden and Marcus is sleeping over with Nathaniel and co, so Abibaal has the roof to himself.

Before they go off to bed in his room, the subdued old ladies sing one of their psalms: 'You prepare a table for me in the presence of my enemies; you anoint my head with oil, my cup overflows.' [18]

Coming round with the wine jug, Farzan translates these words from Hebrew to Latin and winks as he tops up my drink.

In the peace that follows their song, Naomi confesses:

"We're afraid His body will be snatched from us before we can bury him properly."

"Mary Magdalene won't sleep," Salome adds.

"None of us can afford funeral ointments or fine winding cloths," the other Mary finishes.

This is different from the way we Romans deal with our dead and quite diverting, but I am tired and need to go to bed now. As I say my goodnights, Abibaal smiles at me the same way he used to in Tyre when he'd try and come into my flat every evening to check my figures.

There is not much left of me to calculate. In the middle of the night, when everything is purple, I suddenly realise what I have to do; and first thing on the Saturday morning I climb onto the flat roof to shake him awake. My amethyst necklace is clutched in my fist.

"Take these jewels and sell them," I say, "go to Jerusalem because you won't get this in Bethany; I want a pound of pure nard in an alabaster box. Abi just looks at me, (at my bosoms actually), nods assent, gets up and goes to do as I asked. He takes Balthazar with him, and it's Bal who asks why I want spikenard, so suddenly and expensively. I don't tell him; I just give him a brisk breakfast and order him to look after his brother.

Then I look after my sister and wait for them to return with the balm. She's making things for the baby. In fact, Abibaal, him again, has been making a crib, though it looks a lot like a chicken shed. Pubi is stuffing a little mattress with the softest straw she can find and needs me to stitch it up.

The old ladies sit with us, still tense today, worried what will happen to them if Jesus dies. I ask if they've ever seen his mother, then. Hopefully the thought of her will cheer us all up. The mother of God must look great.

Salome has met her, but not the others. She says that once, in Galilee, his mother and brothers came to see him at a synagogue where he was addressing a huge crowd. Peter took him the message, whispering in his ear, and the lord smiled and said to the audience, spreading his hands wide: you are my mother, you are my brothers, for you do the will of my father in heaven. But in fact, his actual family stayed, and were welcomed into the flock, and spent the night with him at some tax collector's house.

When our menfolk return, they bring a jar of nard, suitable for anointing the Messiah. They also give me two bronze talents, change from the amethyst sale. Then, over a cup of Emeshmoon's freshly-steeped leaves I tell them my idea.

See, Jesus is planning to go to Jerusalem in the morning. Everyone who's heard him say his days on earth are numbered, agree this is the place he means to depart from. If he'll be dead tomorrow, we have to embalm his body today. Though it's the Sabbath, we have work to do.

I haven't yet given up all hope of finding my purple toga whole, upcycling it to dress the heavenly king's soul, and I even told the boys that if they could get that instead of the nard, it would be just as grave-worthy. But Abibaal said, seriously, I was being silly. That is not going to happen: Jesus isn't going anywhere. Yet all of us seem to be in unspoken dread that some devastating event will soon come to pass. We might lie to ourselves, and each other, but he wouldn't lie to us.

We send Farzan out on foot, this time, to find out where to find him. He speaks the most languages, so should be able to get the best info from the babble of voices that echo around Lazarus' house permanently now. Then he runs back with the news:

"He's dining with Simon the Leper, tonight."

"Who the hell's that?" says Publia.

"Well, he got better, whoever he is," I reply.

We wait till the eleventh hour, the old women mostly singing, the young ladies mainly praying. Then we cover our hair and slip out of the house. Balthazar tells us where to go; he thinks this guy, Simon, is a priest and gives directions to his place. Abibaal comes with us, cloaked against his striking appearance, but Bal stays behind, disconsolate. He said to Pubi that I'm wasting money we could have put to a more worthwhile cause.

None of the women feel this way, though. Naomi is informing everybody we meet about the alabaster box under my cloak; how beautiful it is, how precious the contents, how crucial the act. Our Mary and Salome are spreading the news, too; and the other Mary and Martha receive it eagerly, standing in the courtyard outside the priest's house, keeping guard over the lord within.

This Simon is actually a Scribe who was cured of leprosy by Jesus about five months ago. Mary says he's been causing big trouble in the synagogue, trying to get the Pharisees to repent, the other Scribes to find enlightenment. The ladies take us round the side of his house, away from the main crowds, where there's a large window onto the dining room. One of the fishermen is on watch, scanning the yard constantly, and there is another keeping guard inside; James, maybe.

From where we are standing, beneath a palm tree, we can see the dining table. Eight men are sitting round it, with Simon at one end and Jesus at the other. Between them, a cityscape of cups and jugs and lidded dishes is built like Jerusalem and gleaming in the lamp glow. A woman moves gracefully from guest to guest, with a plate of bread, a bowl of herbs. As she comes closer to the window we recognise Mary, the Magdalene.

Handing over the nard jar, I watch as Salome takes it to the window and speaks softly to her son. He beckons Maria over and they talk for ages; then finally she looks at us, standing under the tree, and his mother points at me.

Mary's eyes meet mine. I think she knows: I will be in her shoes, if she's wearing any. I will be in her hands, as she opens the alabaster box and pours the ointment onto his skin. I will be in her fingertips as she smooths the spikenard over his shoulders and arms, his shins and calves. I will be in her eyes as she embalms his forehead and cheekbones and chin. I will be in her hair as it swings, in her ear as he breathes, in her tears as they land on his feet.

She smiles at me, now; and I will be in her smile forever. It's like the picture I've known all my life, Pandora with the golden box, painted on the atrium wall of my father's villa. We break that box open together tonight. Then she turns from the window and walks back into the room in Bethany.

At first, none of the men notice what she's doing, as if anointing is the next course. It's not till she kneels that they pay attention. But we don't look at the other men and, from where we're hiding, we can't hear them. We just look at Jesus.

He is love. He is here to love; to give love, to show love, to be love. Not to make love; a single flame trying to kiss the sun, that's how it would be. Mary Magdalene knew it first. God simply needs a pair of hands to feel human.

When she disappears under the table, I trust, now, that Maria is simply at his feet; crying and drying them. As the alabaster box was opened, the last trickle of my dirty thoughts were out. I know, now, that she is saying goodbye to his body because she loves his spirit.

Quite what the men's argument with her is, we're not sure, but the watchers outside the window see their heated debate. If they knew his soul was a rose and nard is just some well-rotted manure there'd be no fight, surely?

Standing in the shelter of tall palms, our group of women are wound round their husbands, brothers and sons. I've woven my arms around Pubi and Emesh, but am also just touching Abibaal as we wait; the whole crowd interleaved under this tree. Our congregation is so powerful, our worship so intense, its branches turn into the arches of a temple.

Nobody goes home that night and when it gets light in the morning we take up the palm leaves that have fallen on us, waving them like banners as Christ's army descends on Jerusalem.

We're hungry and he halts us before we get to Bethphage, finding enough loaves and milk at a quiet farmhouse to calm us down. While we eat, he sends one of the men off into the village, and that man comes back leading a donkey.

At first, Jesus' followers are split over his use of the little ass. We gentiles don't get why he's riding it; is he sick or lame? Our Jewish friends have to explain:

"It is in the scriptures," Naomi says: "'Rejoice greatly, Daughter Zion! Shout, Daughter Jerusalem! See, your king comes to you, righteous and victorious, lowly and riding on a donkey, on a colt, the foal of a donkey.'" [19]

Salome adds: "He told my sons: when he learnt these verses from his teachers, the boy Jesus knew the prophets meant him. The Nazarene saw himself fulfilling their words, first time he heard them."

Balthazar is broody as we set off again. He and Farzan came to find their wives at the ex-leper's house at midnight and were caught up in the excitement.

"See, I knew we should have brought a donkey," he says to Publia as we start the last leg, down the Mount of Olives and across the plain with Jerusalem getting bigger all the time. "Then you could ride, too." The twelve apostles know many secrets and mostly keep silent but today they are shouting and stirring up the crowd; there may be twelve hundred waving the palm leaves in joyous declaration as we arrive at the city gate.

It has several gates, of course, this place; and some are for animals, some are for offal, some are for ordinary men; but this is the gate for kings and wise men and warriors. Built like a fortress, adorned like a whore, with the perfect symmetry of *phylacteria*; we go through the twin arches of the Golden Gate. The beautiful gate, the gate of mercy, the gate of eternal life; it has many names [20] but the souls go under it one by one.

As we enter the city a moving scene unfolds. The followers flow on ahead, laying palm leaves down in the path of our lord, padding the hard cobblestones. We rush through the double-arched gate throwing down the leaves for him to walk on, now leading the donkey. Once he's passed we pick up the holy foliage, hurry ahead and lay it down for Jesus to tread on again.

These leaves didn't all come from the same tree in a Bethany back garden, of course; we started it with the palm fronds last night and, as the crowd has gathered, and the enthusiasm grown, all the trees we've passed on the way have been stripped of their greenery. Earth's flags for the king of heaven; he gets to the temple court without touching the dusty ground. People spread their cloaks and shawls before him, too; and these are every tint of brown, with glints of yellow and I even see a hint of purple.

Somebody lays a cloth of Tyrian twilight beneath his feet but I don't see who. Suddenly, there's the colour of home, at the final step of our journey marked with amethyst pinheads on a map.

I look as close as I can in the crush to see what piece of *purpura* this is, instantly realising, of course, it's not my old dress. But a dealer in the same currency could have sold this. Its vendor might have told the same asking price.

Somebody else in this horde of devotees has, or had, the cash to splash on a wave of murex water; and I've never met them. Another tainted storyline might twine with mine in the vast army entering the city at this time, friend or foe, in the sea of our lord's supporters.

Jerusalem is awakened by a host of a thousand, singing: "Hosanna to the Son of David! Blessed is he who comes in the name of the Lord! Jesus, the prophet from Nazareth!"

The fishermen lead us to the temple steps and up and up, still shouting at the tops of our voices. Some of the Pharisees, who've run out to see what the fuss is about, call to Jesus over the furore; "Teacher, control your disciples." And though the noise is great, we hear him answer quietly; "I tell you that if these should keep silent, the stones would immediately cry out." [21]

And though we keep chanting "Hosanna! Hosanna!" it seems the slabs of temple stone are crying too. The giant-hewn steps, the monster-carved walls, they seem to buzz beneath our feet, hum beside our ears. This holy edifice rings with voices.

The human crowd fills the outer court, held back by the apostles, who link arms against the surging and singing. We're all watching Jesus, in fear for his flesh, afraid this is his earthly end. Our anxiety makes us chant all the louder, as if the sound could shield him; "Hosanna in the highest!"

The priests watch him coming, peeping through the gateway to the women's court; the scribes are frozen as he approaches, and the money changers and dove sellers who do a roaring trade in the porticoes stop what they are doing and stare. Some of them have seen this before. He told them not to turn the house of God into a den of thieves once already, and now he turns their tables over again.

We fall silent as pure white birds fly into the air and their cloth-coloured feathers float slowly back down. Then cascades of coins, Tyrian silver shekels and half-shekels, to pay in temple tax, tumble down the steps past our feet, clinking and chiming on the stone. With them goes all the cash that's ever been changed, in this court, at an extortionate rate. Nobody who follows Jesus bends to pick a penny up.

And in fact, as I watch the money falling, there's another extraordinary thing. Unnoticed by anyone else, and she doesn't know I've seen her, Emeshmoon, the contraceptive queen of Phoenicia, is taking the rusty old coin she uses out of her bag and hurling it down the steps too; mixed with the currency of cynicism, the economy of greed. Standing on tiptoes, she tosses the old Carthage silver into a pot of worthless trinkets.

Then the crowd lets out another roar; a rallying cry which brings almost all of Jerusalem here, to decide whether to scrabble on the floor for spilt change; or whether to join the ones with empty pockets and purses and hearts light as air, shouting again. Our battle chant, "Nazarene! Nazarene!" gradually changes to; "Messiah! Messiah!"

The Pharisees are shouting back at us, or some are shouting between themselves, but nobody can hear what they're saying. He who can calm the storm, whose whisper is heard in a hurricane, whose stillness is felt in a whirlwind; he's not speaking to them anymore and without that they are mute. Jesus comes back to his haloed rabble, through the broken stock and collapsing stalls of the marketplace; while the Sanhedrin, purple tasselled and pomegranate-embroidered, wail curses we can't hear before storming back inside their walls.

Abibaal laughs close to my ear in the maelstrom:

"They can't do anything to him!"

At the end of the day, Jesus leads us out of Jerusalem and back to Bethany in triumph. There, our celebrations last all week. On the Monday, Balthazar goes and buys himself a donkey; not a big boy, like before, but something smaller, almost a colt. On the Tuesday, when no eggs appear for breakfast, Abibaal says he's given them to the hens to sit on, so they can hatch a new family of fluffy chicks. On the Wednesday, we all treat ourselves to a bath at our Roman neighbours (where the green algae grows in the *tepidarium*).

Here, wallowing privately in the darkness, I whisper to Emeshmoon about the coin she threw away; and she tells me, though Farzan doesn't know yet, that it may finally be time for them to have chicks of their own. And on Thursday, Bal takes one of the goats to a backstreet butcher in Bethany to have it dispatched in the proper way, so we can feast that night; though the whole week feels holy...

But early on Friday, there is a hammering at the front door. Publia gets there first; she was the least bladdered last night but the most this morning, so has already been out with the bucket. And in bursts Marcus, his toga torn from his shoulder and his hair in disarray.

"They've got him. They caught him. We thought they couldn't touch him but they took him," he pants. "Jesus is in Jerusalem and they won't let him go."

CHAPTER SIXTEEN

"He gave himself up. Christ could easily have got away if he'd wanted, but he let them get him." The actor's voice is steadier, now; he's wrapped in a blanket, sitting by our hearthside, sipping Emeshmoon's early morning tisane.

The rest of us are racing around, getting ready to rush into town with the thousands who'll be calling for him to be released. I can almost hear them, crying for his freedom outside the *praetorium*.

Set to go before the others, I stand by the fireplace; nothing but my white linen handkerchief folded neatly in my bag, and my long brown hair tucked under a scarf striped amber and ochre.

There I hear a secret that Marcus heard at dawn when Jesus was taken away to the high priest by the Roman soldiers. Someone struck with a sword to defend our lord and cut off the ear of a centurion but our master whispered as he was led from Gethsemane: 'If I wanted to get out of here, don't you think I could call down the angels to carry me?'

Abibaal runs up the garden calling for Alethea but it's Tassos and Tim who come trotting back down with him. Then they make us all run; a flight to fight. Farzan leads up the Mount of Olives; not the sweeping, Southern route we took last Sunday, the slow, curving road to the city; no, this time we go up and over. The steepest, shortest path; I've never walked it before and now we're running.

They say the view of Jerusalem from the top makes people cry. We well up with tears today but not because of its beauty. Truth is in the wilderness; the town is built on lies.

The men hurry on though Publia is stumbling, more tearfully still. My eyes give hers a run for their money when Abibaal spots that she's upset first and pulls Bal over to take care of his wife.

Down the mountain track they carry her between them, their four arms linked to make a single seat. With many ways into Jerusalem, the brothers stop and almost drop my sister as they argue which one to take. I keep legging it forward, in line with Farzan. A great roar is coming from inside the walls and we rush towards it through a more northerly gate than before.

Its narrow archway squeezes us into a dark street with side streets off, each twisting out of sight; but, again, we can hear the direction to go in. A huge tumult sounds round the corner, growing louder the closer we run. The crowds are getting thicker and my comrades are slowing down.

Glancing over my shoulder, I see Publia sheltered by her husband and his brother, who won't risk her safety for God's sake. Farzan's dropped back to protect Emeshmoon. Ahead of me, Tassos and Timothy are plunging deeper into the trouble, Marcus with them and more brick-built men from Bethany.

That wall shields me from punches and kicks as we force our way through the public. I look back desperately at my sister, trying to catch her eye before the darkness closes round me. And when we are inside it, even those burly men can't save me from elbows and fists and feet. I cover my head and bend to feel from the pull of the crowd which way Jesus is.

Because he's here somewhere; and there is still a peaceful sanctuary where he stands. In the melee, there is a guaranteed space to kneel. I crouch to feel which way his feet fall in the stampede. I want to follow in his steps, wherever they lead.

Because I am an ex-assistant priestess to Venus, I understand religious fervour. Because I am a businesswoman, I understand customer behaviour. Because I am a Christian, I understand the way Jesus works. These things combined, I move in a trajectory so well aligned with his, we're soon in the same *via*.

There's a terrifying crush between its narrow walls. It's hard to pick out a single face, so I don't see him coming straight away. My first glimpse is the cross. It dominates the road.

Christ has to haul the crossbeam he'll be killed on up the hill with him. Like a dark and deadweight twin, he brings his heavy Nemesis. Rough-hewn, this wood brother staggers through the crowd. When it comes alongside, I stare at the rugged profile of my beloved lord.

Mud, he must have fallen once already; blood, running in streams from a wreath of thorns on his head. Sweat and tears are trickling from his eyes till he can't see the way.

I struggle to stay by him in the street. He is wearing purple, shredded and blood-stained, over his own tunic, the master's robes, the teacher's gown, the healer's *praecinctorium* all in tatters, too.

I thrust my hand into my bag and grab the linen handkerchief. It's the only thing left in there. I've had it a long time and never been sure what to use it for. I waved it at my sister's wedding, blindfolded a slave and bound myself with it but it's stayed as white as when my father gave it to me, on the quay at Ostia. It was waiting for this moment.

"Here," I hold it out to him. "You've made me clean."

He takes the cloth and wipes mud and sweat from his eyes, blood and tears from his cheeks. I think he even wipes the spit of some virtuous Jew or vicious Roman from his beard.

When he hands back the white linen, he holds my gaze, and I can see myself in his eyes. His lips don't move, but I know he knows my name.

Veronica. The True Picture. Big-nosed beauty, always singing and shouting, staring and sighing; always with a more beautiful sister. Always bathing, with a leap and splash, in the formal Roman *thermae*, in the free-flowing River Jordan, in the illegal dye vats of Bethany. In business with booksellers from Byblos, in trade with tycoons from Tyre.

He knows I was painted purple, once, rich as the murals back home in Roma; then he washed me free of my sins. At the necropolis in Tyre, the night we first met, I sang a dark Persephone and the pomegranate seeds but he saw me in the light. When I stood on the sea wall at Capernaum to listen to him with Publia, our heads popping up above the crowd though our high-rise Latin hairstyles were suddenly flatter; he recognised my potential, then. Selling my purple gemstones to feed the flock as we travelled across Samaria, he knew I was priceless at that point. Bowing my head in a peacock scarf right down to his feet, on the temple steps at Bethany; that gave me right to wipe the purple from his face with my handkerchief now.

I see everything that has happened and then, in one of his blinks, I see some things that haven't happened, yet. I see a new shrine, a small, low temple on the spot we now stand; and I see me, singing on Capitoline Hill. Hymns to Jesus, praise to the lord; spinning a pitch for customers, harder and purer than I've ever pitched before.

I see this in a blink of his eye and then, an explosion of stars as some Roman soldier sends Jesus of Nazareth on again with a sword.

The steel force knocks me sidelong, scrabbling to get my hanky back in my bag and my hand out before I fall. I spin off the centurion's elbow, out of the scene as he raises his weapon again to Christ, staggering beneath the ugly crossbeam.

They can't crucify him. How would we live without his life? How could we survive his death? Watching the centurion's back disappear into the crowd, I give a sob and start going under. They can't kill Jesus. Surely we will all die? I'm getting tossed and trampled by the crowd. I've lost sight of my family and friends. But before I lose it completely, I see something fluttering in the dust where the master has just passed.

A purple feather from his kingly robe, whipped apart by the Romans, ripped to shreds by the Jews; a strip torn from a peacock. I watch the *murex*-dyed scrap flutter under peoples' feet. The last point on a journey way-marked with Tyrian trinkets, I let it lie. The final station on my trade route: I hope to God *purpura*'s bloody tracks stop here. Let the fighters fight for it, the lovers love it, the haters hate it, the gamblers throw dice for it; let the killers draw lots for the illusion of beauty, I wouldn't put my old dress back on now if they paid me.

My sob turns into a song as I follow the cross to Calvary; though I can't remember afterwards how it goes and nobody else can hear me singing, anyway. No-one I know is in sight as we're crowd-swept out of the city through its most northerly gate. We head to that skull-shaped outcrop in the hills where they make examples of men.

Halfway up the hill brow I recognise Joanna, who we travelled with in Galilee, the friend of our Mary and Salome, and the wife of Herod's steward. Grabbing her by the roadside, I beg her to use her influence.

"I have no earthly power at all. My husband is one of the most important men in this kingdom," she swears to me, "and he can do nothing to stop this. We can only pray."

It seems that the great wheels of fate have stopped at an inescapable place. The clouds hang low and heavy in the sky over Joanna's shoulder, the grey light sitting gloomily on her brown headscarf the same as mine. As if to start those wheels moving on, I shove her. In frustration, I beat at her breast as if it were the heart of time itself and I could stop it with my own rhythm, an overriding metre.

Mercifully, at that moment, Marcus and Naomi find us on the crowded road to (what she calls) Golgotha and pull me off. They want to know what I'm doing, and I think I sing again, though I stop pounding. It is unthinkable that the world will kill its own king, put out its own light, destroy its own nature. The wife of King Herod's man must be able to stop them; or Abibaal. Where is Abibaal? Every time I see him now, it's as Mars pacifying his mistress: so surely he'll be able to stop a bunch of sheep crucifying their shepherd.

The procession leads slowly up a green hill, not far outside the city walls, where rock breaks through at the grassy summit like a giant brow bone. This first taste of hard stone foretells the mountain which rises up beyond the foothills, a range of glinting peaks.

And when I turn and look behind me, another breath-taking panorama; Jerusalem is crenelated like the mountains. When I lived in Rome and Tyre, I thought those cities were sublime, but I'd never heard of heaven then. Surely nothing bad can happen somewhere so beautiful, I think; and the sun comes briefly from behind black clouds, sending shafts of dark gold over the turrets and spires of Zion.

I look round again when the line stops moving; up ahead it seems Jesus has been mobbed. It is all the women, weeping well-buckets over him, wanting to be his mother, needing to be his daughter. Far back in the queue, I can't hear what he's saying but I have heard him talk to women many times before, and he always calls them sister.

Eventually the rugged cross starts to move slowly up the hillside again. The crowd thins out and I can see my fat friends, Abibelly and pregnant Publia, silhouetted against the lurid sky.

I rush towards them but what can I say. We've all seen crucifixions before. Why, recently, Abibaal oversaw my slave (or his, in fact) being crucified. There are two other crosses on the hill today and the men carrying them have already passed this way.

Abi has done everything I've asked him lately. Well, for a long time. Ever since I've known him, he's never let me down so when I grab him by the jacket and beg him to do something, he bends his ear to better hear my gabbling in the hubbub.

"Please try and stop it," I say.

He slowly unfingers himself from my grip, nodding grimly. With a last look and a sigh he turns away and sets off at a faster pace up the hill then pauses and calls over his shoulder:

"Just him or all three?"

"Start with Jesus."

I stay with Publia and Balthazar, walking slower with Naomi and Marcus as Abi vanishes ahead of us and soon we come alongside Emeshmoon and Farzan who grab us hysterically, shaking and shouting incoherently in our faces. Clasped thus, we climb higher, meeting Mary and Martha where the big rocks start showing through the grass. They're holding each other up and screaming constantly too.

In this chaos, the dominant beat now is the sound of hammering. Nails, into wood, through human flesh and bone. Mary and Martha are clutching Aunt Naomi.

"Have you seen Lazarus?" they cry. "We've lost him in this crowd."

There's no sign but, as we look around, I do catch sight of Kaspar's turban, higher up the hillside. Everyone is here but hidden in the confusion. Abibaal is there, hopefully, seeing what he can do. I keep hopping up and down for a glimpse of him. Like the astrologer's, his headgear stands taller than the others, and looks different from the rest.

Publia is clinging to me as the hammers sound louder.

"No," she moans, "they can't nail him. Don't they know who loves him?"

"That is why they are nailing him, darling," says Bal, on the other side of her. "Jerusalem is the most jealous city on Earth."

As we carry on up *Calveriae* I see Abi's hat bobbing furiously next to a Roman soldier's helmet in the crowd ahead. They're close to the clearing where wooden crosses are loaded with human prey. I can't squeeze closer; the viewing public are packed tight round the arena of cruelty.

Any moment now there'll be a big surge backwards as the crosses are raised. We've all been at crucifixions before but it has never been for somebody we love, and Pubi's never been pregnant. So I take a step back to help Bal shield her and then we see Abibaal returning towards us too.

He acknowledges his brother with a quick look, ignores the panting Publia, then takes my face firmly in his hand so we can hold eye-contact in the shifting crowd.

"There is nothing to be done," he says. "No need to try and persuade the centurion; he said ninety-nine of them believe that Jesus is the Messiah. No need to appeal to the praetor, Pilatus; he publicly declared Jesus is innocent. The only people we have to persuade are..." he gestures calmly at the masses which seethe around us.

I continue to look at him expectantly.

"But we can't," he finishes. "My words will not be heard. Even your song would be silent now."

I know this. But somehow?

"Your voice," I plead with him. "It is unique. It is much higher than other men's; like your hat, it stands out from the crowd."

His hand grips my face tighter for a moment, bringing it towards his so I see the burning in his eyes.

"I will shout it if you will sing it," he smoulders. Then he looks up and says to Farzan and Emeshmoon, "Help with Publia; we are going forward."

He circles my wrist with his thumb and forefinger, as if I'm a slave in his chain, and leads me towards the crucifixion scene. He is shouting and I am singing, though I don't catch what he says any more than I can keep track of my own wild lyrics in this crisis.

We attract the attention of friends at the front of the crowd; our Mary and Salome are standing by their menfolk. Nathaniel sees me and Abibaal, and reaches between the ladies to kiss us both on each cheek.

"This can't happen," I beg him.

"This was always going to happen," he bawls back. "Yeshua knew it; we finally believed him. None of us should fear the kingdom now."

"It's not fair," I shout, "nailing him next to common criminals."

"They hammered a sign to his cross. We think it's written in his blood. King of the Jews..."

"That's not fair either! He's our king, too."

"Lord, brother, teacher, lover, master, magician, father, friend," Abibaal shrills: "leader, leper, beggar, guru, rabbi, healer, guiding light."

He raises his hands, holds them wide apart: "How big should the sign be?"

So close to the cross, Abi becomes a carpenter. Sweating sawdust, he makes a move as if to say, screw the crucifixion.

The same centurion he was chatting to earlier sees this gesture and pins it instantly with his sword. Without appearing to concede his point, my Phoenician friend steps backwards, carefully keeping me behind him. The whole crowd are stepping back now, anyway. Time has come to raise the crosses. A tight ring around the three, an unholy mix of the highest law-makers and biggest law-breakers in Jerusalem, force the audience to retreat.

I stumble into our Mary and cry on her shoulder, dyeing the black weave of her sleeve with my clear tears. My head is down as the crosses go up. But if I never see the disgrace, how will I know grace when I see it?

And I can hear the creaking and groaning, the tearing of flesh and the breaking of bones. We are all this close to the cross; we can heed the suffering from here. Face it, straight on, and believe, not with the eyes but with the heart. He told us his body would die; he told us our bodies are dead already. Our souls live, our spirits fly. That's what he said.

But the sound of the crowd takes over; rows of men and women, rows of children, booing and hissing, jeering and cheering the execution on. Half-way back down the hill the sightseers stretch, their voices echoing in the mountains and on the city walls.

More than *MCCC*, I reckon. We're standing near the beginning of that number with those who've followed him to the end. All the women, loads of the men, just crying helplessly at the foot of his cross.

Except for one. Our Mary points her out. "Look," she whispers to me: "His mother."

She is surrounded by fishermen, big boys from Galilee, some we've never seen before. They are sea-eyed as they watch their brother die but she does not let a single tear fall. Her look is bright and brimful as she gazes up at the cross; but Mary, the mother of God, doesn't cry.

If he really is who we think, she knew from the first time she saw him, it was all going to end this way. If it really is as we think, her faith in him will be unshakable. He taught her, from his birth, about angels and stars and heaven; his nativity was a lesson in eternal life.

At his death it is her turn to prove her love. To be maybe the one face in the crowd that believes in him steadfastly, right now. From a baby, she knew he could never die; the message conveyed before he was born from the true home she'll return to as his sister.

I stare at her, long time, until my eyes are dry too. Purple couldn't touch this woman; her scarf is a forget-me-not blue. Our Mary and the others around us are starting to calm down now. Big bands of his supporters stand together and out of their gatherings comes the sound of prayer and song. A group to my left are murmuring the 'our father'. Somewhere to my right, women's voices are raised in a hymn I recognise; it's one of mine! A thing I used to sing on the temple steps in Bethany, when we were waiting for him to come back and raise us from the dead.

As more voices are lifted in praise, more priests and praetor's men are raising their swords or fists or spears and forcing the congregation back. Nearby a man is knocked to the ground and continues praying loudly on his knees. A row of women link arms and sing in a soldier's face.

This isn't the worst kind of death we've seen. Stoning is harsher. Being eaten alive by lions is more horrifying. Pyre-burning is hideous. But the cross is so slow and lonely; and everyone can watch for miles around.

Close up, the crowd is getting more violent and I'm worried about where Publia is. Dragging Abi by the sash I start to back away from the action, looking up at the cross as we go. Earlier, he was talking to the thief on his right but now they are just hanging there in agony. Jesus seems to look at the crowd; his eyes appear to move over their faces. A living statue, already elevated to art, watching the audience from a tomb hung above them. We must be out of his line of vision but I believe he feels the heartbeat of everybody there. He sees, without looking directly, how far all his followers have come.

We struggle a few steps backwards before Farzan appears in the crowd and grabs me urgently, pulling us further away, to where the bodies start thinning out and Publia practically falls into my arms. I murmur to her soothingly, as if she'd had a nightmare back home in our father's villa in Rome, where the scariest thing was Cerberus, the three-headed hell hound, with Charon painted on the opposite panel in the alcove behind the front door.

We keep our eyes fixed on Jesus, one of the three heads on the cross, and mutter prayers for him and us. Our master and our friend, no mural; he's sweating blood, he's bleeding tears, his flesh is pierced, his bones are hammered. As we watch, one of the soldiers stabs Christ in the side with his spear. At this point Publia Fabia Pictrix faints.

Bal and Abi carry her off, under the lowering clouds, with a clap of thunder. Abibaal shouts at Farzan and Emeshmoon, letting them know we'll wait by the sheep gate. All the way down the hill, all I can feel is the pain. Stiff and silent, we sit against the city walls, still warm from the late spring sun, as the heat goes out of the day. As the storm passes, the sky turns pink, far in the west, while we sit there watching the three crosses on skull rock. Though we see them growing blacker against the sunset, we can never tell when their victims surrender to the darkness.

Publia lies in the damp grass with her head in Balthazar's lap and her feet massaged by Abibaal. I think we're all dying but are desperately trying to keep the baby alive. I would sing but there is a lump in my throat like all nine muses have swooned inside me.

Then I see something that will help; a wine-seller by the city gate. The red headgear, ruby cheeks and armful of ruddy skins signal him, as he sings to sell his wares. Many people are coming back from Golgotha gasping for a drink and he's doing a healthy trade.

I hurry over before he sells out; rummaging in my bag for one of the two bronze bits, my last coins, ever. Change from the sale of some amethysts, I didn't imagine I'd spend half my worth on wine. But there is nothing else in the world that could make me feel better, if Jesus is dead.

Publia has her child to think of, so she doesn't imbibe much. Abi and Bal have a few long pulls on my new jarful but most of it falls to me to drink, and when I've drunk it I am falling too. It's dark, and everybody is coming down from the hill. But not everybody. The only person I need to see, appearing double before me, won't be seen again. That outline has been our dawn and dusk, the moon path we've followed for seasons; and without Jesus' face, the dark eyes, the straight nose, the pointed beard all showing the way, it is hard to know how to go home.

I never thought I'd spend my last but one penny on booze, but once I had I suppose it was obvious that I should spend my ultimate coin too. Yes, my final bronze talent on a brimming jug that tips us out of Jerusalem; chanting threats that Jesus made about the whole place falling down. In a hundred years it would destroy itself, he said; in three days, he could raise the temple from the ground again. As we finally leave, by the route we walked less than a week ago with Christ triumphant on a donkey, the slogans of his incandescent supporters are turning to inconsolable sobs.

But as we walk across the starlit plain towards the Mount of Olives his spirit rises in us again. How can we, who have heard him talk of heaven as if it were closer to us than Pubi and Bal's house is now, how can we doubt he is sitting in glory and perfect peace in a throne room just through a doorway from that glittering sky?

For the third and last time today, I sing without knowing what the words are. I know there are words, for I can feel my lips moving but, tonight, I read the lips of the wine jar better than my own. I think I might be singing of Hercules, half-man half-god; creator of purple, founder of Phoenicia. Should we just go back there?

Tyre's colour trail ran out in the street where Jesus carried his cross, in torn robes which dropped their kingly threads in his tortured footsteps. The end of the road for purple. To retrace our steps to a place before we knew the lord, picking up riches like spilt gemstones, is still possible; but I would prefer to nail my own hand to the crossbeam.

My song is half-sailor, half-whore as I rollick and roll my way back to bed in Bethany. I know I'm not the only one who's legless; a big group of us stagger over Olivet. But Abibaal must be the other half-sailor, the other half-whore; he matches me sip for sip, swig for swig, gulp for gulp, glug for glug. He sings high and I sing low, in a melancholic harmony, but we both get there at the same time.

We enter the village by a backstreet, and everything is different from the first time we arrived here, from the other direction. Jesus had led us a six hour climb up the mountain road from Jericho as if we were walking on clouds. Publia was about to meet Balthazar again and, who knows, that might have been the night they made their baby. Now she is the only star shining in the sky as we make our way through the quiet lanes. The Passover has come, as if the Messiah had not been and gone.

I don't remember who is there, exactly; who we roar and wail our good Friday nights to, in the square. I don't remember who we hug and hold, whose tears are dried with whose headscarves, or exactly who is looking after my sister. I don't remember what happens to my saleswoman's song and, without that, I rather lose touch of myself.

I remember one more thing, perhaps it is everything, coming back to me in a rush; purple sick. Everything inside me, tainted by the darkness, dyed by the glory, comes out; a splat of the murex, a splash of the sacrificial wine, somewhere on the well-swept floor of Publia and Balthazar's house. The empty shell of me sleeps in their spare *cubiculum*.

I wake up thinking of Christ on the cross. He just wore a loincloth, so each sinew, bone and muscle showed. His body trembled in its fight, minutely detailed and interminable.

First, the image fills me so I can't think about anything else. It seems I slept cruciform. Then slowly I realise it's a hangover; having been unconscious for some time, I come round to find the Sabbath is over and the sounds of work, with a saw or a plane, are resounding nearby. In time again, I understand that of course no one is sawing in my bedroom; it is the noise of my headache. Ages later, I suddenly waken with a shock; it is not the sound of woodwork in my mind, it is Abibaal snoring.

He is in bed with me. My bosom is his pillow. I try to move. How a swallow of water would hiss in the hellish smithy of my mouth. There's a jug on my bedside table but lifting my head makes me dry heave, and Abibaal awakes.

We both act like something bad has happened, beyond the loss of our saviour. He leaps up looking guilty, I hide my face in my hands. I think he speaks to me but I can't piece together what he says. It's like the feeling I had when I was raped in Rome; fragmented.

Abi passes me the water bottle but every drop I drink comes back as a cupful of bile, spat on the floor beside my bed because I just feel too ill to care. I think he leaves shortly but I spend a long time lying on the cross with Jesus, not knowing if I'm alive or dead.

It takes me ages to get off the bed. Late in the afternoon, I make it out of the bedroom. Squinting in the light, I see nobody in the courtyard, which is fine because I don't plan to speak.

I want to read Emeshmoon's latest scroll, to find out what happened on Friday, what was said and what was sung. I shuffle over to the shrine but stop in horror. Strips of papyrus curl on the floor, lengthy shreds hanging off the table's edges, ripped apart. And the carefully arranged stones have been rolled away, all the sacred items spilled or soiled, with burnt sage thrown about. My favourite thing, the original peacock feather, is missing.

Black wings beat at me then, and I sway. From further away than it should be, Publia's voice comes, as she suddenly appears in my face.

"Oh. You," she says.

I can tell by her tone that I stink, even worse than I thought. Left in my bedroom is one of the empty wine jars, filled now with my urine, and probably some of Abibaal's. My sister looks at me as if I am that object.

"What's happened here?" I try to change the subject.

"Farzan tore the scrolls. Balthazar threw the stones. I don't know the exact details; I'd gone to bed." Her voice is dead. "You may wonder why I haven't cleared it up yet. Well, this is the new shrine."

"Where are the boys now?"

"Working."

"What, out there?" I jerk my headache towards the back door, and the outbuildings beyond it. "On the purple?"

"Yes, since they must support people who have no money left," she says pointedly. "People who spent their last talent on the red."

I think she's only saying this because Jesus has gone. The pain in her eyes is too big to be caused by a naughty little sister.

"Publia," I plead. "What did I do?"

"What didn't you do," she starts to waddle crossly away. But then she seems to repent and turns back to me: "You only said what everybody was thinking."

"Did I sing it?"

"No," she tuts. "I wouldn't call it singing." Another pause, then more relenting: "Do you want something to eat?"

My stomach is dead, so no. I do have a burning question, though.

"Do you know where the peacock feather is? From the shrine..?"

She's forgotten there ever was such fluff; like those interred in the necropolis, where I found it, have forgotten too.

"Blown away," she says with a wave of her hand, and disappears into her bedroom.

I stand there for a while, not knowing what to do; then Emeshmoon appears through the back door.

"Oh. You," she says, too.

Christ, it must have been bad.

"I should have died?" I ask her.

She laughs, but quickly stops.

"I'll tell you who is dead. I just heard this," she says. "Lazarus. Again. I saw Alethea in the garden and she heard it from the cheese lady at lunchtime.

"Apparently, he followed the cross with Martha and Mary, but the crucifixion was too much for him. One moment, he was standing with them in the crowd; the next moment, they'd lost him."

That was when we saw Lazarus' sisters, something I do remember, so can nod soberly now.

"But when the crowds dispersed at dusk they found his corpse, lying on the hillside at Golgotha where it had gone unnoticed for hours." Emesh's tone is lifeless as the character she describes. She must know I'm thinking this, somehow, for she looks me in the eye sharply and says: "Would you rather sing it?"

When I shake my head, she's relieved.

"The scrolls are gone, anyway." She sounds like the shredded paperwork went from natural causes, rather than the extreme actions of her husband.

"Do you know where the peacock feather went?" I ask her.

She shifts her gaze across the courtyard to a spot near our bedroom doors. "See over there," she points; "that's peacock feathers. Oh no, sorry, I forgot; that's where a chicken died because it tried to eat your wine sick."

There is a purplish lump on floor, there, but I cannot bear to look closer than that. Or at Emesh who is so pissed off with me.

I must appear suitably mortified, for she softens as Publia did, and gives me a little morsel of consolation on this ill day. She tells me that people are calling it one last miracle; Lazarus died at the exact moment Jesus was nailed, as if to prove the life-giving power he had. Then she starts a small cooking fire.

Next, Balthazar and Farzan come in from work, and stare at me as I haven't been stared at since I was an assistant priestess to Venus. What in her name did I do? Was I topless? Fully nude? Did I show off the arts of a sex goddess like they'd never seen before. Is that why Abibaal was in bed with me?

I don't know whether he had his own way; I used to be so in touch with my body, I'd have known if Hercules had rerouted the rivers while I slept (like in my favourite scene from his famous labours). But I can't tell if Peneus changed course, last night.

Emeshmoon is flowing friendly, again. She calls out casually to her husband; "do you know where the peacock feather went, that was on the shrine?"

He shakes his head but Bal, overhearing, says; "my brother took it, I think."

"It was Veronica's..."

"Never mind," I try to smile. "Do you know where Abibaal is now?"

Normally Farzan speaks to me in my language but now he keeps to theirs, saying: "All the chickens are dead in Bethany. Abi has gone off to weep."

I don't know whether this is true but I have to face the uncertainty; for to get back into my bedroom I must pass a pile of feathers that does, in this dusk, look rather like a dead chicken.

I don't remember if I killed it, if there were others, if it was with vino vomit but I can't stomach the questions and sidle past without looking closer. It's just that they've represented our survival, our growing community, our hopes, and are fragile as an egg.

As soon I get in the chamber, I realise I can't stay here. I'd gladly hide inside but either me or the brimming jug of wee has to go. I wrap my scarf tightly round my head and sling my bag firmly over my shoulder before picking up the pot and carrying it out of the bedroom with my face turned away from the household. Luckily it's quite dark now and people don't look round from the fireplace as I slip out the back door, to the *latrina*.

A full moon is rising over the Mount of Olives, and in the village streets the sound of Passover is resounding. I stand and take it all in, stunned at the thought of this world without Jesus in it. I can't believe that just the other side of the hill, in some rock cave or stone tomb, his body is lying lifeless. Couldn't heaven have come here instead?

So then I go and let it all out; standing on a small tussock above the stinking trench, I tip the night-water away. Strange how it, too, sparkles in the moonlight. While I'm here, I might as well squat; moving to a slightly different spot I start to raise my tunic above the knees.

From the gloom of the garden, a figure steps forward. Broad shouldered and lean hipped; another step toward me and I recognise the gleaming teeth and bushy moustache of Abibaal.

Neither of us know what to say, till he stammers:

"We will get some more chickens. From the egg man."

"I... I didn't know there was an egg man."

"Well, it was me, for a while," he gives a sad smile. "And I can be again."

Another awkward pause, then I blurt out;

"Do you know where the peacock feather went?"

In reply, he starts to fumble with his Phoenician-style pants. Around his waist he wears a sash of grubby silk, folded many times over and elaborately tied. From a pocket in one of its twists, he carefully pulls the green and purple eye that has overseen our adventures from Tyre; a bit ragged now on its cracked white stalk.

He hands the feather to me silently. I don't speak either. Are we both thinking the same thing?

"That's been there since last night," he eventually admits. "It is proof that I didn't take advantage of you."

"I thought it might have been the other way round," I say with a small smile.

He needs a moment to work out what I mean, then his face changes completely:

"No, lady; I wear the trousers."

We go back into the house, me walking in front of him. Though I've felt his eyes on my *posterior* many times before, their touch has never been as kind or comforting.

Inside, Emeshmoon's fire is burning brighter and Farzan and Bal have started on the wine. I finally feel I could stomach a sip of water, so I take some and sit down at the hearth. Opening my bag, I pop the peacock feather safely inside. Then I smell the lord. His scent, musk as incense, comes over me so strongly I close my eyes.

Touching the pale linen handkerchief with the backs of my fingers has set off a list of memories: the dusty hem of his robe and his ankles, the holy weave of his cloak and his forearms, the luxurious wave of his hair. I remember how he looked last time I saw him, in a crown of thorns; what blood, sweat and tears were wiped off his face with this hanky. Feeling his suffering, I well up again. Crying harder, I take the veil out of my bag. With wet eyes, I unfold it, laying it flat on my lap in the firelight, so nobody will see I'm upset.

His face is there. The linen is still ivory-coloured, the creases falling out in the warmth of the fire. But his face is revealed, as clear as if it had been painted yesterday on the wall of the Curia Julia, a state-of-the-art senate house in Rome, by the empire's finest *pictor*.

His face is pictured, as clear as if I'd stepped into that wall-painting with him, on my fabric. When this cloth touched the face of Jesus he was in agony; now, though the thorn pricks, the bloody trickles and tear tracks are imprinted on its surface, he is at peace. The look is serene. The gaze is twinkling.

It might just be the flames dancing; I shift this way and that, angling my handkerchief into the firelight to see if this likeness of my king will dissipate like smoke. The colours of mud and blood have deepened and darkened: purple. However I move, his countenance doesn't change.

"Veronica? Whatever are you doing?" Publia tuts impatiently.

I'd forgotten about her, even her, in my focus on the face of Christ. I look up to meet her accusing gaze and slowly, very slowly, decide whether to show her.

CHAPTER SEVENTEEN

I wait, taking seven swallows of water and watching seven sparks fly from the fire, before I say, "Publia, look!" and hold up the true picture of Jesus.

She screams and faints again. The others' reactions are extreme, too. Farzan says, later, that he first thought I'd raised up his real head, like it was John the Baptist's; only on a tablecloth instead of a plate.

Balthazar, catching his limp wife, looks at the soft image of our saviour in the firelight, and whimpers; "He is here. Jesus is with us. How did you do this?"

Emesh is laughing and clapping her hands with tears in her eyes. She's calling it magic, a miracle, and looking at me to confirm it. I tell them what happened. I'd like to sing it, I'd much rather hymn these words against a rousing tune but my throat is still dead dry and there is not even a hum in me:

"I met him in the street on his way with the cross, as close as we are now, in a massive crowd. His face was a mess, there was so much mud and blood running that he couldn't see," I say. "Even though there was only one way to go, he needed to see the path. So I grabbed this handkerchief from my bag; remember, Bal, I waved it at your wedding. No? Well, I gave it to the master. He wiped his holy face with it."

The men ask me lots of questions; how did he wipe it, one firm downward stroke or side to side scrubbing? Did I roll or fold it, have I specially treated it? I try to explain that I'd forgotten about it until just now when my fingers brushed against it. And how the touch of it is making my hands tingle.

I don't let them feel it, not tonight; but everyone gets close enough to see it's not mud or blood encrusted on the surface any more, but a deep and indelible-looking dye, fixed fast in the fabric.

Abi says his first thought was that it looked like a pattern of chicken wings, a feathered symmetry. "So," he adds, setting off conspicuously to bed on the roof, "tomorrow, I will start hatching eggs."

"Good plan," Emeshmoon yawns as she and Farzan turn in, too, "and tomorrow, I will tidy up this shrine."

Bal blows me a kiss, and walks Publia into their bedroom.

Soon, Abi calls down softly from the roof. The moon, shining into the courtyard, halos his bald head.

"Are you sure you won't come up and check my figures?" he says.

I half laugh, looking up at him, like this:

"There are no figures any more. I deal with a new currency, now. I have no creditors, no debtors, no secret caches."

"I still have something stashed away."

"Maybe tomorrow, Abibaal," I say. "I've been asleep all day, so it's not my bedtime yet..."

Next, I hear him snoring on the roof. I hear a goat bleating beneath the eaves. I hear Emesh and Farzan talking in their room, and Publia crying in hers. The moon shines fully on me, lighting my linen cloth from above; and the hearth is still aglow, lighting its white page from behind. It is as if I am face to face with Jesus and our eyes are in contact. My hands are shaking so much it takes me half the night to fold the illuminated sheet and carefully put it back in my bag.

The true image. Vera Icon. This is what I got my name for. It will be called the veronica.

All night, I wonder what to do with it. First, I imagine taking it to the temple, going as far as the court of women, head covered, on my knees, to show the high priest. I think it will persuade him of the truth. Then, in my mind I take a trip to Tyre; stopping to tell everyone my miracle along the way. And finally to Rome; where I offer this sacred relic to the emperor.

Really, I want to show it to my dad. And my mum. And my horrible younger sister. And the priest and other assistant priestesses where I used to work at the temple of Venus. Oh, and the five men who raped me, while I played her handmaid at the public baths.

I want to tell them all about Jesus. And now he is dead I do not want to live in the land of Judea. I'm going to need to sing on this journey. Previously, I traded my voice for the purple tunic. Not a bad deal; it brought me this pure linen cloth with proof of Jesus of Nazareth, King of Jews, Saviour of Gentiles, Messiah imprinted, in the end.

But I should be singing this now, and instead I'm just thinking. All night, staring at the ripped scrolls that have fallen off our shrine onto the floor. Wondering which format, thought, word or song, he would prefer.

I am still sitting there when a soft knocking comes in the second hour of the morning. None of my housemates stir. I get up stiffly and go to answer the front door. Creaking it open, I see Marcus and Naomi there; he's carrying her but they're both panting from the run up the lane. He steps inside and sets her down.

"Now what?" I whisper.

They don't speak for a long while, just look at me with teary eyes and cheery grins.

"What?"

"He has risen."

"He is alive."

"He came out of the tomb."

I knew some rich *Judaeus* had loaned the lord his grave on the hill outside the city. As we came back over the mountain on Friday night the soldiers were rolling a huge stone into place. It seemed to be so no one could get in; not to stop him getting out. But is this what has happened?

Naomi tells me. She heard it from Mary who'd gone with the other mothers to tend to his body early this morning. They had burial ointments and bandages to prepare him properly for the grave. On Friday night, he'd been quickly wrapped by this Joseph of Arimathea, ahead of the imminent Sabbath; so at cock-crow on Sunday, the Marys and Salome set off to do business at the tomb. They were wondering, as they walked, whether they'd be able to roll that big rock away themselves, if the soldiers had gone.

"The hill of the skull was deserted, and they saw the crosses lying where they fell on Friday," she says. "As soon as the tomb was in sight, though, they blinked and looked twice. It was guarded by a figure in white, who sat on the rock which had been rolled away from the entrance."

"It was an angel," Marcus butts in. "Mary and Salome and the other Mary all saw it."

"She said it spoke to them kindly and knew what they had come for." Naomi takes her story back. "And when the women went inside there was another, sitting where the body should have been."

"And she said that the shroud he'd been wound in was just lying there on the ground, but the piece of linen that was around his head lay separately at the top of the bed!"

Marcus' loud interruptions start to rouse the rest of the household and, over a cup of Emeshmoon's decoction, we all hear the end of the story together: Our ladies ran back to Bethany, to the place they lodge now at Golda's, next door to all the disciples who are lodging at Lazarus' old house. Mary of Magdalene hurried in to tell them and it seems that two immediately set off to see for themselves. Mary and Salome ran to tell Marcus and Naomi and they came to see us at a run.

Bless them, they have bought the whole extended family back to life. As they talk, I see Emesh's lips start to move silently, and her fingers to fidget and her toes to tap. Her eyes flick to the shrine, where lengths of a scroll, as yet unwritten on, hang down in a loop; torn but not a total write-off. Then she suddenly leaps up, like she used to, and rushes into her room for the pen and inkpot.

Our visitors pause to sip their tea, then we talk on and the words are poured in fresh brew. Once Emesh has picked up the unrolling parchment, Publia gets busy on the rest of our fallen shrine to Christ. She dusts off the surface and repositions the found objects of our faith. She bustles outside for a bunch of pomegranate blossom and bosses her husband into relighting the incense.

Sage-green smoke frames the scene for a few slow moments, as Publia sits heavily back down by the fireplace, where Abibaal is whittling a baby toy with his knife, and Farzan helps his wife with the translation of Marcus and Naomi's tale.

I would sing this but I've lost my voice; well, I traded it for the true picture.

It takes seven Sundays before I come up with a song. We're all still hanging around in Bethany, wondering what to do next, but waiting for Publia's delivery date before making any decisions. Some of the disciples are still based here, too, but spending a lot of time at the temple.

After one Sunday, I meet Nathaniel in the street. He puts his arm around my shoulder and walks me into a quiet alleyway whispering urgently; “we have seen him. Jesus came to us at supper last night.” It isn’t the first time he’s appeared; several of the disciples have seen him in different places. But this was the first time Nathaniel had observed his living flesh; Thomas, too, who’d had trouble believing the facts.

After two Sundays, I show him the veronica. I’m ashamed it took me so long to decide. I take the family with me and they do all the talking. Kaspar sees it and Philip, as well as Nathaniel; the voices of my friends tell the story of my *sudarium* but I don’t say a word. The true picture speaks for itself.

After three Sundays, the disciples invite us to their meeting, in an upper room in Jerusalem. There’s a big crowd giving witness; a congregation for prayer and praise. This happy gathering becomes a regular thing; four, five, six Sundays pass.

The seventh is Pentecost. We are praying, that day, when there comes the clap of wind in the room and we feel a hot breeze, though no windows are open. The fishermen are saying, he told us, he promised us; ‘John baptised with water but I will baptise with fire’. This is it.

I feel the warmth rise within me, the thunder rushing through me where I sit; and the breath of the whole room surges upwards, too. It seems to spark flames at the top of everyone’s heads, flickering purple and green like peacock feathers, an iridescent shimmer that could look like it’s not really there. But we all see it, the holy spirit, the blaze of our baptism that nothing can put out.

The master has given us clear instructions; spread the word. The teacher has given us an amazing ability; to speak in many tongues. The lord has given us the fire and we’re going to let it burn.

When we go into the streets of the city, people think we’re drunk; it’s only nine in the morning, but some of us may be slightly tipsy. (Wine tastes like blood to me now, and bread makes me lightheaded.) Then people realise that they can understand what we are saying, men of every race and tribe, without needing translation.

Parthians, Medes and Elamites; residents of Mesopotamia, Phrygia and Pamphylia, Crete and the parts of Libya near Cyrene [22]; wherever they're coming from, they get what we're saying, as a hundred voices start to tell the story of what Jesus did.

It's crowded in those streets again; my friends later said that every Christian who was there that day caused three new believers to be baptised. But I walk away from the crowds, with Publia who can't take the crush and Emeshmoon who doesn't like the shouting, to the end of a street where steps lead up the city wall. While my sisters sit at the shady bottom, I climb; the stairs are narrow and slippery with age, and there's no handrail. When I get to the top, my song comes back.

The view from here spans Calvary, the rocky brow where the sign of a cross is still in my eyes, across the level plain to the mountains between me and Tyre; and beyond that the deep blue sea to Rome. I will be taking the veronica home, I can see it from here.

So I sing like a sales girl; thank God I can still do it, I thought I was losing my touch. My voice sounds high in the Judean air, so I could almost sit on my handkerchief like a flying carpet and get breath-blown back there. But, in fact, I'd better start walking.

From on top of the battlements, I can see some shops in the side street below. I'll need a pair of new sandals. And a way to pay for them. I used to sing to sell my wares. Now, I'll be singing to buy.

Through the traders down there, I watch Abibaal appear, looking for me and finding Pubi and Emesh on the cool bottom step. From here, I notice his hairstyle has changed; the long tail gone and the bald top growing back. (It makes him look more like Jesus.) They tell him I've climbed the wall and he starts bounding up the stairs; finally coming to check my figures. But he's still a bit fat so I'll finish this before he gets here:

'Golden sole, silver straps; this is a song that could sell you a new soul by she who used to trade in prayers of purple, parables of silk, by she who now deals in papyrus hymns.

'God sings it at the same time, melody of Melqart, bass-line of Hercules, with Venus whistling. This is a song played on pipes of amethyst, by she who swam naked from Tyre, and dyed the waters of Jordan with her tune.

'This is the story that started the whole thing, it got the blind seeing, it got the lame walking, it led her away from a paralysed life, out of the purple and into the light; out of the Roman baths and into Bethesda Bath.

'These are the words to the true picture. It has a second verse.'

Footnotes:

[1] I'm grateful to Dr. Deborah Ruscillo for her help with my research into the historical use of purple dye.
http://deborahruscillo.com/royal-purple

There is a fascinating academic debate about the differences between Tyrian Purple and Biblical Blue:
http://pubs.acs.org/doi/abs/10.1021/bk-2013-1147.ch003
http://www.biblicalarchaeology.org/daily/archaeology-today/biblical-archaeology-topics/scholars-study-the-great-tekhelet-debate/

[2] Orphic Hymn to Hercules:
http://www.theoi.com/Text/OrphicHymns1.html#11

[3] Aquarian Gospel:
https://www.sacred-texts.com/chr/agjc/agjc031.htm
It is paraphrased and played with, as well as directly quoted.

[4] Matthew 5:33-37. N.I.V. This is based on the Beatitudes; so would be out of sync with the gospel timeline, here, if Jesus only said it once! I've tried to keep his words and deeds as chronological as can be; but there are places like this where events happen out of traditional order.

[5] Matthew 5:45. N.I.V.

[6] Luke 10:1. N.I.V.

[7] Ovid The Love Books, Elegy IV, Line 21-24.

[8] Neale Donald Walsch (1997) Conversations With God, Hodder and Stoughton, pp 96-97.

[9] The episode of the blasted fig tree typically comes later on the gospel timeline.

[10] Matthew 21: 28-32. N.I.V. Again these words are spoken by Jesus

slightly later in the gospel schedule, once he has entered Jerusalem in triumph.

[11] Aquarian Gospel 29:
https://www.sacred-texts.com/chr/agjc/agjc032.htm

[12] Psalm 139. N.I.V.
http://www.biblegateway.com/passage/?search=psalm+139&version=NIV

[13] Matthew 23. N.I.V.

[14] Aquarian Gospel 22: The background to this text can be read here:
https://en.wikipedia.org/wiki/The_Aquarian_Gospel_of_Jesus_the_Christ

The work was said to have been channelled, or transcribed from the 'Akashic Records', by Levi Dowling in the early twentieth century. The extracts I've used here have mostly been taken from Christ's possible conversations in India!

[15] Cannabis in the Bible? In honour of different spellings I've retained two in my text...
http://cannacentral.com/news/cannabis-christianity-and-the-great-kaneh-bosm-debate-did-jesus-use-pot/
https://en.wikipedia.org/wiki/Holy_anointing_oil
Who knew!

[16] Aquarian Gospel 33:
http://www.sacred-texts.com/chr/agjc/agjc036.htm
http://www.sacred-texts.com/chr/agjc/agjc036.htm

[17] Aquarian Gospel 158

[18] Psalm 23

[19] Zechariah 9:8-10. N.I.V.

[20] http://www.crystalinks.com/jerusalemgates.html
http://en.wikipedia.org/wiki/Golden_Gate_(Jerusalem)

[21] Luke 19: 39-40. N.I.V.
http://www.biblegateway.com/passage/?search=luke+19&version=NIV

[22] Acts of the Apostles 2: 9-11. N.I.V.
http://www.biblegateway.com/passage/?search=Acts+2&version=NIV

Glossary

abba – Aramaic word for father that expresses affection and trust; 'dad' or 'daddy'
ala – Wing. Like alcoves in the hallway, off the atrium, in a Roman villa
alabastrotheca – Make-up case of alabaster jars
anteceptio – Contraception (Veronica uses vinegar!)
argentum – Silver, and also money, like 'cash'
as – Short for assarion, smallest copper coin in Publia's Roman purse
atramentum – Ink
atrium – The open centre of a Roman house, with a pool of rainwater beneath a hole in the roof; statues and wall painting decorate it, and all the other rooms lead off it
bibliotheca – Library, though the books were scrolls
caldarium – The hot tub at the Roman baths
carissima – Most loved, very dear
clementia – Mercy
compluvium – A hole in the roof, over the impluvium, rain pool
cubiculum – Bedroom (cubicle or cubby hole!)
culina – Kitchen (culinary)
curulis – The folding ivory stool that signified a dignified magistrate's status
domus – Home/House
drachma – Silver coin from Greece, one of the earliest known in the world, from an original meaning 'to grasp'
dryads – Tree nymphs, spirits of all trees, particularly oak
duodecim scripta – The Roman equivalent to chess or backgammon, basically, a boy's game (Ludus/Ludo!)
februlis – Latin for purging or purifying: the month February was named after this festival
floralia – The Roman month named for the goddess Flora, in the spring
frigidarium – The cold plunge, final stage in the bathing process
gustus – Taste
hexaplex trunculus – The Latin name for the Tyrian sea-snail, aka murex
homer – A measurement (biblical); ten baths worth of liquid
ima – The Hebrew word for Mum

impluvium – The rain pool beneath the hole in the atrium roof (the compluvium!)
insulae – Blocks of flats, each with lock-up shops on the ground floor, or grander living quarters like Abibaal's, then four or more tenement floors, and balconies, above.
Iudaeus – Jew
kaneh-bosem – Cannabis in the Bible? In honour of different spellings I've retained two in my text...
http://cannacentral.com/news/cannabis-christianity-and-the-great-kaneh-bosm-debate-did-jesus-use-pot/
http://en.wikipedia.org/wiki/Holy_anointing_oil Who knew?!
koskino – Sieve (in Phoenician)
laconicum – Sweat room. The lazy area, or time-out zone, after a hot one at the Roman baths
latrinae – The loos, or toilets
leewan – Three-walled rooms around the courtyard at an inn
'luxoriosa emere cupio' – I want to shop for luxury items, I wish to purchase non-essential things
malum – We might say lemon but it means any juicy fruit, including apple, melon, quince and pomegranate
mane! – Wait, stay there, hold up, hang on
mensula – A little table
mentula – Penis
mingo – Wee, pee, piss, urinate, etc (The modern 'minging' *may* derive from this)
nard/spikenard – Aromatic, amber-coloured essential oil from valerian plant with medicinal benefits
nisan – A month in the Hebrew calendar, around spring time
nominalia – A name-fest, like the naming ceremony we would now call a Christening.
ornatrix – Hairdresser
ova – Eggs
palla – Shawl or cloak
pallium – Shawl or cloak
palliolum – A little shawl, more ladylike
pater – Father
peplum – Tunic, tied to flatter the hips

peristylum – Covered walkway around the internal garden at the Roman villa
Pharisees – http://en.wikipedia.org/wiki/Pharisees
phosphoro – Phosphorescence. Named for the evening star – Phosphorus.
Phylacteria – Pages from the Torah were traditionally worn on the body by Jews while praying
piperatorium – Pepper Pot
plumarius – Embroiderer
posterior – Here it means ass or arse, depending on your accent (Though the proper Latin word is 'culus')
praecinctorium – An apron with lots of pockets, used by pharmacists, for example, to store and distribute their pills and potions
praetorium – Originally the general's tent in the army camp; later the council building
praetors – 'The Government'.
rabiosus – A raving mad man, rabid
Sadducees – http://en.wikipedia.org/wiki/Sadducees
Sanhedrin – Council of Israeli men, up to seventy one; the rabbinical courts
savillum – Roman cheesecake topped with bay leaves. Nom. http://allrecipes.com/recipe/ancient-roman-cheesecake-savillum/
Scribes – http://en.wikipedia.org/wiki/Scribe#Judaism
semicaper – Half-man, half-goat, like Pan
servus – Slave
silphium – A plant Veronica and lots of other Romans used as birth control
http://en.wikipedia.org/wiki/Silphium
http://io9.com/5923071/did-the-romans-drive-a-birth-control-plant-to-extinction
solium – throne, and bath-tub!
Somnus – Sleep
soror – Sister
spikenard/nard – Aromatic, amber-coloured essential oil from valerian plant with medicinal benefits
splendidus – Splendid
stercus bovis – Bullshit

strigilis – Tool used with oil to scrape dirt and sweat from the skin at bath time
sukkah – Tent for Hebrew festival of Tabernacles
suparum – Like the protective layer hairdressers put around your shoulders today!
superanus – Chieftain. Soprano?
tablinum – Study
tekhelet – Blue dye from murex used in the High Priest's tassels and the tabernacle embroideries
tempus – Time
tepidarium – The room temperature or ambient bath, first to come in the three-part bathing process
terabinth – A tree
tesserae – Mosaic tiles
timbrels – Tambourine, from ancient Israel
toga picta – Dyed purple all over and finely embroidered with gold thread, only emperors and generals could wear one
toga praetexta – With purple stripes to show relative prestige
triclinium – Dining room, three couches, each to take three diners, reclining to eat
triumphator – The winner, victor
tzitzit – Tassels attached to the four corners of Jewish prayer shawls, once coloured blue with murex dye
urna infectoria – Dye vat or bath
vale – Bye! Salve is 'hi'. Proper translation is farewell
veneralia – The feast day of goddess Venus, April 1st
vestibulum – Vestibule. The hall or entrance way, in a Roman villa
volcano – The word was actually first used in 1610 CE to describe molten lava – "like in Vulcan's workshop". In fact the Romans didn't know what volcanoes were. Pompeii and Herculaneum were destroyed in 79 CE. But it was too good a reference not to use
Vulcan – Roman god of metalwork and revenge
zaater zejd – Paste of sesame and thyme (I think of it as their equivalent to peanut butter)

About the Author:

Alison's first novel, *Dreamhouse*, was published in 1994 and she's been dreaming up novels, short stories, plays and poems, essays and articles every day since. Course leader for Creative Writing at the University of Portsmouth, she's taught generations of students to do the same thing. Dr Habens holds a PhD on the subject of divine inspiration in literature, and runs a research project into life-writing for wellbeing. She's a tutor at Skyros Writers' Lab.

Alison's life sounds a bit like a story, too; she lives in an old church on the Isle of Wight and commutes to work by hovercraft.

Other novels by Alison Habens: *Dreamhouse, Family Outing, Lifestory, Pencilwood, The Muse's Tale*.

See alisonhabens.com for more.

About this book:

The True Picture has been twenty years in the writing. The first words were sparked in St Swithun's Church, Southsea, when Father Hollins showed Alison a statue of St Veronica and explained how it got its name: *vera icon, true picture*. Notes ripped from her Filofax, penned as she ran excitedly home, were the first pages of the story which for now ends here.

She says: "My plan was to bring that statue to life, and tell the tale as if it were happening today; immaculately researched, intricately crafted, but told in the raucous and relatable tones of a lady you actually know.

I tried to give the most modern voice, and believable account, to the woman who could have conceivably been standing, with a suitable hanky, right there, right then on the gospel timeline. *Ad maiorem Dei gloriam*."

See thetruepicture.co.uk for more.

Acknowledgments:

Deep thanks to dear friend, talented editor and scholar, Matt Wingett.

Much gratitude also to Latin master Will Sutton.

More Fiction From Life Is Amazing

The Snow Witch, by Matt Wingett

A young woman on the run arrives in an English seaside town during a freak snow storm. A refugee from a deeply traumatic past, as she defends herself from a brutal pursuer, she discovers she is a far more powerful woman than even she realised. Both gritty and uplifting. Not suitable for children.
Paperback, £9.99 ISBN 978-0-9956394-5-4
Hardback, £19.99 ISBN 978-0-9956394-6-1

Dark City, Edited by Karl Bell and Stephen Pryde-Jarman

This collection of horror stories is set in Portsmouth, and varies from the spine-chilling through the unsettling to the strange. A gripping visit to the strange and bizarre side of a city.
Paperback, £9.99
ISBN 978-0-9956394-0-9

By Celia's Arbour, A Tale of Portsmouth Town,

by Walter Besant and James Rice

A novel of love, loss, intrigue, spies and revolution, set in the naval town of Portsmouth. "Fascinating – and full of lyrical writing."
Paperback, £14.99
ISBN 978-0-9572413-7-4

Portsmouth Fairy Tales for Grown Ups, edited by Tessa Ditner

A collection of short stories based in the city of Portsmouth, ranging from the hilarious to the bizarre - and all responding to the idea of the Fairy Tale.
Paperback, £9.99
ISBN: 978-0-9572413-3-6

Lightning Source UK Ltd.
Milton Keynes UK
UKHW021016270221
379430UK00007B/110

9 781913 001025